Praise for these
medical susp

"Palmer, the master of medical suspense, captivates readers with [this] stunning thriller."

—*Library Journal* (starred review)

"Of all [Palmer's] novels, this one has the most ambitious plot and a fascinating array of characters . . . [including] one of the best action scenes to ever appear in a medical thriller." —Associated Press

"Take a medical thriller about a strain of bacteria immune to antibiotics, add a disgraced protagonist and a surprising political angle, and the result is a terrifying page-turner that will make readers reluctant to visit a hospital anytime soon." —*RT Book Reviews*

"Palmer's growing audience will find much to enjoy here, as will medical-thriller fans of all stripes." —*Booklist*

POLITICAL SUICIDE

"When you open the pages of a Michael Palmer novel, you know you are in the hands of a pro. This author knows how to weave a plot and keep the action coming, and the readers know it won't all fall apart at the end. Such is definitely the case with *Political Suicide*. Each page adds a new dimension to the characters and a new revelation to the plot. It is action/mystery reading at its best. Palmer just keeps delivering good stories, one right after the other." —*Huffington Post*

"This book goes from great to outstanding . . . a definite keeper!" —*Suspense Magazine*

"Plenty of chills and spills." —*Kirkus Reviews*

"Palmer writes terrific medical suspense, and he has thrown political intrigue into the mix . . . fans won't be disappointed." —Associated Press

"Michael Palmer once again delivers an adrenaline-pumped political and medical action thriller . . . Palmer fans will not be disappointed in this suspenseful and realistic, fast-paced whodunit." —*Jewish Journal*

"A must-read for fans of political intrigue."
—*Fort-Worth Star Telegram*

"The military conspiracy is frightening, while Lou's interactions with his daughter and his blossoming romantic interest in a tough attorney provide some breaks from the merciless pace of the investigation. Suspend disbelief that an ER doctor can, or should, attempt some of these actions and enjoy the ride."
—*RT Book Reviews*

"Michael Palmer mixes politics, medical science, and the military to create another suspenseful medical thriller." —Examiner.com

OATH OF OFFICE

"One of the most exciting thrillers of the year."

—*Huffington Post*

"A shocker." —Associated Press

"This is Palmer at his most terrifying, most plausible and, worst of all, most realistic."

—*RT Book Reviews* (4.5 stars)

"Suspenseful . . . Palmer's easy mix of science and individual courage should please his many fans."

—*Publishers Weekly*

"Compelling." —*Kirkus Reviews*

"*Oath of Office* captures the modern pulse . . . An engaging novel that touches on some of the fears readers may have about big business, politics, and the food supply. Difficult to put down." —*Technorati*

"A darn good read." —Examiner.com

A HEARTBEAT AWAY

"When it comes to inventive plots for medical thrillers nobody does it better than Michael Palmer . . . This premise is explosive and compelling and grabs the readers from the very first page." —*Huffington Post*

"Palmer never fails to thrill when he presents a tautly constructed puzzle, with characters that make readers whiz through pages late at night."

—*RT Book Reviews* (4.5 stars)

"A nonstop action ride . . . Having made a career with medical thrillers, this latest adds political intrigue and terrorism into the mix. . . . Palmer makes what Clancy writes look like the Boxcar Kids." —*Crimespree* magazine

"Perfect." —*Marblehead Reporter*

"Michael Palmer anchors his thrillers in high concept and steeps them in medicine. *A Heartbeat Away* opens with a prologue, and from the opening line, the reader knows things are not going to go well . . . This is the book for readers who wholeheartedly believe politicians are capable of anything." —*Boston Globe*

THE LAST SURGEON

"Prepare to burn some serious midnight oil."

—*Boston Herald*

"Highly suspenseful and compelling." —*Booklist*

"Palmer has always been a good writer but he has never crafted a story as suspenseful as this one . . . This is the kind of book you read with a bright light on and all the doors locked . . . Franz Koller is one of the most deadly villains to grace the pages of a novel since the introduction of Hannibal Lecter." —*Huffington Post*

"Should please . . . all those who enjoy their suspense mixed with medical characters and settings."

—*Library Journal*

"The thrill of the non-kill . . . [is] chilling."

—*North Shore Sunday*

"More twists and turns than a sociopath's psyche . . . inventive and effective, an entertaining and engaging read."

—*California Literary Review*

THE SECOND OPINION

"A heart-pounding medical thriller . . . satisfying, expertly paced [with] enough suspense to keep readers happily turning the pages."

—*Boston Globe*

"The novel is not merely a thriller but also an exploration of its central character's unique gifts and her determination to communicate with her comatose father despite overwhelming odds. Another winner from a consistently fine writer."

—*Booklist*

"A splendid novel."

—*Globe and Mail* (Canada)

THE FIRST PATIENT

"An exciting thriller that is full of surprises and captures the intense atmosphere of the White House, how the medical system works, and how the 25th Amendment could be brought into play. I thoroughly enjoyed it."

—President Bill Clinton

ALSO BY MICHAEL PALMER

TRAUMA

MICHAEL PALMER and DANIEL PALMER

St. Martin's Paperbacks

This is a work of fiction. All of the characters, organizations, and events portrayed in this novel are either products of the author's imagination or are used fictitiously.

TRAUMA

Copyright © 2015 by Daniel Palmer.
Excerpt from *Mercy* copyright © 2016 by Daniel Palmer.

For information address St. Martin's Press, 175 Fifth Avenue, New York, NY 10010.

ISBN: 978-1-250-03088-7

Our books may be purchased in bulk for promotional, educational, or business use. Please contact your local bookseller or the Macmillan Corporate and Premium Sales Department at 1-800-221-7945, ext. 5442, or by e-mail at MacmillanSpecialMarkets@macmillan.com.

Printed in the United States of America

St. Martin's Press hardcover edition / May 2015
St. Martin's Paperbacks edition / March 2016

St. Martin's Paperbacks are published by St. Martin's Press, 175 Fifth Avenue, New York, NY 10010.

10 9 8 7 6 5 4 3

With great respect and admiration, Trauma is dedicated to Dr. David Grass of McLean, Virginia. This book would not have been possible without his dedication to the medical profession, his skill and experience as a practitioner, his imagination, and his support and contributions to this project from start to finish.

To say I couldn't have gotten here without him is an understatement.

D. P.

1

It began, innocently enough, with a fall.

Beth Stillwell, a slight, thirty-five-year-old mother of three with kind eyes and an infectious laugh, was shopping at Thrifty Dollar Store with her kids in tow. She'd been stocking up on school supplies and home staples when she lost her balance and tumbled to the grimy linoleum floor. It was bad enough to have to shop at the dollar store, something new since her separation from her philandering husband of fifteen years. It was downright humiliating to be sprawled out on their floor, her leg bent in a painful angle beneath her.

Beth wasn't hurt, but as her six-year-old daughter Emily tried to help her stand, her left leg felt weak, almost rubbery. Leaning against a shelf stocked with cheap soap, Beth took a tentative step only to have the leg nearly buckle beneath her. She kept her balance, and after another awkward step, decided she could walk on it.

The strength in Beth's left leg mostly returned, but

a slight stiffness and a disconcerting drag lingered for weeks. Beth's sister told her to see a doctor. Beth said she would, but it was an empty promise. Running a licensed day care out of her Jamaica Plain home, Beth was in charge of seven kids in addition to her own, and any downtime put tremendous strain on her limited finances. She rarely had time to make a phone call. But the leg was definitely a bother, and the lingering weakness was a constant worry. She occasionally stumbled, but the last straw was losing control of her urine while in charge of toddlers who could hold their bladders better than she could. That drove her to the doctor.

An MRI confirmed a parasagittal tumor originating from the meninges with all the telltale characteristics of a typical meningioma: a brain tumor. The tumor was already big enough to compress brain tissue, interrupting the normal complex communication from neuron to neuron and causing a moderate degree of edema, swelling from the pressure on the brain's blood vessels.

Beth would need surgery to have it removed.

Dr. Carrie Bryant stood in front of the viewbox, examining Beth Stillwell's MRI. A fourth-year neurosurgical resident rotating through Boston Community Hospital (BCH), she would be assisting chief resident Dr. Fred Michelson with Beth's surgery. The tumor pressed upon the top of the brain on the right side. Carrie could see exactly why Beth's left leg had gone into a focal seizure and why she'd lost control of her urine. It was not a particularly large mass, about walnut-sized, but its location was extremely problematic. If it were to grow, Beth would develop progressive spasticity in her leg and eventually lose bladder control completely.

Carrie absently rubbed her sore quadriceps while studying Beth's films. She had set a new personal best at yesterday's sprint distance triathlon, finally breaking the elusive ten-minute-mile pace during the run, and her body was letting her know she had pushed it too hard. Her swim and bike performance were shaky per usual, and all but guaranteed a finish in the bottom quartile for her age group—but at least she was out there, battling, doing her best to get her fitness level back to where it had been.

Carrie's choice to jump right into triathlons was perhaps not the wisest, but she never did anything half measure. She enjoyed pushing her body to new limits. She'd also used the race to raise more than a thousand dollars for BCH: a tiny fraction of what was needed, but every bit helped.

BCH served the poor and uninsured. Carrie felt proud to be a part of that mission, but lack of funding was a constant frustration. In her opinion, the omnipotent budgeting committee relied too heavily on cheap labor to fill the budget gap, which explained why fourth- and fifth-year residents basically ran the show whenever they rotated through BCH. Attending physicians, those docs who had finished residency, were supposed to provide oversight, but they had too much work and too few resources to do the job.

If the constant budget shortfalls had a silver lining, it could be summed up in a single word: experience. With each BCH rotation the hours would be long, the demands exhausting, but Carrie never groaned or complained. She was getting the best opportunity to hone her skills.

Thank goodness Chambers University did its part

to fund the storied health-care institution, which had trained some of Boston's most famous doctors, including the feared but revered Dr. Stanley Metcalf, staff neurosurgeon at the iconic White Memorial Hospital. For now, the doors to BCH were open, the lights on, and people like Beth Stillwell could get exceptional medical care even without exceptional insurance.

So far, Beth had been a model patient. She'd spent two days in the hospital, and in that time Carrie had had the pleasure of meeting both her sister and her children. Carrie prepped for Beth's surgery wondering when having a family of her own would fit into her hectic life. At twenty-nine, she had thought it might happen with Ian, her boyfriend of two years, but apparently her dedication to residency did not jibe with his vision of the relationship. She should have known when Ian began referring to his apartment as Carrie's "on-call room" that their union was headed for rocky times.

At half past eleven, Carrie was on her way to scrub when Dr. Michelson stopped her in the hallway.

"Two cases of acute lead poisoning just rolled in," he announced.

Carrie smiled weakly at the dark humor: two gunshot victims needed the OR.

"We can do Miss Stillwell at five o'clock," Michelson said. It was not a request. Working at one of New England's busiest trauma hospitals meant that patients often got bumped for the crisis of the moment, and Dr. Michelson fully expected Carrie to accommodate him.

Carrie would have been fine with his demand regardless. Her social calendar had been a long string of empty boxes ever since Ian called things off. During the relationship vortex, Carrie had evidently neglected her apartment as well as her friends, and it would take time to get everything back to pre-Ian levels. Carrie agreed to move Beth's surgery even though she had no real say in the matter.

The time change gave Carrie an opportunity to finish the rest of her rotations on the neurosurgical floor. She met with several different patients, and concluded her rounds with Leon Dixon, whom Dr. Metcalf had admitted as a private patient that morning. She would be assisting Dr. Metcalf with his surgery the next day.

Carrie entered Leon's hospital room after knocking, and found a handsome black man propped up in his adjustable bed, drinking water through a straw. Leon was watching *Antiques Roadshow* with his wife, who sat in a chair pushed up against the bed. They were holding hands. Leon was in his early fifties, with a kind but weathered face.

"Hi, Leon, I'm Dr. Carrie Bryant. I'll be assisting with your operation tomorrow. How you feeling today?"

"Pre—eh-eh-eh-eh."

"I'm Phyllis, Leon's wife. He's feeling pretty crappy, is what he's trying to say."

Carrie shook hands with the attractive woman who had gone from being a wife to a caregiver in a matter of weeks. The heavy makeup around Phyllis's tired eyes showed just how difficult those weeks had been. Carrie had yet to review Leon's films, but was not surprised about his speech problems; the chart said he'd presented aphasic. She doubted he'd stuttered before, but she was not going to embarrass him by asking.

"Leon, could you close your eyes and open your mouth for me?" Carrie asked.

Leon got his eyes shut, but his mouth stayed closed as well. Carrie sent a text message to Dr. Nugent in radiology. She wanted to look at his films, stat.

"He has a lot of trouble following instructions," Phyllis said as she brushed tears from her eyes. "Memory and temper problems, too."

Something is going on in Leon's left temporal lobe, Carrie thought. *Probably a tumor.*

Carrie observed other symptoms as well. The right side of Leon's face drooped slightly, and his right arm drifted down when he held out his arms in front of him with his eyes closed. His reflexes were heightened in the right arm and leg, and when Carrie scraped the sole of his right foot with the reflex hammer, his great toe extended up toward his face—a Babinski sign, indicating damage to the motor system represented on the left side of Leon's brain.

Carrie took hold of Leon's dry and calloused hand and looked him in the eye.

"Leon, we're going to do everything we can to make you feel better. I'm going to go look at your films now, and I'll see you tomorrow for your surgery." Carrie wrote her cell phone number on a piece of paper. Business cards were for after residency. "If you need anything, this is how to reach me," she said.

Carrie preferred not to cut the examination short, but a text from Dr. Robert Nugent said he'd delay his meeting for Carrie if she came now. Carrie was rushed herself. She needed to get to Beth Stillwell for her final pre-op consultation.

Dr. Nugent, a married father of two, was a competitive triathlete who had finished well ahead of Carrie in the last race they had done together. Over the years, Carrie had learned that it paid to be friends with the radiologists for situations just like this, and nothing fostered camaraderie quite like the race circuit.

The radiology department was located in the bowels of BCH, in a windowless section of the Glantz Wing, but somehow Dr. Nugent appeared perpetually tan, even after the brutal New England winter.

"Thanks for making some time for me, Bob," Carrie said. "Leon just materialized on my OR schedule and I haven't gotten any background on him from Dr. Metcalf yet."

Dr. Nugent shrugged. He knew all about Dr. Metcalf's surprise patients. "Yeah, from what I was told, Dixon's doctor is good friends with Metcalf."

"Let me guess: Leon has no health insurance."

"Bingo."

Carrie chuckled and said, "Why am I not surprised?"

It was unusual to see a private patient at Community. Just about every patient was admitted through the emergency department and assigned to resident staff. Dr. Metcalf was known for his philanthropy, and when he rotated through Community he often took on cases he could not handle at White Memorial because of insurance issues.

All the residents looked forward to working with Dr. Metcalf, and Carrie's peers had expressed jealousy more than once. Assisting Dr. Metcalf was the ultimate test of a resident's skill, grace under the most extreme pressure. Dr. Metcalf had earned a reputation for being exacting and demanding, even a bully at times, but his approach paid off. He taught technique, didn't assume total control, and was supremely patient with the less experienced surgeons. Like many world-class surgeons, Dr. Metcalf was sometimes tempestuous and always demanding, but Carrie was willing to take the bitter with the sweet if it helped with her career.

Dr. Nugent put Leon's MRI films up on the viewbox.

"It's most likely a grade three astrocytoma," he said.

The irregular mass was 1.5 by 2 centimeters in size, located deep in the left temporal lobe and associated with frondlike edema. No doubt this was the cause of Leon's aphasic speech and confused behavior.

"So Dr. Metcalf's scheduled to take this one out tomorrow," Dr. Nugent said.

"As much as he can, anyway."

Dr. Nugent agreed.

Carrie was about to ask Dr. Nugent a question when she noticed the time. She was going to be late for the final pre-op consultation with Beth. *Damn.* There were never enough hours in the day.

Carrie made it to Beth's hospital room at four thirty and found the anesthesiologist already there. By the end of Carrie's consult, Beth looked teary-eyed.

"You'll be holding your children again in no time, trust me," Carrie assured her.

Even with her head newly shaved, Beth was a strikingly beautiful woman, young and vivacious. Despite Carrie's words of comfort, Beth did not look convinced.

"Just make sure I'll be all right, Dr. Bryant," Beth said. "I have to see my kids grow up."

At quarter to five, Beth was taken from the patient holding area to OR 15. Carrie had her mask, gown, and head covering already donned, and was in the scrub room, three minutes into her timed five-minute anatomical scrub, when Dr. Michelson showed up.

"How would you feel about doing the Stillwell case on your own?" he asked. "The attending went home for the day, and I got a guy with a brain hemorrhage who's going to be ART if I don't evacuate the clot and decompress the skull."

Carrie rolled her eyes at Michelson. She was not a big fan of some of the medical slang that was tossed around, and ART, an especially callous term, was an acronym for "approaching room temperature," a.k.a. dead.

"No problem on Stillwell," Carrie said. Her heart jumped a little. She had never done an operation without the oversight of an attending or chief resident before.

Quick as the feeling came, Carrie's nerves settled. She was an excellent surgeon with confidence in her abilities, and, if the hospital grapevine were to be believed, the staff's next chief resident. It would certainly be a nice feather in her surgical cap, and helpful in securing a fellowship at the Cleveland Clinic after residency.

"Unfortunately, I'm going to need OR fifteen. Everything else is already booked," Michelson said.

Carrie nodded. Par for the course at BCH. "Beth can wait," she said.

"I checked the schedule for you. OR six or nine should be open in a couple of hours."

Carrie did some quick calculations to make sure she could handle the Stillwell operation and still be rested enough to assist Dr. Metcalf with Leon's operation in the morning. *Three to four hours, tops,* Carrie thought, *and Beth will be back in recovery.*

"No problem," Carrie said. "I'll let you scrub down and save the day."

"Thanks, Doc Bryant," Michelson said. "But you're the real lifesaver here. I don't think there's another fourth year I'd trust with this operation."

"Your faith in me inspires."

Carrie did not mention the promise she'd made to Beth during her pre-op consultation. Michelson would not have approved. If one thing was certain about surgery, it was that nothing, no matter how routine or simple it seemed, was ever 100 percent guaranteed.

2

Carrie had met Beth again in the preoperative area, this time accompanied by Rosemary, a certified registered nurse anesthetist. While Carrie had never worked with Rosemary before, watching her insert the IV into Beth's arm made Carrie confident in the CRNA's ability. Rosemary gave Beth a light dose of midazolam, which decreased anxiety and would mercifully bring about amnesia. Some things were best not remembered, brain surgery among them.

Once in the OR, Rosemary got Beth connected to the monitors that tracked vitals. She delivered a dose of propofol to induce general anesthesia, followed by a push of succinylcholine to bring on temporary muscle paralysis. From that moment on, the endotracheal tube would do all the breathing for Beth.

Dr. Saleem Badami, originally from Bangalore, India, and a highly regarded intern, was to assist with the operation. This was really a one-person show, so

Dr. Badami was there primarily to monitor Beth's neurological status during surgery.

The circulating nurse had painstakingly prepared the necessary equipment, including the Midas Rex drill, which Carrie would use to penetrate the skull and turn the flap. Last on the team was Valerie, a scrub nurse born in Haiti. A longtime vet of BCH, Valerie was one of the best scrub nurses on staff. As usual, Valerie looked in total command of her craft as she prepped her station for the upcoming operation. It was Valerie who had introduced Carrie to the joys of listening to jazz while operating, and over the years the two had grown close.

If there was one drawback to working with Valerie, it was her unwavering commitment to finding Carrie a date. Beneath her surgical cap and scrubs, Carrie had luxurious brown hair down to her shoulders, almond-shaped brown eyes, enviably high cheekbones, and a body toned and muscled from hours of training. All that, combined with her intellect and outgoing personality, and Dr. Carrie Bryant was somebody's total package. Despite Carrie's repeated assurances that she was happily single, Valerie never failed to bring a list of eligible bachelors to surgery.

"His name is James, and he's some hotshot at a biotech startup in Cambridge. My mother knows his family."

"Thanks for the suggestion," Carrie said, checking over the equipment, "but today the only man I'm interested in is John Coltrane. Let's fire up the music, please."

Carrie waited for the first notes from "Out of this World," the first cut from *Coltrane (Deluxe Edition),* to play before she picked up the scalpel and positioned it for the initial cut. The little stomach jitter that had been kicking around was gone. The first solo flight had to happen to everyone at some point, and today was her day.

You've got this, Doc. You trained hard.

Any and all distractions faded. Lingering thoughts of her ex-boyfriend, Valerie's biotech guy, and tomorrow's surgery with Dr. Metcalf were just ghosts in her consciousness. Her focus was intense. She loved being in the zone; this level of concentration was a rush like no other. Prior to surgery, Carrie had managed sundry pro forma tasks, those checklist items requiring no thought or decision. Following standard procedure, she had used Mayfield pins to secure Beth's head in three fixation points.

It was time to operate.

Carrie made the first scalp incision, expertly cutting the shape of a large semicircle over the crown of Beth's shaved and immobilized skull. She paused to examine her work. It was a fine first cut, and Carrie was pleased with the results. The skin flap was certainly large enough.

The growth was sitting underneath the skull, originating from the meninges, the membrane that covers the brain. It was directly adjacent to the superior sagittal sinus, the major venous channel coursing between the brain's hemispheres. From what Carrie had seen in the MRI, the sinus appeared to be open. This was one of her chief concerns going in. If the tumor were adhering to the sinus, Carrie could do only a partial resection, which would mean Beth would need additional treatment, such as radiation therapy or another surgery.

Why did you make that promise?

It was probably seeing Beth's kids, especially little six-year-old Emily with her sweet toothy smile, that had clouded Carrie's better judgment. If the tumor were free from the sinus, the only treatment Beth would need would be careful follow-up to ensure no recurrence, and perhaps an anticonvulsant medication to reduce the risks of residual seizures.

Surgeons were not, in Carrie's opinion, like normal people. They were more like clutch shooters who took the ball with three seconds left and the basketball game on the line. Difficult times seemed to bring out the best in their cool. Sure, Carrie had sweated for just a bit at the start of the operation, but that was normal. Good, even. She was young, inexperienced, and it was smart for her to be cautious. Things could head south in a flash, but Carrie was not overly concerned. By the fourth year of residency, any surgeon who would cower in a decisive moment had been culled from the herd.

Carrie set to work placing the Raney clips around the margins of the retracted tissue to hold the scalp in place. The slim blue clips were atraumatic, designed to minimize injury and limit both bleeding and tissue damage.

Thirty minutes into surgery.

It took another fifteen minutes for Carrie to set all the clips in place. Now it was time for her to drill. Carrie held the high-speed stylus in her steady right hand and made four expertly placed burr holes on either side of the parasagittal sinus.

"Change the drill, please," Carrie said.

The circulating nurse handed Carrie a different high-speed pneumatic drill, and she used that one to

TRAUMA   15

cut through the skull between the burr holes. Carrie took in a breath as she lifted the bone flap over the dura. She carefully handed the bone flap to Valerie for safekeeping until she was ready to reconstitute the skull after removing the tumor.

Valerie, being Valerie, anticipated Carrie wanting bone wax to control bleeding from the exposed skull margins.

You've got a great team here, Carrie thought.

Pausing, Carrie examined the dura, a thick membrane that is the outermost of the three layers of the meninges surrounding the brain, for any signs of damage. Using her gloved fingers, she carefully palpated the hard, solid tumor beneath. She judged the location of the growth to be perfect for resection, and then used cotton pledgets to tamp down the margins of the exposed dura.

Carrie was exceedingly careful with the pledgets, because too much traction on the dura might cause tugging on critical veins over the surface of the brain, which could result in bleeding. When the pledgets were properly positioned, Carrie was ready for her next incision, keeping in mind that she would cut one centimeter away from the tumor.

One centimeter. Exact. Precise.

Done. After her perfect cut, Carrie used the coagulator and Gelfoam sponges judiciously to control hemostasis and limit bleeding. And there it was, the tumor, sitting on the top of the brain, pressing down on the cortex that controlled Beth Stillwell's leg and bladder. It was not too big, but it sure was ugly, and more vascular in appearance than she had expected from the MRI image. Thank goodness it was not adherent to the sinus! Carrie could resect it cleanly. Still, the vascular supply was far more complex than she had predicted.

"James is a heck of a lot better-looking than that nasty thing," Valerie said.

Carrie laughed lightly.

The time was 10:30 P.M. Beth had been in surgery for two and a half hours, a little bit longer than Carrie had anticipated, but not unusually long.

"Vitals?" Carrie asked.

"Looking fine," Rosemary said.

One hour and I'll be done, Carrie estimated.

Working with care, Carrie removed the tumor, along with the adherent patch of excised dura, which would be sent off to pathology for a frozen section. It did not appear malignant by gross inspection. She would want to be sure the margins were clean and there was no evidence of malignancy elsewhere. At this point, Carrie figured she could get to the on-call room by midnight and grab five or so hours of sleep before she needed to be back in the OR by seven o'clock the next morning for surgery with Dr. Metcalf.

Ah, the glorious life of a doctor. Her dad, an internist at Mass General, had warned Carrie about the rigors of residency, but his description paled in comparison with the real thing.

Carrie paused to examine her work once more. Something was beginning to bother her. The margins of the craniotomy looked to be oozing blood, much more than usual.

"More Gelfoam and four-by-fours." Carrie's voice sounded calm, but had a noticeable edge.

Valerie complied with speed. As Carrie dabbed

away the bleeding, her whole body heated up beneath her surgical scrubs.

"Vitals?"

"Blood pressure stable at one hundred over seventy, normal sinus at ninety."

What the heck is happening?

Carrie did everything she could to stanch the bleeding, but the oozing persisted. She started to worry.

Why isn't Beth's blood clotting?

Her pre-op labs had showed a normal coagulation profile. She should not be having this problem during surgery. *What is going on? Where is the bleeding coming from?*

From the beginning of her residency, Carrie had been taught to think on her feet, but her mind was drawing blanks.

Think, dammit! Think!

As if Dr. Metcalf were whispering in her ear, Carrie got the germ of an idea. She recalled a case from back in her internship year. A seventy-year-old woman undergoing a craniotomy for an anaplastic meningioma lost blood pressure during surgery and at the same time developed significant skin hemorrhages.

The body normally regulates blood flow by clotting to heal breaks on blood vessel walls, and after the bleeding stops it dissolves those clots to allow for regular blood flow. But some conditions cause the same clotting factors to become overactive, leading to excessive bleeding, as in the case of that seventy-year-old woman. Carrie recalled the outcome grimly.

Could it be DIC—disseminated intravascular coagulation—causing Beth's bleeding? A tissue factor associated with the tumor could be triggering the cascade of proteins and enzymes that regulate clotting. It was a rare complication of meningiomas, but it did happen, especially if the tumors were highly vascular like Beth's.

"Vitals?" Carrie asked again.

"Stable, Carrie."

Victims of DIC often suffered effects of vascular clotting throughout the body. Once the clotting factors were all used up, patients began to bleed, and bleed profusely—the skin, the GI tract, the kidneys and urinary system. DIC could be sudden and catastrophic.

"Get me a pro time/INR, APTT, CBC with platelet count, and fibrin split products," Carrie ordered. "Saline, please. Rosemary, keep up her fluids."

In a perfect world, Carrie would get a hematology consult pronto, but at such a late hour, nobody would be available. Valerie entered the lab test orders into the OR computer.

"Blood pressure is down a bit to one hundred systolic," Rosemary said.

Carrie continued to control the bleeding at the tumor site as best she could. Now she was in the waiting game. Nobody spoke. Carrie asked Valerie to shut off the music, and the only sounds in the OR were the persistent noises of the monitors and the rhythmic breathing of the ventilator.

Fifteen minutes later Beth's labs came back. Carrie was sponging away a fresh ooze of blood as Valerie read the results off the OR computer.

"Pro time and APTT markedly elevated," Valerie said. "Platelets down to five thousand. Crit down to twenty-two percent—about half normal. Fibrin split products positive."

No doubt about it, Carrie thought, *this is DIC*. Beth

had been typed and crossed prior to surgery. Carrie ordered FFP, fresh frozen plasma, and a transfusion of packed red blood cells.

"Carrie," Saleem said, his voice steeped in worry, "I'm seeing hemorrhagic lesions all over Beth's arms."

Carrie stopped sponging to examine Beth's extremities. Sure enough, blood was pooling underneath the skin, forming ugly bruises marred by bumpy raised patches that looked like charcoaled burn marks. Carrie bit her lip as she cleared beads of perspiration from her brow with the back of her hand.

On paper, she had made no missteps. There was no way for her to have predicted this rare complication of a meningioma surgery. It was just the nature of how the tissue itself could react and explode in the tightly regulated, complex coagulation homeostasis process. One small tip of the scale could have been enough to send the entire well-balanced system into complete disarray. The reduced hematocrit meant that Beth was bleeding internally as well—within her GI and urinary tracts, perhaps elsewhere. Sure enough, the indwelling Foley collecting bag was filling with blood-tinged urine.

"Give me two liters of normal saline."

At this point, the FFP and PRBC were ready for transfusion.

"BP down to ninety over sixty. Pulse one twenty," Rosemary announced.

Carrie took in the information, but she remained calm.

I'm not going to let you die.

At one o'clock in the morning, Carrie had another decision to make. Should she treat Beth with heparin, too? The drug could dramatically worsen the bleeding because it was a blood thinner, but on the other hand, Carrie remembered from her rotation on the medical service that heparin could help by preventing the clotting that caused the consumption of coagulation factors. In some DIC cases, a blood thinner could actually promote clotting. It was a crapshoot. Carrie had been right to give Beth a traditional treatment thus far, but her condition was again deteriorating, and rapidly.

"I want a heparin infusion, now."

The words left Carrie's mouth before she realized she'd spoken them. Though her team was masked and gowned, Carrie had no trouble seeing the astonished looks on everyone's faces. Saleem hesitated, but Carrie barked the order again, and this time he jumped. Everyone held a collective breath as the drug was administered intravenously. Carrie kept a careful watch over the wound and continued to sponge away the bleeding. To her eye, the blood flow seemed to have lessened.

Still not out of the woods. Not even close.

All Carrie and her team could do now was contain the bleeding, keep administering fluids, and pray the decision to use heparin was the right course of action.

At four o'clock in the morning, Beth finally seemed to be stabilizing. Her blood pressure had risen to 110/65. By that point, everyone in the OR was utterly exhausted, with Carrie in the worst shape of all. This was her patient—on her watch! Carrie's feet had swollen to the size of water balloons and her back strained against the tug of eight grueling hours spent standing.

Carrie ordered another set of labs. This time, while the FSP was still elevated, the PT and APTT were definitely showing signs of improvement. The bleeding looked better, too.

Valerie appeared stunned, as did Saleem.

"Carrie, whatever in the world inspired you to give this poor darling heparin?" Valerie asked.

Carrie was breathing as though she had just finished a sprint-distance tri. "Just a thought I had, I guess."

At five forty-five in the morning, Beth Stillwell was handed off from surgical to the medical and hematology teams in the ICU. Her DIC was still a problem and she would need much more intensive work to stabilize her, but the major bleeding seemed to be contained. Fifteen minutes later, Valerie and Beth were changing out of their bloodstained surgical scrubs in the women's locker room.

"She's going to make it because of you, because of what you did in there," Valerie said, brushing tears from her eyes.

Carrie had never seen Valerie cry before, and the sight set a lump in her throat. "But what's the quality of her survival going to be?" Carrie answered. "She bled a lot."

"Carrie Bryant, don't be so hard on yourself. If it had been any other doc in there, they wouldn't have ordered the heparin and we'd be having a very different conversation right now."

"Maybe."

Valerie turned fierce. "Don't you maybe me, Dr. Bryant! You diagnosed DIC quick as you did, and correctly at that. Then treating her with heparin? Girl, in my humble opinion, you are a hero here. Real and true, and I want to give you a hug."

Valerie opened her arms and Carrie fell into her

embrace. The moment she did, the tears broke and would not stop for more than a minute. It had been such a long night. *I made a promise.* . . .

Carrie broke away from Valerie, but could not get the faces of Beth's young daughters out of her mind. She took a moment to regain her composure, then checked the time on her phone. It was six fifteen in the morning. She was due back in the OR for the astrocytoma surgery with Dr. Metcalf in forty-five minutes.

"I've got to go break the news to Beth's sister," Carrie said, her chest filling with a heavy sadness.

The conversation would be briefer than the family deserved, but she'd page Dr. Michelson and make sure he could be there for follow-up questions. At this point, Carrie only had time to take a quick shower and wolf down a peanut-butter-and-jelly sandwich with a black coffee chaser outside the OR.

That was all the time she ever seemed to have.

3

Carrie arrived to scrub fifteen minutes late, expecting to see Dr. Stanley Metcalf already gowned and glowering. Next to medical incompetence, Dr. Metcalf despised tardiness most of all. She was surprised and more than a little relieved to discover he had yet to show up for Leon Dixon's brain surgery.

In addition to making sure the circulating and scrub nurses were at their stations and ready to go, it was Carrie's responsibility to get the patient prepped, properly positioned, and draped correctly. The only part of the pre-op routine Carrie did not oversee belonged to Dr. Lucas Fellows, the anesthesiologist, who would take care of getting the patient anesthetized and intubated. Surgeons and anesthesiologists did not always play nicely in the same sandbox, each guarding their turf with vigor.

Still, when it came time to put scalpel to skin, Dr. Metcalf was the general in charge. Most surgeons with a reputation like his came with a plus-sized ego. The man could be bombastic, often arrogant, always meticulous, and so demanding of his assistants that a healthy dose of fear was advisable for any underling assigned to him.

Despite his intimidating reputation, the advantages of working with Dr. Metcalf were undeniable. He offered the best opportunity for growth and learning, and for that alone, Carrie was grateful to be his foot soldier. But having incurred Dr. Metcalf's wrath once before, Carrie was glad to have a few extra minutes to set up the OR.

Still, she'd have to hurry.

Thinking of Beth, Carrie finished scrubbing in a daze. Breaking bad news was a part of the job, but that did not make the task any easier. Beth's sister, Amanda, had been told the surgery should not take longer than three hours, so she knew something had gone terribly wrong before Carrie set foot inside the waiting room.

"I'm sorry, but I have some bad news." Carrie had been taught to use that phrase, but still, there were few words a doctor despised saying more than those.

I'm sorry . . .

Valerie had accompanied Carrie into the cramped conference room where she had taken Amanda to consult with her in private. Because of Carrie's back-to-back surgeries, Valerie offered to hold the conference with Dr. Michelson instead, but Carrie believed the privilege of caring for sick people came with the added burden of being the messenger.

"Is she going to live?" Amanda had asked after Carrie finished.

Amanda was a sweet-faced woman, five years younger than Beth, and the strain in her kind eyes put a lump in Carrie's throat.

"We're doing everything possible to make sure that she does," Carrie said.

Amanda bit at her lower lip, but could not hold back the rush of tears in her eyes. In response, Carrie reached across the table and clutched the young woman's trembling hand.

"I'm so sorry, Amanda, we're doing everything we can. Please know that. I'm deeply sorry for what's happened here."

A single nod sent Valerie off to get Amanda some water. Carrie did her best to answer Amanda's many questions, though she suspected the young woman would retain little of it. Carrie spoke frankly but compassionately, and promised to follow up with the hematology team looking after Beth as soon as she could.

In the OR, prepping for the next patient, Carrie struggled to push Amanda's tears, Beth's three children, and the complexity of Beth's case out of her mind. A man with a serious brain tumor was waiting for her in the OR, and he deserved her undivided attention.

Margaret, the circulating nurse, was on her first day at BCH, so she was shy and quiet as she assisted Carrie with her surgical gown and gloves. It was just as well. Carrie's guilt and exhaustion left her in no mood for small talk.

Scrubbed and gowned, Carrie entered the OR and headed straight to the viewbox. The films weren't there. She looked around and saw that X-ray had delivered them, but Margaret hadn't put them up, probably because she was new and nervous.

Though the task was the new nurse's, it was easier for Carrie to do it herself. Carrie grumbled under her breath as she removed the MRI image from the protective envelope.

Dammit!

The moment her gloved hand came in contact with the film, Carrie realized her mistake. She had broken scrub by touching a nonsterile object with her sterilized gloved hand. She'd have to go through the sterilization procedures all over again. It would mean being even more rushed during prep than she already was. Dr. Metcalf could arrive at any second, and if he did not see everything in pristine order, ready to drill, there would be serious fireworks.

For now, it was back to Leon's film.

Carrie had given him only a cursory examination previously, but she remembered that Leon had exhibited cognitive and behavioral problems, some muscular control issues, memory problems, and difficulty controlling his temper.

Carrie tossed the film up on the viewbox, a film she had seen only once before, briefly, in Dr. Nugent's office. That felt like a lifetime ago. Based on visual characteristics, the brain tumor was probably an astrocytoma, the most common form of tumor, but pathology would have to confirm. From what Carrie could see, the mass was not characteristic of a systemic cancer, something that had metastasized to the brain. Good news for Leon. Still, she doubted it was a totally unsuspected abscess, something that surgery plus a prolonged course of antibiotics could essentially cure. Dr. Nugent had said something similar during his brief consult.

Regardless, it didn't do any good to speculate. They would sample the tissue, get the pathology report, and go from there.

Carrie saw that the mass was located deep in the temporal lobe. It looked angry, with a good deal of edema. Leon would most likely need additional surgery to debulk the tumor, followed by radiation and chemotherapy treatments. He might get a few more quality years before the tumor came back to take it all away.

Carrie's dry eyes ached from lack of sleep. At least this case would not be difficult for Dr. Metcalf, who had probably done a thousand of these procedures. She'd be home sometime after noon and asleep a few minutes after that. Assuming, of course, that Dr. Metcalf actually made it to surgery. Carrie had never worked a case before where he'd been so late, and she was beginning to wonder if he had the wrong date on his schedule. In an administrative behemoth like BCH, stranger things had happened.

Back at the sink, Carrie followed the proper protocol for the anatomical scrub, and had Margaret help her get gowned and gloved again. Precious minutes lost.

The scrub nurse, Sam Talbot, had done a fine job making sure the operating room was clean and ready for surgery. He had prepared the instruments and equipment and was double-checking his work when Carrie reentered the OR. Carrie was glad Talbot was on the ball so she could concentrate her efforts on Leon.

Leon was on the operating room table, already anesthetized and intubated. Dr. Lucas Fellows monitored vital signs and adjusted the combination of agents used to keep Leon in a state of blissful unconsciousness.

With Margaret's help, Carrie positioned Leon on his back, elevated the head, and turned him toward his left side. Carrie prepped Leon's shaved skull using antiseptic Betadine that turned his dark skin orange. As

Carrie finished with her final swab, the OR door swung open and Dr. Metcalf bounded in, fully scrubbed. Margaret, caught by surprise, shrank a little in his presence. A bear of a man with a full beard, broad shoulders, and a barrel chest, Dr. Metcalf struck an imposing figure in the operating room—or anyplace, for that matter. He held up his arms for Margaret to get him gowned and gloved.

"Sorry for the late arrival," Dr. Metcalf said in his deep, rich baritone. "There was a rollover on I-95 and traffic was backed up for miles. I thought we might have to reschedule, but a friendly cop gave me an escort down the breakdown lane. I can't count the number of angry looks I got."

Dr. Metcalf chuckled and Carrie felt at ease. He seemed to have already observed all of the hard work that had gone into surgical preparation and deemed it fit. He approached Leon and looked over his mask at Carrie, who was standing on the other side of the operating room table.

Dr. Metcalf's brown eyes narrowed. "Goodness, you look terrible, Carrie," he said. "Are you feeling all right?"

Carrie nodded. "Tough operation last night, that's all," she said. "I'm fine."

The persistent throbbing behind Carrie's temple suggested otherwise, but she knew her limits. She could handle one more case.

A few more hours . . . you can do it.

Dr. Metcalf scanned the OR and chuckled again. "Forgot I'm not at White Memorial for a second there. I was looking for the NeuroStation."

Carrie smiled behind her mask. A NeuroStation

was a state-of-the-art workstation for localizing brain tumors using a frameless stereotactic system that gave surgeons an unprecedented view into the operative field while relaying the location of instruments to the preoperative imaging data. It cost hundreds of thousands of dollars—well over a million when factoring in all the ancillary equipment. The fancy folks over at White Memorial could afford such luxuries, but BCH didn't have enough funding for such an extravagant expense.

"No worries," Dr. Metcalf said. "I remember when we used to do these operations without a Midas Rex drill. Hell, the drill and bit set we used during *my* residency looked like something you'd pick up at Sears."

Everyone laughed politely.

"All right, Dr. Bryant," he said. "We'll be finished here in no time."

4

Dr. Metcalf had made the semicircular incision in the temporal-parietal craniotomy site. He was so skilled, had so many years of training, he probably could have done the procedure blindfolded. Nothing was remarkable about his deft handling, except that Carrie could not recall him doing it. It had happened, of course. The skin flap was there, and Dr. Metcalf was busy setting the Raney clips in place, but somehow Carrie had no memory of him actually making the cut. It was like highway hypnosis, only in the OR.

Carrie's body burned with exhaustion that did not justify her lack of concentration. She had pulled plenty of long shifts without her performance suffering. Then again, she'd never been primary surgeon on an operation with serious complications.

Beneath her mask, Carrie gritted her teeth against an onslaught of memories—the blood that kept seeping, the blackened subdermal patches of clotted blood.

Beth's operation was hours in the past. She needed to stop it from affecting her performance here and now. Adding to her burden, Carrie's back throbbed from fatigue. Her calf muscles were bowstring tight, and every two seconds she had to fight the urge to rub at her bleary eyes.

Carrie wondered if she'd ever be able to emulate Dr. Metcalf's level of discipline and focus. How did he never seem to tire, no matter how difficult the operation? One thing Carrie knew for certain: She would need his Zen-like mastery of that particular skill to achieve all her professional goals.

"How about some Gelfoam here," Dr. Metcalf said.

The command snapped Carrie out of her daze. She went to work on the incision area, using Avitene on a pledget and Gelfoam to stanch the bleeding.

"Drill."

Sam Talbot placed the stainless steel handle of the Midas Rex pneumatic drill in Dr. Metcalf's outstretched hand. The specialized air drill was designed to stop drilling as soon as the skull was penetrated, preventing injury to the brain. With enviable control and precision, Dr. Metcalf whistled a low and indistinct tune as he created the burr holes, each perfectly placed, one behind the standard key point, others located posteriorly in the temporal bone.

"Vitals?" Dr. Metcalf asked.

The anesthesiologist checked his monitors. "All fine," Dr. Fellows said.

Dr. Metcalf switched to the footplate attachment and started at the temporal burr hole, cutting in a curvilinear fashion, until this region of bone could be removed. Carrie helped by stanching the annoying small bleeders that cropped up on occasion. Everything appeared to be going exactly as planned. Because Leon's tumor was situated deep within the brain, and not a part of the meninges, the dura would have to be excised, which Dr. Metcalf did with great care.

Soon it was time to locate the actual source of Leon's troubles. In the absence of the NeuroStation, Dr. Metcalf relied on the MRI film Carrie had put up on the viewbox to show him where to insert the needle probes. The needles were not really necessary, and Carrie knew Dr. Metcalf was using them for teaching purposes.

Carrie had done this procedure many times herself, but always under careful supervision. Because Dr. Metcalf could not see the tumor, he used the probes to feel for subtle texture changes indicative of touching a growth. For guidance, he occasionally glanced at the MRI while advancing the needle. Carrie knew from her read of the film that the tumor site was approximately 3.5 centimeters deep within the temporal lobe, and Dr. Metcalf was probing in that exact spot.

Carrie watched him work, admiring his steady hand, calm concentration, when Beth again entered her thoughts. Seeing someone so close to her in age suffer like that was a stark reminder of her own good fortune. It was shameful that it took an incident in the OR to make her appreciate her many blessings: her career in medicine, the mentors like Dr. Metcalf who had helped bring her to this point, her family—and even Ian, for ending the relationship and giving her a chance to learn more about herself.

Dr. Metcalf advanced the probe a bit further, then paused. Lifting his head, he gave Carrie a curious stare—not a disapproving look, but something in his eyes looked nonplussed. He maneuvered the probe some more, but this time without a second glance at Carrie. The bleeders were typical for the surgery. No alarms for the patient's vitals, either.

It must have been nothing, because Metcalf removed the probes and was getting the bipolar coagulator and aspirator ready to go. It was time to get Leon's tumor out, or as much of it as they could.

Dr. Metcalf adjusted the frequency on the bipolar coagulator, an instrument with two electrical poles used to cauterize and remove tissue. The tissue here was soft and would require a lower frequency than something more fibrous. The disposable forceps with two small electrodes decreased risk of thrombosis formation, caused minimal tissue damage without suturing, and were effective at hemorrhage prevention.

Dr. Metcalf carefully advanced the bipolar coagulator through the inferior temporal gyros, using a surgical aspirator, more crudely known as a "sucker," to remove blood and fluids while taking away as little good brain tissue as possible.

Should be at the tumor site any second now, Carrie thought.

The sounds of machinery thrummed in Carrie's ears as her anticipation grew. As Dr. Metcalf shifted his attention from Leon to the MRI image, a shadow crossed his face, and his furrowed brow put Carrie on edge. Focused again on the work site, Dr. Metcalf advanced the coagulator perhaps a centimeter more, then stopped. Carrie tried to read his expression. He was obviously anxious. Could it be another complication? Goodness, she had no stamina to endure another surgical mishap.

Dr. Metcalf adjusted a power setting on the frequency generator. A second later, the persistent hum of the bipolar coagulator came to an abrupt stop. The absence of sound filled the room.

Dr. Metcalf looked up and his eyes narrowed in a way that made Carrie shrink inside. "Carrie, I can't find any abnormal tissue here, and I'm at the tumor site."

A chill raced up Carrie's spine.

No . . . no . . . everything is fine . . . it's not panic time . . . not yet . . .

"Let's take a closer look at the MRI," Dr. Metcalf suggested.

Carrie followed Dr. Metcalf over to the viewbox and saw up close what she had observed from a distance. The mass was easy to spot in the medial temporal lobe. It was obvious Dr. Metcalf was seeing the same thing.

"What's going on here?" he asked, mostly to himself. "Jesus, could this be the wrong patient?"

Carrie and Dr. Metcalf simultaneously looked down at the name on the film. As soon as Carrie saw the lettering, a jolt of horror ripped through her body and her breathing stopped. The name was correct, but the letters were reversed!

Oh, God, Carrie thought. *Oh my God, no. Please no!*

Grim-faced now, Dr. Metcalf let his arms fall limply to his side as he fixated on the text, disbelieving.

"Carrie, do you see this? The film was put up backward."

Carrie staggered on her feet as the room began to spin. She had reversed the film. Following a backwards image, Carrie had set the patient up for an operation on the wrong side of his brain.

She flashed on her brief meeting with Leon, and it hit her. Not only did he have a droopy face, his reflexes were heightened in the right arm and leg, indicative of a left-side problem. But more telling was his speech. He had trouble saying simple words and had not been able to follow one of her commands; those were left-sided problems. If she had remembered, Carrie would have seen her mistake and clipped the image up properly.

This can't be happening . . . this cannot be happening. . . .

The shattered look in Dr. Metcalf's eyes cleaved Carrie's heart.

Leon, who already had damage to the left temporal lobe because of the mass, would now have additional damage to the right side of the brain where Dr. Metcalf had probed and removed completely viable brain tissue. It was all her fault.

Dr. Metcalf glowered at the new circulating nurse, Margaret, with venom in his eyes.

"What happened here? What the hell happened here? Don't you know how to read?" Dr. Metcalf's wrathful voice sent Margaret scurrying to a corner.

Dr. Fellows and Sam Talbot stared at each other in disbelief. Carrie took in a shaky breath, but could barely get a sip of air into her lungs. Her face felt flushed, burning hot, and soon the rest of her skin prickled with sweat as a sick feeling washed over her from head to toe. She opened her mouth to speak but at first no sound came out. Courage finally came to her.

"I put the MRI on the viewbox, not Margaret," Carrie said. "It was my error."

With that, she lowered her head and began a solemn march to the exit door.

5

By the time Steve Abington made his decision, the April sun had hit its midpoint for the day. Steve had hated Philadelphia since arriving there almost a year ago. It wasn't really any worse than Bridgeport, or Manhattan, or East Brunswick, or any of the other cities through which he'd passed. Maybe it was the homeless shelters in Philly that had gotten to him, or maybe it was just life itself.

Still, the Philadelphia shelters were an abomination. Steve hated being jammed inside an airless room with a hundred other misbegotten men. The stale stench of cigarette smoke escaping from the ratty fabric of soiled clothes. Rows of metallic bunk beds like those on a submarine topped with thin mattresses squirming with vermin, sometimes even live mice. Corroded showerheads on tiled walls caked with mold revolted him.

It was chaos, a constant chatter that grated on Steve's eardrums so he couldn't ever relax. Not for a second. Of course a shelter does not pretend to be a Holiday

Inn, but with the reception area located behind reinforced glass, it felt like a country jail segregating the
inmates from the cons. The drunks were the worst.
Screaming, belligerent, and always getting hurt—either
tripping over nothing or cracking their skulls on the
concrete floor after tumbling out of bed. There was food,
at least, breakfast and dinner. But tuna fish sandwiches
most every day could make a man want to give up eating.

Steve preferred the streets.

Or he did until he was robbed.

They came at him in the middle of the night, four
teenagers, while he slept on a heat vent, wrapped inside
a threadbare blue blanket he'd fished out of a trash
can. They came with pipes, steel rods, and a bat. They
smashed the side of his face pretty good and throttled
his leg, but the blows were meant to intimidate, not
kill. They made off with his life savings—a few hundred dollars he had scraped together from change tossed
in his jar and the occasional crinkled bill. The next
morning the bruise on his cheek still stung, his leg felt
a bit lame, and the vision in his eye where one of them
managed to land a solid right hook was blurry. Could
have been worse; he had shocked them when he fought
back. Some skills get drilled into you so hard they
become reflex.

Funny how just a few years ago Steve had a fancy
uniform with plenty of eye-catching chest candy. He
had a purpose in life. Now he had the streets and not
much else. At least the little bastards didn't get his SIG
Sauer, a trophy he'd snuck back from Afghanistan that
was hidden at the bottom of an oily knapsack.

That gun meant the world to Steve. It was like a
time machine. Soon as he gripped the cool steel han-

dle he was right back in his CHU—containerized housing unit—on Forward Operating Base Eagle. In a lot of ways the CHU was a mirror of a Philly shelter. It was a crowded, noisy affair that smelled like a sweaty gym most of the time, but it had been home when he was Staff Sergeant Abington. He had felt at ease inside the chaotic womb, among his friends, his brothers in arms, the soldiers he would have given his life for. Back in the theater they had depended on each other. It was simple, pure, and in a way, beautiful. When he got home, the world stopped making sense.

But now Steve had made a decision. He had a new plan, a little flash of inspiration. He'd had enough of the streets, the shelters, the cold, and the beatings. He used to be somebody—a staff sergeant in the United States Army, a husband to Janine, a father to Olivia. They were phantoms now. Steve did not blame Janine for cutting him out of her life. He had pushed her to it. She feared for their daughter's safety. He had threatened them, been violent at times, sober rarely, and a person could only take so much. No, he blamed the wound in his mind. Not a single drop of his blood had ever spilled in combat, but he was broken all the same. Injured with scars. Haunted.

All he could focus on was survival, and his needs were immediate and simple: Food. Shelter. Money. He had a plan to get those things.

6

The BCH conference room was nearly full. By quarter to eight in the morning, all but Knox Singer, the gray-haired CEO of Community, had arrived for the meeting. Carrie was sandwiched between Julie Stafford, the head nurse for 4C, the neurosurgical floor where Leon Dixon had stayed before surgery, and Emily Forrester, legal counsel for White Memorial Hospital. As part of her official residency at White Memorial, Carrie rotated through various satellite hospitals, including BCH. Her operating room mistake had dragged the neurosurgical departments of two organizations into this legal morass.

Sitting across from Carrie were Dr. Stanley Metcalf and Brandon Olyfson, the CEO of White Memorial. Olyfson was whippet-thin, with a long and narrow face, and hawkish eyes that made Carrie shrivel inside. There was coffee, of course, but the usual platters of donuts and pastries were absent, probably in deference to the gravity of the situation. No one was chatting; periodic, desultory sips of coffee were all that broke the silence.

Olyfson and Dr. Metcalf exchanged a few quiet words. Carrie was deeply unsettled by the tension on their faces. Her actions had not only injured a patient, but she had damaged the credibility of her hospital and the man whose skill and poise she had worked so tirelessly to emulate. Her failure was egregious. Unconscionable. Soon she'd hear it dissected in all its grotesque detail by the higher-ups at BCH and White Memorial.

Until a few hours ago, Carrie had been in the same scrubs she'd worn to Leon Dixon's surgery. Now she had on her most professional-looking outfit: a dark suit jacket, slacks, and a blue blouse. Carrie had returned home to her empty Brookline apartment; fed her goldfish, Limbic, named after a primitive memory circuit in the brain; and passed out on the futon, getting a fitful couple hours of sleep. She awoke mired in self-loathing and disbelief, and the pang in her heart confirmed it had really happened.

She did a reasonable job pulling herself together. After studying the spectral being she'd become in the bathroom mirror—her skin was moonlight pale, with dark circles ringing each eye, and her tousled hair stuck out in all directions—she'd swept her hair into a ponytail and figured they'd at least see she was suffering.

At two minutes past eight, the door to the conference room swung open. In strode Knox Singer, accompanied by Carla Mason, head of legal for BCH. Singer was all alpha male, tall and broad-shouldered, with a finely coiffed mane of silver hair and the swarthy good looks of a guy who made his living doing Cialis commercials.

Mason was pint-sized by comparison, but her severe bangs, ramrod-straight back, and sharply tailored business suit seemed to add a few inches of height.

Emily Forrester grabbed a chair from against the wall and wheeled it over for Mason, while Singer took a seat at the head of the conference table.

"Sorry I'm late," Knox said in a rumbling low voice. His tone suggested this was the worst possible way to start his day. "Let me begin by saying this meeting is privileged. No minutes. The reputation of Community has to trump the glaring negligence from any member of its staff. So, tell me, Stan, what happened in there?"

Mason managed to get Knox Singer's attention, and she gave him a look he understood.

"Wait," Knox said, preempting Dr. Metcalf's response. "Do you want counsel, Stan? You can have it. Just say the word."

Dr. Metcalf sat stone-faced and issued no response. None was necessary. Everyone knew what this meant: There was no defense. As the attending physician, Dr. Metcalf was responsible for everything that happened in the OR, including the negligent actions of his first assistant.

Carrie sat rigid in her chair and felt a tight band pull across her chest. Her throat had gone Sahara dry, but she could not manage even a sip from the glass of ice water in front of her. They might be talking to Dr. Metcalf, but this meeting was about her. She fixed her gaze on her hands, which were clutched together in her lap. She needed to keep it together.

"Got it," Knox said. "So I'll ask again, and pardon my language, but what the fuck happened in there?"

Carrie lifted her head and somehow found the courage to look Knox in the eyes.

"It was my mistake," she said. Her voice came out in a whisper, so she had to repeat herself. Louder. "I'm the one responsible." Carrie pursed her lips against a sob, a few tears leaking down.

Julie Stafford's nursing instincts kicked in, and she put a comforting arm around Carrie's shaking shoulders. Gently, Julie eased the glass of water closer to Carrie and encouraged her to drink. Carrie couldn't; she was nauseated with grief.

Knox appraised Carrie thoughtfully. He bore a sympathetic expression, as did about half of those seated at the table, with Dr. Metcalf being the most notable exception.

"How did this happen, Dr. Bryant?" Knox asked more mildly.

Carrie shook her head slowly, still in shock. On the occasions when Carrie checked her cell phone while driving, she tried to imagine what it would feel like to cause a traffic fatality, as a way of weaning herself from the habit. But now she knew. She knew exactly what it felt like. It was a sickening, horrible feeling she would not wish on anybody.

"I put the film up backward," Carrie said, struggling with her voice. "I should have known—I should have—Mr. Dixon was aphasic, his right side was weaker, he had a right Babinski. All the signs were there to remind me that the problem was in the left hemisphere, but somehow I just forgot. I guess I was tired from my last surgery, but I know that's not an excuse, I know that. I'm so very sorry to everyone involved."

Carrie braved eye contact with everyone at the table, desperate to convey her sincerity. Dr. Metcalf focused on his notepad as if refusing to look at Carrie somehow separated him from her and her mistake.

"Had you reviewed the film prior?" asked Sam Stern, the sixty-five-year-old chief of neurosurgery at Community. It was obvious he would try to shift the blame to another department, and radiology was as good a target as any.

Carrie swallowed hard. "I reviewed the MRI with Dr. Nugent the day before the surgery," she said. "I'd seen the films, Sam. I have no excuse."

The silence that followed lasted several seconds before Knox spoke up and broke the spell.

"Julie, what's Mr. Dixon's status?"

Julie Stafford had been head nurse on the neurosurgical floor for fifteen years, and a staff nurse at Community for fifteen years before that. She essentially ran the place. Jokes abounded about her supernatural ability to know everything that happened on her floor, even before it seemed to happen. It was a well-established fact that Nurse Stafford could make or break the career of any resident rotating through 4C with just a few choice words. But she'd always been good to Carrie; they shared the same work ethic and commitment.

"Mr. Dixon is stable," Julie said. "But he's mute and won't follow any commands. Right now his wife and his brother are with him. They know what happened. Dr. Metcalf hasn't been in to see him, though." Dr. Metcalf shot Julie a stern look.

Carla Mason had been quietly taking notes and looked up over her glasses. "I've told him not to," Carla said.

"I would like to go on record here and say a few words," Julie said.

With a nod Knox gave his consent, and Julie spoke.

"I have worked with Carrie Bryant since the start of her residency, when her responsibilities were limited to doing mostly scut work at all hours of the day. Carrie, more than anyone, took the extra time to get to know her patients and families. I understand that she had been up all night operating on a complicated case. I spoke personally with Beth Stillwell's sister, Amanda, who praised Carrie's kindness and compassion. I've personally seen Dr. Metcalf tear apart residents for any delays that derailed his schedule, so I'm sure that played a role in Carrie rushing to get the OR set up right. Carrie made a terrible mistake. There's no denying that fact, but she's not the only culpable party."

Dr. Metcalf made daggers with his eyes.

"I refuse to be intimidated by any doctor on staff, regardless of their stature here," Julie continued. "In my opinion, I'm tired of the attending physicians using the hospital like a personal garage whenever a physician friend wanted a favor. Look, I sincerely appreciate our close relationship with White Memorial and the excellent doctors from there who otherwise wouldn't be in a position to care for our city's less fortunate. But perhaps if Dr. Metcalf deigned to venture up to 4C to see his patient before operating, or God forbid at least look at the MRI prior, none of this would have happened."

A heavy silence ensued, and Carrie felt somewhat vindicated. Better procedures for double-checking should have been in place, and Carrie believed protocols would change as a result.

"Look, there's really no issue here," Carla Mason interjected.

As chief counsel for Community, Carla was directly responsible for malpractice cases like this one. Unfortunately, they seemed to be happening with greater and greater frequency. The majority of these cases were meritless, but the hospital continued to cough up millions in legal fees defending them, not to mention countless hours of deposition, fact-finding, and copying records. The impact on productivity was now just a cost of doing business. For everyone involved, the expense of a lengthy trial was more than a matter of money; it was years of legal wrangling in terms of time, reputation, and emotional well-being. Carla tried to avoid the courtroom whenever possible, even for the most meritless claims—a strategy Knox Singer fully endorsed.

"The family will sue and the hospital will settle," Carla said. "And the sooner this is done, the better. The last thing BCH and Chambers University need is something like this getting out to the press and the public."

"Carla and I are meeting with the Dixons at eleven," said Emily Forrester, the lawyer for White Memorial. "We will advise them to seek counsel immediately. Knox, I take it you'd agree to our informing the family that the hospital and university will offer a very generous settlement, and will assume responsibility for any upcoming and future medical care that the Dixons might require. I've already discussed this with Brandon, who concurs."

Brandon Olyfson nodded. As CEO of White Memorial Hospital, he wanted out of this meeting, and quick. Olyfson thought of BCH as nothing more than a cesspool. Three-quarters of the patients were drunks or drugged out. No one had insurance. He could give a crap about Leon Dixon, Carrie believed. All that mattered to Olyfson was that Dr. Metcalf, his choice for the next chief of neurosurgery, was now a potential plague on the reputation of White Memorial Hospital.

"So, this Dixon guy. I mean, he was probably going to have problems regardless of any surgery, right?" Olyfson asked.

Dr. Metcalf became indignant. "Brandon, Mr. Dixon has a left temporal lobe tumor, most likely an astrocytoma. But of course, we don't know that for certain now. His tumor may be aggressive, and if so, his prognosis wouldn't be very good. Maybe a few years with radiation and chemotherapy. But just maybe, this could have been an abscess and potentially curable. The MRI isn't definitive. It can't distinguish between an abscess and a tumor. But we can't operate on the other side until we know what damage we caused by this error."

"So was Mr. Dixon going to be compromised regardless?" Olyfson asked.

"The tumor might be less aggressive and potentially more amenable to adjunctive treatments than usual," Metcalf said. "One never really knows. Mr. Dixon was losing control of his speech. Now we've only added to his deficits. He may never speak another word. He may lose all his memory function. His behavior is likely to be very different. Hell, he could lose functional control of his sphincters for all we know. Bottom line is he will now be functionally dependent for the rest of his life, however long that's going to be. Considerably shorter, I suspect. We can do a simple biopsy of his tumor at some point, but because of the damage we've done, aggressive care won't be of any benefit."

Carla Mason and Emily Forrester took copious notes, but Carrie looked only at her lap. She was finished. She sat silent, holding herself together by remaining as still as possible. But she couldn't stop the tears, which cascaded down her cheeks, dripping into her lap. Once again, Julie put an arm around Carrie to comfort her.

"It's going to be okay, sweetie," Julie whispered. "We'll get through this. I promise."

"Carrie, anything else you want to add?" Knox asked.

"Just that I'm tendering my resignation," Carrie said. "Effective immediately."

7

The First National Bank of Philadelphia occupied the lower level of a five-story brick building on the corner of Eighth Avenue and Sutcliff. Abington picked it because he was standing near it when inspiration struck.

As he expected, he drew suspicious looks from his first step inside. With his flyaway straw-colored hair, haggard face, baggy eyes, and mountain man–style beard, Abington made Nick Nolte's mug shot look like a high school yearbook picture.

Four customers were inside the bank when Abington entered, and none made direct eye contact with him as he crossed the marble floor to the teller windows. Though the bank was not crowded, Abington still had to wait in line, which made him edgy. He was especially mindful of the man to his right, filling out a deposit slip. That guy seemed to not notice Abington at all, which was unusual. Could this guy's obliviousness be an act? Abington's gut told him it was a cop, either undercover or off duty.

The brunette behind teller window number five mo-
tioned Abington forward. For a moment he contemplated walking out. He felt naked without a hat or
sunglasses, and the security cameras had already gotten a clear shot of his face. *Oh, what the hell.* He was
here. She wouldn't know the gun in his back pocket
wasn't loaded. She'd give him the money.

As Abington approached, the brunette recoiled sub-
tly, her brow creasing and the corners of her mouth
turning downward. She maintained an air of professionalism, but her demeanor had turned hard-bitten and
judgmental.

"Can I help you?" she asked in a tone that implied
otherwise. Be it a handout, food, booze—whatever it
was, she was not there to assist.

"I would like some money." Abington was surprised
at the shakiness of his voice. He had meant to sound
forceful, but instead spoke in a raspy near whisper.

The teller rolled her eyes and Abington took a moment to look over his shoulder at the man filling out
the deposit slip. *How many checks is that guy cash-
ing?* He had to be a cop.

*Walk away ... head out that door and just walk
away. ...*

Abington was about to turn around when he flashed
on the faces of those bastards pummeling him with
bats and steel rods. He pictured the grate where he'd
slept the night before. He thought of the many shelters
he had called home, and felt a pang of hunger. A tide
of violence rose in his blood as he thought of the VA
that had failed him. He drew his weapon.

The color drained from the teller's face. Before she

could scream, Abington put his finger to his lip, shielding the piece with his body.

"Don't do anything stupid," Abington said, gratified to hear more authority in his voice this time. "Give me the money." From underneath Abington's grimy shirt he produced an equally soiled paper bag, and handed it to the teller.

The teller's hands shook as she filled the bag with thick wads of banded cash, but twice she glanced up to look over Abington's shoulder at the man to his back.

While the teller filled the bag, Abington counted the seconds in his head. *Five . . . then ten . . .*

How much money had she put in there? Maybe a couple thousand. Maybe a little more. It didn't matter. It wasn't like he'd stop to count. He needed to get out of there.

The teller was reaching for another drawer when Abington realized she was stalling. Her hands were steadier, and she seemed less nervous. Maybe she had tripped the silent alarm.

Reaching over the counter, Abington ripped the bag from the teller's hand, leaving her with a little piece of brown paper. He swung around, gun in one hand, money in the other, and saw that the man with the deposit slip had snuck up behind him.

Midforties with short hair and a square head, the guy trained his weapon—a Glock—on Abington's chest. He shouted, "Freeze! Police!"

Abington did not hesitate. The SIG Sauer may have been useless without bullets, but Abington had trained with the SEALs and Delta Force. Even out of shape and practice, he was a fine weapon on his own. Abington dropped his gun and the bag of money and started to raise his hands.

No trouble. I surrender.

The officer started to relax, thinking the fight was over. In a fluid motion, Abington grabbed hold of the Glock's barrel with his right hand while latching his left hand onto the officer's left wrist. Without hesitating, Abington pulled the left wrist toward him at the same instant he pushed on the barrel of the gun. Thrown off balance, the cop stumbled awkwardly, and a fraction of a second later the Glock had transferred into Abington's hands. Abington swung the gun in a wide arc, clocking the cop on his left temple with the butt of the weapon. Two heavy thuds followed: one after the impact, and the other when the cop's limp body crumpled to the floor.

Reaching down, Abington retrieved the bag of money and his treasured gun. He sprang up waving the cop's loaded weapon, shooing the terrified customers back.

"Just leave me alone and nobody gets hurt!" Abington shouted.

Outside the bank, the sun's glare punished Abington's corneas. He blinked to clear his vision, but his head was buzzing and he felt lost. What had he done? Jesus, he hadn't made a plan. No figuring out how he might escape.

In the distance Abington heard a steady whine of sirens. They were coming for him. *Stupid . . . stupid!* His choices were simple: run and get caught, or stand in front of the bank and get caught. He looked at the cop's gun.

He supposed he had a third choice. Abington put the weapon to his temple, closed his eyes, and conjured up

Janine's beautiful face. They had had happy times; he tried to focus on those.

"I'm sorry, baby girl," Abington muttered, thinking of his daughter Olivia. "I let you down, sweetie. I let you down so bad."

Abington pressed the barrel of the Glock hard against his skin and squeezed the trigger ever so slightly. Ironic: with all the bullets flying around him in Afghanistan, this would be the one and only time he'd be shot. Abington took a breath. The squeal of sirens seemed to be coming from all directions.

Can they even identify me? Will they let Mom know I'm dead?

A screech of tires in front of him caused Abington to open his eyes. A windowless cargo van had pulled up, and before it came to a complete stop, a clean-shaven man with short-cropped hair jumped out the passenger-side door. He wore a tailored blue suit and approached with hurried steps. The sirens got louder.

"You don't need to do that, Steve," he said. "You made a bad choice here, but we can help. Just get in the van."

As if on cue, the van's rear double doors swung open, inviting Abington to step inside. Abington hesitated.

"Who are you?" he asked.

"Two seconds, Steve. We've been watching you, and we can help you, but you've got to move, soldier. Now!"

Abington's training kicked in, making it difficult to ignore the command. He dashed to the back of the van, where two arms reached out from the darkness and hauled him inside. At the same instant, the van pulled away from the curb with another screech of tires and made a quick U-turn. The back doors slammed shut, leaving only slivers of dim light. Steve could not get a clear view of the interior, or the person who had helped him aboard.

The van straightened out and drove away from the scene at a measured pace meant to appear inconspicuous. He could still hear sirens, but they were heading in the opposite direction. The interior lights came on, but Abington could not comprehend what he was seeing.

The back of the van was crowded with medical equipment: a stretcher and an IV stand with fluid bags attached, as if this were the rear of an ambulance. The man who had helped him inside wore a surgical mask, head covering, and blue latex gloves. His gray eyes were expressionless.

"Welcome, Steve," the man said from behind his mask. "We've been looking forward to having you."

Steve looked down at the man's gloved hands and saw a needle and syringe. Fast as a cobra strike, the man sank a two-inch needle deep into Steve's neck and depressed the plunger.

A warm feeling swept through Steve's body. He felt light-headed, a bit dizzy, but also at peace. Finally at peace.

8

The town of Hopkinton, Massachusetts, was known—if at all—as the official starting place of the Boston Marathon, but to Carrie it was simply home. The four-bedroom Victorian house where she grew up, with its many gabled windows, wraparound porch, and verdant gardens, was still lovingly maintained by Carrie's parents, Howard and Irene, who were now in their sixties and showed no signs of slowing down. Howard Bryant continued to work at Mass General Hospital, and Irene had gone back to school to become a speech pathologist, which had led to her current job at a nearby nursing facility.

Carrie's visits were limited mostly to holidays, an occasional birthday dinner, and of course Marathon weekend, which had turned into a homecoming of sorts for many of her childhood friends. Aside from Facebook, Carrie did not see these buddies on a regular basis, though when they did get together the night always ended with a promise to do it more often.

Carrie drove her beat-up Subaru down the long driveway. In a few more weeks the tiger lilies would start to sprout and the rest of her mother's gardens would come alive, but right now the desolate landscape was brown and barren in a way that matched Carrie's mood. She parked in front of the basketball hoop, next to her mother's Volvo, in the pullout to the right of the detached two-car garage, mindful not to block her father in.

She stepped out into a chilly afternoon. Spring might have officially arrived, but winter did not seem ready to let go its icy grasp. One of the garage doors was open, and Led Zeppelin blasted from within the darkness. Adam must be in there working on his car, as always; the music was probably coming from the boom box she'd bought to welcome him home.

Adam, who'd aced AP biology and gravitated toward STEM subjects, was expected to extend the streak of Bryant doctors that included two of Carrie's grandparents, but to everyone's surprise he'd enlisted in the army right after high school. Adam's commitment to the military had ended years ago, but in his mind, the war raged on.

Wearing jeans and a fleece jacket over a blue V-neck sweater from Macy's, Carrie wandered into the doorway of the garage, feeling strange not to be dressed in scrubs or sweats. Her brother was bent over the Camaro's open hood, which looked like it was swallowing him. He wiped engine grime from his hands on his already soiled jeans, and only when Carrie cleared her throat did he pull his head out to look her way.

Adam's face lit up. "Hey, sweetie!" He approached with his arms open wide. "What brings you out here?"

Before they hugged, Adam realized he was covered in filth, so he opted for a quick peck on her cheek. "It's good to see you."

Carrie looked at her brother's drawn face and hollow cheeks and tried not to let her worry show. The old Adam was in there somewhere. If she closed her eyes, Carrie could still picture the handsome, sharp-eyed boy she'd looked out for back in high school. He still had his wry smile, but the glint in his eyes and that playful cocky attitude were gone.

Adam had cut his hair short again, a throwback to his army days, and had a whisper of a mustache that was new as well. Carrie did not love the look, but Adam was doing a lot of experimenting, perhaps searching for an outside transformation to make him feel whole inside. The rest of him looked the same. He had a narrow, lean build coupled with a muscular chest, arms, and legs. His pallid complexion called attention to his dark and sunken eyes, reminding Carrie of the drug addicts she used to operate on at BCH.

Used to.

How could it be over? The thought of never operating again stretched a band around her chest so tight Carrie thought she might stop breathing. She was utterly lost, completely bewildered, and had never been closer to understanding how Adam must feel.

"Mom and Dad didn't tell me you were coming," Adam said.

The garage looked exactly as Carrie had expected, a tale of two personalities. Dad's side, with his beloved BMW 325i, was neat and ordered, just like Howard Bryant. Freestanding shelves kept clutter to a minimum; beloved tools were carefully organized on several wood pegboards. Adam's side was like a teenager's bedroom. Tools were scattered everywhere, and the workbench and shelves were covered in oily rags, greasy papers, and indiscriminate mounds of car parts.

"Mom and Dad don't know I'm coming," Carrie said.

Adam gave Carrie a conspiratorial look. "Everything all right?"

Carrie nodded her head vigorously and tightened her lips. "Yeah, it's fine." *Change the subject. Prevent the waterworks.* "Hey, the car is looking really good."

Adam's answer was to stand a little taller. His mouth crested upward as he turned to face the Camaro. He set his hands on his hips and paused to relish his accomplishment. "It's coming along, huh?"

The Camaro had shown up six weeks after Adam left his warrior transition unit, WTC in military parlance, without any definitive cure. He reentered civilian life directionless, with empty, fidgety hands. Fixing up a car that reminded him of his carefree high school days seemed like a good idea, though their parents were not as certain when they saw the mound of scrap towed to their garage. The car sat untouched for a long while, until one day when Adam's inspiration inexplicably kicked in. Now that the body was fixed up and a fresh coat of red paint had been applied, it looked truly special. If only Adam could be fixed up with some elbow grease and determination.

The WTC had begun as an army unit, but a deluge of wounded warriors from two wars had necessitated a rapid expansion. War recovery had become a major cost for the military's budget, and now close to forty of these transition units were fanned out across the country, helping soldiers to heal. Still, they couldn't guarantee Adam would leave his program with a cure. Four years and four different therapists later, Adam had his Camaro and not much else.

"Want to hear it purr?" Adam asked.

Carrie gave Adam two wiggly thumbs up. Anything for her beloved brother. Adam got settled behind the wheel and caressed the dash as if it were a stallion he needed to calm before mounting. He put the key in the ignition and gave it a turn. The engine sputtered, but then it just started to click. A series of loud clicks like the countdown of a bomb.

Click-click-click . . .

He turned the key again.

Click-click-click . . .

Adam's forehead wrinkled in a scowl. Darkness radiated from him as he slammed his fists against the steering wheel and yelled, "FUCK!" so loud Carrie flinched. His inner storm flared and he continued to pound the car with his fists—the seat, the steering wheel, the dashboard. Adam flung open the car door and stumbled out with a look of madness. His face was red with rage.

Adam scrounged on the ground and came up holding a large, rusty wrench.

"No, Adam! No!"

There was no stopping him. Adam brought the wrench down on the side mirror, snapping it clean off with a single strike and sending it to the concrete floor with a clatter. Next he went after the passenger window, shattering it before falling to his knees, breathing hard, spent from his tirade.

Carrie knelt beside him, blanketing him in her arms. She rocked him as he wept, his body shaking.

"I'm sorry, I just—lost it. I'm sorry, Carrie—I don't know why I got so angry. I . . . I just snapped."

"It's okay. It's okay, Adam," Carrie said. "I'm so sorry. I'm so sorry for everything you're going through."

Carrie held her brother while he wept. She did not see or hear her father enter the garage, but when she turned he was there.

For his age, Howard Bryant was exceedingly thin, almost rubbery, with long arms and legs that Carrie was fortunate to have inherited. He wore khakis and his trademark plaid shirt with a sweater vest. Just the sight of him filled Carrie with relief.

"Hi, sweetheart," Howard said from the entrance to the garage. His voice came out raspy, a little aged, but it was soothing in a way only a daddy could speak to a daughter. Carrie held on to Adam; she was not ready to let go, and he still needed her. Howard looked worried, but unsurprised.

"Come on in the house when you're ready," Howard said. "Your mother's made soup. I'll heat you up a bowl."

9

David Hoffman, eyes still closed, stretched out on his futon and sent the stack of papers at his feet fluttering to the hardwood floor. His orange tabby Bosra perched placidly on his chest, undisturbed by the movement. David waited a few seconds, enjoying the special peace of an afternoon nap. Before he drifted back to sleep, David opened his eyes and checked the time on his phone. It was deadline day, which meant Anneke would be calling. He was fine with blowing her off again, but he could not sound half asleep while doing it.

Something about lying on that futon, especially when the fabric was warm from the sun, was like mainlining melatonin. The report he'd been reading was of no help, either. While the Institute of American Medicine was an upstanding organization, their take on PTSD in the military was all jargon and imperiousness. Forty-eight bucks down the drain; Anneke would not be pleased. David could have written in a paragraph what the IAM took sixty pages to convey. *Good on you,*

DOD and VA, for trying to fix this mess. Bad on you, because PTSD in the military is getting worse, and you have no ability to track the outcomes.

David turned his head toward the window and the view, unobstructed by the greenery that would develop with spring. The apartment, though small, felt roomy, and an obtrusive tree branch was a fine tradeoff for cheap rent in Porter Square.

Bosra meowed, and David responded with a gentle scratch between his ears. The cat, a rescue, was named after ancient ruins in Syria. The name reminded David of one of many spectacular sites he had visited as a journalist, and an aspect of his career he missed. Having spent the majority of his professional life chasing political strife, David had become addicted to the rush. Nothing could match the intensity of covering an angry mob, of documenting people's most visceral passion for freedom and security. For someone who'd smoked marijuana only a couple of times and who was rendered tipsy by a single scotch, political upheaval was a different sort of drug, and David missed the high. While some of David's classmates from Columbia embedded with a military unit only to up their profile with a newspaper or network, David honestly enjoyed dangerous assignments, though he preferred politics to platoons.

A knock on the door pushed David to get up. Meowing in protest, Bosra leapt off David's chest and landed noiselessly on the hardwood floor. David ambled over to his front door. "Who is it?" he called, knowing full well.

"David, it's Emma."

David opened the door, grinning. He suspected his

bushy brown hair was standing up like a Chia pet, and he was dressed abysmally in gray sweats and a blue T-shirt, but he was uninhibited with Emma. She had started out as his landlord, became his friend, and then briefly his lover, until both decided that friends was where they belonged. Now he loved her in a way that would have been difficult had they still been dating. Emma was holding Gabby, a delightful four-year-old, in her arms. Gabby had cheeks to cause a chipmunk envy and two animated, big brown eyes. Her shoulder-length blond hair was tied into pigtails. Gabby's whole body squirmed excitedly when she saw David.

"Hi, Uncle David!"

David warmed every time she called him that. Emma handed Gabby to him and the little girl squealed and kicked as David tickled under her chin. Whenever Gabby laughed, a sweet high-pitched chuckle, the world stopped turning.

"Who's gotten so much bigger since the last time I saw you?" He could not resist speaking to her in a high-pitched voice.

"David, you ate breakfast with us this morning."

"Kids develop quickly these days."

"Can I play with the toys?" Gabby whirled her legs instead of asking to be put down.

"You know the spot," David said.

Soon as he set her on the floor, Gabby bounded over to a corner featuring a play mat and a bunch of toys—blocks, Thomas trains, and enough plastic animals to re-create the San Diego Zoo in miniature. Emma did not remove her own brown tweed coat and wool hat, which let David know she would not be staying.

"She sure does like coming up here."

"And I like having her here," David said.

Emma got a wistful look as she watched Gabby playing with the toys.

"No offense," she said, in a quiet, almost conspiratorial tone, "but it would be nice if once in a while she got to visit with her father instead of her surrogate dad."

"None taken," David said. "And it would be nice if her father hadn't moved to California for work." David put air quotes around the word "work," in this case a euphemism for "girlfriend"—the real reason Emma's ex had left them.

"He Skypes with her, just so you know," Emma said. Emma could not resist the compulsion to defend the father of her only child.

David squeezed Emma's hand. "I'm sure he loves her," David said.

Emma and The Ex owned a yellow clapboard two-family home within walking distance of some of the best shopping in Cambridge. They lived on the ground floor, and David rented the apartment above. The Ex had moved out three months after David moved in, and Emma turned to her new upstairs tenant as a lifeline.

With long strawberry blond hair, high cheekbones, and a full, sensuous mouth, Emma O'Donnell was by anybody's measure a stunning woman. But David was not all about looks, and they knew after a month of romance that the chemistry was not there.

"Could you watch her for an hour while I run to the market?"

"Nothing in life would bring me more joy," David said.

Emma looked at him with suspicion. "Really, is it inconvenient?"

David's grin only broadened. "Your needs are my needs, darling. Just pick me up something for dinner. Preferably a food item that won't make me gassy."

At thirty-two, David was still tall and lean, close to his high school weight, and could eat just about anything, to the dismay of his many envious friends.

"Too bad," Emma said. "We're having burritos."

David turned Emma around and gave her a playful nudge out. "Gabby and I are going to work on our Middle Eastern geography while you're gone. Prepare to retrieve a genius upon return."

Gabby overheard her name and came running.

"Can we look at the pictures, Uncle David?"

"Look, she's already a genius," Emma said with more than a dash of pride. "She heard you say geography and thought of your pictures."

David had read somewhere that kids, especially the young ones, love repetition. In a world where so much was new and varied, seeing the same things over again must feel comforting. His walls were adorned with framed photos he had taken, and showing them to Gabby gave him pleasure as well. The pleasure of revisiting memories. The themes, however, were decidedly adult, and it took great concentration to explain them to the child without inducing nightmares.

"What's this one?" Gabby asked.

The photograph, taken a month before former president Morsi was forced out of office, showed a sea of people waving Egyptian flags and holding pictures of the Muslim Brotherhood candidate. *The Guardian* had paid David two thousand dollars for the story, but they went with an AP photo instead of his.

"That's in Egypt," David said. "The city of Cairo." David carried Gabby over to the world map tacked to his wall and pointed to the country.

"Why were they waving flags?" Gabby asked.

"They wanted a new leader."

"Did they get one?"

"Oh yes," David said. "They got one, all right."

Gabby wrapped her arms around David's neck with python force and pointed to the picture on the wall behind him. She always went in the same order, though David varied his explanations.

"What's that one?"

It was one of his favorites—a black-and-white image of a riot in Tripoli right after Gaddafi loyalists managed to kill the rebel leader, Abdel Fattah Younes. *The New York Times* had paid five hundred for the photo and three thousand for his story. It had been a good afternoon.

"That's a bunch of people acting very excited," David said.

"Why are they excited? Did they get new toys?"

David loved the way she said "toys"—her enthusiasm was contagious.

"No, not new toys. They just needed to jump around and yell a lot. Sometimes grown-ups do those things."

"What about that one?"

First, David brought her over to the wall map and pointed to Libya, the location of the last image. She touched the same spot as he did, and then rubbed her hands all over Europe.

"Libya," David said.

"Libya," Gabby repeated, then pointed to the image showing thousands of red-shirted populist supporters of Thailand's ousted prime minister, Thaksin Shinawatra. "Are they excited about the same things?"

"Well, not exactly," David said.

"How come they're all wearing the same color shirt?"

"Because they believe in the same things," David said. "They're a group."

"What group do you belong to?"

"I don't," David said. "I work for myself."

David was a stringer. He had built his career working as a freelancer, forgoing a regular salary in exchange for the opportunity to cover stories that actually interested him. Most of the time that interest took him to places the State Department was advising Americans to avoid. Syria. Iraq. Afghanistan. Yemen. A journalistic tumbleweed, he would probably still be in some red-flagged country had he not been kidnapped.

It was not a terrible ordeal, nor was it an experience he would willingly relive. The opposition forces in Syria had decided that David was part of Assad's regime and, without judge or jury, took him prisoner. For three weeks David lived in a windowless concrete room and had no contact with the outside world. Eventually, he befriended a guard who was looking to learn English. With the guard's help, David was able to contact the State Department. A contact at *The Current,* technically David's employer, spoke by satellite phone to the opposition forces holding him hostage. The editor managed to convince those in charge that David was in the country on assignment and that David's reporting could be of help to their cause back in the United States. A few hours later they let David go, and the next day he was on a plane headed home. Somebody else would have to help the rebels' crusade.

Word of David's ordeal spread quickly to all the people who regularly hired him for stringer jobs. In just a few weeks, David's greatest asset—his willingness to put himself in harm's way to get the story—became his biggest liability. Nobody wanted to bail "Cowboy Dave" out of any more international hot water, and suddenly the only work he could drum up was for local newspapers like the *Lowell Observer*.

A reporter buddy hooked David up with Anneke, a respected editor who had dialed down her career in exchange for some of her remaining stomach lining. Though he was grateful for the work, a feel-good piece about a marine conquering his PTSD was not his dream assignment.

"Are you going to join a group?" Gabby asked.

David's cell phone buzzed. *Anneke*.

"Hmmm, I might be asked to leave another group," David said, setting Gabby down on the floor. "Go play for a bit. I have to talk on the phone."

Gabby ran over to the toys.

"Anneke," David answered, sounding chipper and cheery. "I was just going to call you."

"Because your e-mail doesn't work? No worries. I've got a pen. You can dictate it to me."

"Ha, that's actually kind of funny."

"I'm a real gas. Where's the story, David?"

David could picture Anneke's scowl by the tone of her voice. She was fifty-something, fit and slim from running and Pilates, with shoulder-length blond hair. Poor Anneke walked under a black cloud; everywhere she went, it was raining deadlines. And David was only adding to her misery.

He'd make it up to her. A bottle of Chianti and she'd forget this little lapse. She owed him a pass anyway. His first story for her was supposed to be a puff piece about a bright foster kid from Lowell who won some creative writing contest. The fifteen hundred words she asked for turned into a high-impact story that ran over several days and exposed a huge scandal involving the Department of Children and Families. David could always tell where the real story was, and he knew this particular assignment should not be about one triumphant marine.

"The story is in progress," David said.

"Have you interviewed Sergeant Thompson yet?"

Sergeant Jesse Thompson was a Billerica native who'd lost an arm to an IED and was helping other vets overcome their PTSD symptoms with some success.

"Almost."

"How can you almost interview somebody?"

"I've thought about calling him, but I'm working on a different angle right now."

David was more interested in the staggering numbers of vets with PTSD. The problem was approaching epidemic levels, with one out of four servicemen and -women returning from combat significantly *different*.

"This isn't *The New York Times*," Anneke said. "We're a local paper. We've never won a Pulitzer, and I don't think my boss really cares if we do."

"Never say never," David responded.

Anneke sighed. "How much longer do you need?"

Small community paper or not, he and his boss were

still cut from the same stock. Both of them wanted to do good work, important journalism. If a story were here, Anneke would want David to find it.

"Give me a couple weeks. Sergeant Thompson isn't going anywhere. We can do a flashy piece on him any-time. But I want to explore this a little bit more."

"You're thinking series."

He pursed his lips. "The phone's not ringing to send me back to Syria."

"What's your plan?"

"I'm going to talk to some vets. The guys who haven't been helped."

"Give me some names." Testing to make sure David was actually working.

Luckily, he had his notes handy. "How about I give you three?" David said. "William Bird, Max Soucey, and Adam Bryant."

Click. Anneke had hung up without a good-bye. It was David's signal to get to work.

10

The house hadn't changed much since Carrie left for college. The wall-to-wall carpeting had long ago been replaced with hardwood flooring, and Carrie's bedroom had been converted into a guest room, but those were minor adjustments. Everything here, down to the round oak table in the kitchen, was familiar.

The framed pictures on the walls reflected a close-knit family. Usually they filled her with nostalgia, but today they made Carrie think about Leon Dixon. How many memories had Carrie erased with her mistake?

Carrie broke free of such painful, paralyzing thoughts to look at photos of herself and Adam through various life stages. She especially loved the vacation pictures. Some photos recorded ski trips to the mountains of New Hampshire and Maine, others showed their European adventures, a few had been taken in the Caribbean, and one displayed Howard and Adam riding elephants side by side on an African safari. There were probably as many photographs of Puckels, the shaggy and much-beloved family dog who had died a few years back, as there were of the kids. Carrie had encouraged her father to go to the shelter for another animal, but Howard quoted the comedian Louis C.K., who called puppies "a countdown to sorrow."

Carrie noticed Adam's military portraits were missing. In their place Carrie's mom had hung a couple landscapes she painted herself. Carrie was impressed by her mother's latent artistic ability, though Irene credited her teacher for her rapid progress.

After some time, Carrie wandered into the kitchen, where Howard was warming up the soup. Her dad had a full head of hair, but it was more gray than brown, and thinning. Carrie's mom had once bought him a color treatment, but Howard never opened the box. "Vanity is a young's man game," he'd say. Steam from two hot mugs of green tea fogged up the glasses on Howard's round face, magnifying two of the kindest eyes Carrie had ever seen.

"Your mom will be home in a bit, but you and I can catch up."

When the soup was ready, Howard sat at the table. Carrie joined him. The tea was a perfect temperature, and the soup smelled savory and delicious. Carrie had been living off cafeteria food for so long she'd all but forgotten what home cooking tasted like. She took a sip of tea.

"Your hands are shaking," her father said. "I know it's hard to see your brother like this."

Carrie set her tea down. "It's not just Adam, Dad."

Dad.

The word was a safety net. It allowed Carrie to let

everything out. Her eyes closed tight, a sob escaping, and tears streamed down her cheeks.

Howard pulled his chair close and put his arms around her. "What's going on, honey?"

Carrie took a few ragged breaths. "Something really awful happened. . . ."

It was not an easy story to tell. For most of it, Carrie struggled to get the words out. At first she cried a lot, breathing hard, short of breath, but eventually she settled and managed to tell it all.

Howard looked impressed as Carrie recounted Beth's surgery and the DIC episode. Details about Leon's surgery were fuzzier, perhaps because Carrie had blocked them out, but she remembered Dr. Metcalf's worried expression as he tried to locate the tumor.

Howard did not flinch when Carrie revealed her mistake. His eyes held no trace of judgment. He was full of compassion when she told him about the meeting that followed and her resignation.

Carrie could not have asked for a better confidant. Her father had spent years honing his listening skills. He had long believed that what a patient said, and how they said it, was sometimes more telling than the actual examination. These were skills that he had imparted to his daughter, and they'd been working well. But even Howard, who always seemed to know just the right thing to say, looked at a loss for words. In the prolonged silence that followed Carrie's story, he poured them both more tea.

"I've let everyone down," Carrie said, an all-too-familiar tightness creeping back into her chest.

"Sweetheart, right now is not the time for advice or

instruction. Just know I am here for you. And your mother is, too. And in a way, so is Adam. We love you, and we'll stand by you through all of this."

Carrie embraced her father again, and Howard kissed the top of her head.

"Tell me what you need. Anything."

Carrie laughed because she could not believe what she was about to ask.

"With my student loans and no income, I just don't have the money to afford my apartment. Not without a job."

Howard nodded. "I can lend you whatever you need. Mom and I can cover your rent for a while."

Carrie shook off that idea. "Some doctor I turned out to be. I'm twenty-nine years old and I need my parents to pay my rent. No, thank you."

"Don't let pride get in your way. Think of it as a loan."

Carrie tossed her hands in the air. "It's not pride. It's practicality. How am I going to repay it?" she asked. "I don't know what I'm going to do. I'm completely lost here."

"Then don't repay it."

Carrie shook her head again. "I can't accept that. Not without a plan. It wouldn't feel right to me. I might not even want to stay in town. Maybe I need to go get a research job, something in academia. I don't know."

"Then what do you want to do in the interim?"

Carrie sensed her father already knew. Again her thoughts went to Adam. They had taken two different paths, and yet found themselves at the same destination. It must be discouraging for her father to have worked so hard to raise independent children, only to have them turn out unable to function in the world.

"I spoke to my landlord," Carrie said. "He'll let me break my lease and give me my deposit back."

"That's fine, but where are you going to go?" Howard asked.

Carrie shrugged and tried not to look so crestfallen. "I'd like to move back here for a bit, if that's okay with you and Mom. At least until I figure out my next step."

Howard put his hand over Carrie's. "This is your home, sweetheart," he said. "It'll always be your home."

11

Carrie glanced out the sidelight window at an unfamiliar car, a Zipcar rental, parked in the driveway. The Bryants hadn't had many visitors in the two weeks since Carrie had moved home. No one had rung the bell, so whoever it was must have come to see Adam.

Good. Carrie was still in her pajamas, and didn't feel like making small talk. Since she had gotten home, she'd done next to nothing except watch old movies with her dad. She wasn't feeling cute, clean, or the least bit congenial—hardly ready to face the outside world.

For all the recent tumult, coming home had been seamless. Adam had helped with the move, such as it was. The U-Haul truck she had rented was far too big for her few possessions. Everything Carrie owned—a futon, two bookcases, three boxes of books (mostly medical texts and some fiction), a flea market coffee table, a small color television and scuffed TV stand, some clothes, a few framed pictures, and a dresser— fit into a small corner of her parents' basement. It was depressing to realize her life's accumulations could take up so little space. For so long, her focus had been on nothing but medicine. Carrie wondered what could possibly take its place.

Carrie had settled in her old bedroom, but it was far from cozy or comforting. Limbic, Carrie's goldfish, swam unfazed in his large bowl, which rested atop the same blue dresser she'd had as a kid. It was still her childhood bedroom, even with all her old memorabilia boxed up, and the twin bed covered in the emerald green Tibetan quilt Carrie had bought on her travels to the Far East. Living here again was dispiriting, though better than living in Boston with her parents paying the rent.

Stress had triggered insomnia, which in turn triggered a new dependence on Ambien that left her perpetually exhausted. Her runs, if they could be called runs, were uninspired and dangerously close to being brisk walks. She was probably clinically depressed, but Carrie wasn't going to get help for it. She didn't deserve to feel better. Carrie's actions had substantially reduced Leon's quality of life. It was unclear whether his symptoms would improve over time. Carrie deserved to feel lousy.

Carrie's mother, Irene, a petite sixty-year-old woman, entered the foyer through the dining room, rubbing lotion on her hands. She was dressed in a blue denim shirt and khaki pants, the uniform of a passionate gardener.

"Who's here?" Carrie asked.

"A reporter from the *Lowell Observer,*" Irene said. "Here's here to interview Adam for a story."

Carrie's eyes narrowed. "Adam?" Since his discharge

from the WTC, Adam preferred solitude. Friends rarely came over. This guest was a surprise to her.

Irene said, "I got a call from Everett Barnes, the director of veteran outreach for the Home Base Program, asking to see if Adam would tell his story. I told him about it and I guess he agreed."

Carrie understood now.

Home Base had been set up by the Red Sox Foundation to give clinical care and support services to Iraq and Afghanistan service members, veterans, and their families all through New England. It dealt specifically with veterans and their families affected by stress or traumatic brain injuries sustained on deployment or in combat. Sadly, the organization could not grow fast enough.

"I'll go see how it's going," Irene said, pushing her bangs off her forehead and tucking a strand of dark, shoulder-length hair behind her ear. "Oh, and your father is in the kitchen. He wants to speak with you."

Carrie found her dad sitting at the kitchen table, sipping from a mug of steaming coffee. He drank his coffee no-frills; the whole family did. Was this learned or inherited?

Carrie poured herself a cup. "You wanted to speak with me?"

Howard's face tensed.

Carrie ignored a tic of anxiety and sat down, preparing herself for anything.

"I've been thinking about things," Howard began, choosing each word carefully. "And I think you've come too far to quit now."

Carrie folded her arms and looked away, her instinct for self-preservation kicking in. This felt like an

ambush. She had made it abundantly clear that recon-
sideration was not an option. To be a great surgeon
required great confidence, and Carrie would be a danger in the OR.

Still, this was her dad, and the soul of kindness. He
deserved that she sit still and listen.

"You are a gifted neurosurgeon," he continued, "with
only one more year to complete your residency. I know
that you had your heart set on that fellowship at the
Cleveland Clinic, and then who knows what? I don't
want to say something trite like 'everybody makes mistakes,' but I honestly can't think of one successful person, especially not doctors, who hasn't gone through a
personal hell of some sort or another. Sleepless nights.
A crisis of confidence. Not one." He picked up his coffee cup again and took a long drink.

Carrie's voice caught, and came out a bit shaky. Con-
tradicting her father had never come easily. "Dad, you
don't know how badly Leon is hurt. Honestly, just the
thought of operating makes me anxious. I was never
this way before."

Howard nodded. His eyes brimmed with empathy.
"I know," he said. "You've said that many times. But
there's something I never told you that I think you
should hear." He shifted in his chair. "When I was an
intern, I accidentally overdosed a young man suffering
from a seizure."

Carrie said nothing. In the silence, the revelation
became its own uncomfortable presence.

"I gave him too much phenobarbital. I'll never forget it. He stopped breathing and his blood pressure
collapsed. We had to call a code, and the poor guy almost died. Because of me. Because of my mistake. I

saw him every day in the ICU for the next week, and each time I was racked with terrible, terrible guilt.

"Even today, I always double-check myself when I administer drugs," her father said. "Especially that drug."

Carrie could relate. The last she heard, Beth Stillwell had recovered and returned to work, but Leon had been transferred to a long-term nursing care facility. Not all of Leon's deficits were attributed to Carrie's mistake, but she'd owned all the guilt regardless.

"Unlike Leon, my patient was going to get entirely better before I made him worse," her father continued. "For weeks I couldn't sleep. Barely could eat. Thankfully he did recover, but I think you get my point. My mistake almost cost this man his life. But that's a part of the job. We're expected to be perfect, but no human being is infallible. Not you. Not me. Not Dr. Metcalf. Mistakes happen. But it's how we deal with the adversity that defines our character. You can make peace with this and find a way to move forward. I did. Now, I've a suggestion."

Carrie could guess where he was going with all this, but—it was too soon. Too soon. She could not pick up another scalpel. Not now, and despite what he said, maybe not ever.

"You're a grown woman, and these are ultimately your decisions. But I have some years and some perspective, so I ask only that you hear me out. A couple of weeks ago I went to a dinner on Parkinson's disease sponsored by a pharmaceutical company. I sat next to a man who was taking their drug, a patient. Turns out he had deep brain stimulation to help his treatment and now, with the combination of DBS and his meds, he's doing better. He was able to attend meetings like this one."

Carrie knew all about DBS, a surgical treatment involving the implantation of a brain pacemaker and wires that delivered electrical impulses to targeted areas of the brain. It was used to treat movement disorders such as Parkinson's, but researchers and clinicians were exploring other applications, including treatments for OCD, major depression, and chronic pain.

"This man was very pleased with his results," Howard said. "He talked at great length about his treatment at the VA under Dr. Alistair Finley, whom I know from way back when I did my internship. I haven't seen him since, but why don't you go talk with him? He's right in town. Use my name. We weren't especially close, but I'm sure he'd remember me."

"Thanks, Dad," Carrie said. "I'll give it some thought." She turned her coffee cup in her hands. "I'm not particularly interested in Parkinson's. I mean, that's not what we really do in neurosurgery."

Howard conceded with a nod. "I understand it may seem less glamorous. But maybe, given your . . . your reluctance to get back in the saddle, it could be just what the doctor ordered."

Carrie smiled. She was about to tease him about dads being doctors when the doorbell rang.

Howard got up to see who was there. A moment later, Carrie heard him exclaim, "Oh my gosh!"

Howard returned to the kitchen with a tall, lanky man who was bleeding profusely from the nose. The oily rag he was using to stanch the flow had smeared a good portion of his face with engine grease.

"Adam apparently took offense to something."

Howard spoke without emotion. He'd long since realized it didn't help to get upset about his son's new hair-trigger temper. "Could you please get this gentleman some ice? I'm going to go look for your mother and my boy."

Carrie took the stranger by the arm and led him to a chair at the kitchen table. "Tilt your head back," she said once he was seated. He looked like a boxer ready to concede the fight.

"I'm David. I'm from the *Lowell Observer.*" Between the rag and the injury, his voice was especially high and nasal.

Carrie got a clean roll of paper towel from the pantry, then filled a plastic bag with ice from the freezer. Applied to the bridge of the nose, the bag of ice reduced the swelling and the pressure, and the bleeding stopped after a minute or two.

"What the heck happened?"

David smiled sheepishly and shook his head. "It was my fault," he said. "Really. I'm to blame here, not Adam."

Carrie gave David a fresh paper towel and refilled his plastic bag with ice. She studied her patient. Probably around her age, he had attractively messy hair and a kind face. She suspected he was something of a charmer.

"Go on," Carrie said. "I'm all ears."

"I came here to interview Adam for a story I'm writing about PTSD, but your mother showed up and Adam had a change of heart. No longer wanted to talk."

Carrie grimaced. "You didn't take no for an answer, did you?"

David laughed, and Carrie thought the sound was

warm and inviting. He was obviously embarrassed, but he had enough humility to see a little humor in it.

"No's not my style," he said. "I didn't think I was being pushy, but I don't back down so easily."

Carrie thought of her conversation with her dad. *Neither do I,* she realized.

12

After prying his eyes open, Steve Abington could not make sense of what he saw. He knew this place intimately, but for the life of him could not figure out how he had returned. The last thing he remembered was—was what? Nothing came to mind. He felt as if he had been living in absolute darkness, the blackest infinity, until this very moment, until light flooded his eyes and he saw again the desolate farm field where it all began.

Abington tried to stand, but he felt weighed down. It took a moment to realize he was wearing an ILBE pack, one so fully packed he had to hunch over while getting to his feet.

He also held a rifle, an M4 rifle fitted with an M68 red-dot optic. Where had that come from? And what else did he have on? Cautiously, Abington reached up and felt the Kevlar of an advanced combat helmet. He wore a MultiCam pattern uniform, too. How did that get on him? Why was he here? He thought he was through with all this.

"Steve. Steve, can you hear me?"

Abington spun in a tight circle, but saw no one. The voice, one he did not recognize, came out of the ether. He circled once more, and this time noticed foxholes, several of them. Nearby stood a makeshift structure, like a tree stand but on the ground. It was covered in green camo netting, and he thought he remembered putting it together. It was a command operation center, which meant this place must be the security outpost for Forward Operating Base Darwin. Yes, of course it was. There was the tree line, a hundred meters out. Beyond those trees, the snowcapped Hindu Kush mountain range cut a jagged tear across an endless azure horizon. If he walked west about two klicks, Abington was sure he'd find the remote roadway his squad had been patrolling. The Taliban were setting IEDs along the MSR—main supply route—and his unit used that road to make a quick exit.

"Steve!"

That voice again. Bodiless. Everywhere and nowhere. Where was it coming from?

Lightning bolts erupted behind his eyes, making Abington's head throb. He trotted over to the nearest foxhole. The sunglasses tinted the world, but shielded his eyes against a steady wind's peppering of sand and dirt. Inside the spray of dust, thousands of chiggers and sand fleas took flight in search of soft targets.

"Steve."

The voice. Was it in his head? Had he gone crazy? Had he never actually left this godforsaken place?

"Hello!" Abington called. His voice had the grit of sandpaper, and his throat felt as dry as the ground. *So dry. So thirsty.* "Is anybody here?"

The wind swallowed Abington's words. He crouched and dug his hands into the hard earth. It felt real. He managed to rake up a small pile of dirt using the tips of his fingers. This was how he described the country to anyone who asked: dirt, piles of dirt, dirt everywhere you looked. The soil carried fungus that blew deep into blast wounds to fester and take away limbs that otherwise could have been saved. How was he back in this hellhole? Back guarding FOB Darwin. Had he ever even left?

Abington remembered. He remembered everything about living here, including his squad. But where was everybody?

His gaze fell back to the parched earth, and Abington saw a scorpion crawling by his feet. He crushed it beneath the heel of his well-worn military boot with a satisfying crunch. But what he really wanted to crush was the Taliban. A familiar burning hatred boiled up, warming Abington like Kentucky's best bourbon. There was no better feeling than sending coordinates up the satellite link and watching the ground evaporate where the hardware dropped.

This was a backward country: no real infrastructure. No proper roads. Nothing here except for dirt, and caves, and Taliban. The only thing the Taliban respected was battle. They trained their young children to kill, and in their downtime played polo with dead animals. Pure savagery. Neanderthals with guns.

Abington searched the horizon for any signs of life.

This was a Tier 1 area, no civilians allowed. Any person with a full beard and loose-fitting robes could be legitimately engaged. But the landscape was as barren as the surface of Mars. He was alone. All alone.

"Do you see it, Steve? Do you see what's happening?"

Abington readied his rifle and trained the weapon in all directions. His eyes narrowed and he bared his teeth like cobra fangs. He could see nothing but dirt, trees, and the mountains in the distance.

"He must be seeing it," the voice said.

"I . . . I don't see it." Abington's voice came out as a whisper.

"It's there, Steve. You can see it. You can see everything."

Abington glanced at the foxholes and caught a flash of movement from inside one of them. Was it just his shadow? How could that be? The sun was in front of him. Could he have imagined it? Abington moved cautiously toward that foxhole, his weapon at the ready.

"Is anybody in there?" Abington called out. "Hello!"

Abington took another step forward, then another. He could see a shape now. The silhouette of a figure, but it shimmered like a mirage. Abington advanced a couple more feet.

From out of nowhere, a tracer whizzed above his head. In an instant the air erupted with the sounds of gunfire snapping all around him. Bursts from a Russian PKM machine gun crackled in Abington's ears, rattling his teeth. Bullets pocked the earth, and shattered rock sprayed in all directions. Abington heard a whistle above him, like a screech from a bird of prey, followed by a loud thud somewhere to his back. An ear-splitting boom came next, causing the ground to shake beneath his feet.

Abington turned and saw two billowing dust clouds no more than twenty yards away. This was Afghanistan. One moment all was quiet, and the next it was chaos.

From the foxhole somebody shouted. "RPGs! RPGs!"

Abington broke into a sprint. The foxhole was safety. As he neared, a different shadowy figure lurched up from another hole, and flashes exploded from his rifle. A second later several mortars landed close by and Abington heard shrapnel bounce off the heavy armor of some parked trucks. Wait, had those trucks been there before? Not now. Questions for another time.

Abington dove headfirst into the closest foxhole. He hit the hard ground and felt the breath leave his body. Shock waves from gunfire and erupting mortar punctured the air and echoed across the bleak landscape. The foxhole had room for two, and the man Abington had joined returned fire with his M16.

"Steve! Start shooting! Unless you're hit, put that gun to use, *hombre*!"

Hombre. Only one person called him that. Abington squinted and his eyes strained. He could not see the man's face clearly, but he recognized the thin build and knew that reedy voice anywhere. PFC Rich Phillips—Roach—who, like the bug, couldn't seem to be killed. Eventually the man came into clear focus, and the specter with the M16 was his best friend, all right. The same guy whose guts Abington had stuffed back into his blown-open stomach right after an RPG struck their foxhole.

"Steve? What is it? What are you seeing?" The dis-embodied voice again.

"Look at his face," another voice said. "He's right there."

13

Carrie could not shake the smile off her face. The occasional glint of sunlight slipping through a persistent cloud cover seemed intended just for her, and buoyed her spirits. Her footsteps on her walk to the VA parking lot came quick and purposeful.

She no longer felt directionless or adrift. After two hours with Dr. Alistair Finley, she could visualize some kind of future. It wasn't a fully realized vision, but a sprig of hope had sprung from her despair. Carrie could not help but think of the final line from *Casablanca,* which she had watched with her dad the previous night. *"Louie, I think this is the beginning of a beautiful friendship."*

It was funny that David Hoffman's bloody nose was partially responsible. His passion for his work, undaunted by a violent subject, had reminded her of herself.

I don't back down so easily.

She'd been in no mood to socialize, but after Carrie cleaned David up, it was easy to say yes to an invitation to have coffee later. She was under no illusions about his motives: He wanted information about Adam and their family for his story. But he'd made her laugh.

"I usually only have coffee with rocket scientists," he said. "I guess I could slum with a brain surgeon."

Adam never came back to make amends, leaving Howard and Irene to do the apologizing.

"Don't even mention it," David had said with a wave of his hand. His battered nose would heal just fine. "If it's okay with Adam, maybe we can try again sometime. People need to know what's happened to our servicemen and -women. They need to see the war after the war."

For the rest of that night, Carrie thought only of her father's suggestion and David's persistence. She *had* come too far to quit. She called Dr. Finley's office at the VA the next morning.

To Carrie's surprise, Dr. Finley answered his own phone.

"My name is Carrie Bryant," she said. "My father, Howard, suggested I give you a call."

For whatever reason, Carrie felt at ease with Dr. Finley. His voice was intimate, with no discernable accent, and he spoke to her as a colleague. He remembered her father, and was interested in her background and experience.

"Can you come by the hospital this afternoon?" he asked.

Carrie hadn't expected that. It felt fast, but that was good. No chance to get cold feet. A few hours later, she was sitting in Dr. Finley's office anteroom, flipping through an issue of *People* magazine. Five minutes later, she was in front of Dr. Finley himself.

Unlike his fancy headshot on the VA Web site, Dr. Finley looked every bit the harried professor. His long hours showed in the silver that streaked his mop of wavy, light hair, and in his pale cheeks and burrowed eyes. He might have been intimidating, except for his cheerful expression and a slightly disheveled appearance.

Dr. Finley shook Carrie's hand firmly. "Please, come into my office. The executive suite," he said with a smile.

She wouldn't have called the attendings' offices at Community comfortable, but they seemed luxurious compared to the décor here. Two metal folding chairs faced an L-shaped desk that looked like a Walmart special. An overhead fluorescent light fixture gave off a persistent hum. The walls were bare, except for a couple of diplomas and the requisite pictures of the president and the secretary of Veterans Affairs. The VA reeked of institutionalism, like body odor. Still, the man seated at the desk had a warm and inviting smile.

Carrie gazed out a square window that overlooked the parking lot, focusing on an adjacent multistory brick building under construction. The building was covered in rusted scaffolding and tattered blue tarps, but Carrie could still see signage over the front entrance: VA HOSPITAL ANNEX. Most of the windows on the annex were boarded up, but some remained intact.

Dr. Finley noticed her looking. "That was supposed to be our gleaming new facilities," he said, a bit wistful. "But we've been caught up in a bit of a funding crunch, I'm sorry to say. Work stopped almost two years ago."

"The building has been vacant this whole time?"

"Unfortunately, yes," Dr. Finley said. "There were ambitious plans for hospital expansion, but most everything has been put on hold because of ongoing budget constraints. Perhaps one day the fortunes will change. But we're not here to discuss the fiscal woes of the VA."

"No, we're not," Carrie said, taking a seat on one of Dr. Finley's metal chairs. "My father sends his regards."

"He's a good man," Dr. Finley said of Carrie's father. "That was a great time. Great. Internship was without a doubt the hardest year of my life, but it was probably the best, too. I want you to know he's not the reason I invited you down here. Your call may have come at a fortuitous time for us both, and I'd like to know more about you."

For the next thirty minutes Carrie shared her experience, career plans, and ultimately the incident that had derailed her. Dr. Finley listened with rapt attention. His avuncular interest let Carrie tell him all the whys and wherefores without embarrassment.

"And so I resigned," she concluded. "I couldn't see how I could continue a surgical residency. But now that I've had a few weeks to think about it, I realize that doesn't mean I need to be finished with medicine."

Dr. Finley added some final notes to those he'd been keeping during Carrie's story.

"Well, let me tell you a little bit about our work here."

For several minutes, Dr. Finley detailed what sounded to Carrie like a typical neurological practice. The hospital had a fully staffed neurosurgical department with an accredited residency program. Together with Dr.

Finley's neurology practice, they treated everything from brain tumors to migraines. But of all the work being done by the Department of Neurology and Neurosurgery at the VA, Dr. Finley was most excited about his deep brain stimulation program.

He talked at length and with great enthusiasm about how DBS uses a neurostimulator placed in the brain to deliver electrical impulses to targeted regions, and the great potential it has for treating a wide range of neurological conditions. Mostly he focused its application for treating movement disorders, and he made several references to the patient Carrie's father met during that sponsored dinner on Parkinson's disease. He hinted at other applications for DBS, but kept those allusions intentionally vague, she believed.

"Look, Carrie," Dr. Finley said after his impromptu lecture on DBS, "I can't offer you an actual residency position here. Our program is fully staffed—and besides, it's mid-year."

Carrie tried not to look deflated. In their brief conversation, her expectations had gone from zero to high.

"But I do think I may be in a position to help," Dr. Finley continued. "And I suspect what I have to offer would help renew your confidence."

"I'm interested," Carrie said.

"A stint with the VA would, in my opinion, increase your chances of getting back into a formal neurosurgery residency program next year, while teaching you an awful lot about brain diseases one normally doesn't deal with in the usual neurosurgery program."

If the residency positions were filled, what could he have in mind? "I could certainly do some research on depth electrode stimulation treatment for Parkinson's disease," Carrie said, anticipating what she assumed Dr. Finley would be able to offer, some sort of research position, nothing that involved actual patients. "It sounds like fascinating medicine."

Again Dr. Finley checked his notes. "I tell you what. Better than that, I've got clinic on Thursday morning, and some follow-up patients will be there. Could you come?"

"You want me to come on rounds with you?"

"If you'd be so inclined."

"I'm just curious," she said. "If there's no residency positions, why was the timing of my call fortuitous for us both? How are you in a position to help me?"

"Come to rounds on Thursday," Dr. Finley said. "I'll explain everything then."

14

It felt like divine intervention to be going on rounds again. Carrie thrummed with excitement. A few days ago she had been listless on the couch, trolling Facebook and doing what her mother always advised against, comparing her insides to everybody's outsides. But today she was back in a hospital, about to visit with patients, and feeling both curiosity and confidence return.

Carrie had dressed professionally in a blue blouse and dark slacks, but felt a bit naked without a white coat. She reminded herself that she was here to observe, nothing more. So far.

Patience—first things first. Let's see what this DBS is all about.

Carrie introduced herself to the receptionist. A few minutes later, a nurse took her into the neurology clinic. The aromas and sounds were instantly familiar, and she felt like a shipwreck survivor spotting dry land.

Inside exam room eight, Carrie found Dr. Finley

and an obviously married couple who appeared to be in their late sixties. The man seated on the examination table was heavyset, with a horseshoe head of hair, a weather-beaten face, and loose skin all around. Petite and well put together in a dress suitable for church, the woman kept her hands interlocked in front of her. Concern for her companion was etched on her face.

Dr. Finley's expression brightened on Carrie's arrival.

"Dr. Bryant," he said. "Let me introduce you. Donald and Nancy McCall, this is Dr. Carrie Bryant. She's an accomplished neurosurgeon, visiting today to learn more about DBS."

The compliment boosted Carrie's morale considerably. She *was* an accomplished neurosurgeon. Giving up on her career would do nothing to erase the damage she had accidently inflicted on poor Leon. Every day she would try and make penance. Surgery was and always would be her true calling. In the same way Howard Bryant double-checked each injection of phenobarbital, Carrie would take special care with pre-surgery preparations.

Dr. Finley provided a brief patient history. Donald McCall had well-established Parkinson's disease (PD), and had undergone a deep brain stimulation treatment twelve weeks earlier. Carrie observed the parallel scars on Donald's scalp where cuts had been made to implant wires in his brain. A horizontal scar ran along the base of Donald's neck, and a vertical one on his chest marked the pulse generator's location. Those scars were harder to see. In time, they'd be nearly invisible. Carrie was amazed that so much technology could be so effectively concealed. Even a keen observer would have no idea Don McCall was one of the walking wired.

"This is Mr. McCall's eighth visit to us," said Dr. Finley. "We're just fine-tuning the electrical settings." He turned to Nancy. "Mrs. McCall, would you mind telling Dr. Bryant a little about the changes you've observed, before and after the implant?"

Nancy sparked to life. "At first I thought Don was just depressed," she said. "He stopped talking much, and when he spoke it was like there was no feeling, and his voice got soft." Her own voice softened, as if in sympathy. "I can't say he looked sad—more like he wasn't there. And he started to stare at me for long periods, which was odd and made me uncomfortable. He slowed down, too. It was all very gradual, at first.

"But then he started falling, and my Don had always been so balanced. He used to play ice hockey in an adult league, and now he was stooping when he walked. Then his hand started shaking. A doctor put him on some sort of antidepressant, but that didn't do anything. Don was only fifty-five, but he acted like a man in his eighties."

Carrie nodded. Nancy had her complete and undivided attention.

"It was no surprise when he lost his job at Home Depot," Nancy went on. "I saw that coming miles away. Finally, what—ten years ago now?—we started seeing another doctor, and he knew it was Parkinson's just like that." Nancy snapped her fingers. "He started Don on Sinemet and he got a lot better. But I'm sure you know the story. He started to get worse again, even after increasing his medication. He was taking it almost every hour, it seemed, trying a bunch of new stuff. It got very frustrating." Nancy reached out and caressed Don's shoulder, reminding Carrie of her par-

ents. "Then he started developing these wild movements all over, his arms, legs, neck, and torso."

"Peak dose dyskinesia," Dr. Finley said.

Nancy said, "At other times he seemed almost frozen solid, and it got so you couldn't tell when one state
would change to another. It was like a switch."

"On-off effect," Dr. Finley elaborated.

"We saw a bunch of neurologists, but no one could
do anything new or different. Then Dr. Sawyer learned
about Dr. Finley's program, and since Don is a vet—
two tours in Vietnam—he thought Don might be a
good candidate for the deep brain stimulation." Nancy
exhaled a protracted sigh. "I felt like I was Don's nurse
for thirty hours a day."

Don sat on the table, his expression vacant.

"Don, I'd like Dr. Bryant to examine you briefly, if
that's okay," Dr. Finley said. "Don's machine is off, and
we asked him to hold his medication this morning."

Don nodded, his stare still blank. He'd been poked
and prodded by plenty of strangers before. Carrie
would just be the latest.

Carrie slipped back into the role of caregiver without missing a step. It really was like getting back on a
bicycle, even after an ugly fall.

Don had textbook PD, she thought. Pill-rolling rest
tremor of right upper limb, dystonic turned-in postur-
ing of the right foot.

Don gazed unblinking out the window and showed
little expression. It was easy to empathize with Nancy.
The poor woman had to care for a ghost of her husband. Carrie asked Don a few simple questions—his
name, birthday, and home address. His voice came out
soft and stuttered, barely intelligible.

Carrie helped him down from the exam table and tested his mobility. He followed her movement instructions with all the grace and fluidity of the Tin Man: classic cogwheel rigidity in all limbs. Positive glabellar tap response, classic flexed posture of the trunk. The Parkinsonian shuffle was on full display as he attempted to walk, and it was no surprise when he froze midway while turning to his left.

Carrie recounted all that she had observed, and Dr. Finley looked pleased.

"A lot of neurosurgical residents who rotate through my program don't seem to know a thing about movement disorders or show that they can conduct a decent neuro exam," he said. "You're already two steps ahead."

From a nearby countertop Dr. Finley retrieved a compact device, approximately the size of a deck of cards. It had a plastic case, several buttons, and a small display screen.

"This programming unit will help us fine-tune Don's stimulation settings," Dr. Finley said. "It uses radio communication to adjust the stimulus parameters of the surgically implanted unit. Last time we set the frequency at one hundred and forty cycles per second, and the pulse width at eighty milliseconds. Today, we're going to increase the voltage amplitude just a bit, to two and a half."

Dr. Finley peeled away the paper covers over the sticky pads on the back of a plastic dock and adhered the unit over the scar on Don's chest. He snapped the programming device into place on the dock, then spent some time making sure the programming unit worked properly. When he was satisfied, he said, "I'll be back in a while to take another look at you, Don, and we'll see how you're doing 'plugged in,' as they say. And then we'll put you back on your medication and see how the whole package is working.

"As you know, Nancy, this is going to take some time," he added. "I'll be here checking on other folks for a while. Why don't you get yourself some coffee?" He turned to Carrie. "My job is to make sure the patients receive the proper dosage of medicine and stimulation. It would be up to you to get those wires precisely where they need to be. And believe me, Dr. Bryant, this is no simple feat."

Up to you. Did he mean it? Could she work here?

The VA's cafeteria, even down to the food, was about what Carrie had expected. "Institutional" was apparently a flavor, as well as a design aesthetic. Still, so far, she was enjoying every minute of her time with Dr. Finley. They had looked in on several more patients, and Dr. Finley suggested they take a coffee break before concluding with Don McCall.

"So, what did you think?" he asked once they were seated.

"Well, the management of movement disorders is far more nuanced than I appreciated," Carrie said. "It's interesting, and really necessary work."

Dr. Finley looked pleased. "Let me be very candid with you, Carrie," he said. "I've checked your references, and I know even more about the incident we discussed in my office. Believe me, everyone at Community and White is heartsick over what happened. They really like you, and I know you saved a woman's life the night before. I've got to tell you, Metcalf is still pissed—but he's all massive ego anyway."

Carrie shrank at the mention of Metcalf's name. "I hope you didn't ask him for a reference."

Dr. Finley laughed. "I don't think you'll ever get back into his good graces. But I don't need his commendation to know talent when I see it."

"I'm really glad to hear that, but I guess I'm a bit confused," Carrie said.

"Why is that?"

"When we met in your office you said there were no residency openings available, but you also said my timing was fortuitous. Can you explain that now?"

A shadow crossed Dr. Finley's face. He spent a moment stirring the cream in his coffee. When he looked up, his eyes showed strain and more than a hint of sadness.

"A few weeks ago our DBS surgeon, Sam Rockwell, was in a terrible, terrible car accident coming back from his vacation home in Maine. I saw the photos. His car crumpled like a tin can. His condition is too tenuous to MedFlight him to White Memorial, so his family has been keeping vigil at his bedside in a Bangor hospital. He's in a drug-induced coma with multi-organ failure and sepsis. There's a good chance he won't make it. It's a definite blow to our program."

"That's horrible," Carrie said, feeling a stab of sadness for Dr. Finley and for Rockwell's family.

"Sam and I were extremely close, and I'm—I'm just devastated. Anyway, there's no way Sam is coming back here any time soon, and we need someone to take over his responsibilities. I know you would be an excellent replacement. There is some time sensitivity to this offer. I'm afraid we may lose funding for a very special initiative if we don't get someone into the role post-haste, but I can't take just anybody. And, as you know, most of the qualified candidates are currently employed. We can't wait for them to become available to us."

Carrie nodded grimly. "I see now why you said my call was fortuitous." Medicine was a Darwinian world. One doc's misfortune was another doc's golden opportunity. Still, it felt ugly to profit from tragedy.

"Listen, Carrie, I know this seems wrong, given Sam's unfortunate circumstance, but a person with your considerable skill and talent would be a huge asset to us. You'd be able to jump right in without missing a beat. I've got the funds, and while this would not be a formal residency, it might help you get your groove back, so to speak. The surgical schedule is not too demanding, not at all like what you're used to. We try to limit the surgeries to one or two per week. There simply isn't a large staff to conduct proper patient evaluations and handle follow-up care."

"That's a wonderful offer," Carrie began, but Finley stopped her.

"But here are the restrictions," he said. "You're my hire. You work for me on this, not the VA. I'd be able to pay you out of the DARPA funds, and that includes benefits. Those funds give me a tremendous degree of clout with the VA's leadership team, including the acting medical director. You won't be part of the residency program, but that's no issue. I know you're a good surgeon, and your reputation precedes you. I know what you did for Beth Stillwell, and I thought it was remarkable. I truly believe you'd make an incredible addition to our team."

"How do I get credentialed?" she asked. "It's going to take so long to get on board here."

Dr. Finley showed no concern. "Carrie, you have a medical license. You got that when you graduated medical school. Your residency is for training, but legally, if you wanted to go out and start a practice, you could have done that. Some people need five years of residency to get where they need to be, some get it after three, but my inquiries have persuaded me that you got it after one or two. You've got enough talent, enough training to do this job. Even though I run the neurology residency at the VA, I'm hiring you under private funding for this program. It's a very unusual opportunity, and you'll be able to use this experience to enhance your credentials if you wish to get back to formal residency—though my hope is that you'll stay with my special initiative for years to come."

"And what exactly is the special initiative?"

An inscrutable look came to Dr. Finley's face, then it morphed into a grin.

"Come with me," he said.

Carrie followed Dr. Finley back to Don McCall's hospital room, where Nancy McCall greeted them with a bright smile.

"Already much improved," Nancy said.

"Have a look for yourself," Dr. Finley said to Carrie.

Right away, Carrie noticed the rest tremor was significantly decreased.

"How are you feeling, Don?" Carrie asked as she checked the mobility of his limbs. It was not enough to get him back on the ice, but the degree of movement made Carrie think somebody had replaced one Don with another.

"I'm feeling much better, Doc," Don said.

The stutter was gone and his voice was strong and intelligible.

After her brief exam concluded, Carrie followed Dr. Finley back into the hallway.

"Impressive, isn't it?" Dr. Finley said.

"Yes, very much so," Carrie said. "But treating Parkinson's with DBS isn't all that new, at least not according to my research. So I'm still curious about that special initiative you mentioned."

"What if I told you that we could use DBS to cure PTSD—not treat it, but cure it?"

Adam came to Carrie's mind with a flash of wonder. How was it possible? Could it be possible?

"If that were true, Dr. Finley," Carrie said, "I'd say you had yourself a brand-new DBS surgeon."

15

On Wednesday afternoon, a week after her coffee with Dr. Finley, Carrie followed a crowd of doctors into the cramped VA hospital auditorium for the monthly grand rounds conference, which was usually a welcome break from the grind. This gathering hummed with extra excitement because Dr. Finley was expected to make a big announcement regarding the deep brain stimulation program. The room was packed with neurosurgery, neurology, and psychiatry attending and resident physicians, as well as a number of other parties who were interested in hearing what Dr. Alistair Finley had to say about DBS. Dr. Finley, who'd been working at this VA for years, was considered a pioneer in applying the technique to a variety of brain and mental disorders. Perhaps that was why this GR was so well attended.

Or maybe it was the free pizza.

Carrie settled into one of the cushioned seats in the

second row, where she had a good view of the rather small screen used for the PowerPoint projection. Most everyone was dressed in scrubs and white coats, except for two men Carrie had noticed in the back of the hall. One was bald, with close-set eyes and a round face. The other had a square head, broad shoulders, and a football player's neck. His stone-hard gaze held all the joy of a funeral, and Carrie got a shiver when they briefly locked eyes.

For the past week Carrie had been obsessively studying the software that did most of the heavy lifting in the OR. When it came to DBS procedures, precision, surgical skill, and patience were the chief operational skills required, and she would have to work as part of a team. It was painstaking, complicated work; a typical procedure could last five to six hours. That explained why nobody was available to assume Sam Rockwell's responsibilities.

The entire Department of Neurology and Neurosurgery at the VA consisted of only three full-time physicians. Three! It was microscopic even by BCH standards. Dr. Finley was the staff neurologist, and Dr. Sandra Goodwin and Dr. Evan Navarro comprised the surgical team. Dr. Goodwin, a severe-looking woman in her late fifties with a broad forehead and aquiline nose, was the head of the neurosurgery department and therefore perpetually bogged down with administrative work. As a result, most of the actual surgical responsibilities fell to the staff attending, Dr. Navarro.

Dr. Navarro, a thin man with a small face, dark hair, and ferret eyes, was also in charge of the residents who rotated through the VA from satellite hospitals, much as Carrie had done at Community. Carrie and Navarro had not quite hit it off. She found him cold and disinterested—a typical ego on legs. Goodwin was more affable, but harried by the constant demands on her time. The good news was that Carrie's involvement with Navarro would be limited. For the DBS program to flourish, Finley needed the dedication of one committed, exclusive neurosurgeon. That role would be Carrie's, her sole responsibility.

At five minutes past the hour Dr. Finley strode to the lectern and slipped on his half-moon reading glasses. His hair was tousled as usual, but with his starched long white lab coat, crisply pressed white shirt, and classic repp tie, he shone with authority. The attendees, largely sleep-deprived residents, made the effort to stop eating and pay attention.

"Show the video first, please," Dr. Finley called.

Carrie noticed a resident to her right spontaneously close his eyes with the dimming of the lights. The rigors of a residency program were universally brutal, and Carrie understood his fatigue. She hoped none of the VA residents would ever have to endure the nightmare she and, more importantly, Leon Dixon had suffered because of her own exhaustion.

"This gentleman, we'll call him Patient X . . ." With the start of Dr. Finley's lecture, Carrie cleared her troubled thoughts and focused on her new boss's narration.

"Patient X developed signs of Parkinson's disease in his early forties. He had been exposed to Agent Orange while in Vietnam in his late teens."

The video was a series of home movies. A life well lived, but as the film soon revealed, one quickly diminished by the ravages of disease. The symptoms were a mirror of Don McCall's ailment. The footage went on to show the crippling nature of PD—frozen movement, violent tremors, spastic limbs. Dr. Finley reviewed the anatomy of the basal ganglia and its interconnections, structures deep in the brain that were affected in Parkinson's disease. Then he began to discuss the DBS treatments.

"We first stimulated the right ventral lateral nucleus of the thalamus. That benefitted his left arm tremor, but not much more. That electrode has been removed, and six months ago we placed electrodes bilaterally in the globus pallidus interna. This next video shows his current status."

The audience, impartial before, was captivated by Patient X's freedom of movement. Had Carrie not witnessed Don McCall's dramatic improvement for herself, she would have had a hard time believing the footage.

"Deep brain stimulation is a form of stereotactic neurosurgery," Dr. Finley continued. "We insert electrodes guided by a stereotactic frame, as well as CT and MRI imaging, deep into brain nuclear complexes that are involved in complex movement patterns. Lights, please."

As the lights came on, some in the audience began rubbing their eyes. Dr. Finley removed his glasses. "The value of DBS has been proven in Parkinson's disease. But what's particularly exciting for us at the VA is that we're exploring the use of DBS as a new chapter in psychosurgery. We believe we are at the vanguard of hope in treating conditions that have defied the most comprehensive drug and counseling programs."

Dr. Finley smiled. Everyone was there to find out

about the planned DBS program expansion. Sam Rockwell had done a number of procedures, but the pilot program had been operating in stealth mode.

Dr. Finley said, "As many of you are well aware, here at the VA, both outpatient and inpatient psychiatry have become overwhelmed by the number of PTSD cases."

For several minutes Dr. Finley presented a sobering array of statistics. "One-third of veterans from the wars in Iraq and Afghanistan have contemplated suicide." When he compared this to the 3.7 percent of the general adult population who had serious thoughts of suicide, the military stat looked stark. He coupled these statistics with the numbers of actual military suicides: "Twenty-two per day by current estimates, which also far outpaces the rate from fifteen years ago," Finley said.

"Long-term mental health care is perceived by many to be detrimental to military career advancement. Misguided as that is, it remains a fact. Close to fifty percent of servicemen and -women suffering from PTSD will not seek treatment because of this stigma or—and I say this knowing who pays my salary—the challenges of navigating the VA's antiquated bureaucracy."

Dr. Finley paused until the chuckles died down.

"An operation, I believe, would be far more attractive to those afflicted, and thus would dramatically increase the numbers of those willing to be treated."

Dr. Finley fell silent to allow the notion to sink in.

"It has been reported that the economic impact of PTSD, limited to just the military, is anywhere between four to six *billion* dollars. And this does not take into account the spouses and children whose lives are further traumatized. I would argue that four billion grossly underestimates the economic toll."

Of course Carrie thought of Adam: his lost wages and diminished potential, coupled with the burden on her parents emotionally, financially, and in scaled-back career plans for themselves. Her family was just a tiny fraction of that billion-dollar crisis.

Dr. Finley showed a schematic of the limbic system, a complex network of structures ringing the ventricular system deep in the brain. Its functions were many, including regulation of emotion and basic drives and motivation. It also regulated the initial processing and emotional aspects of memories, and the body's response to stress including blood pressure, pulse, and respiratory rate, as well as sleep patterns. Tiny as it was, the almond-shaped amygdala nucleus, located deep and medially in the temporal lobe, was accountable for a whole host of critical functions.

"We believe the basolateral nucleus of the amygdala represents the most promising target for DBS in treating PTSD. Here is where fear and its memory converge."

Dr. Finley advanced the slide. The amygdala was now circled in red.

"This is the epicenter—where our primitive fight or flight reactions form in response to a threat, where unchecked rage can be unleashed in response to a disturbing memory. Regardless of how much we try to alleviate these terrible memories through therapy or pharmaceuticals, we know that PTSD symptoms are structurally imbedded, literally imprinted, in the brain. And we believe this processing involves the amygdala nucleus significantly."

Dr. Finley came out from behind the lectern. He made eye contact with Carrie, and she smiled.

"We have realized something that you may find counterintuitive. Traditionally the goal of treatment has been focused on the mitigation of disturbing thoughts and memories, analogous to the way we treat many phobias. Think of the man who is afraid of heights, for example. We may subject him to systematic desensitization by gradually introducing him to higher heights. And indeed, such treatment is often effective, at least partially, for phobias, but war zone trauma is something else entirely.

"We are discovering in controlled laboratory experiments that electroshock therapy administered to animals in close proximity to a traumatic event greatly suppresses those animals' behavioral response when immediately re-exposed to the trauma. In other words, they seem to have forgotten their emotional response to the initial trauma."

Dr. Finley went on to discuss a group of human test subjects who were involved in a different memory experiment involving electroshock therapy, more commonly known as ECT. These patients were first shown images of terribly unpleasant events and asked to recall them. Surprisingly, the researchers found that the patients were not able to remember any details of the disturbing event the day following their ECT, even though they had been told explicitly to remember the event in as much detail as possible. The shock treatment seemed to interfere with storing a new memory in the brain. The researchers concluded that there was a period of time when stored memories were accessed, in which they could be vulnerable to manipulation. They could be modified, changed in some way, reconfigured or "reconsolidated."

Dr. Finley continued, "We know the intense connections of memory tied to emotions sends the amygdala into overdrive in PTSD. If we can dampen that
hyperactivity in the amygdala, all the social and psychological consequences we see in PTSD—the nightmares, depression and apathy, anxiety and fear, the
likely drift into drug and alcohol abuse, the emotional
roller coaster, potential flashes of aggression—all this
can potentially be negated."

Dr. Finley went on to present a series of slides referring more specifically to the anatomy of the amygdala
and its connections to other limbic structures.

"Our goal is not to erase the memory per se, but to
erase the emotion associated with the memory. Let me
repeat: The goal of our DBS program is emotional
erasure. To do this, we first need to reproduce the
soldier's trauma, as vividly as possible. And just then,
after the memory has been reproduced, we suppress
the amygdala by deep brain stimulation of the amygdala's basolateral nucleus, interrupting its emotional
and physiological connections to that memory, and in
so doing, reconsolidate the memory without the emotional context."

A hand shot up from one of the psychiatric social
workers seated directly behind Carrie.

"How would you do that? How do you plan to
re-create these memories so vividly?"

Dr. Finley's expression brightened as if this question had been planted and anticipated.

"Glad you asked, Wanda. Today I am officially an-
nouncing a very exciting pilot program, initiated with
the assistance of DARPA."

Dr. Finley's gaze traveled to the back of the room,

where the two men in suits were seated. Carrie guessed they were from the government.

"By a show of hands, how many of you have heard of DARPA?"

Fewer than half the hands in the room went up. One person felt a need to clarify. "The initials, yes, but I'm not sure what it stands for."

Dr. Finley gave a slight nod. "It stands for Defense Advanced Research Projects Agency. Their mission is to create breakthrough technologies for national security. They're the folks who gave us the Internet—sorry, Al Gore."

The reference inspired scattered laughter.

Dr. Finley continued. "PTSD is approaching epidemic levels in the military, so DARPA has been experimenting with exposure therapy using virtual reality simulations."

Carrie felt a jolt. DARPA was remaking the war in pixels.

"We can re-create that IED event when a soldier's buddies were killed or maimed." Dr. Finley spoke to a hushed audience. "And while the brain is forcibly agitated, we have an opportunity to treat that individual with deep brain stimulation with the hope that we will actually erase the emotion associated with those terrible memories forever. I'm not talking suppressed. I'm talking *gone,* forever. Ladies and gentlemen, I am pleased to see Calvin Trent from DARPA has joined us today. Cal, could you please stand up?"

Cal, the man with Atlas shoulders and cold eyes, glanced briefly at his companion and stood up slowly. He acknowledged the audience, then sat right back down. Dr. Finley either did not recognize or did not know the other suit that had accompanied Cal Trent. Either way, the bald guy with a round face and beady eyes got no introduction.

Dr. Finley said, "Cal oversees all aspects of the program, including the virtual reality simulation, which is used prior to the DBS surgery to reconsolidate the negative memory. The virtual reality does leave many patients highly agitated, but that's a temporary state. We need the emotion heightened, the negative memory fresh, as close to surgery as possible. Once the electrical stimulation commences, the emotion gets dampened. It's as simple as that. Cal's pulled together an amazing team of people to run this program, and I know you'll extend him your every courtesy."

Carrie could sense excitement building in the audience. Just about everyone there had had some contact with a returning soldier who was devastated by PTSD, or his or her family. She thought again, always, of Adam.

It had been eye-opening to live with her brother, and see the difficulties he and her parents had been enduring. Sometimes his nightmares were so savage it sounded like he was being murdered. She saw how Adam avoided going out, especially into crowds. Even walks in the woods behind the house were an ordeal. Everywhere he went, he was scouring the ground for IEDs. At least he had started going running with her—well, more like she followed Adam as he sprinted. Poor kid could easily outrun her, but not his demons.

The hope she saw in Dr. Finley's eyes, the enthusiasm in his words, buoyed Carrie's commitment. Dr. Finley had told her about the program after she had accepted the position, but seeing everyone else respond with excitement reinforced her own enthusiasm. She was proud to be on the cutting edge of such critical care. Funny that she'd named her goldfish Limbic, the system the amygdala resided in.

Was fate at work here?

16

The operating room was Carrie's amphitheater, and she was the violinist about to dazzle. She was back in uniform: green scrubs underneath a white lab coat. Soon she would enter the preoperative holding area to visit a patient, her first at the VA. His would be the first burr holes she would drill in almost two months.

Jealousy from the other resident physicians had been an initial worry. Other residents had competed for their positions, while Carrie had been handed what many would perceive as a post-resident fellowship, working directly with one attending on a single project, without the onerous responsibilities of taking call or being responsible for patient care. It was a plum assignment for sure, but Dr. Finley made it clear to everyone that Carrie would not receive credit toward her residency requirements. No, this was a different trial for her. Would she perform to her ability?

While the DBS procedure she would perform would be relatively simple and straightforward, it was by no means free of complications. Opening the brain involved significant, life-threatening risks, every time. Still, implanting wires was not like sucking out blood clots deep in an already swollen brain where the surgeon had to be both swift and meticulous. DBS required a tremendous amount of patience and an OCD-like attention to detail. Carrie took a few calming breaths. She ought to wait for Dr. Kauffman, the anesthesiologist, but felt she could handle the preoperative consultation just fine.

Five minutes later Carrie entered the preoperative holding area, where she was struck by the sight of a man who could have been her brother's twin. Seated on a beige armchair, reclined ever so slightly, the man looked like Adam not before the war, but after. He had Adam's strong jaw and sharp-featured face, but his shaved head called attention to his concave cheeks, and he appeared frail and skeletal. His arms were spotted with ugly purple bruises that spiraled outward like mini nebulas. But it was the eyes that truly alarmed her. They looked hollow, a stare that seemed to stretch out into space.

Carrie was not sure what to expect from patients after they'd been subjected to the virtual reality therapy, but it certainly was not this. Her patient had the dazed look of a car accident victim. She knew he would be sedated, but it was tough to see his suffering. Carrie usually treated the sorts of injuries and ailments that appeared on an MRI. This man's wounds were just as significant, even if they couldn't be imaged.

She checked her chart. She knew the soldier's name, but wanted to double-check to make sure she got it right. Her father's lesson on the importance of details had taken root.

Abington. Staff Sergeant Steve Abington.

Carrie helped Abington out of the chair and onto the exam table, positioned kitty-corner in one end of the room near a counter with a built-in sink. Above the sink was a steel medical supply cabinet affixed to the wall. At first Carrie thought Abington was too thin, but once he was standing she could see he was rippled with muscle. He had the minimal body fat of an athlete.

"How are you doing today, Steve?"

No response.

Abington had fixed his gaze on the framed print of the Boston Common on the wall before him, but he seemed to be looking through it, not at it. Carrie was close enough to smell detergent and cleanser; he smelled institutionally clean. She checked her chart again. No address listed. No emergency contacts. He could have been homeless, and now in the care of the VA system. What did they use for soap where he lived?

"I'm the surgeon who is going to perform your DBS procedure today. I wanted to meet you before the operation in case you had any questions for me. Do you have any questions, Steve?"

Abington turned his head slowly, dreamlike, as through pushing through molasses. His mouth began to twitch, perhaps to form a word. But all that came out was a guttural noise like the clearing of a throat.

Carrie knew that the DBS had to be done within a window of opportunity immediately following the virtual reality simulation, when the negative memory was most fresh in the mind. She did not know exactly where

DARPA conducted the simulations, or who had escorted Abington to the exam room, or where that person had gone. Those questions were well outside her area of responsibility.

"There are lots of bruises on your arms, Steve. Can you tell me how you got them?"

Abington shifted his gaze to one of his battered arms. He lifted the limb slowly, like a marionette whose string was pulled, and studied the arm with detached, vague curiosity. Then his face slipped back into that dead-eyed gaze.

Carrie moved to check his vitals, and he did not resist. Blood pressure: 90/60. Perfectly normal. His temperature was 98.6 degrees, and his reflexes were normal. Heart rate was also in normal range for a resting adult. She put a penlight up to his eyes—five-millimeter pupils, a bit dilated but equal, and briskly reactive to the flashlight. *Good.* All the consent forms had been signed. There was no reason not to proceed with the surgery.

"Steve, do you understand what's going to happen? You're scheduled for a very important operation."

Once again, Abington's mouth began to twitch with words he could not quite form. Then, surprisingly, he started to move his body, bouncing where he sat like an anxious child, and massaging the bruises on his arms. To Carrie it looked as though his drained battery had somehow sparked back to life.

"You don't know—you don't know," Abington mumbled. He periodically stopped rubbing to run his fingers over his newly shaved pate.

"What don't I know?" Carrie asked.

"I don't belong here."

"I know you're scared, Steve. But we're here to help."

Abington shook that off. "It's not all right. I don't belong here." His voice rose in pitch and volume. "You don't know."

"Steve, take it easy."

Abington went still. His arms dropped to his lap.

Carrie let out a relieved breath, wishing that she'd waited for Dr. Finley or Dr. Kauffman before starting the consultation. Dr. Finley had warned her that patients could be highly agitated pre-op. They were fragile following the virtual reality treatment.

"Steve, let me explain what—"

Abington reached out and seized her by the throat, pressing on her windpipe. Shocked, Carrie started to panic, her eyes bugging out, able to take only tiny gasps of air. She reeled backward, pulling Abington off the exam table. As he dropped to the floor, Abington let go of her throat, so Carrie whirled around and sprang for the door. But Abington charged her. With speed that belied his earlier torpor, he snatched the back of Carrie's flapping lab coat just as she was within reach of the door handle. He pulled her toward him and she fell back into his arms, then he spun Carrie around to face him.

His mouth formed a fearsome snarl—from lifeless to rabid in a matter of moments. His sedative must have worn off, revealing murder in his eyes.

"I don't belong here," he hissed in her face. "Got to get out!"

His back was to the door she had closed for their interview, and hers was to the counter and medicine cabinet. Carrie wriggled free from Abington's grasp.

"Somebody please help me!" Carrie yelled, though it was doubtful anyone would hear her. The walls were made of thick concrete, and the nurses' station was located way down the hall. Carrie flashed on an idea and turned her back to Abington to focus on the locked supply cabinet.

"Help!" Carrie cried out again. "Somebody help!"

From behind, Carrie heard Abington gibber unintelligibly. Carrie fumbled in her pocket for the keys. Did she dare risk turning her head? She could not resist. Abington paced in front of the door like a caged animal. He took a step toward Carrie and said, "I'm not here. I don't belong here."

He could have left the room, but he wanted something else. He wanted her. Carrie retrieved the keys, but her hands shook so violently it could be impossible to work the lock. *Which key opens the damn cabinet, anyway?*

Carrie fumbled with the keys some more. There were too many attached to the ring. She heard Abington take another step toward her. One. Single. Step. Carrie's throat ached where he had grabbed her. The soldier's labored breaths seemed to come from every corner of the room.

Carrie located a small key among the jumble on her ring and tried to jam it into the lock. No good. Wrong fit. She searched for another. The cabinet was made of metal; otherwise she would have broken the glass.

"Help!" Carrie yelled.

There was another small key on the ring. But was it the same one she had just tried?

Abington muttered, "Listen to me. I don't belong here." Carrie jammed the second key into the lock, and this time it fit. The lock turned easily and Carrie ripped open the door. Mixed in with a number of medical supplies she found various vials of medication and several wrapped syringes.

"I don't belong here," Abington said from someplace behind her.

Carrie fumbled through many vials of medicine, until she found the Valium. She held the Valium in one hand, and used her teeth to rip open a syringe package. Carrie kept her back to Abington as she worked to get the syringe inserted into the top of the vial.

"Steve, it's okay. You're going to be okay. Please believe me. I'm going to give you a shot to calm you down."

Carrie filled the syringe just as Abington charged and struck her in the back. His momentum slammed Carrie against the lip of the counter hard enough to take away her breath. Abington wrapped his arms around her waist and together they tumbled to the floor. Carrie held on to the syringe with her life. She twisted underneath him, intending to claw at his face. But Abington flipped her onto her back and dug his knees into her ribs hard enough she feared he'd snap her sternum.

Once again Abington took hold of Carrie's throat, but this time he did not squeeze. "Where's Smokes? Hunter. Is Hunter here? What about Roach?" His voice was plaintive. "Roach!"

Carrie forced herself to stop struggling.

Just don't squeeze . . . please don't squeeze.

Years of surgery gave Carrie tremendous hand dexterity. She was able to position the syringe for an effective strike without drawing Abington's attention.

"Please, Steve, I'm not here to hurt you."

"That you, Roach?" Abington said. "You got to get me out of here. I don't belong."

Abington tightened his grip around Carrie's throat

like a python readying to squeeze. She had one chance. One. It was hard to hit under normal circumstances. But induction time was everything. The drug needed to work and work fast. Abington squeezed some more. Carrie could still get air into her lungs, but it was barely a breath. Gurgling noises bubbled up from her throat, from all the saliva that had no place to go.

One chance . . . one . . .

Abington's jugular vein pulsed like a thick blue target. Carrie swung her arm in a wide arc. Abington leaned away from the strike and his body position shifted. Instead of hitting his neck, Carrie slammed the needle into Abington's shoulder, right into the muscle. It would delay induction, but she depressed the plunger anyway.

Carrie tried to speak, but no words came out. She left the syringe dangling in Abington's arm and used her fingers to try and pry Abington's hands free. Abington acted unfazed. He pressed harder on Carrie's throat. The loss of oxygen started to get to her, and she couldn't control her panic. She kicked and bucked wildly, but could not toss him. Her legs began to spasm and her eyes watered.

This isn't how I'm supposed to die. . . .

Gripped by panic, Carrie thrashed beneath Abington, kicking over a metal stool that clattered noisily to the floor, but it was no use. He would not let go. She felt herself slip into unconsciousness. Her body became heavy, novocaine for blood. Carrie closed her eyes. She did not want the last thing she'd see to be the face of her murderer.

And then she was filled with a sense of profound peace, of weightlessness. She felt her fear fall away as the darkness grew deeper and darker.

In the very next moment Carrie could breathe again, and the room went from dark to bright. The feeling of weightlessness slipped away as she blinked her eyes open. Dr. Finley knelt beside her. He looked as worried as her father might.

"Carrie, are you okay? Can you hear me?"

Through her blurred vision, Carrie saw Dr. Kauffman and a sizable orderly restraining Abington.

17

David Hoffman carried two drinks over to the table where Adam Bryant sat waiting. The young veteran had called unexpectedly and invited him to coffee in Hopkinton, so David, worried that Adam could easily return to his shell, canceled his plans with Gabby and Emma. David didn't like to disappoint Gabby, but he'd bring her to the children's museum some other day.

"You take it black, right?" David said, setting down a steaming mug.

Adam took a sip in response.

"Usually, I drink tea these days, the chosen beverage of the Afghan people, but for whatever reason I'm in the mood for a good cup of joe."

David had shown up fifteen minutes early and found Adam already there, his jean jacket and faded T-shirt fitting the coffee shop's bohemian vibe. Adam's darting eyes and alert posture told David he'd chosen their seats deliberately, with the best sight lines and quick access to the exit. Adam's training and caution had kept him alive during the war. His body might be thousands of miles from Afghan soil, but certain instincts remained.

David settled in his comfy chair with his espresso. Compared to the stuff they served in the Middle East, this coffee tasted like water.

He'd thought he had a shot at a Reuters job that would send him to Saudi Arabia, but evidently his reputation still preceded him. David knew he would get back in those good graces eventually, so the setback was not overly discouraging. Besides, his story on PTSD was too important to rush. He wanted to tell it right, and Adam's perspective would help.

"I'm glad you called," David said. "I didn't think you would."

"Yeah," Adam replied. "I wasn't sure myself. Figured the least I owed you was an apology."

"You don't owe me anything, Adam. I just want to get your story out there. If you're willing to share."

Adam inspected David's face. "Nose looks pretty good," he said. "Look, I'm really sorry I lost my cool."

"I was pushy. I asked for it."

Adam didn't disagree.

"Do you mind if I take notes?" David asked.

"No, man, you gotta get it right."

David took out his pad and pen. "So how do you want to begin?"

"I'm not sure. Hard to say what got me all screwed up."

"You mean there wasn't a specific incident?"

The corners of Adam's mouth ticked up a couple degrees into the hint of a smile. "It was *all* a specific incident, man."

"Start wherever you'd like, whatever feels natural." David acted as if they had all the time in the world.

If Adam had been privy to the terse conversation David had had with Anneke on his drive to Hopkinton, he would know that was not the case. She continued to hound David for the story, and he continued to come up with appropriate delay tactics. So far he had interviewed the two other vets he'd mentioned to Anneke, spoken with an administrator at Walter Reed, networked with a retired brigadier general, and read several books on PTSD that covered everything from science to sociology. The books were enlightening, but they could not adequately convey the depth of pain David saw in Adam's eyes.

Adam seemed lost for words.

"What was it like for you over there?" David said. "How about describing a typical day."

Adam thought. "Well, I guess on a typical day you'd do PT from zero five thirty, and it could go until the CO wanted to puke. Most of the time it was just an hour, though. PT, that's physical training."

"Got the reference, but thanks."

Adam said, "Then it's SSS—that's shower, shit, shave—before breakfast. Just the normal stuff. A lot of time it was real quiet. You know? Funny, because the quiet was the toughest part. It gave you time and space to think about stuff, home, all the things you missed, but mostly you focused on your friend who got blown up the other day. You had time to think that you were going out on patrol soon enough and maybe you'd get 'blowed up' yourself." Adam put the words "blowed up" inside air quotes.

"Basically, that was the life. It was patrol and post," he continued. "We'd go out four or five hours in the morning, come back and eat something, then back on patrol, and then you'd have dinner and maybe do another patrol after that. Or sometimes you go out on patrol and some T-man is shooting your ass up. Or sometimes you didn't come back."

David guessed "T-man" meant Taliban. He would check later, as he did not want to interrupt Adam's flow.

"You can come back from patrol so racked up," Adam said. "Good luck getting any sleep. And then before you know it, you got PT all over again. And then boom—you're back on patrol, same as the day before. It's Groundhog Day over there."

"Even the firefights?"

"Yeah, well that's the only break in the routine, but on a COP even that becomes routine. You know?"

David nodded as he jotted down the word "COP" in his notebook, something else to look up. "Can you tell me about one of the patrols where things did not go well?"

Watching Adam, David was reminded of friends who had embedded with U.S. forces in Iraq and Afghanistan and got shot at, or navigated an IED (or worse, did not), and who all came back haunted. David did not believe in ghosts, and his religious views bordered on agnostic, but those who came back often seemed burdened by a malevolent spirit that would not let them find peace.

Adam's expression shifted, like a shadow that crossed his face, as he seemed to settle on a particularly unpleasant memory.

"On my last tour we set up a COP in an abandoned school." Adam's voice turned softer. "A COP is combat outpost, in case you were wondering."

David made a note next to the abbreviation in his notebook.

"We were sleeping on cots with our guns and packs tossed around like a bunch of school kids on a camping trip," Adam said. "The air there never circulated. It was so damn hot at night it was like sleeping in a sauna. The only breeze you'd catch is if the guy next to you cut wind. But you know the drill, right?"

"Patrol and post," David said.

Adam looked pleased. "So I'm on patrol. The day before, we had some T-men shooting at us, and some kids from the village said they knew where they were. For ten bucks and a few Twix bars you can get all sorts of good intel from the locals. We took two fire teams out on a hunting expedition. We got an AK, RPK, RPG, lots of firepower with us. Going to get us some T-men."

Adam's leg began to bounce, fast enough to shake the table. David kept his eyes on Adam while he silently moved their drinks to an adjacent table to avoid a spill.

"So we're following these kids on some shitty nothing road." Adam's voice gained energy with the telling. "Moving west to east. The whole time I'm looking for upturned dirt. You see, predeployment training teaches you that upturned dirt could mean an IED. But let me tell you, the dirt's upturned everywhere you look. Everywhere. So any step could be it. Boom! Any single step."

It was cool inside the coffee shop, but a sheen of sweat coated Adam's forehead. His eyes darted in all directions, as though he were scanning the tiled floor in search of upturned dirt.

Adam said, "By the time we reach the village we're all sorts of jacked, and most of the kids we're following go on back to their little mud huts. Of course the villagers come out to greet us, but it's hard to know which are allies and which are Taliban. Now, in addition to IEDs, we're keeping eyes out for guns poking out of robes, because rules of engagement say we can't shoot anybody who's unarmed. But it's a kinetic area—violent, I mean. You just don't know who's there to kill you and who wants help. It's a constant Charlie Foxtrot. That would be 'cluster fuck,' in your vernacular."

Adam reached for his coffee and took a long drink, then returned it to the adjacent table. David could relate distantly to Adam's ordeal, having been in some dicey situations of his own, but what Adam had endured was on a different level. The idea that any step could be one's last was truly terrifying. David could not see how anybody could return from that sort of grinding stress unchanged.

"So we're back moving, with just one guide now, a twelve-year-old kid, maybe fourteen. He's skinny and dirty and waving frantically to us to hurry."

Adam waved his arms, pantomiming the kid's gestures. His breath turned shallow.

"He points to these trees maybe a hundred meters away, just past the outskirts of the village. Hell, even the trees are brown over there. Sometimes when I get stressed I have to look at something green to remind myself where I am." Adam paused to gaze out the window at the green of Hopkinton, but when he looked back, he did not appear convinced he was safe.

"Anyway we follow this kid a bit further down the road, but every step, you know, we're doing our check. That upturned dirt. And then the kid turns around and he just smiles at us. I'll never forget that look on his face. It was pure joy. And then he reaches into his robe, takes out a pistol, and he fires. PFC O'Malley is right there in front, and he takes the bullet in the side. Damn kid gets this lucky shot. Bullet doesn't even nick O'Malley's SAPI plate."

Adam was breathing harder now. His eyes darted about, seeing phantoms everywhere. The sweat on his forehead began to drip down his face, as if he was back in the Afghani heat.

"A couple guys jump on O'Malley right away. But I'm focused on the kid. He fires again, but we're all moving now so he doesn't get a clean shot. Now I've got good lines on him. My AK is up, and I get off a burst. *Rat-tat-tat. Rat-tat-tat.*"

Adam raised his hands as if he was holding his gun. He trained the imaginary weapons on patrons at the coffee shop. A few noticed and flinched in response. Adam's voice choked with raw emotion, and he sucked down air in gulps.

"I ripped him apart. You know?" Tears streamed down Adam's face. He wiped them away with the back of his hand.

"I fucking tore this kid in half. Pink mist everywhere. And we're all scrambling for cover, thinking T-men are right there and now it's an ambush. But there weren't any T-men—just IEDs all over the side of the road. The kid knew he was going to die. He just wanted us to scamper. To be careless." With the tears, the sweat, the snot, Adam was clearly reliving the moment, as he probably did most every night in his nightmares.

"Sure enough I heard the boom, and then another, and then somebody's arm hit me in the face. There were limbs everywhere, man. Fucking flying everywhere. Bodies aren't supposed to be blown apart like that. Blood and limbs and guts everywhere you looked."

David's heart was racing now as well.

"So we're all over it, you know. *Fix our wounded! Fix 'em!* Four things. Restore the breathing. Stop the bleeding. Protect the wound. Treat for shock. We got this QuikClot shit, and I can see Doc P working on O'Malley, using it like caulk on a leaky window. But blood's spurting out of him like a whale shoots water out a blowhole. And I'm just looking around. My ears are ringing. It's like I'm underwater. And LT Carlson is coming toward me, doing a commando crawl, but then I can see his legs are blown off and he's dragging his intestines behind him."

Adam fell silent and bowed his head. When he looked up his eyes were ringed in red, but the tears had stopped falling.

"Bodies aren't meant to be broken apart that way."

18

Steve Abington was breathing comfortably, twelve times each minute, heavily sedated, his oxygen delivered via an endotracheal tube. Just hours ago he had been rabid, but now he looked peaceful thanks to the combo of propofol and fentanyl, which the anesthesiologist, Dr. William Kauffman, titrated expertly. The patient was hooked to a ventilator as well as the usual monitors for ECG, blood pressure, and pulse oximetry. Abington's labs came back within normal limits. Still, he almost hadn't gotten to this operating table.

The whole team had met for a lengthy discussion in the conference room down the hall from where Carrie had been attacked. For the first several minutes Dr. Finley apologized profusely to Carrie for not having been clearer about security and safety measures. He promised a thorough review of all practices and standards, and said he would have new protocols in place by the end of the week.

In the meantime, there was the matter of Abington.

This was a medical meeting, but Cal Trent from DARPA was present, along with Dr. Finley, Dr. Kauffman, and Carrie. Trent was dressed nattily in a tailored blue suit that showed off his muscular frame. At the grand rounds, she'd thought him cold and distant, but here he acted warm and conciliatory.

"I'm really sorry for what happened to you," Trent said in his low, gravelly voice. "You must still be very shaken."

"I'm doing all right," Carrie replied, which was only a half-truth. She was shaken, but perfectly functional. She'd had a brief medical exam, and despite some bruising on her neck, she was unharmed and experiencing no shock. She had recovered her composure rapidly.

"Timing here is everything," Dr. Finley said. "Abington is active right now."

"Active?" Carrie asked.

"He's been subjected to the VR simulation program. This is the time when those re-created memories are being enhanced emotionally by connections through the amygdala. The DBS has to block those emotional connections, and we'll lose our chance if the memory evaporates. It's not like PD, where we have the luxury of making subtle adjustments over weeks and months."

"There's no telling if the virtual reality would be effective again," Trent added. "We don't have any data on this. Essentially it could be a one-shot deal for him. If we don't get a DBS system installed and working, Abington might miss his only opportunity to lead a normal life."

"Carrie, I want you to know that it is up to you," Dr. Finley said. "Medically speaking, I see no reason not to proceed. But obviously we need our head surgeon to be at the top of her game."

All eyes fell on Carrie. She was starting to develop a conference room complex; the last time she'd been in one with all eyes on her like this, the conversation went horribly.

And again, Carrie had an important decision to make. Should she go ahead with the procedure? Though the decision was hers, there was no mistaking what Dr. Finley and the rest of the team wanted her to choose. As for Abington, it was clear that the hyper-realistic virtual reality simulation had triggered his rage. Carrie felt deep empathy for her attacker, and would not hold him accountable for his actions. But she wondered what he had seen during the simulation. Was Smokes there? Roach? What had happened to them over there?

While Carrie had come to the VA to recover from a devastating professional setback of her own, this procedure might be a way to truly help people like Adam and Steve, whose minds and lives had been turned into a daily nightmare. Right now, Carrie was the only surgeon here. It was her job, and the window was fast closing. If DBS could ease Abington's grievous memories, in a Don McCall miracle way, Carrie owed it to him to try.

"I'm fine to proceed. Let's do it."

Carrie could not believe how natural it felt to be back in the OR. This was an environment where she could feel herself in control. The old adage of riding a bike was not lost on her. Unlike the vets whose PTSD she hoped to cure, Carrie had no trouble blocking out the memory of Abington's assault. She was focused on the task, summoning not only her recent training, but her years of residency work as well.

As she prepared to drill the burr holes, Carrie thought back to the time, not long ago, when Beth Stillwell's life had rested in her hands. Today's procedure was technically a breeze by comparison.

Acting as the team's neurophysiologist, Dr. Finley was in the operating room to record the electrical discharge patterns from nerve cells when Carrie worked the electrode, ever so slowly, toward the basolateral nucleus of the amygdala.

Intraoperative neurophysiological monitoring was a demanding discipline, and obtaining certification required years of additional study. Carrie was impressed by Dr. Finley's dedication to his calling. There was no question that the doctor brought world-class medical skill to the VA.

In addition to Dr. Finley and Dr. Kauffman, the team included Dr. R. T. Patel, a first-year neurosurgical resident. Though Patel was primarily there to observe, he was also scrubbed, should Carrie require any unforeseen assistance. Intracranial hemorrhaging remained Carrie's chief concern during the operation, and post-op she would be vigilant about monitoring for signs of infection.

Also present was Donna Robinson, the scrub nurse, who looked of an age to have treated vets from Vietnam, and Louise Phillips, who, as a circulating nurse, was not scrubbed. Carrie doubted she'd find anybody quite like Valerie on the VA staff, but she was optimistic about the skill and diligence of these women, and hoped over time to develop a rapport with her new colleagues.

The real art of DBS work was developing leadership and communication skills in order to bring the team along with her during each operation. Fortunately, though everyone made it clear he was loved and missed, she sensed no lingering resentment over her replacing Sam Rockwell.

For what it was worth, during scrub, Donna expressed her admiration for Carrie's toughness and grit. Hours ago Carrie had been afraid for her life, but instead of retreating, she had brushed off the experience like a kid after a playground tumble. Having spent most of her career working for the VA, Donna measured a person by their ability to endure.

Carrie attached the stereotactic frame to Steve Abington's shaved head with four screws using a local anesthetic, just to be sure, even though he had already been sedated. Then, he was wheeled next door where an MRI dedicated exclusively to OR protocols had been waiting, and a series of ultra-thin-cut T1 and T2 weighted images of his brain were acquired. Abington was wheeled back to the OR while the scans were loaded onto the planning station. Computer images provided exact XYZ coordinates of Abington's amygdala, giving Carrie all the information she would need to guide the stimulating electrodes to her target by the least invasive path. This sort of equipment would have prevented the Leon Dixon disaster, Carrie thought ruefully. It was a supremely expensive setup, and she wondered how much of the bill DARPA was covering. Probably most of it.

Dr. Kauffman kept Abington unconscious with propofol and fentanyl. He would add isoflurane if deeper sedation became required. With Parkinson's and dystonia patients, who had to be awakened intermittently in order to assess their motor function, agents like propofol were ideal. But the last thing anyone needed was another violent outburst during surgery, so it was best to keep this patient insensate.

Carrie made a curvilinear, right precoronal scalp incision and penetrated the underlying skull with the Midas Rex, making a standard fourteen-millimeter burr hole. A Stimloc was screwed in. The electronic drive system was attached to the frame and Carrie sliced open the dura. Next, the long metal cannula, guided by the drive platform, was ever so slowly introduced through the brain. Carrie took her time. She made certain the drive plane avoided any sulcus where some juicy artery or vein might be lurking.

Carrie inched the cannula another millimeter forward. She checked her computer and inched it some more. Long minutes passed as Carrie meticulously worked the cannula toward the target area. By now, Carrie's legs ached, and a glossy sweat coated her brow and had to be dabbed away. The pull on her back left an unpleasant and persistent dull ache. As the hours passed, Carrie began to feel every stitch of Abington's assault. She blocked out the throbbing of her throat and the hurt in her shoulder from when she hit the floor. Her concentration had to be total, and it was.

While this was still neurosurgery, it exercised a different set of muscles, which compounded Carrie's fatigue. She pushed, persevered, and tapped into the kind of mental toughness she'd taken up triathlons to build.

At the start of the operation, Dr. Finley and others did frequent welfare checks with Carrie. Her two-word answer, "I'm fine," never varied, so the last check had come more than an hour ago.

Three hours into the surgery Carrie announced softly, "I'm pretty sure we're at ground zero." She removed the stylus and replaced it with three micro recording electrodes.

"Wow, I'm getting an excellent signal," said Dr. Finley. "I'm getting a typical pattern of neuronal firing from the basolateral amygdaloid nucleus. Great job, Carrie! You're right on target with the first pass. The anatomical and physiological coordinates could not be more perfect."

The microelectrodes were replaced by the stimulating electrode, and its surrounding stylet was removed. Carrie placed on the locking clip. All that was left would be to tunnel the exposed lead component into the chest. Four hours had ticked off the clock. Abington was shifted onto his left side. The right side of his neck and chest were bathed in Betadine. Carrie made an incision in the scalp and another five-centimeter cut in the right side of his chest, just under the collarbone.

Carrie inserted her fingers to enlarge a pocket where the subcutaneous pulse stimulator would fit. Then she inserted a t-tunneler and pushed it under the scalp and through the neck to reach the chest wound. The exposed lead was next introduced through the tunneler and connected to the generator in the chest. The scalp and chest were closed. The system was now in place, and potentially operational.

Five hours of surgery were complete.

Abington would spend the night in neuro recovery. Then it was home, wherever that was, and back in three weeks to follow up with Dr. Finley, who would assume responsibility for adjustments of the stimulus generator signal.

Dr. Finley checked the signal readings once more. "Dr. Bryant, you've just hit a grain of rice in a three-pound mass of Jell-O. Congratulations!"

Carrie removed her mask and grinned.

19

During the day the canteen in the basement of the VA hospital buzzed with activity, but at this late hour it was a ghost town. Food service stopped at three o'clock for everything except K-cup coffee and whatever the vending machines supplied. Food at the VA was partly subsidized by the government, which could explain why there was no dinner service for the staff.

Carrie had slipped on a fresh pair of scrubs and joined Dr. Finley at a long table. Steve Abington was in neuro recovery and, Carrie figured, emerging from the effects of anesthesia about now. She could enjoy a cup of coffee and then go check up on her first, and most eventful, DBS patient.

Dr. Finley was all smiles. "Carrie, that was just splendid. You were like a veteran in the OR, no pun intended."

Carrie's face lit up with a genuine smile and she blew on her coffee to cool it. "Thanks, I appreciate the compliment."

"The microelectrodes are perfectly placed,"

he continued, "right in the basolateral nucleus of the amygdala. The neuronal firing pattern, the post-op CT, everything's perfect. You were so calm and focused. I knew you could do this work."

"It was a team effort, like you said it would be."

"Ha! A modest neurosurgeon—now that might be a first."

One small step for Carrie Bryant, one hopefully enormous leap for Staff Sergeant Steve Abington.

"Given all that you've been through, and I don't just mean the attack, what you did today was nothing short of astonishing. I really can't say enough good to you, Carrie."

Carrie tried to keep her composure, but blushed at his praise. She'd fought so hard to find her way back to her field, she was amazed to be here. Now, given the extent of her day, Carrie figured she'd be bone weary, but it was the opposite. Maybe she'd crash later, but for the moment Carrie felt electrified.

After about twenty minutes talking about DBS, the surgery, and Abington's prospects for recovery, Dr. Finley glanced at his wristwatch. "Whoa. It's after eight. I mean, I love this place, but I gave up on the idea of using any hospital as a bunkhouse back in my residency years. So will I see you tomorrow?" Dr. Finley winked.

It was his way of asking if Carrie was coming back. Given the threat to her life, it was a reasonable question.

"You couldn't keep me away," Carrie said with a smile.

"Well, no more unaccompanied consultations," Dr. Finley said. "We need our best DBS surgeon safe, if we're going to fix the PTSD problem one patient at a time."

Carrie saluted. "Dr. Bryant will be reporting for duty, sir."

Dr. Finley chuckled as he stood. The crow's-feet marking the corners of his eyes seemed to have deepened. "We're lucky you're both resilient and dedicated. But I suggest you go home and get some rest. It's been an eventful day."

Carrie nodded. "You go on ahead. I'm going to nurse this coffee a while longer and catch up on some e-mails."

Dr. Finley gathered his briefcase and gave Carrie's shoulder a couple of friendly pats before heading for the door. Carrie sipped her drink and watched him go. She took in the quiet; it was one of her favorite times to be at a hospital. At Community, Carrie had been responsible for a whole team of patients, any of whom might turn for the worse at a moment's notice, and too often did. She had always been grateful for any fifteen-minute respite.

Maybe this job would be a stepping-stone back into other types of neurosurgery, but maybe not. Her mother preached mindfulness, living in the moment. Carrie was not opposed to the idea of making a long-term commitment here. Perhaps after she spoke with Abington, once Carrie could see the impact the procedure had made—a Don McCall miracle—it would encourage her transition to becoming a career DBS surgeon.

Carrie laughed at herself as she got up to throw her coffee cup away. Who knew how long Carrie would last at the VA? Hell, she was happy just to be back in the OR. But the same ambition that drove Carrie into neurosurgery had climbed back into the driver's seat of her mind.

From now on, Carrie would focus just on her patients. She'd barely started this job. She needed to be here a while and experience the whole program before making any decisions. Best to get her head on her task. And right now, that was checking up on Steve Abington before checking out for the day. This crazy day.

Even though Carrie functioned as an attending physician, her instinct was to go see her patient post-op. It had been ingrained in her for the past four years. One of an attending's privileges was being able to do the surgery and leave the scut to the residents. But Carrie was still a resident in both her heart and mind, and so a check on Abington was almost like a reflex. Steve Abington might well have taken Carrie's life, but he had also been instrumental in giving back her career.

Inside the elevator Carrie pressed "3" and headed up to the neuro recovery floor.

The hall outside the elevator was dim, quiet, and empty as she walked down to the four-bed unit. Hospitals could be lonely places in the evenings, but the VA seemed especially dormant.

Carrie pushed the intercom and waited for the double doors to buzz open. Inside, three of the four glassed-in rooms were empty. Steve Abington was in the bed at the far end of the last room, extubated and resting comfortably, reclining with his head up fifteen degrees, IV in place, a bedside gooseneck lamp illuminating his face.

Marianne, the full-figured night nurse, sat behind a wide desk with her face buried in a book. In front of

Marianne was a row of monitors, all dark except for the one reporting Abington's heart rate and BP. Taped to a wall in the nurses' station, easy to read from a distance, was a list of phone extensions for ordering various tests. As if Carrie needed another reminder she did not belong on the floor, at the bottom of the list, in bold lettering, was Evan Navarro's ordering number, as well as his user name and password to the system where lab orders and such were entered. This was clearly his domain.

"It's all quiet tonight." Marianne spoke in a reedy voice, alert to her surroundings, despite keeping her eyes on her book, a bodice-ripper romance. Carrie grabbed Abington's chart and walked toward his bed.

"I'm not used to seeing docs up here at this hour," Marianne called out. "Usually, I just call 'em if things go bad, and they usually don't with these DBS folks. Anesthesia extubates them and they breathe just fine. Haven't had a problem yet. Hey, you new here?"

Carrie came back to the desk. With a smile, she extended her hand. "I'm Dr. Carrie Bryant. I work with Dr. Finley. I'm the new DBS surgeon."

Abington's hospital room held little warmth. With a crush of high-tech gear and monitors, the place was intimidating at best, and not intended for long-term stays. The electric hum of equipment buzzed, and in the quiet of the floor every beep could be heard in perfect clarity.

Carrie paused at the door and eyed her attacker with compassion. She reminded herself that the man who hours ago had his hands wrapped around Carrie's throat was not the same person who lay on this hospital bed. The image of Abington's crazed-eye look flashed through her mind and sent a chill down her spine. She could recall every detail of the attack: the feeling of pressure on her throat, the coursing terror as her windpipe closed. The smell of his hot breath when he hovered over her, his eyes aglow. But—it wasn't with hate, was it? It had been fear. Yes, Abington was terrified when he attacked. In a way, the assault was more like a drowning person flailing at a would-be rescuer.

She went to Abington's bedside and pulled a penlight from her coat pocket.

"Good evening, Mr. Abington," Carrie said. "I'd like to check your pupils. Would you kindly follow my light?"

Steve Abington opened his eyes ever so slowly and stared vacantly toward his doctor. If he remembered Carrie and what he'd done to her, it did not register on his face.

Carrie quickly checked his pupillary reactivity and then his eye movements. "Now please follow my light. Up . . . good. Left. Right . . . good."

Abington's shaved head was dressed in bandages, but the stereotactic frame had been removed and he looked handsome now that he was free of the elaborate computerized apparatus.

"Well, you've had quite a day. We haven't had a proper introduction. Do you remember anything about meeting me?"

Abington, who appeared quite groggy still, didn't respond. Carrie checked his reflexes, and made sure he was moving all fours pretty much equally.

"You were extremely upset when they brought you in," Carrie said. "Do you remember? You were very confused, telling me you didn't belong here."

Abington mumbled something under his breath. He looked utterly lost and alone. Confusion smoldered in his darting eyes.

"Steve, can you tell me the last thing you remember?"

Like a veil had been lifted, Abington came alive and looked wildly about. His jaw set and a snarl overtook his face. He covered his ears with his hands and began to shake his head as if something was lodged inside his ears. Carrie worried he would rip the IVs out of his arm.

"Enough. Shut up, shut up, shut up," Abington said. His speech came out thickly. His expression was that of a cornered animal.

"Steve, what's wrong? What's going on?"

Abington continued to turn his head frantically from one side to the other, keeping his hands over his ears.

"Where are you? Stop it! Stop saying that! Follow my light, follow my light, follow my light! What light? What light? Stop it!"

"Steve, calm down. You've got to calm down. Everything is all right."

Abington appeared to have heard Carrie, but his expression became even more agitated.

"Why do you keep saying it's all right? Nothing is all right. Nothing is all right! Nothing is all right! Stop saying that!"

Abington flipped onto his stomach and buried his

head under the pillow. But Carrie could hear him muttering the same words over and over.

"Follow my light . . . follow my light . . ."

Carrie bolted for the door. It would be easy to get Abington sedated. The question was, could she ever get him cured?

20

The badge dangling from a red lanyard identified the nurse as Lee Taggart. He wore crisply pressed white scrubs and unblemished matching canvas sneakers that carried him down the long hallway at a brisk pace. He stopped in front of Marianne's workstation and leaned forward, hoping to catch her eye.

"Reading anything good?"

Lee's warm voice drew Marianne's attention. When she looked up, he flashed her a brilliant smile. Marianne smiled back. Lee had an athletic body and smooth ebony skin, and was not unaccustomed to flattering looks. He had never met Marianne before, but that was not so unusual here. Staff seemed to change as often as shifts, and Marianne would need only to see the red lanyard and white uniform to believe he was a staff nurse.

Marianne glanced down at the cover of her book, which featured a bare-chested Adonis riding a stallion with a scantily clad buxom woman clutched in his massive arms. She laughed flirtatiously.

"Oh, just something to pass the time," she said, embarrassed enough to cover the book jacket with a clipboard.

The look in Lee's brown eyes turned conspiratorial. "Another slow night, eh?" he said.

He knew it had not been slow in the least. Everything that could have gone wrong with Abington had gone wrong.

"I prefer that to the alternative," Marianne said as she glanced at one of the dark monitors and caught a glimpse of her reflection within. She noticed her hair was a bit tousled, which she promptly corrected, using her hand as a comb.

"Well, I got assigned to Dr. Goodwin's staff tonight," Lee said. "Just got to go in and check on the patient. He's in four, right?"

"That's right. He's in four."

Marianne was having a heck of a time keeping her eyes off this new nurse. She was also struggling with Tinder, and every other dating site where she'd posted a profile. The VA offered slim pickings when it came to the opposite sex, so she was enjoying this pleasant surprise to the fullest.

Before Lee headed off to room four, Marianne checked Abington's vitals in the only active monitor. His heart and pulse were optimal, but the patient had been in a blissful haloperidol stupor for the past couple of hours, with not a peep since his earlier outburst. She had been told to be extra vigilant for any Q-T prolongation or incidence of arrhythmia, but so far he and the drug were working well together.

Dr. Bryant had ordered ten milligrams of diazepam

IV after Abington went crazy, and Marianne had bolted from her chair and gotten the syringe promptly. Within a few minutes, the patient was relaxed again, and his eyes closed.

"Looks like he didn't need too much on top of that residual anesthesia," Dr. Bryant had said.

Having had enough excitement for one night, Marianne had been satisfied with that explanation, but Dr. Bryant still looked perplexed.

"I've never seen anything like that," she had said. "It's like he was hallucinating. Hearing voices, the same phrase over and over again. He repeated what I said, and then he answered my question multiple times. I only said it once, but somehow it never stopped for him."

Marianne was not concerned. "They're all agitated in some way," she said, not sharing Carrie's concern. "It's not unusual for them to get extra sedation. The residents are used to it and they're trained for it, so I can see why it was a shock to you."

Marianne's words did not seem to have much impact on the new DBS surgeon.

Dr. Bryant wrote a prn sedative order, administer as needed. She told Marianne to call if there was a problem, and to give the phone number to her relief at the eleven o'clock shift change. Sam Rockwell used to do the same. Marianne had looked in on Abington twice since then. He seemed a bit restless, his limbs moving involuntarily, shaking, but those were common side effects of the sedative.

"He's been a handful, that's for sure," Marianne said to Nurse Taggart. "Very agitated. Not sure what's going on with him."

"Well, that's why I'm here to check up on things."

"If he starts to give you trouble, you just holler," Marianne said.

"I sure will," Lee replied, "but I'm pretty good at handling most any situation on my own." With a wink, Lee headed to Abington's room.

Marianne focused her gaze on his well-defined backside as he walked away.

I bet you are. She smiled and went back to her book.

Relentless heat bathed the back of Abington's neck, and sandy grit somehow wormed underneath his eyelids to scratch at his corneas. Place? Time? Where was he? What had happened? Somewhere off in the distance, Abington heard the thunderous roll of artillery shells detonating as the ground beneath him rumbled and shook with each massive blast. He felt around for his weapon, but his arms responded spastically like they had a mind of their own.

One of Abington's pawing hands felt something made of steel. He clutched his M16 and pulled the weapon close to him. He managed to get onto his hands and knees, but each breath came at a price. Something was wrong. Something was horribly wrong with him.

The air parted as bullets whizzed overhead. Abington forced open his eyes and blinked in response to the oppressive sunlight. When his vision cleared, he saw he was still in Afghanistan. Again, he was back where it all began, inside the foxhole, and Roach was with him just as before. Only now the indestructible Roach had had his guts ripped open by a peppering of bullets and he was bleeding out.

In lumbering, agonizingly slow motion, Abington flipped onto his belly and crawled over to his wounded comrade. He could not understand why his movements were so labored, dreamlike. But this could not be a dream. It was all too real. He could feel the heat scorching his skin, and a stench of gunpowder mixed with blood was visceral and genuine.

Gasping, Abington made his way toward Roach, who groaned and clutched at his injured stomach. If Abington did not stop the bleeding soon, his friend would die. All over again.

From close by, Abington heard a spit of gunfire. In the same instant, sand and dirt sprayed his face. With a burst of surprising adrenaline, Abington brushed his face clean and lurched forward, landing almost on top of Roach. With nothing to stop the bleeding, Abington placed his hands over the pulsing wound. He cried out in horror as his fingers sank deep inside the bloody cavity. Muscles and tendons pulsed around Abington's probing fingers, but the blood continued to ooze out. Roach moaned deliriously, fading in and out of consciousness.

Abington was about to scream for a medic when he noticed a shadow looming. He looked up just in time to see the figure of a man leap into the foxhole with them. Abington blinked to clear his vision. He had thought the dark-skinned man was wearing white hospital scrubs, but now there were no scrubs. The man was dressed in camouflage, with the combat medic's Red Cross insignia sewn onto his sleeve.

"What's happening here, Steve?" the man asked.

Abington had so much to say, but he could not utter a single word.

Instead, the medic's voice tumbled about his head and Abington heard the words "what's happening . . .

what's happening . . . what's happening" like a scratched record.

Abington pulled his hands from the gruesome gut wound and covered his ears to try and block out the sound. His red-stained palms lathered his face with warm blood, but those words kept rolling about his head like an endless echo.

What's happening . . . what's happening . . . what's happening . . .

"Steve, you're going to feel a little funny in a moment."

Steve you're going to feel . . . Steve you're going to feel . . . Steve you're going to feel.

"Stop! Stop saying that! Just fix Roach!"

Now it was Abington's voice providing the echo.

Fix Roach . . . fix Roach . . . fix Roach . . .

The medic moved inches from Abington's face as he produced a syringe full of clear liquid from his pocket. At first the medic appeared to be injecting the syringe into thin air, but Abington's vision altered and he saw the needle had penetrated the tubing of his own intravenous line. How did he get a line in his arm when it was Roach who had been shot?

"It's called potassium chloride, and while it's not fatal, you're going to feel very uncomfortable," the medic whispered benevolently. "I'll see you in a minute, Steve."

The medic climbed out of the foxhole and was gone—but not his voice, which remained and echoed mercilessly in his ears.

I'll see you in a minute . . . see you in a minute . . . in a minute . . .

Seconds later, a new sensation came over Abington, something strange and unnerving. He inhaled sharply and fought against the tightness in his chest, curling into a fetal position and rhythmically rocking. He rubbed Roach's blood all over his head, hair, and neck in an effort to stop the noise in his head. Nearby, Roach lay on his back, mouth open, with a dead-eyed gaze up to the heavens.

The tightness changed into something else. Abington's heartbeat began to flutter, then it morphed into a pounding. Abington could feel the palpitations in his chest, throat, and neck. He turned his head and locked his gaze on his dead friend, certain he would soon be joining him.

Lee Taggart had made it to the elevator bank when Abington's alarm went off. While he was not at all surprised, Lee still made a show of it, and raced back to Marianne, who had a look of panic on her face. Some of the nurses were stoics—they could handle any stressful situation thrown at them—while others were not at all adept at managing crises. They tended to relish the relative calm of the neuro recovery floor.

"Something is wrong," she said. "His heartbeat just went crazy."

"He's on haloperidol, right?" Lee said. "Arrhythmia can be a side effect. I'm here, let me rush him down to the med ICU."

Marianne looked relieved. She was definitely not the good-in-emergencies type.

21

The house was quiet when Carrie got home. The front porch light was on; it was always on when Carrie stayed out after her parents had gone to sleep. Traffic on the Mass Pike had been mercifully light, but it was still almost midnight when Carrie pulled into her parents' driveway.

She'd spent the drive running Abington's surgical procedure through her mind. It had been an exhilarating, terrifying, and utterly strange first day on the job and she was glad to be home. Carrie had given some thought to moving out now that she had an income stream again, but opted against it. Until she had some permanence she was not going to make any big changes.

When Carrie walked into the kitchen, she was delighted to find a card waiting for her on the table, propped against a small vase of flowers—daisies mostly, her favorite. The handwritten note from her mom and dad congratulated her on what they assumed had been a successful first surgery. She had debated telling them about Abington, but worried they would worry.

Reading her parents' note, Carrie became keenly aware of the soreness around her neck. It was tight, and every time she looked to the left, she felt a sharp, gripping pain that stretched across the back of her head. It was the pain of a muscle spasm, not a fracture. She also had additional pain along the outside of her right knee, but not with every step. In the morning she'd probably wake up with visible signs of the day's violence. Those would need to be explained, or perhaps just covered up.

Carrie heard a floorboard creak behind her and turned to see Adam in the entrance to the kitchen. He was wearing a T-shirt and sweats. For a moment she saw him as her little brother again, but that vision was blown apart by his haunted, hooded eyes. Eyes that resembled Abington's.

"Hey Carrie," Adam said as he trudged over to the fridge. "How'd the first surgery go?"

"Pretty good," Carrie said. "Nobody died."

Adam returned a fractured smile. "Well, I'd call that a big success." He chuckled. "Want some OJ?"

"Love some."

Adam poured two glasses and joined Carrie at the kitchen table. Carrie moved the flowers and card to the side to make room, surreptitiously checking her arms to make sure there were no visible marks or scratches. If her parents found out, they'd certainly be concerned about safety, but Adam could go ballistic.

"Can I ask you something?"

Adam took a swig of OJ. "Anything."

Carrie softened her voice. "What do you think

would happen if you saw a virtual reality simulation of something that happened to you over in Afghanistan?"

"What do you mean by that? Like a computer simulation?"

"Along those lines," Carrie said. "But hyper-realistic."

Adam tossed his hands in the air. "I dunno."

Carrie thought not only of Abington's initial assault, but of his second outburst after the surgery, which required a haloperidol drip to calm him. Having experienced Adam's explosive temper, it was not a stretch to envision her brother in Abington's place.

"Could you maybe . . . become violent?" Carrie asked.

This was a sensitive subject for the family. Adam owned several guns, including a pistol and rifle, and threatened to move out before he'd give them up. He was a lawful and responsible gun owner, and nobody disagreed, but nobody wanted him to have those weapons either. The worry was for Adam's safety, since PTSD and gun ownership were often a lethal mix. Adam returned an indifferent shrug.

"I hit a reporter for no real good reason. So I suppose anything is possible."

Carrie laughed. "Did you call to apologize?"

"I did better than that," Adam said. "I met the guy for coffee. Gave him everything he could possibly want to hear, and probably more than he expected."

Carrie made a mental note to call David Hoffman; she'd agreed to a coffee date as well. Seeing sadness in her brother's eyes, Carrie reached across the table and took hold of Adam's hand. "Even I haven't heard those stories."

Adam squeezed her hand. "For a reason."

"If you ever want to talk about it—"

"You're here for me. I know that, Carrie. You've always had my back." He raised his hands in a pantomime of a pneumatic drill. "Hey, what do you think of this work you're doing? Should I have you drill into my head and stick me with wires?" Adam gave a cartoon evil scientist's maniacal laugh.

Based on Abington's reaction to the treatment, Carrie could not say with certainty, but she still believed in the program and its promise. It might be worth the pain of reconsolidating bad memories through virtual reality therapy to get positive results, though Carrie had reason to worry about potential side effects.

Her mind picked at the odd verbal exchange with Abington right before he went off the rails. The man's voice had sounded so distressed as he repeated, "Follow my light, follow my light." *It was like he heard my voice in his head over and over again,* Carrie thought.

"I don't know yet," she said to Adam. "I need more time to see it in action before I can say, though I do think there's tremendous promise."

Adam swallowed his orange juice in a long gulp and pushed back his chair to stand. "I'm beat." He stretched and yawned.

"Hi Beat, I'm Carrie." She held out her hand and Adam shook it, smiling at their long-running joke. "Have a good night. I'll see you in the morning."

"Night, Carrie." At the doorway Adam paused and turned. "Hey, it's good to have you here. It's good for all of us."

Carrie blew him a kiss. "When are you going to take me for a ride in that Camaro of yours?"

"I almost got it running today."

Carrie grimaced as she recalled the last time Adam almost got it running.

Adam noticed her reaction. "Don't worry," he said. "I'm not going to go all *Christine* on it."

Christine, the film adaptation of the Stephen King novel, was Adam's favorite movie these days. He'd seen it on cable after he came home from the war. He was referring to the scene when the high school kids trashed the car named Christine using aluminum bats, only to be killed after the car magically repaired itself and sought revenge. Adam seemed to like the idea of a thing that was indestructible, perhaps because he felt so vulnerable.

"Good night, Adam," Carrie said, crossing the room to give her brother a warm embrace. God, she hoped the DBS treatment worked. She hoped it was the cure for PTSD. She wanted her brother to feel whole again, but he was more like his Camaro he could not get running than Christine, which could magically put itself back together again.

Upstairs in her bedroom, Carrie went to put her phone on the dresser, and saw by the display that she'd missed a call during her drive home.

"Dr. Bryant, this is Marianne from the VA. You asked me to call if there was any problem with Patient Abington. He was rushed down to the medical ICU by a nurse on Dr. Goodwin's staff. Abington developed an arrhythmia and his blood pressure fell. The monitor showed ventricular tach with a wide QRS. I'm sorry to have to leave you this message. I tried you a couple times, but I couldn't reach you."

Carrie felt her own heart start to race. She checked

the call log, and sure enough: two missed calls from the VA, including the call where Marianne had left her the voice message.

Carrie muttered to herself, "The haloperidol, dammit."

She probably should have just given Abington more Valium, since it was already in his system from before. Except she had checked his ECG, and the Q-T interval was not prolonged or anything, and it had calmed him down. She felt physically ill. She had made the call, she had ordered the drug, and Steve Abington in the ICU was on her.

Carrie thought of other ways she could have handled the situation, but kept returning to the haloperidol. He had seemed so crazy, beyond agitated. She had never experienced a post-op patient with symptoms resembling anything like Abington's. His repeating the same phrase, and that look in his eyes—that was fear and terror she saw. It was different from the confused agitated state or delirium she'd seen time and time again, whether someone was in the throes of DTs, or suffering the consequences of acute stroke, or sepsis, or, well, a host of other medical and surgical disorders. This was something unique, and she did not know what to make of it.

What else could have caused the arrhythmia?

A hemorrhage?

Goodness, that was always a risk after surgery. And Carrie had seen at least one case where a subarachnoid hemorrhage had resulted in a serious arrhythmia. While negative drug reaction remained the most probable event, other considerations besides a hemorrhage dotted her thoughts. It could be an infection. Fever.

Perhaps a seizure, or even a stroke. A CT of the brain would be the logical first step.

However, she could do nothing about it now. Abington's welfare was in the hands of the med ICU team. Before she could do anything, Abington needed to be stabilized. His blood pressure, heart rhythm, vital signs in general had to be under control. To go barging in there at this late hour would be counterproductive. They would take all the necessary precautions. She could picture Abington lying in an ICU bed, intubated again and hooked to a ventilator, IV fluids and antiarrhythmic drugs flowing through his veins. Dopamine and other vasopressors keeping his blood pressure up. The baton had been passed; Abington was not a neurosurgical post-op case any longer.

Still, she would go see him first thing in the morning.

22

It was dark when the alarm went off. Cocooned in her bed, Carrie thought about hitting the snooze button, but decided to get an early start. Despite the aches in her body and neck—the result of a buildup of lactic acid and inflammation—she managed to arrive at the VA a little after seven thirty. She wanted to check on Abington before her day officially started. Even though the med ICU staff was more than capable, she had done the invasive procedure and felt ultimately responsible for his outcome. It could be that all she did was give them her thanks and a pat on the back, but she had to do something. Either way, she had to know the outcome.

Carrie had just flashed her security badge at the front desk when her phone began to vibrate. To her surprise, it was a text message from Dr. Sandra Goodwin, head of neurosurgery. *Come see me as soon as you arrive. I'm in my office now.* The text came across as a bit edgy. Carrie belonged to Dr. Finley, head of neurology and his DBS program, so even though surgery resided under Dr. Goodwin's purview, the line of responsibility to her was a dotted one at most, and thus far Carrie had had little interaction with the woman. Still, Abington could wait. Carrie stopped by the cafeteria for coffee before making her way to Dr. Goodwin's second-floor office.

Seated behind a metal desk that had probably been manufactured in the 1970s, Dr. Goodwin eyed Carrie with contempt. Carrie had not expected to see Dr. Evan Navarro, who ran the residency program, there as well. Navarro sat on one of two uncushioned folding chairs set in front of Dr. Goodwin's desk. The concrete brick walls were painted a sorry shade of yellow, and the low ceiling covered with cheap acoustic tiles made Carrie feel uncomfortably confined. Other than a couple of struggling plants, Dr. Goodwin's home away from home had all the life of a pathology lab.

Dr. Navarro turned the chair next to him slightly and offered it to Carrie. She sat down gingerly, which had more to do with Navarro's hard stare than with her aching knee. Dr. Navarro was short—Carrie probably had two inches on him—but he had a reputation for being pugnacious and for bringing residents to tears. His dark hair was gelled back, showing off a prominent widow's peak.

Dr. Goodwin looked every bit her fifty-five years. She wore her hair in a bob that called attention to her face's sharp features, and nothing warm or fuzzy showed in her hazel eyes. She was all business and all about maximizing every minute in her day. Wearing a white lab coat over a set of blue scrubs, her clothing implied she would touch a scalpel at some point in the day, which Carrie highly doubted. Dr. Goodwin was an administrator. But maybe she liked looking the part of a surgeon.

Dr. Goodwin spoke bluntly. "I heard you went to see Steve Abington in the neuro recovery floor yesterday."

No "Hello." No "How are you adjusting to the new job." No "I heard you almost got killed." Dr. Goodwin was as efficient with her words as she was with her time.

"I did." Carrie did not know what else to say.

Dr. Goodwin's glowering expression said that the chief of neurosurgery did not approve. "Yes, I see," Dr. Goodwin replied. "I heard about yesterday, and I'm aware of the circumstance. I'm sorry that happened, though I do believe Dr. Finley expressed to you beforehand that the PTSD patients should never be seen without accompaniment."

Carrie felt a bit ashamed by the accusation, but she bristled. It sounded like victim-blaming.

"I guess I didn't fully appreciate the need for the warning," Carrie said.

"That may be," Dr. Goodwin replied coldly, "and because of the extenuating circumstances here, Evan and I thought it would be appropriate to review our department policies with you with respect to post-op care, among other things."

"That's the job of the residents," Navarro said in a sharp tone. "You may think of yourself as one of the gang, but you're not."

Dr. Goodwin shot Navarro an admonishing look, perhaps to call back her attack dog. "What Evan is trying to say, Carrie, is that you are basically an employee of Dr. Finley. Your situation here is highly unique. Unusual, is the word I would choose to describe it. To be blunt, the hospital has a well-organized residency program, and you're not part of it. Surely you understand that we have procedures in place for patient care, and a hierarchy for addressing emergent situations. You show your face and nurses don't know who to call if there's a problem. Do they call you? You're not even insured here if something does go wrong. You expose this program to added risk by this behavior."

Carrie's face felt hot. "I was simply curious to see how my first DBS patient was doing."

"That's understandable," Dr. Goodwin said. "Which is why we're having a friendly chat about it."

Doesn't feel friendly, Carrie thought.

"If the residents think you're undermining them, it will throw my entire program into disarray," Navarro said.

"It was certainly not my intention."

"Yes, well, our best intentions may have unintended consequences."

"Well, how is Abington doing?" Carrie asked. "All I know is that he was moved to medical ICU."

"And that's all you need to know," Navarro answered curtly.

Dr. Goodwin held up her hand again. Navarro apparently needed an even shorter leash.

"I guess I'm a bit confused," Carrie said. "I just wanted to see how my patient was doing after *my* surgery."

Dr. Goodwin's intense expression ticked up a few notches. "Let me take a moment to clarify your role here," she said. "You are the DBS surgeon. Period. You did your surgery just fine. Dr. Finley brought you on board exclusively for that purpose. And I, for one, did not support your appointment."

No kidding.

"I would have preferred we bring in somebody who had gone through a formal residency program *successfully*," Dr. Goodwin continued. "But Dr. Finley is the one who has the funds, and he insisted your skills as a surgeon trumped any concerns we may have had regarding your . . . unfortunate history."

Carrie tensed at the reference, and in doing so caused a stab of pain in her aching knee.

"Your job is to do the DBS installations, and that's it," Dr. Goodwin said.

"And the next link in that chain is me," Navarro added.

Carrie felt like she had just been body-slammed.

"So you see, Carrie, you're here because the DBS surgeries are lengthy and do require a dedicated resource. You're quite simply a hired hand, and it's best if you keep your involvement to that."

Carrie's cheeks flushed. She could feel her anger starting to percolate. Digging deep, she mustered restraint. "I understand." She directed her attention to Navarro. "Would you mind giving me an update on Abington's condition? I understand he's been moved to the medical ICU. I did the procedure. I feel a responsibility for the patient outcome. I think I deserve that professional courtesy."

Dr. Goodwin and Navarro exchanged an inscrutable look.

"Let's make sure we got this clear, Carrie," Dr. Goodwin said. "You do the surgery and you're done. The residents and Dr. Navarro will do the post-op care. If a patient is moved to another unit, that patient becomes the responsibility of others. Not us. We take care of our responsibilities as they apply to neurosurgery, and do not go chasing after patients when they become the province of a different department. This is the way our organization is effectively maintained. Do I make myself clear?"

Carrie was shocked. She could not believe the tone Dr. Goodwin was using with her, the utter disdain. It was as if Carrie, by acting in a thoughtful and caring manner toward a patient, had violated some sacred oath and thereby single-handedly put the entire system in a state of dysfunctional disrepair.

Carrie knew all about "turfing," the idea that a patient who was moved off one floor and brought to another became OPP, other people's problem. But she had never worked in an environment where the hush-hush practice was so openly supported and, in fact, endorsed. The notion made Carrie sick to her stomach. This was not what she had signed up for, and she had every intention of making her feelings known to Dr. Finley.

For now, the best, most politically expedient strategy for this meeting was to appear compliant and retreat. *Never poke an angry bear.*

"You've made yourself clear," Carrie said. "So if I'm not scheduled to do any DBS surgeries, what then?"

"As long as you respect our procedures, that is not my concern. You do what you feel is best for you and your career, Carrie," Dr. Goodwin said.

Dr. Goodwin's smile held all the warmth of a snow cone. Carrie didn't have to be told to stand; this meeting was clearly adjourned.

23

Carrie spent fifteen minutes in her cramped, window-less office trying to decompress. Her blood pressure had settled, but she was having enormous trouble concentrating on her DBS research. She was halfway through a difficult paper on dysarthria in Parkinson's disease, but the words jumbled on the page.

She was ruminating on that contentious conversation—ambush was more like it—with Drs. Goodwin and Navarro. The insinuations were absolutely infuriating. Carrie had not taken the job just to be a surgical tool. A hammer for a nail, so to speak. Dr. Finley had told her she'd be part of the team, and that was how she'd envisioned her role.

I would have preferred we bring in somebody who had gone through a formal residency program successfully. Dr. Goodwin's words bit hard.

Out of frustration, Carrie balled up the printout she'd been reading and threw it against the wall. That woman had been cutting, disparaging, and downright offensive. Something odd had happened with Steve Abington, something potentially related to his DBS treatment. It was more than the agitated state the duty nurse had described. This was something—but what? She was focused mostly on his strange response. In her mind, she could still hear him muttering the same phrase over again, repeating what she had said.

Follow my light . . . follow my light . . .

Abington seemed to experience some form of auditory hallucination. It was unusual, not the type she had seen in schizophrenics where disturbing voices outside the head seemed to speak directly to victims. She was keen to try and understand. Even if she were prohibited from seeing Abington, her time was her own, and Carrie could still work his case.

Take that, Dr. Goodwin!

Carrie squeezed into the crowded elevator. Her finger hovered over the button to the medical ICU floor before she resisted the temptation. It was one thing to do some research in the library on a "turfed" patient, but she couldn't flagrantly ignore Dr. Goodwin's instructions minutes after they had been issued. It was best for now to keep her investigation academic.

The library at the VA was located on the first floor, just off the lobby, and it did not look like it got much use. The floor was covered with a threadbare carpet, and though it had a few wooden carrels, none had a chair. Unlike the gift shop, which was staffed by volunteers dressed in brightly colored smocks adorned with patriotic pins, the library reception desk was unattended. In place of a human, a sign in an acrylic holder provided instructions on how to obtain a password to access the computer and navigate to the home

page. Some of the more recent medical journals—
what limited print supply was on hand—were stuffed
haphazardly into a standing magazine rack, but the library's shelves were notably barren.

Carrie located a plastic chair and set it facing a ter-
minal. A thought of her dad flashed across her mind.
How would he go about this? Her father loved doing
research. To him, it was a major part of the challenge
of medicine. He and Carrie could not have been more
different in this regard. As a surgeon, Carrie preferred
her puzzle pieces manifested not as words, but rather
lab results, machine readouts, and whatever visual
cues she could derive from inside the human body.

She was typical of the field; few surgeons loved doing research. Carrie recalled her third year in medical
school, during her clinical clerkship, when she was on
hospital rounds with the attending physician and a host
of medical interns and residents. The resident would
summarize the previous day's events, what the blood
work or imaging studies revealed, while the rest hovered over the patient's bedside like spectators at a
sporting event.

While these bedside rounds may have been a bit in-
trusive, they were always interesting and instructive.
Until, that is, some suck-up student or resident would
inevitably blurt out something like, "Thompson et al.
in last week's *Lancet* . . ." Then they'd go into detail
about some study that was published and how it might
relate to the patient before them.

Inwardly, Carrie would groan her displeasure. To
Carrie, rounds on surgical services were about practi-
cal information and hands-on study. The book learning,
though important, was no longer the focus. Instead,

her attention was on the ins and outs of active treatment. She held nothing but respect for internal medicine docs, or "fleas," as the surgeons called them. Her dad was one, for goodness' sake, and he would always be her idol. But from day one Carrie felt more comfortable in her skin as a surgeon.

An old joke came to mind: an internal medicine doc, a pathologist, and a surgeon are out duck hunting. Suddenly a flock of birds goes by. The internist says, "They quack like ducks, they fly like ducks, they've got the coloring of ducks. They're probably ducks." The surgeon glances over at his friend, raises his shotgun, and shoots the birds out of the sky. Then he says to the pathologist, "Go see if they're ducks."

Carrie was a surgeon.

After about a minute of aimless clicking and browsing, Carrie called her dad.

"Hi, sweetie," Howard Bryant said.

Carrie smiled at the sound of his voice. "Hi, Dad. I could use some help."

After she'd explained what she was after, Carrie's father pinpointed the problem: She was at the wrong library. It felt liberating to walk out the front doors of the VA, leaving the building Dr. Goodwin occupied, for the Orange Line T stop. Carrie could have driven to the Harvard Medical Library, but parking at this time of day would be a hassle. Thirty minutes later, Carrie traded the warm spring day for the cool interior of the Francis A. Countway Library of Medicine.

The Harvard library was a sprawling, multifloor building, with a winding marble staircase and a spacious courtyard gloriously situated beneath a massive atrium ceiling. It took Carrie some time to find the

Index Medicus, which had stopped publication in 2004, toppled by medical search engines, but respecting her dad's library research attack plan, she'd start with the tried and true.

Two hours into her effort Carrie still had not found anything useful, but she remained dedicated to the task. It was some relief that Carrie could find no cases of DBS-induced arrhythmia, which quieted the voice in her head that wanted to blame her for that part of Abington's condition. As for his delirium, the medical search engines offered up a host of unusual types of hallucinations that took her nowhere: hypnogogic hallucinations associated with sleep stage alterations, peduncular hallucinosis associated with brain stem diseases, musical hallucinations that seemed more benign and could even be pleasurable, but nothing that seemed like Abington's case.

Carrie examined a few old textbooks: *Noyes' Modern Clinical Psychiatry* from the '60s. Useless. She got up to stretch her legs. Another hour slipped by. And then another. Carrie's stomach was rumbling, but she was not ready to stop. She recalled the pure terror on Abington's face as she filled out a reference request card for an obscure medical journal. Her hunger for lunch seemed small next to the needs of the patient.

"I'll be sitting over there," Carrie said to the delicate and bony eighty-year-old woman working the desk, who hefted enormous tomes with seemingly little effort.

"I'll get it for you . . . I'll get it for you," the librarian said, repeating her words in what was probably a lifelong habit.

It reminded Carrie of Abington.

Follow my light . . . follow my light . . .

That was when it struck her. Carrie had been so focused on calling Abington's symptoms hallucinations that she had found articles specific only to that condition. But Abington was not exhibiting hallucinations. These were not totally false perceptions. It was more of a misperception of what Carrie had said. She had asked him a question and he had responded multiple times. He only thought she was saying it over and over again, when in fact she had uttered it only once, a simple single phrase.

As a neurosurgeon, Carrie was well aware of the difference between an illusion and a hallucination. She had focused on the wrong issue. A hallucination is a *false* perception, with no external stimulus involved. Whatever the individual hallucinates is an internal, personal experience. But an illusion is a *misperception* of reality, and in these cases an external stimulation is always present. With Abington, the external stimulation was Carrie's voice.

Carrie raced back to her desk and grabbed a standard textbook, *Principles of Neurology* by Adams and Victor. She had already read up on hallucinations, but this time she aimed elsewhere.

Illusions.

Carrie rifled through the index until she found: illusions, auditory, page 759. There, down toward the bottom of the page, was a reference to auditory illusions associated with lesions of the temporal lobe, where "words may be repeated, a kind of perseveration." Yes! Perseveration, the uncontrolled repetition of a word or phrase that was associated with brain injury. He was not hearing things, but rather he had a misperception of what was heard. It was a subtle twist, but it made all the difference.

Carrie's pulse jumped. She was onto something. She read about palinacousis, a condition first described by Bender in 1965, and elaborated by Jacobs with a number of case studies in 1973. Came from the Greek, *palin* (again) and *akouein* (to hear). All cases were attributed to lesions in the temporal lobe, where sound was processed in the brain. Some cases were due to a form of seizure, like a type of localized epilepsy. Single words or more extensive phrases would be repeated several times—in other words, perseverated.

The sounds could even be louder and more vivid than the original. Many patients became upset and quite disturbed by the event. Carrie read about several patients who were coherent enough to figure out that the sounds seemed to come from one particular side of their head. As it turned out, doctors were able to determine that instances of palinacousis manifest on the side opposite the brain lesion. If that were true, Abington would have heard Carrie's words, "Follow my light," only in one ear—more accurately, the left auditory field, on the opposite side of the lesion.

Palinacousis was extremely rare. Carrie could find only a handful of described cases despite an extensive literature search. She spent some time contemplating possible reasons why Abington had developed the condition. He certainly did not exhibit it prior to his surgery. Then again, he was not in any coherent state during her pre-op exam. Perhaps he was having the illusion then. Maybe that had triggered his rage. Could it have been seizure-related? Or did he have a hemorrhage in the temporal lobe post-op? The amygdala was not in the anatomical area that processed sounds, but could the DBS have done this, in some indirect way?

Carrie's head was spinning. Was this auditory illusion somehow connected to the arrhythmia, or did the haloperidol bring it on? Perhaps it was a combination of factors. At least Carrie had one possible answer, and a name, palinacousis, to account for Abington's strange behavior.

Such a bizarre and unusual disorder; she could imagine how anyone would get agitated, believing someone was yelling the same thing over and over again in your ear. And you could not see the person who was doing the yelling or where it was coming from. It was an illusion. The implications were troubling. The condition indicated a localized disturbance in the brain, specifically the part of the temporal lobe that processed auditory information.

Carrie returned to the idea that the condition could be a side effect of DBS. It would mean Abington's confused agitation was not the commonly encountered post-op delirium, a temporary consequence of anesthesia or other drugs. Carrie needed to see Abington, to examine him further, but obstacles blocked her way, namely Goodwin and Navarro.

She saw another path forward. This one involved a friend, perhaps her only one at the VA.

24

The timing could not have been better.

Functioning as Dr. Finley's private DBS surgeon, Carrie had no clinic responsibilities, but he had sent her an e-mail to ask her to join him this morning because of a specific case on the schedule, one of his first patients who had undergone DBS for PTSD. The stars appeared to have aligned just for her.

Carrie had replayed her conversation with Abington dozens of times in her head. She had no doubt that he had repeated the phrase "follow my light" numerous times, and seemed to answer her question each time he thought it was asked, but that was not proof of palinacousis. Since Abington was off-limits, the best way to learn more, Carrie concluded, was to see another patient like him. Dr. Finley's e-mail was like manna from heaven.

At this point, Carrie's investigation into palinacousis was nothing more than an intellectual challenge. She simply wanted to know if the behavior ever manifested

in others, or if Abington was truly an outlier. She was
not in a position yet to broach the subject with Dr. Finley. Her confidence was nowhere near where it should
be, and any claims made had to be based on evidence,
not conjecture.

She had found nothing that reported auditory illusions in DBS cases treated for Parkinson's or other
movement disorders. But with these PTSD patients,
electrodes were being placed in a completely different
area of the brain, the amygdala nucleus.

Carrie pondered this. The amygdala was not gener-
ally associated with hearing perception. She knew
that. But this was an experimental program, and the
brain was still an organ of profound mysteries.

Carrie was scheduled to meet with Dr. Finley on
Wednesday morning, after the general neurology clinic.
Dr. Finley was supposed to supervise the neurology
clinic, which was otherwise run largely by the residents
who rotated on three-month shifts through the VA. But
Finley's increasing commitments to the deep brain
stimulation program had gradually displaced his direct
teaching and supervisory obligations, and on a typical
Wednesday he would hold court from his office, making himself available as needed for residents. For the
most part, the residents preferred to leave him alone and
solve clinical problems by themselves.

Carrie had attended just one clinical round since
she joined the VA's rank and file, but the DBS patients
she saw that day were being treated for movement disorders, not PTSD. She had no way to correlate those
patients to Steve Abington's condition. Traumatic brain
injury patients comprised the majority of cases Carrie
observed, with cognitive, perceptual, and language

deficits usually accompanied by a hemi- or quadripare-sis or seizures. Those patients whose foremost symptoms were post-traumatic stress were often referred to the psychiatry clinic, which was bursting through its seams.

Everyone realized these veterans were suffering from a brain disorder, but treatment was limited to antidepressants, antianxiety medication, or ineffective psychotropics. Acceptance into the DBS program was extremely limited during these early clinical stages, and the pent-up demand dwarfed the number of operations performed to date. Unless humanity put an end to war—likely only if humanity put an end to itself—a cure for PTSD seemed the only palliative measure for the VA's mushrooming resource woes.

Carrie arrived at Dr. Finley's office five minutes after the clinical rounds concluded and gently knocked on his door. She worried about interrupting him, but he threw the door open, as if in anticipation. A reassuring smile eased much of her concern, and he was filled with effervescence.

"Really exciting day, Carrie. I've just been reviewing the neuropsych tests on Ramón. We are clearly on track. Look at this."

He handed Carrie a bulging manila folder full of test results and graphics referencing one Ramón Hernandez, a thirty-two-year-old male, and a veteran of war in Afghanistan. Carrie leafed through the studies.

"He was one of our first DBS cases, because he failed all the usual therapies," Dr. Finley said. "I remember that Sam Rockwell had some difficulties with his surgery, and actually had to reposition the stimulating electrodes several times before we got adequate signals from the amygdala, but fortunately there were no obvious complications."

No follow my light, Carrie thought. *No arrhythmia.*

With an expression like a proud papa's, Dr. Finley went on.

"Ramón Hernandez has gone from living on the streets, or in jail, to holding a respectable job as a logistics analyst for a Target distribution center. He's still on sertraline one hundred and fifty milligrams, but the Oxycontin, benzos, and beta blockers are gone, and he regularly attends the weekly counseling sessions with his clinical social worker. Last I heard, he's even got a girlfriend."

Lifting the folder, Dr. Finley said, "This battery of psychometrics documents Ramón's impressive progress. In addition to the MMPI, we concentrated mostly on tests of all aspects of memory function, emotional intelligence, and executive functioning. There's an alexithymia scale."

Carrie was familiar with the Minnesota Multiphasic Personality Inventory, or MMPI, but had not heard of the alexithymia scale and asked Dr. Finley to clarify.

"It's when people have difficulty describing and expressing their own emotions," Dr. Finley said. "Kind of a measure of how much people are in touch with their feelings. It's a useful addition to other tests of emotional intelligence and frustration tolerance. They're far from perfect, but we get a pretty good picture of someone's personality when we analyze the entire test battery results."

Adam didn't seem to have that much difficulty there, Carrie thought. He seemed as caring and understanding as ever. But she could not deny his explosiveness, as seen in David's bloodied nose and the damage Adam had inflicted on his Camaro. Adam was a firework of violence, awaiting only a match.

"You thought Don McCall was impressive," Dr. Finley said. "Wait until you meet Ramón."

25

The Department of Neurology and Neurosurgery at the VA occupied an H-shaped section of the second floor in the main building. There was some talk that the department would move if they ever finished construction on the annex, but that was a very big "if." While it was a bit cramped, there was a certain convenience to having the surgical suites and the neurology exam rooms all in close proximity.

Dr. Finley led Carrie at a brisk pace to exam room five in the neurology unit. The exam room was like most Carrie had been in over the years; not that different from the one where she'd almost died. It had a waist-high counter, a sink, and various instruments for checking vitals.

Seated in the aluminum chair next to the examination table was a clean-cut, neatly but casually dressed and well-groomed Hispanic gentleman, who stood and shook hands with Dr. Finley. He was powerfully built and quite handsome, Carrie noted.

"Hey, Doc. Good to see you." He spoke with a youthful and vibrant voice, the voice of somebody excited for the future.

Carrie had to look carefully to see the slight asymmetry of the neck where the stimulating wires had been tunneled from the scalp, running down beneath his right clavicle to attach to the battery pack in his upper chest.

"This is Dr. Carrie Bryant, who has taken over for Dr. Rockwell."

"Yeah, I heard about his accident," Ramón said. "Terrible. He was a terrific guy. Nice to meet you, Dr. Bryant. You've got big shoes to fill." Ramón's hand, half the size of a baseball mitt, swallowed Carrie's as he gave her a firm but gentle handshake.

"I've heard only great things about Dr. Rockwell," Carrie said.

"Mind if she examines you, Ramón?"

"Be my guest," Ramón said. "But I can probably examine myself by now."

Carrie resisted the urge to come right out and ask if he ever heard the same words spoken over and over again. Her old pal Val would say Carrie possessed all the subtlety of a jackhammer.

Carrie proceeded through a series of questions pertaining to Ramón's current lifestyle. It was clear that he was socially appropriate, concentrated well, and attended to questions with insight and flexibility. He enjoyed his work, and even gave some thought to getting married to his longtime girlfriend.

"Considering she could have charged me with domestic assault not that long ago, I'd say I've come a long way." Ramón's smile projected the kind of cocky confidence required for the battlefield.

"Can you elaborate?" Carrie asked.

How far had Ramón really come, she wanted to know.

"I used to get drunk and jealous. I hit her. More than once. Not something I'm proud of, obviously. Once I got my anger under control with the DBS I could actually listen to what the therapists were trying to tell me."

"And that is?"

"That I was trying to control her because I was really afraid I was going to lose her."

The insight impressed Carrie, but she was curious to see how he would react to questions about his war memories. "What happened during that ambush? Do you mind talking about it?"

Ramón's eyes flashed, but he just shrugged. "Honestly, I don't remember all of it."

"Share what you can," Carrie said.

"I was stationed at Camp Dwyer in the Helmand Province, a place we lovingly referred to as 'Hell, man.' Luxury there was a sandbag that could double as a couch," Ramón said, with the detachment of a newscaster. "We were on a scouting mission, looking for a terrorist named Nasser Umari. He was a big-time anti-Coalition dickhead, pardon my language—hooked up with the Taliban, and other militant groups, too, I suppose. We had just fast-roped from an MH-47 helicopter, did our patrols, and after that, exfiltrated back toward our extraction point. There were about fifteen of us in the fire team." He paused to remember. "Yeah, about fifteen. It was the usual oven hot that day. A few more degrees and the sand would have turned to glass. We had just vaulted a mud wall in what looked like an abandoned town when machine-gun fire seemed to come out of nowhere. Me and three other guys fell back into an alley where I figured we'd get a better read on the enemy position. But the Taliban had machine-gun positions all around and next thing I knew I got shot in the arm. Hurt like a mother, you know what."

Ramón rolled up the sleeve on his white cotton T-shirt to show Carrie a scar on his bulging trapezius a little bigger than a quarter. She was sure his body was riddled with other scars that had nothing to do with DBS surgery.

Ramón continued. "We were returning fire, but I had crawled into a doorway to try and clot the wound. Next thing I knew, an RPG struck our position and two of the guys in the alley with me couldn't have an open casket at their wakes. It was that fast. But, I guess that's war. The bad guys are after us, and we're after them. Kill or be killed, right?"

Carrie was taken by how calm and controlled Ramón seemed. She saw no reticence or protectiveness. He remained focused, his mind targeted in the present, the past trauma mitigated by perspective. She was duly impressed. If emotion was a color, Ramón's ambush had been rendered in simple black and white.

"So, what sort of problems are you having?" Carrie asked.

Ramón gave this some thoughtful consideration. "Well, sometimes I don't seem to care about things all that much," he eventually confessed. "I don't get as worked up about a lot of things that used to bother me, either. Mostly that's good, but I wonder if sometimes

I'm too relaxed. If I get behind in work, I don't seem to care or worry as much. That's not me. And I don't remember a lot about my time in Afghanistan. I mean I do, but I don't. There's lots of holes. People have to tell me things, and sometimes it doesn't make sense. But I can live with that."

"What about your hearing? Do you hear voices?" Carrie asked.

"No."

"How about hearing sounds or voices that you know are real, but they seem to go on and on in your head, like an echo that never stops?"

Dr. Finley looked at Carrie, nonplussed. She knew these questions would produce that kind of reaction. They were way off base for this sort of exam, but Dr. Finley did not intervene.

"No," Ramón said.

Carrie went on to complete her examination, standard bedside tests of memory and cognition that she knew he would pass with flying colors. She analyzed his vision and eye movements, his hearing, speech, and swallowing. His motor functioning, gait, sensation, and reflexes were all perfectly normal.

"Thanks," she said. "It was a real pleasure meeting and talking with you. And thank you for your service."

"My pleasure. See you again. And good luck with the program."

She shook hands again and Carrie followed Dr. Finley out of the exam room. Dr. Finley had more to discuss with Ramón, but he said he wanted to speak with Carrie in private first.

"Amazing, right?"

"I'm truly astounded," Carrie said.

Dr. Finley's pride and enthusiasm were infectious, but Carrie could not embrace the moment to his degree. Ramón had reinvigorated her mojo, but her curiosity had not been fully satiated.

"Was Steve Abington ever diagnosed with schizophrenia? Any history of the disease in his family?"

Dr. Finley thought on it and shook his head.

"No, why do you ask?"

"Just curious," Carrie said.

The answer was expected and did nothing to waylay her concerns. Post-op delirium or some strange side effect to DBS? It was impossible for her to say. Carrie contemplated her next move. She was scheduled to be back in the OR on Friday, for a DBS surgery on a marine named Eric Fasciani. Before she could share Dr. Finley's enthusiasm completely, she had to see whether the condition happened again.

If she were careful, Carrie could go see that patient post-op, and Goodwin would never be the wiser.

26

Carrie had never acquired much of a taste for alcohol. She seldom drank, but on Friday night, two days after meeting Ramón Hernandez, she sat alone in a booth at Bertucci's and sipped from her glass of Sauvignon Blanc. Her thoughts were dim from fatigue. She had spent seven grueling hours on her feet performing another successful DBS surgery on Eric Fasciani.

The operation had gone smoothly enough, and it was easy to see how her job could become routine. Two Parkinson's cases were already on the schedule for next week, and they would be virtually identical procedures. Today it had been Eric Fasciani's turn on the table, and depending on what Carrie found out, it could change everything.

A middle-aged waitress with a kind face and friendly smile scuttled past Carrie's table, but backtracked when she noticed the empty wineglass.

"Do you want another?" She cleared the glass along

with the remains of Carrie's salad meal. "Maybe some dessert? The chocolate mousse is amazing."

"Sounds tempting," Carrie said, "but I'll just get a coffee. Black."

The waitress departed and Carrie checked the hour on her smartphone, then frowned. She was eager to get to Fasciani on the neuro recovery floor, but it was too early to see him. Her latest DBS patient represented a possible answer to the Steve Abington mystery, but he would be too heavily sedated for Carrie to properly evaluate. She needed him more alert.

Fasciani's operation had been long, but without incident. At the advice of Dr. Finley, Carrie had skipped pre-op consultation altogether. Better for her nerves, it was thought. Instead of greeting a troubled and nervous patient, Carrie saw only a shaved, bald-headed young man, deeply sedated and intubated with his endotracheal tube tied to a ventilator, and an IV drip open to KVO. It was probably better this way, and it fit right in with Dr. Goodwin's view of her role as hired help. Carrie was a technician, not a doctor. At least Dr. Finley had briefed her on the poor fellow's history.

"Three tours in Afghanistan, but it was the last one that did him in," Dr. Finley had said. "Apparently, the attack was highly organized. A hundred fifty Taliban came running down the hillsides from four directions and riddled his base with gunfire and RPGs."

Carrie wondered if anybody came back from the war unchanged.

"The outpost went up in flames," Dr. Finley continued. "After this, he was a quivering wreck. He couldn't sleep without his dead buddies waking him in a sweat. They MedFlighted him out of there and eventually

got him back home to Worcester. But he failed reentry
miserably. He suffers from horrible flashbacks and daily
panic attacks. We actually found him on the street,
living out of an old shopping cart. We've got him in a
shelter now, but he's made little progress."

Carrie felt a fleeting sense of gratitude. Adam had a
home, loving and helpful parents, and her. She looked
over at Fasciani and saw the scars and needle tracks in
his arms and neck, and the dozens of skin-raising scars
on his limbs and trunk. One of his demons was heroin.

"He hasn't done too well with talk therapy," Dr. Finley added. "And most of the time, his blood work comes
back with no evidence that he's even taking the antidepressants we've prescribed. Just Valium, alcohol, Oxycontin, and other opiates. So in this case, Carrie, DBS
is not just a treatment, it's his only hope, a prayer."

The surgery was Abington redux. The small burr
holes for fixing the stereotactic frame, the CT scan and
superimposed computerized mapping with his earlier
MRI images. The 14mm burr hole placed just where
the images told her to drill, the cannula driven through
to the basolateral nucleus of the amygdala, finally
the electrodes, only to await Dr. Finley's confident
voice coming up from the monitor on the other side of
the table: "Great, Carrie. Precise and perfect signals.
Lock 'em in."

After, Dr. Finley and Carrie had met outside the OR.
Her boss was beaming with pride, overjoyed.

"This is your second case this week, and you are, in
a word, terrific," Dr. Finley said. "Trust me, Carrie, you
have what it takes to do this. You're a machine. I mean
despite all those computerized gizmos, a lot of times
Dr. Rockwell had to reposition the cannula, three or

more passes at times, and I always worried about an increased risk of infection or hemorrhage. But with you, I'm sure we've got those electrodes placed where they need to be, and I'm just that much more confident in the results."

From the corner of her eye, Carrie could see Eric Fasciani's stretcher being wheeled into the elevator on its way up to the third floor, neuro post-op ICU.

"Thanks for the vote of confidence," she said.

"Rockwell's a fine doc," Dr. Finley said. "And I pray he makes a full recovery. But no matter what happens, I think you've got his job."

Carrie blushed, a little uncomfortable that her good fortune had come at another's misfortune. She politely refused Dr. Finley's invitation to dinner, instead heading off on her own to kill time.

That was three hours ago. Carrie checked her smartphone once more, paid her bill in cash including a hefty tip, and slid out of the booth. As she hurried to her car, she thought: *If Fasciani exhibits the same symptoms as Abington, nobody is going to have Sam Rockwell's job.*

27

The doctors' parking lot at the VA was virtually deserted when Carrie drove up in her trusty Subaru. She parked some distance from the entrance, out of the way of prying eyes. Only the residents' on-call spaces were occupied, and somebody working for Navarro might recognize Carrie's car. That could lead to questions, and Carrie's workday had technically ended the moment Fasciani got wheeled out of the OR. A little extra precaution was the right prescription for this evening's unsanctioned jaunt.

The VA was not in the best neighborhood, and the quiet of the surrounding streets set Carrie on edge. A biting wind rippled the plastic sheets draped over the long-neglected scaffolding that framed much of the darkened annex. Carrie did not know if the VA's administrators were counting on continued DARPA funds to get construction going again, but she had her suspicions.

Carrie pinned a clipboard to her side with one arm, and shielded her hands from the cold within the thin fabric pockets of her long white lab coat. *Some spring.* Beneath her coat, Carrie wore a clean pair of blue scrubs. She needed to look official, here on hospital business.

The automatic doors of the rear hospital entrance swooshed open as Carrie approached. Once inside, Carrie scuttled past the lone security guard stationed at a wood podium with a quick flash of her hospital ID. To him, she was another doc on the job and nothing more. The VA's empty corridors amplified Carrie's footsteps. At this hour, BCH would have been bustling, and Carrie was reminded of the days when ambulances arrived in steady streams hauling everything from panic attacks to gunshot wounds.

On her way to the elevator, Carrie spied a young woman dressed in green scrubs who approached from the opposite direction. She could have been one of Navarro's, but Carrie did not take a close look to confirm. With the clipboard to her face, Carrie lowered her head and pretended to study something important.

The ruse worked. Not a glance. Not even a hitch in the other woman's stride. The experience made Carrie feel a little bit foolish. She was a surgeon, not some fly-by-night medical detective. It was all a bit absurd, but exhilarating at the same time. Most of her life Carrie had been a rule follower, not breaker, but in this instance she felt justified, and believed her actions were absolutely necessary. Carrie quickened her pace and was a bit breathless when she reached the elevators.

Moments later, Carrie was back on neuro recovery. She pushed the intercom and waited for the duty nurse to unlock the double doors securing access to the unit. Carrie heard a faint click, pulled on the door handle, and headed inside.

Marianne was off tonight, apparently, and a different nurse occupied the nurses' station. Carrie did not recognize the attractive black male in his thirties who was too busy charting to bother to look at whom he buzzed inside.

"Good evening," Carrie said.

The man glanced up from his monitor. He had a handsome face and almond-shaped eyes the color of dark caramel. Carrie's eyes dropped to his ID badge, but it was concealed by shadows and impossible to read.

"Quiet night tonight," Carrie said.

Only one doc was supposed to be doing rounds, and it was certainly not Carrie. For this reason alone, Carrie would have preferred to avoid conversation altogether, but that would have come across as odd. Nurses expected a bit of small talk from the doctors.

"Only got one patient on the floor tonight," the nurse said. His resonant voice sounded neither pleased nor bothered by the lack of activity. Abington had also been the only patient on the floor the night Carrie visited, which pinged her curiosity. Were vets slated for DBS surgery specifically on days when no other major neuro surgeries were scheduled? It would make sense to isolate them, given how agitated and volatile these patients could become. Either way, the scheduling practice worked in Carrie's favor.

"How's our patient doing?"

"He's been pretty quiet. But these vets aren't in the best of shape to begin with."

"I'm just going to pop in and check on him. I'm the surgeon who did his DBS installation."

"Um-hum." The nurse could not have sounded less impressed if he tried. On a whim, Carrie decided

to secure a little extra insurance on her clandestine
visit.

"What's your name?" she asked.

The nurse returned a wary glance. Docs do not always bother with such pleasantries. "Lee Taggart," he
said, holding up his badge for Carrie to see and read.

"Look, Lee," Carrie said, leaning over the nurses'
station to deliver her message. "I'd appreciate it if you
kept my visit here a secret. I'm really supposed to let
the residents handle things, but I guess I'm a bit of a
control freak."

Carrie flashed a playful smile that did not appear to
soften Lee any. She got the distinct impression that
Lee Taggart did not care about hospital politics in any
way, shape, or form, so long as his checks cleared.

"You do what you need to do," Taggart said as his
focus returned to his charts. "I don't tell people anything they don't ask or need to know."

Carrie gave Taggart an appreciative smile he did
not see, and left.

Fifteen steps later, she was inside Fasciani's room.
These hospital quarters were nothing but glass cubi-
cles with a freestanding wardrobe closet and a flimsy
curtain for privacy. The patients were kept isolated to
reduce the spread of infection, and while there were
not many rooms to choose from, Carrie observed that
Fasciani occupied the same bed as Abington had before his transfer to med ICU.

A gooseneck lamp mounted above Fasciani's hospital bed illuminated his face enough to show Carrie his
glassy-eyed stare. He was awake, and Carrie com-
mended herself for getting the timing of the anesthesia

right. She closed the door, pulled the curtain shut, and turned on the overhead fluorescent.

Fasciani's eyes were sunken and ringed with dark circles. His hollow cheeks, missing teeth, and shaved head made him look more like a POW than a hospital patient. At least Fasciani did not have that accusatory stare and look of terror she had seen in Steve Abington's eyes. Maybe this was all for naught. She would know soon enough.

Carrie approached Fasciani's bed and spoke in a whisper. "I'm Dr. Bryant, Eric. I did the surgery on you earlier today."

Nothing. If anything, his vacant gaze worked harder to penetrate the wall in front of him.

"I just came to check on you," Carrie said, resting her hands on the bed railing. "I hope you're doing okay. Sometimes, patients feel a little nauseated from the anesthesia right about now, and I suspect you have a bit of a headache."

More silence. Fasciani's only response, if it could be called that, was to turn his head away from Carrie. His movements came in slow motion. Carrie's stomach tightened and her earlier confidence fell away. She thought of only one cause for such languorous motility.

He's still too sedated, dammit!

She was certain she had given him enough recovery time. This many hours post-op, Fasciani should have been coherent enough to play checkers. In his current condition, there would be no way for Carrie to effectively evaluate him. She doubted Fasciani would spend another night in the neuro ICU. If Carrie was going to evaluate him, it needed to be tonight. She had no other option. Carrie would have to retreat and come back later. Her curiosity had become its own gravitational force. She hoped whoever worked the overnight shift would be as accommodating as Lee Taggart.

Carrie came around to the front of the bed and examined his chart. With a quick scan of his meds, she saw the problem right away: Valium, a lot of it. Fasciani must have become agitated at some point and the nurse had wisely put him under. Evidently Lee Taggart thought an infusion of a major sedative was a detail Carrie did not need to know, and certainly she had not thought to ask. Well, at least she could trust the tight-lipped nurse to keep her visit here a secret.

Dammit again!

The situation was essentially hopeless. Fasciani was going to spend the night sedated. Carrie could come back at midnight or two in the morning, and it would not make a difference.

Though daunted, Carrie was not ready to give up. She had inherited her mother's willful determination. Addressing Fasciani from the foot of the bed, Carrie asked, "Eric, can you tell me how you're feeling?"

He gave no response, but Carrie expected none. She went around to the left side of the bed to check Fasciani's pupil reaction to her penlight, and saw that his lips looked dry and chapped. She smoothed an ice chip taken from a plastic cup at his bedside over his cracked lips like a healing balm. Fasciani's empty stare went beyond a thousand yards. After several passes with the ice, Fasciani turned away from Carrie, his movements slowed by the drugs in his system, and came to a rest with his head facing the door. Carrie wondered if he was going to call for the nurse, but Fasciani was so doped up she doubted he even knew where he was.

She decided to make one more attempt, though it was an obvious sucker's bet. She went around to the other side of the bed so she could look him in the eyes.

"Eric, I want to help you," Carrie said. Her voice cracked slightly under the strain of emotion. The pang in her chest felt like heartbreak; her deep compassion went far beyond her duty as a doctor. The rawness of these feelings came from Adam. She heard echoes of her brother in Fasciani's struggles. Abington's, too. And while Adam seemed to be coping, a distinct possibility remained that he could one day fall into the abyss—first to the streets, then to drugs, the shelters, and eventually maybe to some hospital bed at the VA, with or without wires in his brain. In this way, Fasciani was not just another wounded vet. He was like family.

Fasciani's bedsheets rustled as he turned away from Carrie to face the wall opposite the door. This time his movements struck Carrie as a bit strange. *Did he just turn away intentionally?* Carrie waited a moment, perhaps as long as two minutes, purposefully silent. When enough time passed, she repositioned Fasciani's head so he again faced the door. He offered no resistance and stayed with his head in that direction, unmoving, hardly blinking. She took a couple steps toward the door.

"Eric, can you hear me?" she asked.

One second . . . then two . . . then three . . . then . . .

Fasciani turned his head and faced the wall opposite the door.

Twice. That's nothing, Carrie thought. I spoke and he turned his head away from my voice twice. Could just be a coincidence. For a third time Carrie repositioned Fasciani's head to face the door. Again she spoke. "Eric, can you hear me?"

To herself, Carrie counted: *One . . . and two . . . and three . . .*

Fasciani showed Carrie the back of his head as he again faced the wall opposite the door. She repeated the test again with the same result. She spoke to Fasciani from the right side of the bed, and he turned his head to the left.

Carrie said, "Holy crap. It's as though he's hearing my voice from that side of the room!"

Carrie tested him one more time, but in a different way. "Eric, I want you to answer me each time you hear this," she said.

Fasciani repositioned his head to face left and mumbled in a groggy, drug-slurred voice, "I hear you, I hear, I hear you."

Carrie's breath caught. This was classic and just what she had read in the literature. Many patients were able to localize their illusion to the side opposite the pathology in the brain. She felt certain the auditory processing of the right temporal lobe in Fasciani's brain was not working right.

Carrie's training kicked in as she battled to slow her thinking. She did not want to be reactive, but found it hard to control her emotions.

Abington and Fasciani both exhibited symptoms of palinacousis, and the commonality was DBS. But was that the root cause? Carrie could not say with certainty. Again she went back to a hemorrhage, but could there be a stroke from a blocked blood vessel? She wanted a CT scan or MRI, stat. An EEG, too. Could it be a seizure? Something else? Why didn't Ramón experience anything like this? Or had he, and his memory was fogged?

Carrie felt urgency and curiosity, but also anger. She was trapped. She had no business being here, and had no one to call on for help. She couldn't even order these tests without Goodwin torpedoing her career.

She had no authority to intervene, unless she went to Dr. Finley. But what then?

Hi boss, sorry I put your program and the hospital at risk by acting like a resident when I haven't been credentialed.

That could create all sorts of problems. At a minimum, Dr. Finley would have to make some excuse for Carrie examining Fasciani, or he'd simply lie and say that he himself had followed up on the patients. But Dr. Finley was not even a surgeon, and that explanation, Carrie knew, would not wash.

Before Carrie could approach Dr. Finley, she needed more specifics. The worst thing she could do would be nothing at all. The second worst thing would be to make some wild claim about a huge DBS side effect, one that nobody else had noticed before, without any supporting evidence. Her credibility was still in the repair stages, and Carrie was already on unstable ground. She thought she was onto something, but what? She could not do anything about it at nine thirty at night.

Unless . . .

An idea came to Carrie so ingenious her whole body tensed. The next shift was due to come on at eleven o'clock. Carrie could go home, call the duty nurse, and order a CAT scan using Dr. Navar's hospital ID. It was pinned to the nurses' station for everyone to see.

It was a risky move, but asking for a scan was not like ordering narcotics. She could say that Navarro had personally asked her to call in the labs. Chances were nobody would question the order. If the nurse on the next shift was anything like Lee Taggart, it was almost a certainty. The scan could be done overnight or very early in the morning. Carrie would go by radiology first thing and have a look at the films herself. No one was likely to see her if she showed up early enough. Once she checked out the CAT scan and the EEG, she'd decide what to do from there. Carrie gently touched Fasciani's face. His skin felt spongy, no give. Her heart ached for him. Something had to be done.

It was not perfect, but at least it was a plan.

28

A glance at the speedometer showed Carrie was going seventy. Her thoughts raced, and it was no surprise the surge of adrenaline had her driving so fast. Carrie checked the time on the dashboard clock. In thirty minutes she could make the call she had rehearsed into memory.

The radio was off, but Carrie's fingers drummed an erratic rhythm against the steering wheel as she exited the highway. Her thoughts returned to Fasciani, Abington, and this bizarre palinacousis. The implications of the discovery both exhilarated and bewildered her. DBS sat at the epicenter of a renaissance in psychosurgery, a groundswell that Carrie's discovery might disrupt. It was the last outcome Dr. Finley had imagined when he brought her on board.

Carrie kept to the speed limit and arrived home at quarter to eleven, leaving fifteen minutes until shift change and showtime. It was difficult not to project into the future. If DBS proved detrimental in the way she suspected, it would put an immediate halt to Dr. Finley's pilot program, and put her right out of a job. What she was about to do carried a burden of guilt, lots of it. Dr. Finley had given her a second chance, and here she was going behind his back, working covertly to dismantle what might be Nobel Prize–worthy work in the treatment of PTSD.

While the surgical community had embraced DBS as a neurosurgical treatment for a variety of ailments, the public would key in on the brain damage it caused, and would have a hard time not seeing the procedure as a harkening back to the days of rusty implements and drooling, mindless patients. Some side effects to experimental surgery would be tolerable, but palinacousis was not one of them. The extremely rare condition made it impossible for anyone to function, with bodiless voices constantly shouting in one ear. If it was not a fate worse than death, it sure was close.

Irene Bryant was in the living room working on a painting when Carrie arrived. Adam was stretched out on the sofa. Dressed in gray shorts and a loose-fitting T-shirt, he struck a Rubenesque pose as he munched on an apple. If only he were as plump and healthy-looking as those models. After hanging up her coat, Carrie came around to the front of the easel. She fully expected Adam would be part of her mother's creation, but Irene had painted only the bowl of fruit on the coffee table. It was so realistic-looking it tricked Carrie's mind into smelling citrus mixed in with the scent of fresh oil paint.

"It's beautiful, Mom," Carrie said.

Standing beside Carrie, Irene appraised her work

thoughtfully, body akimbo. "I'm thinking of calling it *Bowl of Fruit*."

"Very clever title," Carrie said. She pointed to an apple in the fruit bowl. "May I?" Carrie asked. She had eaten only a salad for dinner, and her belly was rumbling. She needed something to settle her stomach before making the call, and her mother's painting had given her a craving for fruit.

"My work here is done, so be my guest."

Adam tossed Carrie an apple. She noticed the tips of her brother's fingers were blackened with engine grease, which he somehow managed to keep off the furniture but not her apple. Carrie tossed the apple back to her brother.

"I'll get my own. Thanks."

"I almost got the beast running today," Adam said.

The distant look in Adam's eyes and his downcast expression caused Irene's bright smile to retreat. It made Carrie sad, thinking how this must be for her mother. Adam's past was stunting his potential, his future, and the mental shackles he wore kept him in a seemingly inescapable limbo. Here was Carrie, at the helm of a major mental health breakthrough, in a position to help Adam and others like him, but she was about to do the exact opposite.

Irene turned her attention to Carrie and fixed her daughter with a worried stare. Irene's ability to see what others missed made her gifted at the canvas as well as a difficult parent to hide from. Carrie had learned that lesson the hard way in her rebellious middle school years, most notably the one and only time she came home a little tipsy from a friend's house. Her mother's powers of observation never failed to amaze. Perhaps Carrie had inherited some of that talent, and it allowed her to see in Abington and Fasciani what others at the VA had not.

"Is something wrong, sweetheart?" Irene asked.

I'm just about to blow my future up again, Carrie thought. *Mine and Adam's.*

"No. I'm fine," was all Carrie managed.

"Good day?"

"Great. But I'm going to turn in. Big day tomorrow." *Maybe the biggest, depending on what those tests show, or don't show.*

"Yeah, me too," Adam said, sounding sarcastic. "I'm going to do nothing, and then in the afternoon I have a big heap of nothing on my plate."

Irene shot Adam a slightly disapproving look, only because the truth in his humor hurt. Adam had nothing to do except work on that car of his. He could not hold a job, see his friends, or concentrate on a task without his frustration and pent-up anger getting the better of him.

Carrie crossed the room, wrapped her arms around her brother, and gave him a kiss on the forehead. "I love you, brother," Carrie said. "And we're going to get through this together."

Adam returned a weak smile that seemed to contradict her conviction. "Maybe in my next life," he said.

The guilt returned. The ache of betrayal, of secrets Carrie would have to keep, weighed heavy and would probably grow more burdensome over time. As she headed for the stairs, Carrie paused to apply a quick peck on her mother's cheek. The look Carrie got in response said her loving gesture hadn't lightened her mother's lingering concern.

Carrie bounded up the stairs and closed her bedroom door behind her. *Home again, home again.* But not home. No, no really. This was transient living; Carrie's life was in flux, much like Adam's.

Carrie sat on her bed with her smartphone in hand. She did not know the VA's phone number by memory, and after looking it up, wrote it down on the same scratch paper where she had earlier jotted Navarro's hospital ID and his user name/password combination. Navarro had posted those numbers as a personal convenience so he would not have to approve and enter every lab order from a resident. It was a bit lazy, but not at all an uncommon practice. Still, Carrie did not want to keep Navarro's login credentials on her smartphone, lest Goodwin employed hackers as spies. She could not be too cautious.

Carrie knew without checking that her pupils were slightly dilated and her heartbeat accelerated, all neurological responses to stress. Intellectually, she understood that her sympathetic nervous system was causing a biochemical imbalance, not that the knowledge reduced her anxiety any.

The phone rang. Her hands turned clammy.

The operator answered. "VA, can I help you?"

"Yes, neuro recovery ICU, please."

"One moment."

A beat of silence preceded the phone ringing once again. Carrie took a breath and exhaled slowly. She studied Navarro's ID number, committing the digits to memory.

You can do this. Just sound confident.

Another ring. Carrie tensed, gripping her phone even tighter. But the phone kept on ringing. No answer. *Where's the duty nurse?* Carrie considered the possibility that Fasciani had suffered a setback. Maybe he was being triaged at that moment, or he could have coded. Naturally, Carrie's mind went to the worst possible outcomes. Was it related to the DBS?

Carrie waited fifteen minutes, then called back. The operator connected her to the unit for a second time. By twelve thirty, after three attempts to reach the duty nurse, Carrie was an emotional wreck. Something horrible was happening to Eric Fasciani, she felt certain of it. She dialed the operator once more.

"This is Dr. Carrie Bryant," she announced. "Could you please page the duty nurse on the neuro recovery ICU and have whoever it is call me back ASAP."

Carrie gave the operator her number and waited anxiously for the call back. When her phone finally rang some seventeen minutes later, she was on the floor trying to stretch out a bit of tightness in her legs and back. Days after Abington's unprovoked assault, Carrie still felt a persistent ache. She should have gone downstairs and grabbed something to eat, but Adam was up watching television and Carrie was in no mood to confront her guilt again.

She staved off a bout of light-headedness from having stood too quickly, and answered the call. "This is Dr. Bryant," Carrie said into the phone.

"Yeah, Dr. Bryant, this is Mandy, the operator here."

"Mandy?" Carrie was confused. *Where's the duty nurse?*

"Um, okay," was all Carrie could think to say.

"There's nobody up on the ICU neuro recovery floor."

The light-headedness Carrie had experienced returned with a vengeance. "What do you mean? That's impossible. I was just visiting a patient there not more than a few hours ago."

Mandy made a bit of an exasperated sigh as if to imply the docs never knew what was really going on.

"That may very well be," Mandy said. "But there ain't no patients up there now. Security checked it for me. The lights are out, the doors are locked, and nobody is home."

29

Carrie kept a light foot on the gas on her early-morning drive back to the VA. She had espresso for blood. The notion that Fasciani had somehow gotten up and walked away from neuro recovery simply did not compute. Could Fasciani have had a medical emergency like Abington's? Perhaps he coded, maybe an arrhythmia like Abington, and had been transferred to the med ICU—"turfed," as Goodwin would call it. DBS-induced palinacousis and arrhythmia? Carrie could not dream up a more bizarre set of symptoms.

If Carrie could have called Lee Taggart or the duty nurse for the eleven o'clock shift from home, she would have. The problem was, Carrie did not have access to the scheduling application. She was Dr. Finley's employee and had no IT privileges. If she wanted to speak with the nursing staff, her only option was to return to the hospital. Not a problem. Carrie had reheated a burrito in the microwave, and a Red Bull would keep her alert for hours.

Besides, this would give her an excuse to go to the med ICU to look for Fasciani and personally check up on Abington, assuming he was still a patient there. It would be easy enough to walk the floor without raising too many eyebrows. Her goal was modest and obtainable. She would get to work hours before everyone else, find out what she needed to know, and maybe grab a few hours' sleep in a vacant on-call room.

A little past one thirty in the morning, Carrie arrived at the VA and parked in the same spot she had occupied hours ago. Then it was back through the rear entrance with a head nod and a flash of her badge, this time to a different security guard. She raced down the hallway, eager to confirm what she already knew to be true. The hospital, like most of the patients here, seemed fast asleep.

The elevator stopped on the third floor and Carrie hurried out. In no time she was back at the double doors to the neuro ICU. They were locked, but that was standard procedure. More unusual was the view through the windows built into the swinging doors. The hallway lights were off. The glow from various screen savers illuminated the nurses' station enough for Carrie to see it was unoccupied.

Unoccupied, but why? What had happened to her patient? Not her patient, but rather Navarro's and Goodwin's.

If Fasciani was still in the hospital—and where else would he be?—Carrie reasoned she would find him in the med ICU. He'd coded, or something. The arrhythmia. It was the only logical explanation.

Soon Carrie was standing outside the locked doors to the med ICU, looking through the glass into a well-lit, active unit. Carrie buzzed the intercom and announced herself as Dr. Bryant. The doors unlocked and Carrie strode over to the nurses' station. A black woman in her late twenties, hair pulled back, high cheekbones, pretty and slight, looked up from her monitor and gave Carrie a quiet smile.

"Morning, Doctor, what brings you here?"

"I just wanted to see if you had a patient by the name of Eric Fasciani brought here this evening?"

The woman, Dot according to her name badge, clicked at her keyboard and shook her head slightly.

"The name doesn't sound familiar. No, I'm sorry. He's not here."

Carrie's brow furrowed and her eyes narrowed into slits. Where could he have gone? She asked, "Is Steve Abington still here?"

Dot executed more key taps than a ticket broker at an airline counter. That slight frown returned. "We don't have a Steve Abington here, either," she said.

"Well, he was transferred to the floor the day before yesterday."

Dot checked her screen again, thinking she might have missed something. "I'm sorry, we don't have his record, so I can't tell you where he went."

"Can we check the computer?" Carrie asked.

"Sorry, I can't do that," Dot said. "This new electronic medical record system is great in some ways, but we're still in classes for access authorization. I've spent about a hundred hours and all I'm allowed to do now is input vitals and other nursing data."

Carrie was not the least bit surprised. She understood this all too well.

"I can look up labs," Dot offered. "But I still can't

see things like patient demographics. Don't ask me why. Most everyone hates it, but I suspect we'll get the hang of it soon enough."

Carrie brightened. "Could you check for any labs you might have done for Steve Abington in the last day or two?"

Dot nodded and her fingers went flying over the keyboard. "There's nothing in the system."

"Nothing? Is that common? I mean, he was a patient here."

"Honey, at the VA we see it all. The only thing common is that nothing is common, if you get my drift. By the way, who are you?"

That was it. The last thing Carrie needed was a leak of her presence getting back to Dr. Goodwin or Navarro. She had to bring her concern to somebody who could really help.

30

Clutching a cup of coffee, Carrie made her way to Dr. Alistair Finley's office after making sure his midnight blue E-class Mercedes coupe was parked in its assigned space. The parking lot was already half full, and the hallways around the main entrance were starting to bustle with activity. The hospital had yawned and stretched, and was coming to life like a once dormant giant.

Around her the gloom of the early morning gave way to sparkling sunshine and a pleasing warm breeze. By all accounts, it would be a glorious day. Carrie wondered where Fasciani and Abington might be experiencing it.

She walked to Dr. Finley's office in a bleary-eyed daze, having secured just two hours of sleep on a lumpy mattress while baking inside a stuffy on-call room. Dr. Finley always began his day at eight; Carrie rushed to get there without any primping at all. This had to be the first news of his morning.

When she arrived at five minutes to the hour, Carrie found Dr. Finley's office door was closed—the equivalent of a hotel's Do Not Disturb sign—but she knocked anyway.

Typically genial, Dr. Finley came off a bit gruff when he summoned Carrie inside. As she entered, she noticed that he hadn't yet turned his laptop on, and she doubted he'd finished his first cup of Starbucks. The action was happening before he was officially ready to face the day.

Dr. Finley looked surprised to see Carrie. He took a quick glance at the surgical schedule, tacked to a cork bulletin board that hung on the wall over his computer.

"We don't have surgery today, do we?" he asked, picking up his coffee.

"They're gone," Carrie said. "Abington and Fasciani. They've disappeared. I can't find either of them."

Dr. Finley squinted. "What are you talking about?" he said as he gestured toward one of the metal office chairs. "Carrie, sit down, please. You look awful. Have you had any sleep?"

Carrie had not checked her appearance in any mirror, but suspected it bordered on grisly. She'd slept in her lab coat and scrubs, and it showed. Her hair was a tousled mess. By contrast, Dr. Finley was well-groomed and dressed neatly in a striped oxford and sharp red tie.

Realizing she had barreled in like a hurricane, Carrie sat down as directed. She worked to slow her thoughts. Neurologists of his stature at White Memorial would have panoramic views of the Charles River, but here, Dr. Finley had a view of an abandoned construction site. He was uncelebrated and understated, and Carrie wanted to do right by the man who'd brought her under his wing and given her a chance at redemption.

Dr. Finley swiveled his chair to face Carrie. He leaned back and rested his chin on his thumb, his other arm folded across his chest. "Now, just what are you talking about? Can I get you some coffee or something?"

Carrie showed him her coffee. "No, thanks. I've got some."

Carrie's stomach used that particular moment to rumble like approaching thunder. She had not had a decent meal in hours. After her visit to the med ICU, Carrie had spent some time sitting practically alone in the cafeteria, nursing a cup of coffee and staring at a scoopful of powdered scrambled eggs and canned fruit that stared back at her.

"What's on your mind?" Dr. Finley asked.

"I checked up on Steve Abington after his surgery," Carrie said. "I didn't think anything of it. It's something I've always done with my patients. It's something you would do, too. You feel responsible when you order tests or perform a procedure on someone to follow up on their status, right?"

"Of course. I think I know where this conversation is headed."

"Evidently that's frowned upon here. Dr. Goodwin and Dr. Navarro both told me—no, make it *insisted*—that I not follow up on my patients. But I only heard that after I went to see Steve Abington."

"You went to the ICU post-op?"

Carrie nodded. "I've got to tell you, Abington was not doing well at all. He was still confused and agitated when I saw him, but that's probably because he was just coming out of anesthesia. But then it got worse.

The nurse and I ended up having to give him a drip of haloperidol in addition to Valium."

Dr. Finley grimaced. A line had been crossed. "Yeah, Goodwin accosted me in the hall and spoke at length about your conversation," he said. "But I didn't know you had done any post-op care. Now I know why she was so pissy with me."

"What did she say?"

Dr. Finley chuckled. "Nothing I need to repeat. I promised her I was going to speak to you, but as a point of protest I decided to not bring it up at all. You're an adult and I trust you to follow department protocols. That said, I think Goodwin possesses all the tact of a wrecking ball."

Carrie deflated in her seat. She had more to share, but Dr. Finley's look of sympathy was a sharp stab of guilt to the chest. Instead of being a team player, taking her probationary period seriously by following the departmental rules, Carrie insisted on creating chaos.

"Well, I didn't set out to violate hospital policy," Carrie said in her own defense. "After I got home, that's when I learned Abington had been moved to the med ICU because of a cardiac problem, but before I could go in to see him the next morning, Dr. Goodwin confronted me and told me I should stay away, that he was somebody else's concern now."

"As much as I hate to admit it, she's right, Carrie," Dr. Finley said, trying to not sound overly reproachful. "The day-to-day care of patients has to be maintained by a coherent and well-organized staff, and that has to be under the direction of those two. Even though you're kind of my private hire, you technically fall under her department's responsibility. The truth is, I stay away from them as much as possible, and I suggest you do the same. It would just be too confusing otherwise. Besides, Goodwin can make a mess of things if she decides she doesn't want you on the staff."

Carrie looked alarmed. "She could do that?"

Dr. Finley did not appear overly concerned. "Your salary may come out of my private funds, but ultimately it's all the government's money. So technically it's Goodwin's show to run," he said. "That said, if we're successful here, you and I will share all the accolades and honors and Goodwin will have to take a backseat."

Carrie could not quite grasp the logic. But, if Dr. Finley agreed to the policy, it made a little more sense for her to retreat. However, two patients were missing. Surely Dr. Goodwin would not be satisfied by that outcome.

Dr. Finley chuckled. "Trouble seems to find you wherever you go, doesn't it? So how much damage control do I need to do here? And what's this talk about missing patients? I thought you said you only went to see Steve Abington."

Carrie shrank further in her seat. "Well, I have to confess I couldn't keep myself from at least following up on Eric. I know, I know—I shouldn't have done it. But I had only done his surgery a few hours before and I was worried he was going to have the same post-op reaction as Abington. Wouldn't you do that, too?"

"Maybe."

Carrie cringed at his disapproving tone. To violate protocol inadvertently with Abington was one thing, but to blatantly disregard Goodwin to check up on Fasciani pushed the boundaries of what Dr. Finley could condone. But Carrie couldn't do anything about that now. She had to press her case.

"When I went to see Fasciani, he wasn't there. The unit was empty and closed," she said with measured composure. Carrie left out the part about going home to order the labs. Now was not the time to bring up her larger concern. "Since I was at the hospital, I decided to pop down to the med ICU to see Steve Abington."

Dr. Finley slapped his hand to his forehead. "Good gracious, Carrie! You're trampling all over Goodwin here."

"But Abington wasn't there," Carrie said, ignoring the rebuke. "And Dot, the nurse in the med ICU, had no record of him *ever* being there."

"What time did all this start?" Dr. Finley asked.

"It was probably after ten," she said. "I grabbed a bite to eat after the surgery, and then I came back to get something I left in my office. That's when I decided to check up on Fasciani."

"Carrie." Dr. Finley was obviously displeased.

"I know I shouldn't have done it," Carrie said. "But I was curious. I'm just not used to letting go of my patients. It's hard for me."

At last, something Carrie said seemed to sit well with Dr. Finley. A trace of a smile put her slightly at ease.

"I get it," he agreed. "You have a unique job in the VA's unique culture. There's a lot of bureaucracy to navigate, and your position here doesn't make it any easier. So after you couldn't find our patient in neuro recovery, you went to see Abington in the med ICU—do I have that right?"

"That's right," Carrie said. She had knowingly bent

the truth, but did not break it. "Call it professional curiosity."

"I'd call it very, very strange," Dr. Finley said, rubbing his chin. "Not what you did, but these patients going missing. Honestly, I don't know what to tell you at this moment, but I promise you that I will look into this right away. Let's meet again this afternoon. I'm booked all day, but I'll make room for you at four. That will give me time to get to the bottom of this. But you, my dear, should take advantage of your day off and go home and get some sleep." He rose from his chair. The solicitude reminded her of her father. "Let me do the work. And take my advice and stay away from Goodwin. She has fangs."

"Navarro too, I suppose."

"That one also bites."

"In that case, I'll see you at four."

Carrie walked out of Dr. Finley's office, glad she had not shared her worry about palinacousis. She'd thought about it, but resisted the temptation. Her concern about the cause behind the condition—a stroke or hemorrhage, a seizure or some unrecognized complication of the DBS procedure itself, or who knows what—remained unchanged. All of medical literature held only a handful of palinacousis case reports, and seeing it in two patients back-to-back was more than coincidence. For this reason she would need evidence before calling Dr. Finley's entire program into question. She would need to see the cold, hard facts. She needed the CAT scan and EEG to help exclude a more common explanation for what she observed.

Instead of driving home and driving back, Carrie decided to grab a few more hours of sleep in the on-call room, and spend the afternoon doing research before her four o'clock meeting with Dr. Finley. After downing a protein bar purchased at the cafeteria, Carrie had no trouble finding a vacant on-call room this early in the morning. She fell down on the mattress and closed her eyes.

Her thoughts kept her from falling asleep right away. She had so many possibilities to consider. What if the condition no longer presented in Abington and Fasciani once they were found? It might suggest the palinacousis was temporary. In that case, Carrie could push for a neurological post-op exam as a component of the DARPA program to see if it manifested in others. The plan was not optimal, because Carrie hesitated to do any more surgeries until she could rule out the potential side effect. A lot would depend on her meeting at four.

Unable to focus, Carrie closed her eyes. She took a couple of calming breaths and tried to clear her mind. Exhaustion made her wired, and she could not let it go. Again she focused on the idea of the condition being temporary. The more she thought about it, the more it made the most sense. Otherwise, Dr. Finley would have come across it by now and said something to Carrie. Perhaps Goodwin knew about the side effect and was keeping it a secret. But why would she do that? Carrie could not come up with anything.

A thought occurred to her and she bolted upright in bed. Her stomach lurched. What if nobody had seen the condition because it had never happened before? What if Carrie had caused it during surgery? What if *she* was the problem, and not DBS?

31

The Humvee hit a ditch at a high rate of speed and almost bounced Steve Abington to the floor. He scrambled back into his seat and peered out the square window on the left side of the vehicle. The horizon seemed a million miles away and the parched landscape zooming by stretched out like an endless blanket of brown. The unrelenting sun stood high in the sky and roasted the cracked earth like the inside of an oven. Where was this place? What province? Paktika? Khost? Hell, it all looked the same.

Outside the vehicle Abington heard the pop of small-arms gunfire blended with the familiar *rat-tat-tat* of automatic weapons. The bullets seemed to come from all directions, impossible to pin down a source. Abington had fired an M2 Browning from the open roof of a Humvee more times than he could count. But now he looked up and saw this vehicle was not equipped with a canopy. They would have to drive through the firestorm. Maybe catch up with a convoy if they were out on their own. One thing for certain: Whoever was doing the driving did not appear to be in any real hurry.

"Hey, put some zip in this pig," Abington shouted.

Somebody chortled to Abington's right. Only now did Abington become aware of the other passenger sitting beside him. He was a muscular white male, with a square, chiseled face, and prominent nose. The man's mouth broke into a crooked smile and beneath his shades Abington imagined a playful glint in his eyes. Abington had never seen this man before. Or had he? He was confused. Disoriented.

Where had he been before riding in this Humvee? Abington searched his memory, but came up blank. In fact, he could not come up with anything at all. His brain felt like a sieve trying to collect water. He knew only that this was Afghanistan, though he could not recall how long he'd been there, or when he'd arrived. It felt like the whole shit mess had blended into one endless day. Maybe that was why he could not remember how he got here. The sameness of it all made it easy to forget one moment from the next.

Abington blinked to clear his vision. For a second, the man to his right looked to be wearing civilian clothes—black shirt and pants under a dark zip-up jacket. A second later that changed, and Abington saw the man wore camo and Kevlar like everyone else. But why was he wearing a boonie hat. He should have had on a Kevlar helmet.

Steady gunfire ripped up the air and pockmarked the ground on the side of the road. Spires of red clay and dust sprayed skyward like earthy geysers. Abington could not believe this vehicle was not riddled with bullet holes, nor could he understand why the driver seemed so unconcerned.

"Hey, the speed limit here is get the fuck out. Let's step on it!"

The driver nonchalantly craned his head and cocked a quizzical eyebrow in Abington's direction. The driver was a black man with short hair and almond-shaped eyes. He had a pleasant face, showing no grit, grime, or even traces of fatigue. He looked soft, like someone who did work other than the business of war. He showed no particular concern about the bullets, either. If anything, Abington detected an officious air about him. Maybe this man was someone important, an LTC or even a full-bird colonel. Whoever he was, Abington withered slightly under the man's hard stare.

"We're going fast enough," the driver said. His tone served to placate Abington and end the discussion at the same time.

The man seated to Abington's right—Boonie Hat—started to laugh.

Abington heard, "We're going fast enough . . . we're going fast enough . . ." repeating in his left ear. But the voice, like the bullets, seemed to come from nowhere and everywhere.

"This guy might be the most gone of the whole bunch."

"Yeah, he's struggling for sure," the driver said.

It was difficult for Abington to follow the conversation, because everything they said kept repeating.

Boonie Hat said, "Well, at least some of them come out all right. For a while anyway."

Driver chuckled. "Yeah, it'd be a pretty messed-up gig if they were all like him."

Abington squinted, straining to make sense of the odd exchange.

"What do you mean?" Abington asked. "Did Roach make it? Is he alive? Where's Roach? Where are the others?"

Abington heard, "Where are the others . . . where are the others . . ."

Boonie Hat laughed even harder this time. A stab of pain focused Abington's attention. He looked down at his leg in time to see the man extract a needle from his thigh, the contents of the syringe evidently emptied into his bloodstream intramuscularly.

"Hey, what's that all about?" Abington cried out.

Boonie Hat smirked and tapped the driver's shoulder. The driver looked back at Boonie Hat and the empty syringe.

"I can't listen to this nut job for the next five hours," Boonie Hat said. "I just can't do it."

Nut job? Why would he say that?

Abington asked, "What did you give me?" Already his speech sounded thick and slurred as his tongue swelled inside his mouth. A bitter taste soured the back of his throat.

"Just a push of adrenaline," Boonie Hat said in a semi-mocking tone. "Um . . . all the Special Ops guys are using it."

"Special Ops? What are we doing? Where's Roach? I was with Roach when we took fire."

Took fire . . . took fire . . . took fire . . .

"Yeah, you were with Roach," Boonie Hat said,

sounding unconvinced and uninterested. "Whatever you say."

Abington blinked in rapid succession, trying to keep alert, but his eyes grew heavy just the same. He wanted to sleep. Soon enough, the sound of gunfire receded into the background until, like Abington's other senses, it all just faded away.

When he came to, Abington was lying on the ground. He recognized this place right away. This was where he and Roach had done battle with the Taliban, the same place where his best buddy got his stomach shredded by bullets. The Humvee was parked nearby and the sound of gunfire still filled the air, but Abington could not see any tracers. Boonie Hat and Driver sure did not act like two guys about to get shot.

"We got heat coming in!" Abington shouted. His voice came out thick and garbled. His body felt flulike, achy joints and all. He still heard the echo, but it was fainter, easier to ignore.

Abington looked around for a place to take cover and saw a hole dug in the earth, but it looked different than what he was used to seeing. This hole was longer, more rectangular, more like a coffin.

Boonie Hat approached, his face hidden in shadows. "Climb in," he said, pointing to the hole. The driver leaned against the Humvee, feet out in front of him, arms folded across his chest, looking as unhurried as a Sunday morning.

Abington hesitated. Something was wrong here. Something was horribly wrong. But his thoughts were scattered. He was seeing something between the slivers of his recollections. For a moment, he seemed to be experiencing a different reality. There were trees, tall pines encircling an open enclosure. Sure, Afghanistan had large forest trees, but this terrain had been more desert. Or was it? The strange image Abington saw fell away, and the desert returned. Then the trees came back. It was like a light switch being turned on and off, and each time it happened the scenery would change. Could it be from that adrenaline shot?

Boonie Hat rolled his eyes. He looked frustrated about something.

"Enemy fire," Boonie said without a hint of anxiety or enthusiasm. "Get in the foxhole, asshole."

Abington held his ground. The man's appearance changed with his surroundings. It kept shifting between tactical gear and black-colored civilian clothing.

What the hell is happening to me?

"Maybe it's wearing off," the driver said. "Talk him up, Curtis. Play it real. I don't want to have to chuck him in there by force. I'm beat from all that driving."

Curtis. Boonie Hat's name is Curtis.

Abington had the distinct impression he had seen this man before. The name was familiar and it had triggered some memory. The memory felt real, not like the shifting scenery, but it was not from this place. No, it had happened elsewhere. A dark place. A cubby, almost. No, more like a cell. Why would he have been in a cell? Who was Curtis? He was feeling for something that was lost within an impenetrable fog. For a second he thought he had latched on to it. The name Curtis came at Abington like a speeding train, but the clarity lasted only a moment, and soon it tumbled off into the dark corners of his mind.

Curtis . . . Boonie Hat is Curtis . . . who is the driver?

"Get in the hole!" Curtis shouted.

No, Abington was not going to budge. Not without answers. Like where was Roach? Why did these two not care about getting shot?

The driver and Curtis exchanged looks.

A sly smile creased the corners of Curtis's mouth just before a panicked look overtook his expression. "Enemy fire!" Curtis shouted, in true terror. "Get in the foxhole, Stevie! Hurry!"

The ground around Abington's feet erupted with bullets. Nothing made sense to him anymore, but he jumped into the hole anyway.

"Stay there! Stay there!" Curtis yelled. "Help is coming."

Then Curtis laughed. Inside the hole Abington clutched his legs to his chest, taking an almost fetal position. This was a womb of sorts, a safe place. Above him he heard footsteps whenever the spatter of gunfire died down enough.

Something liquid poured down on him. Was it a chemical strike? It smelled like gasoline and it got into Abington's eyes and stung. His vision went white and the horrible burning sensation continued no matter how hard he rubbed.

"You're a sick freak, you know that?" the driver said. "We can do this the humane way. Like shoot him first."

Abington yowled in agony. The gas stung his eyes and singed his mouth as if he had dove headfirst into a pool of man-o'-wars.

Curtis said, "I've been thinking about it. I just want to know what happens."

"I repeat, you're a sick freak," the driver said. "I'm going to wait in the car. I don't want to see this. Make sure to pulverize the bone into ash before you finish burying him."

Through a film of tears, Abington saw Curtis toss a metal lighter into the hole. The top was open and the flame was lit. The lighter touched gas and bright orange flames erupted all around. Abington screamed as his skin began to bubble. It peeled first down to muscle and then to bone. His cries turned into something animal-like, savage, primal. Curtis watched from the lip of the hole.

At some point the driver reappeared. Abington saw him, but his brain could only process the pain. He saw the driver take out a gun and point his weapon into the hole, but didn't understand it. Abington could smell his own burning flesh and hair—an awful, abhorrent odor. His bubbling, iron-rich blood gave off a coppery, metallic smell.

"Man, you are really messed in the head, Curtis."

The driver fired a single bullet that ended Steve Abington's misery.

32

"That just doesn't make any sense," Carrie said. She studied the papers clutched in her hand, head shaking slightly, incredulous.

Dr. Finley's deeply troubled expression mirrored Carrie's growing dismay. He bit the tip of his reading glasses, and rotated his chair to face Carrie.

She looked up from the medical discharge forms to see his puzzled expression. "Goodwin signed off on this?" she asked.

"She did," Dr. Finley answered.

Carrie lowered her gaze and rested her chin on her knuckles, striking a pose reminiscent of Rodin's *The Thinker*. She recalled a lecture from medical school that included the fact that 1 to 2 percent of all hospitalizations resulted in the patient leaving AMA—against medical advice. The percentage was skewed to those with alcohol and substance abuse problems, which applied to both Abington and Fasciani. It was not an entirely surprising statistic, given how powerfully some patients needed to get back to whatever substance they abused. But her two DBS patients had exhibited no notable withdrawal symptoms. Something else was going on with them—confusion and agitation for sure, but she did not believe they left AMA to go get high.

Carrie leaned across Dr. Finley's desk and pointed to the box on the AMA form indicating the date for a follow-up visit. "Do you think they'll show?"

Dr. Finley looked sad. "This is a large program," he said. "Cal Trent has a number of different specialists involved. I do my part, but that's certainly not the whole. We're a part of a much larger effort involving VR technicians, accident reconstruction specialists, psychiatrists, psychologists, and even biochemists. Each patient knows they're going to receive monitoring and study over the course of many months. But not everybody is diligent about coming to the VA or DARPA's other facilities for the follow-up appointments. In this case, I'm afraid we might have lost two of our participants. And it's not going to reflect well on us. Cal will be most displeased, I'm sure of it."

Carrie thought back to the presentation Dr. Finley had given in the grand rounds during her first week on the job. She remembered the bald man with close-set eyes and a round face who'd sat next to Trent. At the time she'd found it interesting Dr. Finley did not introduce him, but it made more sense to her now. The scope of this effort extended far beyond the confines of the VA, and Dr. Finley probably did not even know Trent's companion. The insight did nothing to assuage her concern for these missing patients.

"Why would they leave? Where would they even go?"

"I'm as troubled as you are. We've got two guys out

there with wires stuck in their heads who are technically our responsibility. I want to find them as much as you do. Goodwin had no choice but to let them walk. This isn't a prison. But the behavior is highly anomalous. We've treated dozens of vets in the DBS program, and these are the first two who have done anything like this. Sure we have to coddle and remind them to come in for follow-up appointments from time to time, but to leave like this? To just walk out? It hasn't happened. Not ever."

Carrie shrank in her seat, but Dr. Finley did not appear to take notice. It was his word choice that had really struck her. *Anomalous.* The palinacousis was beyond strange, but now each patient had exhibited what appeared to be extremely poor judgment. If it had never been observed before, then the only common factor, the only real link, was Carrie. She had done both surgeries only to discover each patient had presented with the same bizarre set of symptoms.

"Well, I don't have any idea what Abington was like when he requested to be discharged," Carrie said. "But I had just seen Fasciani last night, and I don't think he was coherent enough to do something like that."

"I know what you say you saw, Carrie," Dr. Finley said. He took the papers from Carrie's hands to look them over again. "But here are the forms. Signed by Abington and Fasciani. Look. Their signatures match with the pre-op releases." Dr. Finley turned the pages so that Carrie could see where his finger was pointed. "Both have been countersigned by Dr. Goodwin. She told me she tried to convince them to stay and admitted they both seemed a bit wifty, but she made the judgment call that they were sufficiently compos mentis to leave AMA. Evidently, after you left, the overnight night nurse called Navarro and he went to Goodwin because Fasciani was demanding to be discharged."

Carrie stiffened.

"Don't worry," Dr. Finley said. "I didn't get the sense Goodwin knew about your after-hours visit. And from what I'm reading here, Abington had signed himself out earlier in the day. His cardiac condition had stabilized. In fact, she said he had no more arrhythmia and his mental status had cleared dramatically. They sent him to the neuro unit and he demanded to be discharged, just like Fasciani."

"Well then, why wasn't there any record of Abington in the med ICU?"

"That's a good point. I forgot you told me that. Let's have a look, shall we?" Dr. Finley logged into his computer. Moments later he was able to access Abington's electronic medical record. Carrie stood and looked over Dr. Finley's shoulder as he navigated a series of menus and forms displayed inside various gray-colored boxes.

Right away Carrie could see a long list of medical treatments and corresponding chargemaster codes pertaining to his care. Toward the bottom of the ledger was an entry for Abington's transfer to med ICU. It was all there. Everything the med ICU nurse could not find, including treatments, nursing notes, physician notes, and lab tests ordered. The last entry was the AMA request and signatures. Abington had not gone missing after all. He had simply wanted out.

A fresh spike of anxiety put a tight band around Carrie's chest. Could the DBS be affecting their judgment, too? The electrodes had been placed in the amygdala, that almond-shaped nucleus deep in the anterior medial temporal lobe. That section was at the heart of the brain's processing of fear and its memory. This type of DBS work was uncharted territory, and Carrie's concerns about having caused post-op complications had doubled. The need to locate the missing vets and gather the pertinent data felt even more pressing than before. She had to rule out all other possibilities before she'd willingly shoulder the blame.

"What now?" Carrie asked.

"Now we have a new vet scheduled for surgery later this week. I guess we'll have to proceed as planned, and hope these two missing guys turn up."

Another person for me to injure? Carrie thought. *No, thanks.*

On the spot, Carrie made herself a promise. If she could not locate Abington and Fasciani in time, there would be no more surgeries. Simple as that. She would resign and the whole program would be cast into limbo. Her deadline was set, and would not move.

"Are you worried about infection?" Carrie asked. "What about trouble with the DBS system itself?"

"Well, of course, I'm worried," Dr. Finley said. "On both those counts. But what do you suggest?"

"Looks like I have some days off before our next surgery. Let me see if I can find them."

Dr. Finley gave no apparent objection. He mulled over the idea a moment, humming softly with a tip of the glasses back in his mouth. "I do think the situation warrants a bit of extreme measures, if you're willing to put in the effort."

"What about Goodwin? Should I go speak with her?" Carrie asked. "Maybe she has some thoughts on where they might have gone."

Dr. Finley scratched at his head. "To be honest, I'm not sure that's such a great idea," he said. "She doesn't know you went looking after her patients."

"What if I told her?"

"If you speak with her, what would you say?"

"I'd ask what the patients were like when they requested the AMA," Carrie said.

Dr. Finley raised his eyebrows. "And how do you think she'll respond?"

Carrie thought a beat. "She'll want to know why I care. It's not my problem. It's none of my business."

"And then?" Dr. Finley was goading Carrie, encouraging her to play out the scenario to its inevitable conclusion.

"She'll wonder why I haven't understood my job here."

"And that will put us right back to square one, that being Goodwin doing her very best to get you ousted. So I'll have two missing patients and no DBS surgeon, and that might just put an end to my involvement with DARPA. I think I liked your other plan better."

"Go looking for them?"

Dr. Finley smiled and returned a playful wink. "I know it's outside your job description."

"I'm highly motivated," Carrie said. *For reasons you don't even know,* she thought.

Carrie's phone buzzed inside her lab coat pocket. The sound startled her. She retrieved the device and saw a text message from David Hoffman.

I'm at the VA for an interview. Can I buy you a cup of coffee?

"Well, it's our lucky day," Carrie said with a slight smile.

Sure. Java du Jour, 15 minutes?

She sheathed the phone back in the pocket of her lab coat.

Dr. Finley returned a curious look.

"And why's that?"

"Well, I may not be a detective, but I just got invited out to coffee by an investigative reporter."

"Will he help you?"

"I can be pretty persuasive," she said. "I'm going to find them, Alistair. It's a promise." *And with luck, I'll prove it wasn't me who did anything wrong.*

Leon Dixon seemed destined to loom over Carrie like a shadow she could never discharge. Her thoughts went from Dixon to Abington, and her mind flashed on Abington's terror-filled eyes during the attack. She saw him hovering over her, and felt his strong hands around her throat applying exquisite pressure.

She paused at the door, thinking. What had triggered Abington's insane outburst? She knew prior to surgery Abington had been subjected to his most traumatic war memory via virtual reality. At that moment, Carrie wanted to know as much about these vets and the DBS program as she could. Goodwin could think what she wanted, but Carrie would never willingly put herself into a silo.

"Dr. Finley?"

He turned to face her.

"I'd like to try out that virtual reality device."

33

Java du Jour, the quaint and cozy coffee shop a block away from the VA, was surprisingly only half full. The place was usually jumping with activity, so perhaps four thirty was a slow time. Carrie stepped inside and saw David sitting alone at one of the few wooden tables adjacent to the stone fireplace, tucked invitingly beneath the large bow window. Their eyes met. He got to his feet and held out a chair.

Nice touch, Carrie thought. Her ex hadn't been given to such chivalrous behavior—nor were most of her contemporaries, for that matter.

"Thanks for meeting me," he said. "Cappuccino?"

Carrie took notice of David's style of dress. He had on a blue oxford shirt, dark jeans, and polished black shoes. He was taller than she remembered, and his outfit revealed a pleasing fit and trim frame. Not a gym rat, but clearly somebody who liked to keep his body in shape. As for the coffee, Carrie usually went for the black gold, but the way David said "cappuccino" somehow made it seem like the perfect choice.

"Yeah, a cappuccino sounds great."

Carrie took a seat and was already starting to doubt her plan when David went to place the order. Maybe it was foolish to go looking for these men, but she didn't know what else to do. She could not shake the thought that somehow the DBS, and more specifically her technique, might be behind the singularly rare complications of palinacousis and poor judgment. These conditions would surely have presented before in other PTSD patients. Since it had never been reported, Carrie could look only at the mirror for a culprit. She struggled to fit all the pieces together.

Carrie glanced up and saw David already seated, looking soothingly at her with two cups of cappuccino in front of him.

"Twenty seconds," David said with a glint in his eyes.

"What?"

"That's how long it took for you to realize I'd come back."

Carrie gave an embarrassed little laugh. "Sorry. I was just thinking. Excuse me."

"No worries," David said. "I've been accused of doing that from time to time."

Carrie laughed again as David pushed her cappuccino across the table. She picked up the cup and the aroma came at her with force. She savored it before taking a sip. Maybe she was a cappuccino girl after all.

"I'm glad we could meet up," David said. "To tell you the truth, I'd been meaning to give you a call. I thought we could talk about Adam, but I'd first like to find out what's going on with you."

Carrie found something very comforting about David. The way he'd handled her brother's assault was impressive enough. But more was going on here than that. He radiated confidence, and perhaps that was what intrigued her. He seemed so comfortable in his journalistic skin that she held no reservations about confiding in him. It did not hurt that he was damn good-looking, too.

Carrie knew her work at the VA would be of great interest to David and his story, but she had a different agenda. The conversation hit a lengthy lull as Carrie contemplated how to proceed.

"Are you always silent as a lamb?" David asked playfully.

Carrie laughed a little.

"Sorry. Lost in thought again. And that was an utterly terrifying movie, by the way. Couldn't watch it."

David pretended to look offended. "It's only one of the best."

"What about *Titanic*?"

"Knew the ending going in. Kind of spoiled it for me," David said with a wink and a smile. "What about *The Killing Fields*?" he asked.

"Never saw it," Carrie admitted. "And my father and I watch old movies all the time."

"*New York Times* journalist covering the civil war in Cambodia?" David said. "No? Doesn't register? Now that's a film after my own heart."

"Have you always worked for—" Carrie looked somewhat embarrassed. "What's the paper again?"

"That would be the *Lowell Observer*," David said. "And no. I'm a stringer, what you might call a freelancer. I go to places like Cambodia and Thailand, and pretty much anywhere the government would warn us against visiting."

David went on to talk at some length about his adventures overseas and his kidnapping episode in Syria that led to his taking a job with the *Lowell Observer*. Carrie found this facet of David's personality quite intriguing. In medical school, she had done a research paper on why some people were drawn to intense, often fear-inducing thrills while others shunned the thought.

Evidence exists to suggest that dopamine stimulates the insular cortex, a portion of the cerebral cortex deep within the temporal lobe. The trait was thought to be a carryover from the earliest humans who'd risked everything to feed and shelter their families. Carrie had often caught herself analyzing her ex Ian's behavior based solely on what she imagined was going on in his brain. She was doing the same now with David, after only minutes alone together. Carrie had wished she and Ian had more adventures together, and David's active insula fascinated her.

"So enough about me," David said. "Tell me more about your work at the VA."

"I don't know quite where to begin," Carrie said. She slowly circled the rock sugar swizzle stick in her cappuccino, and looked up directly into his hazel eyes. "This is pretty confidential stuff and you're a reporter."

"Meaning you don't trust me."

"But I'm desperate for some investigative expertise. My career may depend on it."

"Oh, a conundrum. I love it. Do you know the term 'deep background'?"

"No, but if you hum a few bars I can fake it."

It took David a minute before he smiled.

"Cute," he said.

"Old family joke."

"Deep background means you can't be quoted in any story I might write. You're just enhancing my view of a topic."

"This might turn into a story, but for now, I'd like to talk friend-to-friend—or maybe as colleagues on the issue of PTSD."

David was cautious. "All right, I'm not taking notes. But if you tell me something I think I can use, I'm going to be pushy about asking for permission to use it. That's my job."

"I understand that," Carrie said. "And I wouldn't tell you any of this if I didn't think it might eventually turn into a story for you."

"Go on, then," David said.

"DARPA and the VA have launched a joint pilot program to try and cure PTSD. Not treat it, cure it."

David's expression brightened as if a movie star had walked into the coffee shop. He leaned forward with an ardent air. "You might be my new hero," he said. "Although my editor will think otherwise."

Carrie pulled back. "Why is that?" she asked.

"Because if you have something really interesting here, I'll have to push out my deadline again, until you give me permission to use this. Anneke will be none too pleased."

"Until I get permission from my boss, this is off the record," she repeated.

"Deal," he said.

"No, I'm being serious, David. I need your help with something and I'll trade information for assistance, but we have to do everything aboveboard. If word leaks about the program, it could jeopardize funding. A lot of vets are counting on this, my brother included."

"Helpful is my middle name. Well, actually it's Charles."

"We're off the record," Carrie reminded him. "Because I need your help."

David held up two fingers and said, "Scout's honor."

Carrie appeared dubious. "Adam was a Boy Scout," she said. "I think it's three fingers, and your hand is supposed to go the other way."

David took his hand down and gave Carrie a sheepish look. "You get the point," he said.

Carrie smiled. For whatever reason, she trusted him. "Well, I'm the surgeon responsible for inserting electrodes into the brains of vets with PTSD. We're using DBS—that's electrical deep brain stimulation—to try and eliminate the emotion from memory of what's causing the PTSD."

David looked incredulous. "Um, you can do that?" he asked.

"It's very experimental, leading-edge stuff. For it to work, we have to reconsolidate the fears and horrible memories these soldiers have suffered."

"Reconsolidate how?"

"With virtual reality," Carrie said. "Those memories, and especially the fear and other emotions associated with a traumatic event, are processed to a great extent in a nucleus of cells deep in our brains called the amygdala."

"Is it cheesy to say I like it when you talk science?"

"A little," Carrie said, not bothered at all. "Anyway, we reconsolidate the memories by subjecting the patients to a virtual reality program that is supposed to vividly reproduce that bad memory, and right after that we stick an electrode into the amygdala. In theory, when we then stimulate the amygdala, we hope to erase any fear associated with that memory, and perhaps the memory itself."

"And it works?"

"Four major successes so far, and one who I examined personally could be called a total cure without much of a stretch."

"Who qualifies for the surgery?"

"The program is only for vets who have failed all other forms of conventional drug and psychotherapy. Some of the participants are homeless, but I understand that they've got living support from this program. I think they're housed somewhere on the VA campus. I'm sorry I can't give you more specifics."

She stared at David, but no need to worry. He hadn't taken his eyes from her, nor sipped his coffee. Carrie felt bad about being a tease, but she would reward him with the scoop by getting Dr. Finley and the folks at DARPA to agree to let David cover the story. *After*.

"Carrie, are you telling me that you may be curing these folks?"

Everyone was familiar with post-traumatic stress—called shell shock in World War I—at least to a degree of having sympathy for these vets, and although the problem was probably bigger than anyone wanted to admit, the idea of having a possible targeted and effective treatment was beyond exciting.

"Well, that's the idea. But some things don't seem right, David, and that's why I really wanted to talk to you."

"And I thought it was my infectious personality that got you to go out with me for coffee," he said.

"Honestly? It was the bloody nose."

"Oh, that."

"And my problem," Carrie added.

"What's going on?"

"I've operated on two patients so far," Carrie said. "I thought the surgery went well, and so did Dr. Finley."

"I'm guessing it didn't," David said.

Carrie spent some time going over the cases of Abington and Fasciani, and in the telling gave a detailed accounting of Goodwin and Navarro's ambush. In doing so, she felt compelled to vaguely explain her unorthodox hiring, while omitting all details about Leon Dixon and her decision to leave residency. She did not know this man well enough to share such a painful experience. After three coffee dates maybe, but certainly not on the first.

"A persisting echo? That sounds like a nightmare," David said when Carrie described palinacousis.

"There are only a handful of case reports in the literature," Carrie said. "I have no idea what could be causing it. In the cases I've read about, some patients had a stroke. In others it was attributed to a seizure or a hemorrhage in the part of the brain where auditory information is processed. Some may have had an unusual encephalitis, or even a rare form of migraine. The point is, I doubt whether a neurologist or a neurosurgeon would ever see a single case, let alone two in a row. So I can't help but think this is something I've done. Did I put the electrodes in right? I can't say for sure. But they're not placed anywhere near where the brain deals with acoustic processing. Did I cause a bleed? Could it be the first sign of a brain infection? These are things I have to wrestle with. But there's more."

Both cappuccinos were getting cold. David wiggled his chair a bit closer.

"Both of these patients have disappeared," Carrie said. "They signed out against medical advice, and I have no idea how to find them."

David's expression became slightly strained—evidence of deep thought. The compassion and steely determination in his eyes set Carrie further at ease. She felt right to have confided in him.

"So what can I do to help?" David asked.

"I need to find these guys—Steve Abington and Eric Fasciani. I don't even know where to begin to look."

David leaned back in his chair with a confident air. "You need help finding people? Well, I'm your man for that gig. . . . I'm guessing my getting the scoop on this DBS program is contingent on patient location?"

Carrie held up her hands to show him that was her plan, straightforward and simple.

"This is even more up my alley than you know," he said. "I've been working on this story for a lot longer than my editor wants. I know the shelters, the different services they might go to. And by 'services,' I mean flophouses and crack dens. It's lovely how we let some of the people who fought for our freedom waste away—but we're not here to fix the system, right?"

Carrie bristled a little. "I am," she said.

David finally took a sip of his too-cold cappuccino.

"I get your worry about these guys," he said. "The only things I can hurt are people's reputations and feelings."

"The pen is mightier than the sword."

"But perhaps less potent than the electrode."

Carrie's smile was genuine. "Are you always this clever?" she asked.

"Only when I'm having coffee with an intellectual dynamo I'm trying to impress."

"You only want the scoop," Carrie said. "I know your type."

"I want to help," David said in a serious tone. "You're telling me nobody has ever seen this condition before?"

"I'm telling you that the DBS surgeons aren't supposed to check up on the patients post-op, per Herr Doktors Goodwin and Navarro. We are persona non grata outside the OR."

"*You* are," David corrected. "You told me Goodwin's beef was with you. She wanted a more traditional hire, right? And you've kept your concern about the palina-whatever-it's-called a secret from your boss because you think you might have caused it."

"Palinacousis," Carrie corrected. "And sort of. It's not a secret. It's a theory. I need more data before I start making unsubstantiated claims that could put an end to this whole program. It's a quandary, and I'm not doing another DBS surgery on a vet until we find these guys. If we can't find them, I'll come forward about my concerns and resign from the program. Essentially, I'll hammer the last nail in the coffin of my career."

"These two are important to find. I got it."

"And you're right about Goodwin having it out for me. But why is that important?"

Things were clicking for him; Carrie could see that

in David's eyes. At that moment, Carrie suspected David Hoffman was a supremely competent reporter, which only enhanced his attractiveness.

"Maybe somebody else has seen the same symptoms, but didn't even know what was happening. You're a bright doctor; I'm guessing more observant than most."

Carrie blushed a little. "I don't know about that," she said, and felt forced to look away. "But I've thought the same."

"Who was the surgeon before you?" David asked.

"Sam Rockwell. He was in a car accident, and he's still in the hospital in a medically induced coma."

David took the information in. "I'd put in a call to that hospital of his if I were you," he suggested. "Doc Rockwell wakes up for some reason, maybe he has answers. In the meantime, get your best walking shoes out of the closet. Tomorrow you and I are going on a hunting expedition."

34

After six hours of driving around and hunting for parking spaces, Carrie and David had acquired two sizable parking tickets and no leads. They had already been to the Motel 6 where Dr. Finley thought the vets were staying. DARPA covered the bill, but the manager said that Abington and Fasciani had not returned to their rooms all week. Carrie and David would have to keep looking.

Their current stop, the Pine Street Inn, was located in a multistory redbrick building tucked away on a quiet section of Harrison Avenue in downtown Boston. Two words on the placard mounted beside the front entrance communicated the nonprofit's singular mission: ENDING HOMELESSNESS.

The day had been as eye-opening as it was frustrating. At BCH, Carrie had treated many of the city's poor, but the shelters were an entirely different world. They housed hope and despair in equal measure. Having dealt with the bureaucracy of BCH, Carrie could only imagine the budget battles taking place at these shelters to keep the lights on and the people fed. After things settled down, she vowed, she'd donate her time and her funds, when possible, to do more to help. She had no doubt David would join her effort if she asked.

Carrie had seen some run-down, grungy-looking shelters throughout the day. The inside of the Pine Street Inn was, by contrast, a breath of fresh air. The building was clean, and the rooms she could see from the lobby looked airy, well lit, and filled with people of all colors, from all walks of life.

Carrie and David went straight to the reception area. From a plastic bag, Carrie removed colored print-outs of the two missing men, taken from their veteran ID cards, which were on file with the VA. The photos were small and bore only a vague resemblance to the haunted men Carrie had operated on. She presented the printouts to the fresh-faced, mocha-skinned woman at the reception desk.

"Hi there," Carrie said. "I'm searching for these two men. I was wondering if they've been here recently."

Furrowing her brow, the receptionist gave each image a careful look. She handed the printouts back to Carrie with a pursed lip and a shake of the head.

"I don't think so," she said. "But we see a lot of folks coming and going. I suggest you keep checking back."

David removed a small stack of printouts from his canvas carry bag and stepped forward.

"Could you take these and circulate them among the staff?" he asked.

"These fellows aren't in any trouble, are they?" the receptionist asked. A wary look crossed her face.

David smiled as he produced his press ID. "No, not in the least," he said. "I'm working on a story for my paper and I could use their help. That's all."

The receptionist accepted the explanation without question. Perhaps it was David's charming smile, or the way he was dressed in a tailored blazer, crisp slacks and shirt, and blue patterned tie. Conducting the search under the guise of a reporter's story, and not Carrie's medical concerns, proved to be a winning idea. If confronted, Fasciani and Abington might be leery about anything having to do with leaving the VA against medical advice. But it had been strikeout after strikeout, everywhere they went. The Pine Street Inn was the last place on their list of Boston-area shelters.

Carrie and David ambled back to her Subaru in grim silence. By now, her legs had begun to tire, and after settling in behind the wheel Carrie massaged a bothersome knot out of her right quad. Another casualty of her troubles at the VA had been her commitment to her tri training. Her ligaments seemed to have shortened, and her joints were achy and stiff. Adding to the discomfort, the humid day had turned the car uncomfortably warm, and Carrie rolled down the windows without firing up the engine. No reason to waste gas, because she had no idea where they might be headed next.

David set his blazer down neatly on the backseat and picked up his clipboard of maps and notes. Looking over his shoulder, Carrie watched David draw a thick line with his Sharpie through the Pine Street

Inn. The sheet of paper was full of thick lines—lots of places they had looked, dozens in all.

"What now?" Carrie asked. The dashboard clock said it was close to three o'clock. They had been out searching for seven hours without so much as a lunch break.

"We can drive to Worcester or Fall River," David suggested as his eyes scanned the map.

Carrie was about to suggest they go get something to eat when David's cell phone went off. His ringtone was a series of wind chimes, very new-agey, and not at all what Carrie imagined he would have set as the default.

David noticed Carrie's look. "My downstairs neighbor has a four-year-old. She liked that ringtone best," he said.

Carrie accepted the explanation with a smile as David glanced at the number. His expression changed. He clearly knew the caller and liked whoever it was. "Speak of the neighbor," he said.

David put the caller on speakerphone. "Emma, light of my life, tell me you've got something."

"Hey, you," answered a female voice. "Listen, if I get fired for this, you have to find me a newspaper gig. Deal?"

"Deal," David said. "As soon as I find one for myself."

Carrie did not know who Emma was, but the woman, and more specifically her relationship to David, had her intrigued. Perhaps it was David's reaction to her that piqued Carrie's curiosity. She sounded young, and if a voice could make somebody attractive, it was Emma's. The twinge of jealousy surprised Carrie. She did not know the first thing about David or Emma, or their relationship, but the feeling was undeniable.

"Now, what did you get for me?" David asked.

"Are you with that cute doctor you told me about?"

David's face turned a shade of red. "Whoa, whoa, whoa," he said. "I'm with Carrie right now, and *you* happen to be on speakerphone."

Emma laughed. Carrie felt relaxed with this woman, as if they could be friends.

Carrie raised an eyebrow and gave David an amused grin. "Hi Emma, I'm Carrie."

"Delighted," Emma said. "And yes, I have some useful intel."

David's reddened face returned to its normal pallor as he reached for a pen on the seat beside him.

"Go on," he said.

"Steve Abington's mother lives in Bangor, Maine. She has an unlisted phone number, I'm afraid; I checked. But I can text you the address."

"Oh, Emma, you're a lifesaver."

"You can thank the DMV and the fact that I know my supervisor's passwords."

Carrie thought of her own bit of subterfuge with Navarro's pass code, and her opinion of this Emma person spiked.

"Text what you got," David said. "You're a treasure."

"That's dear of you to say. But it was easy. You knew her name."

"How did you know Steve's mother's name?" Carrie asked David.

"I'm a journalist," David said with a shrug. "It's my business to find stuff out."

"And he's good at it," Emma said. "Careful with this one, Carrie. If he gets out of line, you call me."

Carrie laughed. "I will."

"Oh, Gabby wants to say hello," Emma said. "Hang on a moment."

Seconds later, a small, high-pitched voice squealed through the phone. "Hi, Uncle David!"

David's whole face went supernova. Carrie's heart swelled at seeing his reaction to the little girl's voice. At this point she assumed Emma was David's sister, and oddly, it felt like a relief.

"How are you, sweetheart?" David said.

"Good."

"Are you being helpful to Mommy?"

"Yes."

"Okay, I'll see you soon."

"Bye."

The call went dead.

"All our calls are like that," David said.

"So Emma is your sister?" Carrie asked.

"My landlord," David said, and added, "It's a long story."

"And just who was that cute doctor your landlord was talking about?"

"What say we skip Worcester altogether and take a drive to see Steve's mother in Bangor, Maine? She might know where he's gone." The redness in his face had come back.

"What time would we get there?" Carrie asked.

"If we leave now, we'd arrive around seven," David

said. "We could swing by her home, get a hotel, and come back in the morning."

Carrie said, "Sure," before she realized she'd spoken the word.

35

Squatting with his palms on a thin mat in the center of his Spartan living room, Braxton Price pressed his knees into his arms and slipped into a crow pose, getting both feet off the ground. He was nearing the end of what had been an invigorating ninety-minute yoga workout.

Braxton had the build of an elite athlete, though it was difficult to see under his nurse's uniform. Before he became a nurse, Braxton had worn a different uniform, that of a Green Beret in the United States Army. After twenty-one continuous months of combat in Afghanistan, Braxton joined a small combat team tasked with training and arming Afghan fighters who wished to rebel against the Taliban.

It was good work. Honest work. Bloody work.

He was part of a somewhat loosely organized counterinsurgency effort promoted by General David Petraeus to win the locals' hearts and minds. As a weapons sergeant, Braxton served a key role in the Green Berets' twelve-member Alpha Team, the A-team. Before his deployment to the Middle East, Braxton had attended forty-three weeks of Weapons Sergeant School, where he learned how to adapt to any situation and improvise on the field. He could speak Pashto better than Dari, but was conversant in both.

Braxton came to appreciate his interaction with the locals, but it was nothing compared to the high he got as part of a hunter-killer team, smashing down doors and putting bullets into targets. Killing was just a part of the job, and he did it without remorse.

Braxton's time in Afghanistan might have come to an end, but he was not lacking for work. His new role required a dozen weeks of training, during which he learned all about charting, taking vitals, administering drugs intravenously; rudimentary knowledge, at best. He could hardly be considered a registered nurse, but one day, just like that, he had a badge with the name "Lee Taggart" and was on staff at the VA. No questions asked.

Even though he did no real nursing, he knew it was good work. Honest work. Bloody work.

Braxton got into a plank position on his mat. Thirty seconds into the hold, he could feel every muscle fiber start to twitch. Closing his eyes, Braxton let his mind replay Steve Abington's final screams.

Fucking Gantry, he thought.

Curtis Gantry was a thug, prone to violence and lacking professionalism, but he was also Braxton's best friend, former A-team member, and the guy who had saved his life more times than he had fingers. But this part of the operation was Braxton's to run as he saw fit, and not Gantry's. In hindsight, he should have made

Gantry put a bullet in Abington's head. The screams did not bother Braxton in the least, but Abington was a brother in arms and he deserved to go quick.

Braxton knew all about the long suffer. Some of his interrogations in Afghanistan had lasted for weeks. The job description was "information extraction," not torture, but the line was a blurry one at best. Braxton kept his enjoyment of the work a secret, thinking he otherwise might not get it.

A minute and a half holding the plank and Braxton looked like a bronzed statue. His core was on fire, but there was no noticeable shake in his arms or legs. Fitness was always a passion. He could be sent back to war tomorrow and do just fine over there. In a way he was still at war, doing battle of a different sort.

At the two-minute mark one of Braxton's cell phones rang, the important one. Braxton cursed; he had two more minutes to go in his hold. But only one person had that phone number, and the call needed to be answered.

Braxton sprang to his feet and padded across the two-bedroom condo's gleaming hardwood floor. Light spilled in through a bank of bay windows that framed a glorious view of the Charles River. It would be impossible to afford this place on a soldier's salary, but his current employers were more than happy to pay the bill. In return, he was more than happy to answer their phone call.

"Speak," Braxton said.

"The girl."

"I figured."

Braxton recognized the baritone voice with a distinctive rasp. He saw no reason not to speak freely.

Besides, these were stealth phones that used a machine-generated international mobile equipment identifier to make calls more secure and virtually untraceable. A warning system would alert Braxton if somebody were trying to intercept the call. In that case, he would turn his phone off and on to reset the IMEI number. Dive back into the shadows.

"She's proving to be a problem."

"I'm not surprised," Braxton said. "She's tenacious. Is there an order, sir?"

A pause. Braxton made no inference. He waited for his next instruction as he had been trained.

"Can Gantry be trusted?"

"To not hurt her?"

"We're not there just yet."

"Yeah, I think Gantry can be trusted." Braxton's mind flashed on Gantry's twisted grin as he stood at the lip of the pit, lighter in hand, Abington moments from immolation. "He can be trusted, for sure."

"I'll call back when we know what we want him to do."

"Very good," Braxton said. "What about the next one?"

"We still need him."

Fine with Braxton as well. He got paid regardless.

"You know, I'm scheduled for a shift. But there's no removals pending."

"We can take care of that. You're sick until further notice."

"I'm sick, all right," Braxton said with a laugh.

"Just make sure Gantry does what we want."

"You know you can count on me, sir," Braxton said.

Braxton called him "sir" because anybody over him

in the food chain was a "sir." It was not meant as a show of respect.

"Very well. I'll be in touch."

Braxton ended the call and returned to his mat. He got back into the plank position and began his hold once more.

Thirty seconds into it and Braxton was questioning his endorsement of Gantry. While he considered Gantry a friend, Braxton knew he *would* do something to Carrie Bryant before he killed her, and he doubted it would have anything to do with fire.

36

Rita Abington lived on a busy street in a ramshackle ranch home with a sagging roof and paint-chipped front stairs. The yard was just a small square, a bit more brown than green with nothing to spruce it up, no landscaping of any kind. Shrubs grew as they wished and a few of the taller trees might have been bent by ice storms, never straightening.

Carrie followed David up the narrow front walk. She noticed that all of the curtains were drawn. The only indication someone might be home was the Chevy Cobalt parked in the narrow driveway, battered-looking as the house.

David pushed the doorbell, but nothing happened. No rings. No chimes. He knocked. Carrie heard footsteps from within, and a moment later the door came open just a crack to reveal part of a woman's hard-bitten face.

The woman said, "I don't want to buy nothing, save

a whale, or go to heaven, so I figure you've got no business being here."

David laughed.

The woman spoke with a notable Down East accent. She also had a throaty voice, and Carrie suspected an X-ray of her lungs would reveal at least a pack-a-day habit.

"Are you Rita Abington?" David asked.

"Depends if you're looking for money."

"I'm looking for your son, Steve."

With that, the door came fully open to reveal a tiny woman, thin up top and below, wearing a sleeveless white blouse that showed off moles like archipelagos dotting her arms. Her skin was brown and wrinkled, but it appeared to be from hard living rather than too much sun. She had sunken cheeks and a neck thin enough to give Carrie a good look at the tendons. Rita's hair came down to her shoulders and was thin like the rest of her, with all the color and luster of what might be found in one of her ashtrays.

Rita said, "You seen Stevie?"

"We were hoping you had," Carrie said.

Rita stepped aside. Carrie figured this was her way of inviting them in and she went, with David following.

The living room was not much more than a few pieces of Goodwill furniture spread out over a well-worn rug. The stale smell of smoke hovered in the air and taxed Carrie's breathing some, but she managed to ignore it after a few minutes. Plenty of pictures hung on the walls and stood on tables; apparently Steve was not Rita Abington's only child.

Carrie and David waited on the plaid sofa while

Rita got a pitcher of iced tea from the kitchen. She poured three glasses and took a seat on an armchair covered by a patchwork quilt. She lit up—Benson and Hedges—and took a puff. This was her home, and she saw no reason to ask anybody's permission.

"Forgive me," Rita said. "I haven't had a lot of visitors come around. It's been quiet here since Winston died."

"Was Winston your husband?" David asked.

"My dog," Rita said. "I got more love from that little dog than I ever did my ex, rest his soul."

With that, Rita rose from her chair, the cigarette dangling in a practiced way between two long fingers, went to the hallway, and removed a picture from the wall. She handed the framed photograph to Carrie and used her hand to fan away the smoke.

"He's so cute," Carrie said of the tiny, silky-haired dog with ears reminiscent of furry satellite dishes. "What kind of dog was Winston?"

"I don't know," Rita said, as she took a puff. "A good one, that's enough."

Carrie showed the picture to David, who acknowledged Winston's cuteness with a smile. Carrie hung the picture back on the wall and noticed another framed photographed, long and rectangular—this one of a group of soldiers, some wearing shirts and others without. Not all the guys had beards, but everyone had guns.

Carrie pointed at this photo. "Is this Steve?" she asked.

Rita came over, squinting, to take a look. She took the rectangular photo off the wall. "Eyes aren't so good these days," she said, almost apologizing. Her expression brightened. "That's Stevie, right there." She pointed. "How do you know my Stevie, anyway?"

"I'm his doctor," Carrie said. "I was treating him and, well, he sort of took off."

Rita carried the photograph back to her seat. "He's always taking off," she said.

"Have you heard from him?" Carrie asked.

Rita spit out a laugh. "That's a good one. No. No, I haven't," she said. "My two other boys haven't, either. Ben lives over to Orono. Comes to visit from time to time with the grandkids. Ian, well, let's just say he likes fishing more than he likes people."

Tough life, hard living, Carrie thought of the Abington clan. Rita would have no idea about Steve's DBS operation, or his involvement with the DARPA program, and Carrie was not about to violate his privacy by sharing those details. Her vague answer about being Abington's doctor had seemed to satisfy Rita's equally vague curiosity. Carrie got the sense all Rita really cared about was hearing Steve's voice one more time.

"Would you have any idea where he might have gone?" Carrie asked.

Rita let her gaze travel to the floor. "I haven't seen him in years. I couldn't tell you."

"So he had no contact with his family?"

"None," Rita said. "He came back from that war broken. No other way to put it. Stevie used to be my sweetie pie. Light of my life. He was the example for his brothers. But when he came back, it was just a ghost of that boy. Not the kid I raised. He took to the drink and the drugs, for sure, but there was more. He left something back in that desert."

"What's that?" Carrie asked.

A shadow crossed Rita's face. "His soul," she said.

Carrie stood, crossed the room, and put her hand on

Rita's shoulder. The woman gazed up, clutched Carrie's hand, and batted back some tears.

"He was a good boy," Rita said, looking at the framed picture in her lap. "The sweetest."

Carrie stooped and pointed to the thin, muscular man in the photograph who had his arm around Steve. "Who is that?" she asked.

A sad smile of some memory deepened the wrinkles on Rita's face.

"Why, that's Roach," Rita said. "Stevie's best buddy. They called him Roach on account that nothing ever could kill him. Nothing. Then he died in Stevie's arms. Honestly, I think that's when it all began to go bad for him."

Roach.

The name meant a lot to Carrie, but she kept quiet about the terrifying ordeal during which Steve had asked for his departed friend. Carrie's eyes fell on another man in the photograph, this one taller than most, with broad shoulders and a handsome face. He had the neck of a football player, but without the asymmetry of the stimulating wires she had observed during her examination. Ramón Hernandez's dazzling smile contradicted the photograph's harsh setting.

Carrie's thoughts reeled. How was it two people who'd had contact with each other over in Afghanistan ended up in the same DARPA DBS program? Did Hernandez refer Abington, or was their involvement coincidental?

"Did Steve know this man?" Carrie said, pointing to Hernandez.

Rita shook her head. "If he did, he didn't mention it to me."

As Carrie studied the photograph one more time she noticed a figure in the background, tall and lean, shirtless and rippling with muscles, his face partly obscured by shadows. She could not make out the visage, but the man called to mind Lee Taggart, the nurse working the neuro recovery floor the night Eric Fasciani disappeared.

The green Garden Inn was just off the highway, and was the kind of roadside motel Carrie's father seemed always drawn to on long family drives. It was nothing special: green vinyl siding, black shutters, and landscaping that looked like a PGA golf course compared to Rita's place. Night had fallen and Carrie was ready to let go of the day, the endless, fruitless search—put on some bad television and drift off into oblivion. David brought in the plastic bag with two toothbrushes, some sweatpants, and T-shirts they had bought at Walmart, and the paper bag with takeout Chinese food.

Though she was ravenous, Carrie took a fifteen-minute shower. She thought about Ramón Hernandez. She'd told David about seeing him in the photo and he thought it could be a coincidence. If she'd been sure the other man was Lee Taggart, she wouldn't have let David convince her.

Out of the shower, Carrie put on her new sweats. Her hair was tangled and stringy, and a quick check in the bathroom mirror confirmed she looked as exhausted as she felt. Not the impression she had wanted to make. Not even close. When she emerged from the bathroom, David was slurping noodles from a paper carton and drinking Heineken from a glass bottle, lying on one of the two twin beds and watching ESPN.

"Your dinner is on the table," he said. "Happy to change the channel if you want."

Carrie scooped up a bowl of chicken and broccoli, grabbed a Heineken David had opened and set on ice, and climbed onto the empty bed, feeling better than she had all day.

"Do you want me to change it?" David asked.

Carrie looked up at the television and shrugged. "It's fine," she said. "I've been watching a lot of ESPN with Adam since I moved back home."

"You know, I was going to ask you about that."

"About why I'm twenty-nine and living with my parents?"

"You forgot brain surgeon."

"You really want the whole story?"

David gave Carrie a sidelong glance. "I'm a reporter. I may write the CliffsNotes version, but I don't ever ask for it." He shut off the TV.

For the next twenty minutes Carrie provided a detailed accounting of everything that had happened at BCH, starting with Beth Stillwell and ending with her resignation. She could not fathom why it felt so comfortable, so natural to share with him, but it did. Once she started to open up, she could not stop.

David sat on the bed facing Carrie, with his feet on the floor and his food going cold. On occasion, he'd sip from his beer, but mostly his eyes were on her the entire time, and Carrie thought that was just fine. When she finished, Carrie gave a little shrug because she had nothing more to say.

David took a final swig of his beer. "You didn't have to quit," he said. "Dr. Metcalf was in charge. You were just a resident."

"It was my fault," Carrie said.

"But you're a damn good doc."

"You can't say that for sure. I've never operated on your brain."

"But if I needed brain surgery, I would totally want you to do it. I have a really good gut instinct for this sort of thing."

Carrie chuckled. "Yeah, well, talent isn't everything. You were good at your job and look where that got you."

"What's that supposed to mean?"

"It means you were a great stringer, if that's the right term, putting yourself at risk, doing more than the others, always pushing the boundaries. And because of that, you were taken captive, held hostage, and suddenly your maverick ways turned you from an asset to a liability. Our stories aren't so dissimilar, if you think about it."

David gave this some serious thought. "We both pushed ourselves out of the jobs we loved."

"And now here we are in a motel room in the middle of Maine."

"Yeah, here we are," David said.

A lengthy silence followed. David swung his feet back on the bed and turned up the volume on the TV a couple clicks to hear a report on how the Pacers had outlasted the Celtics in a grueling overtime match. The scrollbar along the bottom of the screen was nothing but a string of abstract letters and numbers. Carrie had no focus, and her thoughts became fuzzy as her arms and legs seemed to melt into the bed. Her eyelids were shutting, voluntarily or not. They snapped back open when David spoke up.

"Goodwin," he said.

"What?"

"Why doesn't she want you to see the patients post-op?"

Carrie shook her head and dislodged a few of the cobwebs.

"I don't know," she said. "It's her policy. She's a control freak, I guess."

"What if she's not," David suggested.

"What do you mean?"

David returned to his earlier position, feet on the floor, eyes on Carrie.

"I guess what I'm getting at is what if the palino—you know."

"Palinacousis," Carrie said.

"Yeah, that. What if it only happens in a few patients, not all of them? And that's why Goodwin doesn't want you or Dr. Finley to look after her charges. She doesn't want you to know."

Carrie mulled this over. "But there's been a lot of patients, David. Somebody would have found out by now."

"Not if it's temporary," he said. "She makes sure nobody knows about it. Or if they do, it gets reported to her or Navarro, and that information doesn't get back to you."

"But why?" Carrie asked.

Here David shrugged. "That's the big question, isn't it?"

"So why did Abington and Fasciani check out AMA?"

"Maybe something was different with those two, and Abington and Fasciani had to disappear. Some-

thing about their symptoms wasn't going to be temporary."

"Then explain to me how she got them to leave?"
Carrie asked.

"She could have paid them off. Or maybe she took
them."

"Kidnapping?"

"It's a possibility."

"Goodness, you're a conspiracy theorist, David.
Who knew?"

David held up his hands, evidently pleased to embrace the label.

"I think there's a reason Goodwin wants to keep
you from looking at those patients, and that it goes beyond protocol. That's all I'm saying."

"We would need a motive. Why would Goodwin
want to hide a potential side effect, and then purposefully work to remove patients not only from the program, but the hospital?"

"I know a way we could find out," David said.

"How? By asking her?"

"As a reporter I've had to learn things about people
they wouldn't say directly to my face," David said almost apologetically. "So, let's just say I have access to
some devices that could aid our effort."

"Elaborate, please."

"If you want to know Goodwin's private conversations, you've got to listen to them."

"You want to bug Goodwin's office?"

"Think about everything you've experienced so far.
It all points back to Goodwin. She's up to something,
Carrie. The question is, what?"

"I'll think about it," Carrie said.

"You can help get me inside, and I can set it up. The offer is on the table."

"I appreciate it," Carrie said, and she meant it.

David went back to watching television. Carrie turned her gaze to the ceiling. She was not thinking about bugging Goodwin, or any possible motive for hiding the patients. She was thinking about David. Part of it, she knew, was driven by loneliness. While Carrie did not regret putting her career first and foremost in her life priorities, she was also a woman with needs. But she was not ready to act on the impulse—not yet, anyway. The focus had to be on Abington and Fasciani. It had to be on saving her career.

Mind reading, Carrie knew, was nothing but a parlor trick; even so she caught David looking at her and sensed he was having similar thoughts. Carrie held his gaze a moment, then said, "Well, it's late and I'm pretty tired. I'll see you in the morning. Thanks for being there for me, David. It means a lot."

Carrie shut off her bedside lamp and turned her back to David.

David said, "You know, I would have helped you even without getting the story."

In the darkness, Carrie smiled.

37

Carrie used the VA locker room to change into her running clothes. Her sneakers, size nine Newton's the color of watermelon with electric blue piping, felt stiff from nonuse. Soon enough, she imagined, her legs would be aching from nonuse as well. She had no particular destination in mind, just a desire to get out there and slap some pavement. Her body ached from a bad night's sleep on a crummy mattress, plus all those hours of driving, and a good run would hopefully loosen her up.

She and David had returned from Maine late morning, and Carrie had gone straight to the VA to visit with Gerald Wright for his pre-op consultation.

Wright, a sixty-five-year-old grandfather of eleven and a fighter pilot during the Vietnam War, had been on the surgical schedule for months. His advanced-stage Parkinson's disease couldn't have cared less about two missing vets and Carrie's growing concern about DBS therapy. She had contemplated backing out of the surgery altogether, but worried that might make Goodwin overly suspicious, more careful of what she was willing to say behind closed doors.

On the drive south, Carrie had given David the green light to get whatever equipment was necessary to conduct the surveillance. She trusted his instincts about Goodwin, among other things, including his belief that the Wright operation would go without a hitch.

"It's not Parkinson's that's the problem," David had said. "There are too many DBS procedures involving patients with that condition. Something would have surfaced by now. It's got to be related to PTSD."

It was strange to be back at the VA. Everything felt so normal. Dr. Finley had joined Carrie for the pre-op consultation and he seemed to be in a jovial mood. Immediately following her meeting with Wright, Carrie gave Dr. Finley a briefing on her search, and expressed regret at not having made more progress.

"I appreciate your efforts," Dr. Finley said. "But as I told you back in my office, not everybody who has had the procedure returns for follow-up appointments. We are dealing with very fragmented individuals here."

When Carrie mentioned seeing Ramón Hernandez in a photograph with Abington, he did not seem at all fazed by the discovery.

"It could be that's how Steve got involved. I can check with Ramón, or Cal Trent, but there is a referral component to the DARPA program, so it's not entirely surprising to find a connection between them."

Something that was probably nothing.

All this did was get Carrie's thoughts churning even faster. Maybe what she had observed in Abington and Fasciani was an aberration, and her theory about palinacousis was entirely groundless. After all, Fasciani never actually articulated what she assumed was the condition. It was his behavior that had made her suspect it. Perhaps she was projecting symptoms on these two men to fit a puzzle she'd created.

Her doubts were not enough to call off David's plan to bug Goodwin's office. She was willing to accept Ramón's connection to Abington as potentially coincidental, but there were too many other unusual happenings for Carrie to discount. In any event, a good run might pound some clarity into an increasingly murky situation.

After some light stretching in the parking lot, Carrie tightened the laces of her shoes and set off at what she thought was a ten-minute-mile pace. The cityscape provided the perfect backdrop. She had enough to look at to keep her interested, but not so many cars and pedestrians to make it dangerous or distracting.

She turned right on Brynmar Street, thinking it might be nice to run through Healey Park. Evidently, she was not the only one with this idea. It was not the starting line in Hopkinton on Marathon Monday by any stretch, but plenty of joggers, bikers, and walkers were catching the final rays of sunshine on what had turned into a pleasantly cool afternoon.

Carrie's mind was beginning to let go and she remembered why she had fallen in love with running. Twenty minutes into her jog, her lungs felt great. Concern about her out-of-shape legs became an unfounded worry. The pitch was mostly level, but a few hills challenged her breathing and form.

Out of the corner of her eye Carrie caught a flash of movement. In the next few seconds a couple, fit and trim and dressed in fancy athletic gear, zipped past her on the right. Carrie quickened her pace to keep up until her lungs begged her to retreat. She slipped back to her natural gait, slowed her speed considerably, and laughed at her competiveness.

Always trying to be the best. Always pushing the limits.

It reminded Carrie of her conversation with David in the motel room, about the symmetry of their circumstances. She had almost succumbed to impulse and climbed into bed with him. It probably would not have been something she'd have regretted. Part of her wondered if that had been on David's mind as well.

Carrie was not sure what drew her attention to the jogger behind her. She glanced over her shoulder at the muscular man, who wore blue Nike training pants and a dark running jacket. A Red Sox baseball hat and sunglasses concealed most of his head and face. Carrie ran on, but she could hear the man behind her, his footfalls landing like soft taps against the pavement.

Curious if he was going to pass her, Carrie looked again. He had not gained a step. He also did not appear to be breathing very hard. This guy with tree trunks for legs must have another gear, but for whatever reason he'd opted not to use it. He evidently preferred to run behind Carrie, in that dead space where he was not a stalker, but not invisible either. There was plenty of room for all runners, and after a hundred yards with him on her tail it got irritating. She decided to put some pep in her step and lose this guy.

Her muscles responded, and soon she was running at what felt like a nine-minute-mile pace. Carrie's heart rate jacked and her lungs felt squeezed, but it was a manageable pace, at least for a while.

After about a minute Carrie took a peek behind and saw the same man running the exact same distance away from her. He had not fallen back, not even a few feet, which meant he had increased his speed to match Carrie's. It did not look like he was breathing any harder, either. Once again he maintained the exact distance that allowed him to be a presence, but not a threat.

Carrie switched sides of the road and picked up her pace a little bit more. She was probably running a sub-nine-minute mile now, well outside her comfort zone. Whatever her exact speed, Carrie's form suffered as a result, and she no longer landed with the mid-foot strike that helped prevent injury. The bad form caused joint strain, and made her breathing even more labored. But she pushed on, refusing to look behind her, not wanting to give in to curiosity or fuel her growing unease.

Her resolve lasted all of ten strides. As she passed a tall oak tree, Carrie craned her neck to look over her left shoulder and immediately spotted the same man running behind her. He had crossed the road with her and picked up speed to keep pace.

His arms pumped effortlessly, and his legs looked as if they could go on moving that way forever. This run was nothing to him, she could tell. He acted completely nonchalant. To anybody else, it would look like two runners working out. Maybe he was using her as a pace car, or for motivation. Since other joggers were around, Carrie was not too panicked. But she had moved beyond just being annoyed.

It's your mind playing tricks, Carrie assured herself. *Nothing more.*

She ran another fifty yards with the man in the dark

hat and sunglasses behind her before she decided to turn around. She slowed and made a wide, arching turn, and a few moments later she passed Hat Man on her left. He kept his head forward and his running rhythm steady with no change in direction. She took one glance behind her and saw Hat Man was still running away from her, just a guy out doing his own thing.

Carrie laughed at her paranoia and kept her gaze forward as she ran. The urge to look back once more felt almost oppressive, but she refused to cave in to her paranoia again. The incident was innocuous, she decided. She continued at a pace still above her norm, but the urge to look back would not let go.

Just take one look—one quick check—one . . . little . . . glance . . .

Carrie turned her head and her body followed. As her gaze traveled back, a feeling of relief came over her. Nobody was there.

Once again, Carrie laughed at her perceived ridiculousness. Fear was easy to catch. This made her think of Adam, and how he lived with that sinking feeling almost every second of the day. Like Abington and Fasciani, Adam was caught in terror's unrelenting grasp.

Ahead, she spied a turnoff to a cut-through that bisected the park. The path was narrow and paved with dirt, less demanding on the joints, and Carrie went that way. The sides of the path were lined with tall grasses and trees with budding leaves. Carrie absorbed the scenic beauty, appreciating every bush, cloud, and birdsong.

Behind her, a new sound entered her ears: the soft crunching of dirt. Somebody running. The tall grasses became a long green blur in Carrie's peripheral vision.

It's nothing, Carrie said to herself.

Five yards became ten, but Carrie still did not look back. Fifteen. Then twenty. The impulse to check was irresistible. She turned her body and gave a look. A sinking feeling swallowed her gut and Carrie's pulse took off. He was there, running behind her, hat on his head, sunglasses in place, keeping the same distance as before. Carrie had no idea how he'd snuck up on her, but she believed he wanted her to notice him.

Fear uncoiled as a surge of adrenaline hastened her strides. Carrie's heart hammered in her throat. She looked ahead, but the dirt path was vacant, no other joggers or bikers in sight.

She broke into a sprint, panting. Her eyes started to tear, and her thoughts turned black with terror. Her burning lungs needed more air. She opened her mouth wider, but that did little to help.

Straining her ears, Carrie heard the persistent patter of footsteps. Panic set in. She looked left, then right; would the tall grasses give her an escape route, or would they just slow her down? She decided to keep to the path. Run as hard as she possibly could.

Her only chance was to get to the main road and find someone to help. Carrie staggered sideways, unable to keep a straight line. Her eyes stayed fixed to the ground as she navigated around roots and rocks. Despite the intense exertion on her legs and lungs, Carrie managed to find still another gear. Her arms were pumping wildly to keep up the pace.

Ahead, she saw an opening where the cut-through path intersected the main road. People would be there, and safety.

Carrie risked another check behind her. He was

still there, running at a brisk pace, but as before, he did not appear to be gaining. Why? Was he toying with her? Did he get off on her fear?

She saw a smile on his face, and a flash of something in his hand—a knife, or perhaps even a gun. The tall grasses that she'd thought might aid her escape would be the perfect place to hide her rape or murder.

A fresh blast of terror filled her. She wanted to scream, but her battered lungs needed every bit of air and left nothing for her voice.

The path ended maybe a hundred yards ahead. He could still catch her. She sprinted in a blind panic. How could she have been so stupid, to take this cut-through?

The road was about seventy-five yards away.

Her focus wavered. In the next instant Carrie's ankle twisted, sending her sprawling. She landed on the hard, packed ground and skidded several feet on her knees. Momentum carried her forward and she got back to her feet, almost without breaking stride. Her only recourse was to keep running, and she refused to waste a second to see if he was gaining. Of course he was—he had to be. The ankle burned, as did her knees where she skidded, and every other stride hurt like running barefoot across shards of glass.

Don't look, don't look! Just run!

But Carrie could not resist. Her back and head turned and the man was there, five feet away, sporting a broad grin on his face. A scream of sorts escaped from her lips, more like a low moan that grew increasingly louder. Sweat glossed her skin and her thoughts became gummed with terror. Her legs kicked furiously, arms swinging in wild arcs. The numbness in the legs turned intense, beyond unpleasant. Her lungs screamed for her to stop, but Carrie blocked out the pain and she urged herself on.

Faster! Faster!

She wondered if it was the man's breath that made her neck so hot. She could almost feel his fingers gripping at her clothes.

Five more steps . . . five more.

As Carrie stumbled from the path, she collided with a female jogger who had no time to react. The impact was not too much, but Carrie's weakened ankle sent her tumbling to the ground. The other jogger let out a gasp, and once she figured out what had just happened, turned back to Carrie.

"Are you all right?" she asked, without offering to help her to her feet.

Carrie was down on her stomach, unable to see the path, but she still managed to get out a warning.

"Behind you, behind you!" she yelled. "He's behind you!"

The woman turned to look as Carrie scrambled to her feet. A moment later, the man in the baseball cap emerged from the cut-through with a worried look on his face. He came over to Carrie and she saw now a scar like a jagged lightning bolt on his cheek, and a shamrock tattoo that decorated the side of his neck.

"Nasty tumble you took there," he said.

Carrie skirted back several feet.

"Get away from me," she snapped.

The man looked only slightly aggrieved.

"Hey, I was just trying to help," he said with a shrug and a what-can-I-do kind of smile. He turned on his heels, and started back down the same dirt path.

"Do you need me to call the cops?" the woman jogger asked.

"No," Carrie said. "I'm fine. Thanks for asking. Sorry to run into you."

The jogger waved and went on her way.

Favoring her good ankle, Carrie watched Hat Man run away from her. Soon enough he was a pinprick on the horizon, and then he was gone. All she saw were the tall grasses swaying in concert with the gentle breeze.

38

Adam was shooting hoops when Carrie got home. She parked her car in the pullout and ambled over to him, trying to not favor her swelling left ankle. Worried about alarming everyone, especially Adam, Carrie had decided to keep the incident at the park a secret.

Adam took a shot, swished it from fifteen feet out, got his rebound, and bounced the ball with a display of his substantial dribbling skills. He appraised Carrie warily.

"What happened to you?" he asked.

Carrie was taken aback. She thought she'd done a good job concealing the minor sprain, and glanced down to make sure her pants hid the scrapes from her fall. "I'm fine. Why do you ask?"

"You're limping," Adam said.

Irene had passed her keen observation genes to her son as well as to her daughter.

"It's nothing," Carrie said.

Adam tossed Carrie the basketball, with a little heat

on the pass. He never held back when it came to playing sports. He loved competition, as did Carrie, but he took it to a whole different level. It was one aspect of his personality that had driven him into the military.

Carrie took a shot, but her balance was off on account of her ankle, and the ball clanged off the rim. Adam snagged the rebound, and in a fluid, dancerlike motion, turned and fired a jump shot that sent the ball in a high arc before it eventually found the center of the hoop.

Everything about Adam's body was in perfect working order, Carrie observed. He was lithe, agile, and quick on his feet. It was a bit surreal to see how able he appeared when Carrie knew he was anything but.

"You seem a little shaken," Adam said, dribbling once more. "Everything all right?"

On a whim, she decided to tell the truth. The experience had been truly frightening. Who better to share it with than someone who understood fear so well? "Oh, I just had a really creepy, scary incident at the park, while I was running. It's nothing."

Adam's stern expression indicated otherwise. "What happened?"

Carrie had not spaced on Adam's overly protective tendencies. The dark expression that overtook Adam's face after she had finished was more than a little unsettling.

"You sure he was just using you to set the pace?" Adam said.

"I don't know. I think so," Carrie said, not sounding at all convinced. "He came up to me after and seemed to feel badly about it."

Adam said, "Yeah, well, don't trust anybody, and

run with somebody else, will you please? I told you that like a thousand times. People do terrible things to each other, Carrie. Really terrible things."

Carrie was not sure whether Adam was talking about the jogger in the park, or himself. She set her hands on Adam's shoulders. "Look, it's nothing," she said. "I'm fine. And I'll be more careful next time."

Adam took a couple dribbles to get centered, and looked at Carrie the way she might examine a patient during a pre-op exam. She could tell he was looking for any hint of deceit. Adam said nothing, but it seemed he had picked up on Carrie's lingering apprehension.

"It really was harmless," Carrie said.

In the back of her mind, though, she wondered about the timing. The incident with the jogger came on the heels of her plot to bug Goodwin and in the middle of her search for two missing vets.

Still unconvinced, Adam said, "Just remember, I'm your brother. I'm always going to look out for you. Always."

Adam slugged Carrie playfully in the arm, and she slugged him back with an even lighter tap. During this exchange, the garage door came open and Carrie snatched the ball from Adam's grasp while he was distracted. She launched a solid ten-footer that found the net, no problem.

Howard Bryant emerged from the garage, carrying a tray of gardening tools, dressed for that sort of work. He set down the tools and sauntered over to his kids.

"Who's up for a game of Horse?" Howard asked with a star-bright smile on his face. Like their mother, Howard wanted his two children living on their own, but the sparkle in his eyes said he would cherish every moment spent together as a family under any circumstance.

Adam passed the ball to his father with maybe a little less zip than his delivery to Carrie. Not missing a beat, Howard caught the ball with two hands, took a couple of dribbles, and fired off a shot that could have been a mirror of Adam's earlier jumper. It hit nothing but net.

The game commenced as the sun beat a final retreat and birdsong filled the sweet-smelling air with joyful chatter. Howard started off the game with a layup, made it, and passed the ball to Adam, who also made the shot. Carrie, still favoring her left ankle, dribbled awkwardly to the hoop and clanged the ball off the rim.

"Carrie's a bit lame," Adam said.

Carrie acted indignant. "We're *playing* Horse," she said. "I'm not one."

"Just keep the move-and-shoot to a minimum, Dad. I'd hate for us to have to put her down."

Howard made a face, but the truth was that he'd been encouraging Adam to lighten up, to relax. Any show of levity was a minor victory in an otherwise endless war. Howard saved his expression of concern for Carrie.

"Did you hurt yourself, sweetheart?" he asked.

Carrie shot Adam a nervous glance, fearing he might say something about the incident in the park. Her dad might not think it was so innocuous, either. The world was full of predators, and Carrie was not interested in a lecture on safety. Adam gave Carrie a look that said she could trust him.

"I'm fine," Carrie said. "It's just a slight sprain, that's all. I fell while jogging. I can still take you boys on."

The winner of the game was basically predetermined.

The real contest was between Howard and Carrie for second place. Adam seemed to relish his expected victory, and a fraction of a grin overtook his face, until his gaze settled on the dysfunctional Camaro visible in the garage. Adam stomped over to the garage, pushed the button to shut the door, and returned to the basketball game with a look of disgust.

"Come morning, I'm turning that pile of metal into scrap," he said.

The glower on Adam's face remained until he buried three free throws in a row. Neither Carrie nor Howard reacted. They had heard the same threat many times before.

Carrie tried another shot and missed. *H-O*. Not wanting to earn the final three letters, Carrie decided her ankle needed a more supportive sneaker. She excused herself to go inside and change footwear.

Carrie could not locate the sneakers she wanted in her closet at first, but eventually saw them to the left of her black riding boots. It was a bit odd; Carrie was normally fastidious about her closet, and those sneakers were always to the right of her boots, kept in order of size. She sat on the bed and put on her sneakers, then got up to feed Limbic.

While Limbic gobbled every flake of food offered, Carrie opened her dresser to change into a different T-shirt. Right away she could tell someone had rifled through her clothing. Her shirts were folded, but not exactly as she would have done it. Close, but not perfect. Not her stamp.

Carrie was on high alert, every muscle tense. She scanned her bedroom for other anomalies. They were not especially difficult to spot. The sheet on her bed had not been pulled as tight as she would have done, and a stack of papers on her desk seemed closer to the window by about six inches. All these details were minor, but Carrie cut her teeth obsessing over the minor details. She noticed everything. Somebody had been in her room. Not just in her room, but looking through her things.

Carrie tried to make sense of it and arrived at one disturbing conclusion—Adam had spied on her. Who else could have done it? As much as she tried, Carrie could not come up with another logical explanation. His mental state was obviously fragile, but he had never done anything this strange, this out of character. Carrie's pulse accelerated as she descended the stairs, but at the bottom step she paused.

Deep breaths . . . deep breaths . . .

The surge of anger subsided like the tide rolling out to sea. There was an answer, Carrie assured herself. It would just take a conversation with Adam to clear things up.

Outside, Carrie found her father and brother shooting around. She approached tentatively, hands on her hips.

Howard stopped dribbling and said, "What happened to you? You look pale."

Carrie's heart fluttered as the anger returned. "Was somebody in my room?" She looked right at Adam, and her composure vanished.

"What are you talking about?" Howard asked.

"Somebody went through all my things. My clothes, under the bed. Somebody was in my room."

Adam's eyes narrowed and his face reddened like

a boiled lobster. "Why are you looking at me?" he asked.

"I'm just asking," Carrie snapped. "I'm trying to figure it out."

Howard said, "No. No. Of course not. Nobody went into your room."

Adam took a step forward. "Are you accusing me of something?" His voice held violence. His eyes were like pools of lava bubbling just below the surface and about to go volcanic.

Carrie changed her approach. One slight push might be enough to send Adam over the edge. "I'm trying to figure out if somebody went into my room, or not, that's all."

The answer, of course, was that *somebody* had been in there. The question was who.

Adam was not about to beat a retreat. He had been accused of wrongdoing and felt victimized. "Maybe you're getting paranoid," he said. "First you think a guy is chasing you in the park, and now they're rummaging through your stuff?"

"What guy?" Howard asked, turning to Carrie.

"It's nothing, Dad."

Adam let the basketball roll into the woods and approached Carrie in a menacing, threatening manner. His shoulders were forward, his arms out in front of his body, palms facing up. "Maybe the jogger is the guy who went into your room," he said.

Maybe, Carrie thought.

But that seemed incredible. It was too bizarre to reconcile. Why would somebody go into her room? What could they be looking for?

"Were you here all day?" Carrie asked, not yet ready to back down.

Easy, Carrie . . . Easy . . .

"Yeah, I've been here all day. Going through your crap."

"Adam, that's not necessary," Carrie said in a softer tone. "I'm just trying to understand what happened."

"Understand this," Adam said. He held up two hands with his two middle fingers fully extended, then turned and marched his indignation all the way down the driveway.

Carrie felt sick to her stomach, but it had been the most logical conclusion. While her father and mother were out and about, Adam had free rein around the house.

Howard appeared crestfallen. "You have to be careful with him, Carrie," he admonished.

Now she felt even worse. Disappointing her father, her hero, even a smidge, put a crimp on her heart.

"I'm sorry, Dad, but somebody was in my room."

"Well, obviously it wasn't your mother or me, and I'm willing to believe Adam. You're under a lot of strain, Carrie."

Carrie took a sharper tone. "Are you suggesting I'm making it up? I know what I saw, Dad."

Howard did not take the bait, and he was not going to get into it with her. "Just go easy on your brother," he said. "You two need each other. And I need to know that you're there for him in case we're not."

Carrie understood the subtext. She nodded glumly at the thought of her parents' demise. It would be many years away, she prayed, but one day they would be gone, and her dad was right: She would be Adam's lifeline.

"You can count on me, Dad," Carrie said. "I won't ever let him go."

Howard leaned forward and kissed his daughter gently on the cheek. "Good," he said. And with that, Howard headed down the driveway to go looking for his son.

39

At five thirty the next morning Carrie was back at the VA for Gerald Wright's DBS surgery. Parkinson's disease had crept into and enveloped the retired lieutenant colonel's life over the previous fifteen years, and as with all the other PD candidates for DBS, medication management had become unreliable. The surgical team, including Carrie, Dr. Finley, and the anesthesiologist, Dr. Kauffman, met to review Wright's MRI from the day before and the CT scan from that morning to determine where best to insert the leads.

To Carrie's surprise, Dr. Evan Navarro showed up for the meeting. The images had just been brought up on the computer when Navarro entered the conference room without knocking, as though he belonged there. He gave Carrie a cool smile as he walked through the door.

"What are you doing here, Evan?" Carrie asked.

"Sandra wanted me to observe this morning," Navarro said. He fell silent, feeling no compulsion to further elaborate.

Carrie's heart began to thunder. In the aftermath of yesterday's tumult in the park, she gave serious consideration to the possibility that the missing vets, the encounter with the jogger, and the ransacking of her room were all somehow connected. Now that Navarro had shown up unexpectedly, this notion took deeper roots.

Navarro looked snappy in his white lab coat, red-and-white-striped tie, and dark trousers. His hair looked extra oily, slicked back as if in homage to Eddie Munster, widow's peak and all. Carrie bristled at the thought of him joining her. A glance told her that Dr. Finley was equally displeased.

"Why would Dr. Goodwin want that?" Carrie asked.

"Surgery is her department, Carrie," Navarro answered coolly. "I don't ask how she runs it. I just do my job." His tone was condescending, implying Carrie would benefit from doing the same.

Dr. Finley stepped forward. "This is entirely inappropriate, Evan." His face was a shade of crimson Carrie had never seen on him before. "Nobody cleared this with me."

Navarro just shrugged. "You'll have to take that up with Sandra, too, I guess."

"And I damn well will do just that," Dr. Finley said. "We both know what this is about, don't we, Evan? And it's total bullcrap."

Navarro's smarmy expression set Carrie's blood on fire. "Well, Alistair, last I checked, this is surgery that you're doing here. And that would be my boss's area of responsibility. So I can only offer the same reply to you that I just gave to Carrie, which is if you don't want me here, you'll need to take that up with Sandra. Otherwise, I'm not interested in pissing her off today— or any day, for that matter."

Navarro set his beady little eyes on Carrie. She glanced over at Dr. Finley, who glowered at Navarro until he softened. No value in wasting energy, his expression conveyed. He pulled Carrie aside.

"I suspect this is a bit of payback for questioning her AMA orders," Dr. Finley said in a whispered voice. "I know her style. She's letting you know you're on notice. Don't worry about it, and try to ignore Navarro if you can. I'll speak to Sandra after and see if I can smooth things over. Nobody wants to work under a microscope."

Carrie gave a nod. She had her own payback in mind for Goodwin, and after the surgery she would help David make that plan a reality. For now, Carrie would dedicate all her attention to her patient and ignore Navarro as Dr. Finley advised.

The question now was where to place the electrodes.

Wright's facial inexpressiveness, unblinking vacant stare, and almost inaudible whisper of a voice belied a reasonably intact intellect, but significant personality and behavioral problems had influenced Dr. Finley's decision. The apathy and depression, for example. Were these behaviors a direct consequence of his disease, or an understandable psychiatric reaction to the devastations of a failing motor system?

Wright had had enough problems for Dr. Finley to decide on the right globus pallidus interna for the stimulating electrode target. This would seem to afford the best opportunity to reduce the left arm tremor and improve Gerald Wright's overall motor status. Dr. Finley and Carrie considered other target placements, but the risk of psychiatric complications favored the GPi as the better choice.

"He may be a bilateral case," Dr. Finley told Carrie as she went in to scrub for the surgery, "but let's see how he does with this side first. He's pretty intact cognitively, but I'm concerned about his behaviors and the neuropsych testing reports we've gotten back."

Carrie was still schooling herself in the subtleties of Parkinson's disease and the options of DBS surgeries. Like everything else in medicine, this was a rapidly evolving discipline, meaning patient and doctor alike were on steeply ascending learning curves. Carrie reprimanded herself for not spending more time studying about PD, even though she was still new to the program. She'd had too many distractions.

Like missing vets.

The familiar harsh smell of Betadine scrub and the lather up above her elbows brought her mind back to the problem at hand, retired LTC Gerald Wright. She smiled slightly beneath her mask. Despite all that was going on, she was still a surgeon at heart, and she could focus all her attention on her profession and the task at hand.

Funny how at the most unpredictable of times, she became aware of the transformational effects of training. No one had ever taught her to feel like a competent doctor, a leader. But that was how she felt as she did her second scrub midway up the forearms, and then the third, just the hands.

She entered the OR not feeling as comfortably in the zone as she was accustomed.

The procedure was becoming commonplace, which played in her favor: affix the stereotactic frame with four screws under local anesthesia first thing in the morning, then down to MRI for ultra-thin slices, with the images sent over to the planning station in the OR. Carrie selected the optimum XYZ coordinates to minimize risk of brain injury or hemorrhage as the needle advanced its way to Gerald Wright's globus pallidus interna.

He was awake for this procedure, kept comfortable with just the right amount of propofol. That way, Dr. Finley could monitor the patient's motor status directly and also use the electrode recording techniques that signaled their specific placement. They were a team now, Dr. Alistair Finley and Dr. Carrie Bryant. They were able to carry out the extended, time-consuming procedure with little back-and-forth dialogue, as if they were reading each other's thoughts, despite the fact that they had worked together on only a handful of cases.

Evan Navarro's presence was as innocuous as the familiar sounds of the operating room machinery. Maybe the choice of music helped Carrie block out the unpleasant distraction. Gerald Wright was also a jazz fan, and he had requested Bill Evans's *Portrait in Jazz* for his big day in the OR. The melodies reminded Carrie of her life at BCH, and friends like Valerie, with whom she was no longer in touch. Even in the Facebook era, friendships forged at work faded quickly once that bond was broken. But now she had a new community, a new team she counted on and who counted on her.

"Are you doing all right, Carrie?"

Carrie's focus had been so total that Dr. Finley repeated himself.

"Yeah, I'm fine. Why?"

"You're about to go off your line by about three mi-
crometers. Do you need a rest?"

"I'm sorry," Carrie said. "Maybe just a minute and
some water."

Navarro's black eyes seemed to be smiling.

Carrie was not 100 percent, and Dr. Finley seemed
to know it. A thin film of grit blanketed her eyes, left
behind from a bad night's sleep plagued by nightmares
of men chasing her in the dark. Adam had crashed on
the couch watching TV, and Carrie woke him by accident getting ready for work.

Yesterday's fight was in the past. He had smiled
warmly at her and wished her a good day without having read the long note of apology Carrie had left on
the kitchen table. Seeing Navarro's wicked look made
Carrie more willing to believe her brother. Could Evan
Navarro have been in her bedroom? Could Goodwin
have put him up to it? And if so, why? Carrie had a gut
feeling that bugging Goodwin's office would get her
some answers.

After a short break, Carrie resumed her work. Dr.
Finley recorded the electrical discharge patterns as
Carrie sank the electrodes on the sweet spot. Navarro
did not stay for the entire show. Evidently, he had made
his point and was off to other things. Soon enough he,
or one of his residents, would be looking in on Gerald
Wright, and Carrie would probably never see this patient again. Even if everything that had been happening
lately had a logical explanation, Carrie doubted she
could continue to work under such rigid constraints.

In total, it took seven hours to drill the holes and close up the skull, and in that time Carrie developed knots in her shoulders the size of walnuts.

"You seemed a little off today," Dr. Finley said back in the scrub room. "You sure everything is okay?"

"Navarro had me a bit rattled," Carrie replied.

"Well, leave that to me. I'm going to speak with Sandra right now. That won't happen again, I assure you."

Carrie went to the locker room to take a shower and get changed. After that, she stopped by the hospital cafeteria for her second coffee of the day. Next, it was on to the front desk where Carrie would arrange a temporary ID for David Hoffman. They had settled on the ruse that he was a medical student coming to the VA tonight to help with some research. To keep their activities as covert as possible, David asked Carrie to use an alias, and she picked "Michael Stephen," which were the first two names that had popped into her head.

She texted David her chosen moniker and headed to an on-call room to grab a few hours of shut-eye on the narrow, industrial bed before Mission Possible commenced.

Carrie's cell phone buzzed in her lab coat pocket, which she assumed was David responding. She checked the number, but did not recognize the caller.

"Hello, Dr. Carrie Bryant speaking."

"Dr. Bryant, I'm Dr. Abbey Smerling from Seacoast Memorial Hospital in Maine."

Carrie's entire body came alive. "Yes, Dr. Smerling. What can I do for you?"

"You placed a call regarding a patient, Dr. Sam

Rockwell, and asked to be notified if there were any developments."

Carrie braced for the news to come. A potential link to the mystery of what might have happened to Abington and Fasciani had probably just died.

"Yes, that's correct," Carrie said.

"Well, I have some good news to share."

This was what Carrie had hoped for. It was common practice for doctors to share patient information with other doctors irrespective of the new privacy laws. Some habits were harder to break than others.

Dr. Smerling said, "The brain swelling had begun to recede, so we lightened up the coma to see if he could come back."

"And?"

"And we got something," Dr. Smerling said. "A lot more than we expected."

40

At precisely seven o'clock that evening, David arrived at the VA ready to get to work. As far as he knew, Carrie was already on the road, headed back to Maine. She had called with the exciting news about Sam Rockwell and suggested they reschedule tonight's activities, but David saw no need. He could get the job done as long as Carrie did her part to help.

At the front desk David almost forgot to use the alias "Michael Stephen," but remembered at the last possible second, before the conversation with the receptionist turned decidedly awkward. Carrie had assured him nobody would ask for ID, and she was right. Even so, for backup, David had printed a bogus one using a template procured off the Internet, and had it laminated for authenticity. It proved an unnecessary precaution, but David seldom left anything to chance.

"Here you go, dear," the kind-faced receptionist said as she handed David his temporary badge.

One obstacle cleared, thought David.

He headed to the third floor, following a rudimentary map drawn from Carrie's brief description of the hospital layout. Walking these institutionalized halls, David felt suffocated at the thought of having to work in such an antiseptic environment. Journalistic stringers were free spirits, and David relished the uncertainty of his chosen profession. He was all about new possibilities, and shied away from anything that could anchor him—a permanent job, a mortgage, a car, material possessions, and yes, even love. He often wondered if the issues between him and Emma were a product of mismatched pheromones or his wandering spirit. Guarded as he was, something told David one kiss from Carrie Bryant might be enough to tame his wanderlust permanently.

Carrie's office was third to the last down a long hallway lined with ordinary wooden doors without any markings on them. She had left the door unlocked, as she said she would, and David went inside.

His first impression was that Carrie essentially worked in a closet. His prison cell in Syria had been only slightly bigger. She had enough room for a chair and a metal desk, which Carrie wisely kept uncluttered. A small, square window offered a narrow view of a gritty construction effort under way. All in all, David found it a depressing place. He much preferred the dangers of the field.

Carrie had left a pair of scrubs on the door hook, and they fit David fine. He turned the lock on the doorknob before he closed the door, and checked the hallway to make sure nobody was coming. Carrie had rightly said most everyone would be gone by now, and the halls were museum-quiet.

From the pocket of his pants David retrieved a leather case that contained a tension wrench and set of picks. He tested his picking chops on Carrie's door. It was open in less than a minute. Having worked in dangerous locales over the years, David had acquired a unique set of unsavory skills. In addition to picking locks, forging documents, and planting bugs, David was competent with a gun and could also hot-wire some cars.

Returning to the main hallway, David passed a few people on his way to Goodwin's office, but nobody gave him a second glance. The modest disguise more than sufficed.

Following Carrie's directions, David took a right turn at the first hallway branch, and stopped at a door with a mounted placard that read: DR. SANDRA L. GOODWIN, CHIEF OF NEUROSURGERY, M.D.

David put his ear to the door and gave a listen. Not a sound. He gave the knob a gentle turn. Locked. *Good.* David had the door open in less time than it had taken him to manipulate the pins on Carrie's lock. He entered quickly, closed and locked the door behind him, and flicked on the light.

The office within was larger than Carrie's by a good amount, with nicer furniture, and a bigger window, too, but the intuitional stamp was just the same. David fished the Sonit-21 mini voice recorder from his pocket. The device had cost five hundred dollars, a fortune for David at the time, but the investment had paid back ten-fold in the information covertly obtained. The voice-activated rectangular device was a bit larger than a Bic lighter, weighed just eight grams, and could record for 120 hours on a single charge.

David searched the office for the best place to

hide the recorder. The Sonit's black case blended well with the dirt of one of Goodwin's ailing plants. After he turned on the voice activation mode, David covered the recorder with a thin layer of soil to better conceal it, and took a seat in Goodwin's chair.

"Testing one, two, three," David said in a normal speaking voice. "Testing. Testing."

He retrieved the device, cleared away the dirt, and pressed the playback button. His voice echoed loud and clear. David returned the recorder to the pot and flicked enough dirt to make it disappear.

He got halfway to the door when he heard footsteps coming down the hall. He moved behind the desk, feeling sweat bead up on his brow. The doorknob to Goodwin's office turned from the outside.

David looked around for anyplace to hide. The ceiling tiles could be removed, but the chance of him climbing up there before the door came open was slim to none. Keys rattled. Color drained from his face. David had to act quickly, rationally. The only place he could think to hide was under the desk.

He moved the chair back a foot to squeeze his body into the small crawl space underneath the desk. The desk's metal front would partly shield him from anybody walking in, but half a foot of space between the legs and the metal sides left him horribly exposed. All somebody had to do was look down, and they'd see David huddled in a little ball on the floor.

To get his body off the ground, David pressed his back against one side of the desk and put his feet up against the other side. Next, he engaged his core, arched his hips, and raised his body off the floor. The strain on his stomach muscles was instant and intense. It took all of a few seconds for the spasms to begin, his midsection shaking like an earthquake.

David swallowed a breath and concentrated on relaxing. He heard the key go into the lock and a slight noise as the doorknob engaged. David worried his bottom might be sagging a bit, and he lifted it up higher. The burn intensified. He heard two sets of footsteps enter, and then a man's voice.

"I just need to grab a file for Sandra and then we'll be out of here."

A female voice said, "Maybe we should stay a while longer."

David's heart pounded in his ears. Every muscle in his core was fully engaged, and his joints ached from the oppressive strain. The crawl space under the desk was unpleasantly cramped, but David elevated his hips some more without making a sound. Closing his eyes, he breathed through his nose and began to count in his head.

One . . . two . . . three . . .

"Got it," the man said.

"I got it, too, Evan," the woman said.

David heard a groan of pleasure escape Evan's lips. This had to be Evan Navarro, Goodwin's minion Carrie had told him about.

"Residents are not supposed to fraternize with their boss," Evan said in a breathy voice.

"Is squeezing and rubbing the same as fraternizing?" asked the woman.

David snapped his eyes closed and fought against the growing fatigue. Sweat poured out of his body and began to drip on the floor. Evan groaned again and

David heard the sounds of sloppy kissing. David's mind began to quit on him.

Just give it up . . . drop to the floor . . .

He felt his grip slipping, and the desperate urge to let go intensified. His violent body shakes persisted and threatened to dislodge him.

Sixteen . . . seventeen . . . eighteen . . .

"Maybe we should skip dinner tonight," Evan said.

"I know what I want for dessert," the woman cooed.

The kissing resumed while tears of pain streaked down David's cheeks. Both legs burned equally, and it felt like sharp needles were being jammed into his stomach. He kept his eyes closed tight and kept counting.

Thirty-five . . . thirty-six . . . thirty-seven . . .

David feared he might black out. He had to let go. There was no way to hold on. His body was screaming as the agony turned exquisite.

The kissing sounds abruptly stopped.

"Let's take this to a more comfortable location," Evan suggested.

Please . . . please . . .

A consuming blackness came over him. David's back was slipping. His legs were giving out on him. His whole body was drenched in sweat. The traction simply was not there. He slid down an inch.

"Maybe we should do it here?" the woman suggested.

A beat. David slid some more. His legs had turned to Jell-O.

"If you want to do it in an office, let's use mine," Evan said. "I'll have visions of Sandra in my head, and that's just not a turn-on."

David dropped another inch. His back began to sag,

and if somebody glanced at the floor they would have no trouble seeing him. His lower back and hips were clearly visible.

"Let's just go to your place," the woman said. "A bed would be far more comfortable than a desk."

David heard a thunderclap sound when somebody slapped the top of the desk. The vibration nearly dislodged him, and his body dipped even more. He kept his gaze fixed upward. A biting on his tongue helped him regain focus.

Hold on.

His muscles went into full spasm. David was going to drop.

I can do this . . . just hold on a few more seconds . . .

"Couldn't agree more," Evan said.

In the back of his mind, through a fog of pain, David heard footsteps and the sound of a door opening. The office lights went out as David's body let go. He crashed to the floor at the same instant the office door slammed shut.

41

Seacoast Memorial Hospital was south of Bangor, overlooking beautiful Elkhorn Lake. According to Carrie's navigation app, it was a four-and-a-half-hour drive from Boston, mostly a straight shot up I-95 North. The sameness of the route had lulled Carrie into a trance, and the classic rock station she found did a marginal job at keeping her awake and alert. She rolled down her window and took in a refreshing blast of fresh air. Sunset was approaching, and off in the distance Carrie spotted a helicopter making lazy circles against a sky brushed with hues of pink and yellow. She figured it was a news chopper, but traffic on this stretch of highway was light and it would have to fly elsewhere to find any congestion.

On a whim, Carrie exited the highway at Brunswick, and merged onto Route 1 headed north. The detour would add only twenty minutes or so to her drive, but would take her along the gorgeous scenic coastline.

A few miles down the road, Carrie's phone rang and gave her a start. She checked the number, thinking it might be David with news, but the ID came up as Dr. Abbey Smerling.

"Hi there, Dr. Smerling," Carrie said, fumbling with the phone's settings to activate her Bluetooth and make the call hands-free.

"Hi, Carrie, you had asked for an update on Sam Rockwell's condition."

There was no small talk. Abbey Smerling, like most every doc Carrie knew, squeezed phone calls in the way they did meals. Carrie again braced herself for a disappointing report.

"We just did his Glasgow score and it came out a six."

Carrie's mouth fell open. *A six!* She could hardly believe her ears. This was up two points from when she had last spoken to Smerling.

The Glasgow score provided neurologists with a way to gauge the severity of an acute brain injury. By measuring various functions, including eye opening, verbal response, and motor response, a patient's prognosis could be predicted with surprising accuracy. Anything eight and above had a good chance for recovery, while a score between three and five was most likely fatal. A six was the nether world—not great, not dismal. Perfectly in between.

Sam Rockwell had suffered a massive hemorrhage that went below the arachnoid membrane and into the cerebrospinal fluid, according to what Dr. Smerling had told her. The hemorrhage had grown, too, in part because of a course of anticoagulant medication. The increased swelling from fluid collection around the hemorrhage site caused further pressure on the brain structure and additional neurological injury.

For Rockwell to have emerged from his coma and get a six on the Glasgow score was about as likely as Goodwin inviting Carrie on a girls' weekend.

"So what's driving the number?" Carrie asked.

"We've got a little more verbal response than before, but his speech is still incomprehensible. He's a two there. His eyes have opened in response to pain, and he's got the same decerebrate posture as before."

Based on that alone, Carrie pictured Rockwell in his hospital bed, arms and legs held straight out, his toes pointed downward, and his head and neck arched back. The abnormal posture was a sign of severe brain damage and earned him a two on the widely used scale. The eye movement was the new development, having gone from a plus one to a plus two in under a day. It was encouraging progress.

While there was no real reason for Carrie to rush up to Maine, Rockwell's scores were not low enough to keep her from making the drive. As Dr. Smerling confirmed, his scores could improve at any time, and perhaps the verbal could get up to a four. The conversation in that case might be confused, but he might be able to answer some simple questions.

Did you ever see palinacousis in the vets before?

Did you notice any side effects from the DBS surgery?

Did any of your patients ever go missing?

As long as there was hope for Rockwell's further improvement, Carrie could stay a day or two before her next scheduled surgery.

"Well, I appreciate you keeping me in the loop," Carrie said. "I'll be up there in a few hours."

Carrie ended the call and her foot got a little bit heavy on the gas. She noticed the helicopter high up in the sky, hovering like a dragonfly as it made several passes over the highway. *You're not going to find any traffic here either,* she thought.

Twenty minutes later, Carrie made a pit stop at a roadside gas station, an oasis on a lonely stretch of road. She filled the tank and took a much-needed stretch. She got a chicken salad at an attached restaurant, and was back in her Subaru thirty minutes later, enjoying a glorious sunset.

Up ahead, Carrie noticed a red Ford F-150 truck pulled over to the side of the road. She checked for oncoming traffic, wanting to give the truck a wide berth as she passed. She was maybe fifteen feet away when the Ford's engine revved, its taillights flashed, and the pickup spun out into the road in front of her.

Carrie shrieked and slammed on the brakes, burning rubber that left long black trails behind her. She had been going forty-five, and avoided a rear-bumper collision by inches. Carrie leaned hard on her car horn to let the pickup driver know exactly what she thought of that maneuver. The F-150 sped on ahead, and Carrie released her white-knuckled grip on the steering wheel. Her hands trembled slightly as the adrenaline rush lingered.

"What an asshole," Carrie muttered under her breath.

The F-150's brake lights lit up as if the driver had heard her and wanted to escalate the confrontation. Carrie tapped on her brakes to keep distance, but the truck had slowed to a crawl and the gap between them closed in a blink. Clenching her jaw tight enough to hurt, Carrie braked some more, but the truck had come to a near standstill; before she knew it, the bumpers were almost touching.

Carrie hit her horn again, but with a little less force. The beeps were meant to urge the driver to pick up speed, not show her anger. She noticed the license plate was from Maine. Probably some local kids who did not take kindly to tourists who dared use the horn on them.

The truck picked up speed, and Carrie did as well, but inexplicably the driver braked again. The next time it accelerated, Carrie kept some distance that she would use to try and pass on the left. She had no desire to play this obnoxious game for the remainder of her drive.

She checked the traffic, moved over a lane, and gunned the accelerator to pass. All four of the Subaru's engine cylinders worked overdrive to build up some speed. Carrie glanced to her right as she passed the truck, but the driver was just a shadow. She drove on ahead and felt her blood pressure spike when a check in her rearview showed the truck gaining. The truck was flashing its lights and slamming the horn. Carrie had one chilling thought.

Road rage.

She accelerated, but the more powerful pickup easily kept pace. The truck's horn blared and its headlights flashed. Carrie rolled down her window and waved her arm to encourage the pickup to pass. The truck gained speed, but did not change lanes. The driver got so close to her Subaru the bumpers nearly kissed. Carrie's heartbeat accelerated. She brought her arm back inside her vehicle. If the driver was not going to pass, she might have to get to the side of the road and let him go by.

A flash of fear came over her. What if she stopped and he did as well? There were no other cars on this stretch of highway. She checked her phone: no signal. Carrie could not imagine being in a more vulnerable position.

She put her arm out the window and gave another urging wave. This time the truck veered left into the oncoming lane, and then right, then left again, weaving down the road. Before Carrie could make sense of it, the pickup switched lanes and accelerated again. Carrie punched the gas, but the F-150 easily kept pace. They were driving alongside each other, but only the Ford was at risk for a head-on collision. Carrie dared a glance to her left and saw a single broad-shouldered driver in the cab. His face was an empty shadow, or so she believed. For a second, Carrie thought he had on a black mask. She did not get a chance for a better look.

Panic gripped her. Carrie floored the accelerator around a sharp bend and her car shot forward like a rocket. Her tires skidded, but never lost grip of the road. The Ford stayed in the left lane and kept pace as it inched closer to her car. She would have to leave the road to get any distance. Ahead was a long, straight stretch of highway with no oncoming traffic. Again Carrie leaned on her horn, giving it a long and angry blast, and then intentionally let up on the accelerator, hoping the Ford would decide to pass. The pickup's driver anticipated her plan somehow, and slowed as well.

The truck kept parallel to Carrie's car as it maneuvered yet another inch closer. The distance between them was no greater than a hair's width. Carrie heard a sudden and tremendous crack as the truck snapped off her side mirror. The piercing scrape of metal on metal followed.

Instinctively, Carrie turned the wheel hard right as the pickup swerved away. She straightened out her course just as the pickup came back again. This time, the truck slammed into the side of her car. Carrie gave a yell and swung the wheel right. Her only thought was to get away from danger. She did not contemplate the consequences of making such a violent and sudden turn. Once the skid started, it was not going to stop.

Carrie screamed as her car veered off the highway going forty and headed for a dense copse of trees. Everything was a blur of green. She heard tree branches snap violently and metal and glass shatter. There was a huge crash, and a crack of splitting wood louder than thunder. Carrie's head snapped back and she heard another sickening crunch of metal and plinking glass as the car stopped abruptly. A gunshot sound followed as the airbag deployed. It happened so fast, Carrie could not even register what hit her, but it felt as if somebody had slapped her face as hard as they could. Chalky dust went into her eyes and up her nose as she choked on a pungent stench.

For a moment, Carrie could see nothing but the white of the airbag. But then the pain came and the whiteness of the bag gave way to black.

42

Braxton Price and Curtis Gantry used the police scanner in the pickup to listen in on the aftermath of Carrie's accident. The accident drew two fire trucks, two police cruisers, and an ambulance to the scene. The driver was conscious and reported that a red Ford F-150 with Maine plates had driven her off the road.

The APB included no plate number, so Carrie had not seen, or could not recall it. Either way, Braxton was not worried about the police pulling them over. They were driving Gantry's blue Chevy pickup with Massachusetts plates. Braxton had ditched the Ford on a prearranged side street off Route 1 about ten miles from where the accident occurred. Gantry had picked him up there, per the plan, and together they resumed the drive north. The whole operation had been improvised when they got word Carrie was headed to Maine.

Braxton took the chopper north, secured a car to use, and got behind Carrie's Subaru with help of the chopper and Gantry, who had tailed Carrie all the way from Massachusetts. Braxton figured on taking her down near Bangor when she left the highway, but Carrie had opted for a scenic detour, so he and Gantry had arranged a different meeting place. It helped that Carrie had stopped for something to eat. Braxton was able to pull ahead and wait for her while Gantry got even farther down the road. The transition from one truck to the other took no time at all.

Gantry was acting like a boy at the skate park—all smiles and pumped full of adrenaline. He loved missions, any missions, but especially successful ones.

"So she didn't die," he said. "Does that mean we get a bonus?"

"No, it means we didn't screw up," Braxton said.

"What's the worst thing that could have happened?"

"We're about to permanently take out Rockwell. We don't need two docs going dark on the same day from the same hospital who happen to work for the same program. It's not the sort of coincidence our employers are interested in explaining away. What we did wasn't optimal, but we had to do something. Besides, she's still considered an asset to the program—at least, that's the word from up high. I figured if Rockwell didn't die after we ran him off a cliff, Carrie could survive a little action in the trees. Maybe we got lucky here, but we did all right."

Gantry went silent. He seemed almost reflective, though Braxton knew his friend's thoughts seldom strayed far from guns, sex, and money.

"Good thing we had the bird in the sky," Gantry said. "I had lost her for a while there."

"There are no helicopters where we're headed next. No backup, either. We get caught, we've got to go dark ourselves. You carrying?"

From the pocket of his denim jacket Gantry fished out a white pill the size of a Tic Tac and popped it into his mouth.

"Hey, don't screw around with that!" Braxton snapped.

Gantry hid his teeth and pressed the cyanide capsule between his lips. He flashed Braxton a toothless smile. "I t'ank you're purty, Braxton. You like me?"

"Get that out of your mouth before you bite it and die."

Gantry spit the pill into his hand and tucked it back inside his jacket pocket. "Who did you give the money to?" he asked.

"None of your damn business."

"I'm guessing it's Jesse."

"Guess all you want."

"How long since you've seen him?"

Braxton thought a beat. "Maybe five years. Maybe more."

"So he's what, fifteen now?"

"Something like that."

Gantry gave a long, low whistle. "Imagine being that young and getting, what is it, half a million dollars? Just like that? Shit, if I had that kind of money at that age I'd have screwed myself into a coma deeper than Rockwell's."

"He's not going to get the money, because we're not going to get caught."

"Maybe I won't take the pill," Gantry said.

"Who did you give the money to?"

"My mom," Gantry said.

"So we get caught, you're dead regardless, and instead of your mom winning the lottery, somebody other than you will be planning her funeral. Look, Gantry, the poor woman had it hard enough raising your sorry ass. Give her the peace of mind she deserves, man."

Gantry nodded. He saw the logic in Braxton's thinking. Always did.

"Speaking of piece, Carrie's got a great ass," Gantry said.

"That's a different kind of piece," Braxton said.

"Whatever. I'm just saying I followed her on a jog in Healey Park, and she has tremendous assets. I'd love to tag that."

"That's how you conduct surveillance?"

"Hey man, I'm just doing my job. Checked out her room, too. Nothing there, but I did have a nice time lying down on her bed and thinking dirty thoughts."

"Nobody saw you?" Braxton asked.

"Nah, man. Her brother is a drone. He was watching TV and didn't hear me come in. I think that guy could use the wires, if you get my drift."

Braxton shook his head dismissively, turned on the radio, and eventually found the local NPR station.

Gantry listened for all of three minutes before he tired of hearing about the struggles of life in Libya and switched to a pop station. "You and your freakin' NPR. I don't know how you listen to that crap. We're like the Odd Couple, man," Gantry said.

Braxton shot Gantry an annoyed look. "Have you ever even seen that show? I know for sure you didn't read the play. Do you even know what you're talking about?"

To Braxton's surprise Gantry returned a broad, sloppy grin and hummed in perfect tune the opening bars to the show starring Tony Randall and Jack Klugman.

"The Internet has everything, asshole," Gantry said, and he resumed humming. On they drove, speeding into the twilight on their way to Seacoast Memorial Hospital, with Gantry humming *The Odd Couple* theme as if it was his favorite show of all time.

Gantry pulled into the hospital parking lot a little after nine o'clock. The two-story, mostly brick structure appeared to be undergoing a major renovation, and Gantry drove around until he found a parking space out of the way, near a loading zone. He cut the engine only after making sure that no surveillance cameras were around to record them.

Meanwhile, Braxton maneuvered inside the cramped cab and pulled off his loose-fitting sweats and T-shirt to reveal the green custodial uniform he wore underneath. He had in his possession an employee badge from Seacoast Memorial with his picture on it, but Lee Taggart's name. The uniform and badge were precautions taken a while back, as soon as they'd known Rockwell would be a patient at Seacoast Memorial for a while. In the shadows of some scaffolding he checked his supplies: a syringe and a vial of clear liquid.

"I'll be out in ten minutes," Braxton said as he filled the syringe with liquid to the last marked line.

Gantry winked and blew Braxton a kiss. "Careful, sweetheart. I'll be thinking of you."

Braxton ignored him and headed for the main entrance. Inside the hospital, he flashed security his ID and continued on his way. No problems there. Braxton's badge opened all the doors, a modern miracle courtesy of some supremely competent computer types who worked for his employers. Deep pockets bought a lot more than aerial surveillance.

Braxton walked the halls until he found a janitor's cart—complete with a broom, cleaning supplies, and a twenty-gallon vinyl bag for trash—tucked away in an unobtrusive nook. He wheeled the cart over to the long-term-care wing on the first floor. The diffused fluorescent lighting, powerful stench of cleansers, beeps of various machines, and unpleasant stale air reminded Braxton of the VA. All hospitals were essentially the same, and the people who came to them were the same as well: They got better, got worse, or got dead.

Braxton went in and out of several rooms, emptying the trash and wiping down furniture. The two duty nurses did not give him a second look. He was the help, one of the invisibles who worked behind the scenes to keep the place clean enough to cure.

"Good evening," Braxton said to a stout nurse who sat behind a desk covered with monitors.

Same shit, different location.

"Evening," the nurse said. She gave Braxton only a cursory glance before her focus returned to those monitors.

Braxton wheeled his cart into Sam Rockwell's room. For a guy who had been in a coma for so long, Rockwell actually looked pretty good. The bruises and cuts had mostly healed, and he appeared to be sleeping peacefully.

With practiced skill, Braxton injected succinylcholine intravenously and titrated the flow to speed up induction. Beneath the skin, invisible to the eye, Rockwell's muscles had begun to twitch and spasm. Almost immediately Rockwell's heart rate accelerated to help get oxygen to the brain. But the neuromuscular blocker, widely used by anesthesiologists and easy for Braxton to procure, would stop that heart in short order.

A patient as injured as Rockwell would not be subjected to an autopsy, Braxton had been told, and there was little chance of discovering the breakdown product, succinic acid.

Braxton counted to thirty before he wheeled his cart out of Rockwell's room and over to the nurses' station. "I'm no doc," he said, "but that guy in there looks like he's having a real hard time breathing."

As if on cue, an alarm sounded. The nurse leapt up from her chair as though it were on fire, and rushed into action. Braxton heard the code call come over the loudspeaker. A moment later, a crush of doctors and nurses headed for Rockwell's room like galloping racehorses.

Braxton became invisible again as he wheeled the janitor's cart nonchalantly down the hallway, whistling the tune from *The Odd Couple* as he went.

43

"It looks a lot worse than it feels," Carrie said.

Using the tips of his fingers, gentle as possible, David touched the large bruised area that marred much of Carrie's right cheek. His face expressed sympathy and heartfelt concern.

The Starbucks was packed at the bustling strip mall near the VA where the two had met. In less than an hour, Carrie was scheduled to see a demonstration of the virtual reality program that had sent Steven Abington off the rails. David had plans of his own at the hospital.

Carrie removed her sunglasses to show David the full extent of her injuries, but bright sunshine stabbed her eyes, and she quickly slipped the shades back into place. The ER doc who had treated Carrie in Maine warned that her sensitivity to light might last a few weeks. After she showed the doc a picture of her crumpled Subaru he added, "Be grateful that's your biggest concern."

Carrie had spent a few days resting at home after

the accident, but her body still ached in every conceivable way—stiff joints, throbbing pain in her knees and wrists, tight muscles, pounding headache. David's touch, at least, made her forget the discomfort for a moment.

"I wish you'd called me from Maine," David said. "I would have come to get you."

Carrie had actually given the idea some measured consideration, but opted for her brother instead, in part because of vanity. Days after the accident, Carrie's left eye was still swollen, her split lip had not fully healed, and her nose, though not broken, looked like a doorknob squished on her face. Most of the damage was the result of airbag deployment, but without it Carrie knew her injuries could have been fatal.

As for Adam, her brother had been incredibly supportive throughout the ordeal. He had dished out all the expected brotherly jabs: "You look hot," he'd said, and, "It might be an improvement." But those had come later, on the drive home. The first thing he did was to give Carrie a long embrace, and the first words he spoke were, "I'm so grateful you're all right." Carrie managed to hold back the waterworks until Adam kissed her bruised forehead and told her how much he loved her.

Howard's treasured BMW was off-limits to all, so Adam drove Carrie home in their mother's Volvo.

"If I had that stupid Camaro running, I could have picked you up in style," he had said.

"I'm just glad you came," Carrie said.

"Anything for my favorite sister."

"Um—I'm your only sister."

"Yeah, semantics, whatever," Adam said.

During the drive home, Adam pulled alongside any

red pickup truck so that Carrie could get a good look at the driver. She was almost glad it never was the guy who ran her off the road because her brother had a murderous look in his eyes.

The Subaru was a total loss so Carrie had co-opted her mom's Volvo to get to the VA. Arrangements to see the virtual reality demo were made with Cal Trent before the accident, and Dr. Finley had suggested they reschedule. Carrie convinced him otherwise. All DBS surgeries were on hold until Carrie was medically cleared to operate, and she felt useless just sitting around at home. More than anything, Carrie wanted to keep this appointment. Her suspicions were in full bloom, and she needed to learn more about the DARPA program posthaste. The best place to begin, she believed, was at the point in the process where those negative memories got reconsolidated.

Carrie checked the time to make sure she was not running late for the demo.

David saw her preparing to go and gave her a concerned look. "Are you sure you shouldn't just be in bed?" he asked.

Carrie brushed aside the suggestion. "I'm fine. Really."

David read something in Carrie's eyes. "You don't think it was road rage, do you?" he asked.

"A lot of things have happened since Abington and Fasciani went missing. The timing is more than a little unusual, don't you think?"

"But you told me Rockwell died of heart failure," David said.

The call with the sad news had come while Carrie was at the hospital waiting for Adam to show. Though she had never met Sam Rockwell in person, Carrie's emotions vacillated between stunned and heartbroken. The intensity of her feelings came as a surprise, but Carrie understood their origin. She and Rockwell were connected in ways that went beyond the operating room at the VA. Ways Carrie believed she was on the cusp of discovering.

"His body was incredibly damaged, and for the heart to stop was not a shock to anybody. Normally I would agree—but again, the timing makes me highly suspicious. I get run off the road, and suddenly he dies. Think about it."

"What about an autopsy?"

"There's not going to be one, according to Dr. Smerling. The family doesn't want it, and I can't start spouting conspiracy theories. The best way to find out what really happened to Sam is to keep the pressure on Goodwin."

"You really think there's a connection to Rockwell?" David asked.

"I don't think," Carrie said. "I know."

"You're sure Goodwin's not around?"

"I checked her schedule. She's in an all-day meeting. Are you sure you can get inside her office?"

David fished out the lock-pick kit from his pocket and showed it to Carrie with a smile. "Of course," he said. "I have the key."

Carrie wore her lab coat, and for that reason alone garnered plenty of curious looks while navigating the halls of the VA. It was one thing to see an injured person in a hospital, but something else entirely when that individual also happened to be a doctor. It set people on edge.

Dr. Finley, who had only spoken with Carrie by phone and had not seen her injuries, grimaced at the sight. "My goodness," he said, rising from his chair. He gave Carrie a warm embrace that conveyed utter relief.

"It looks worse than it feels," Carrie said, repeating what she'd told David. It was the same lie she told everyone.

"Well, I just hope they catch whoever did this to you."

Carrie thanked him, and he sat back down.

Dr. Finley glanced at the letter on his desk, written on his personal stationery. "I've spent the last hour trying to figure out what to say to Sam's wife," he said. "I'm just devastated. Nothing I write expresses how I really feel. I let my hopes get up when he came out of the coma, but now—" Dr. Finley slipped off his glasses and rubbed at his reddened eyes. Carrie got the feeling he had been crying. "Now, I just have memories."

"I'm so sorry for your loss. I wish I had gotten to know him."

"We were pioneers in this together from the start," Dr. Finley said. "We owe a lot to Sam. I owe a lot to him."

"He sounded like a wonderful man," Carrie said, and then fell silent. If anything, her eyes were even wider, her expression more empathetic. "Listen, Alistair, there's something I'd like to talk with you about."

Dr. Finley noticed Carrie's apprehension. "You look upset, Carrie. Please take a seat. I'll let Cal know we're running a few minutes late."

Carrie's anxiety bubbled like uncorked champagne

while Dr. Finley texted his message to Trent. He put his smartphone away and locked his gaze on Carrie. "Go on," he urged.

Although Carrie had planned what to say, the reality of the moment felt weighty and more difficult than anticipated. "My car accident happened in Maine," she began.

"Yes, you said you were there following up on an Abington lead."

"Yes and no," Carrie said. "I was headed to the hospital to see Sam."

Dr. Finley looked confused. "Sam? Heavens, why?"

Carrie said, "I wanted to know if he'd ever seen palinacousis in a DBS patient before. Specifically one of the PTSD patients."

Dr. Finley seemed mystified. Carrie watched him mull over the word "palinacousis," as if it was something he had heard before but could not put into any context. When it finally came to him, a surprised look came over his face. "Palinacousis? Good gracious, what on earth would make you want to ask him that?"

Carrie explained her encounter with Abington and later with Fasciani, and noted how both patients had disappeared. She also revealed her own self-doubt about causing the auditory hallucination in addition to the impaired judgment issues exhibited by both patients in their choice to leave the hospital AMA.

When she finished, Dr. Finley said, "And you thought you caused all this?" in a way that absolved Carrie of any responsibility.

"I admit my confidence was shaken when I started working here. And when they both presented with palinacousis, well, I naturally questioned my technique."

"To be honest here, Carrie," Dr. Finley said in an even tone, "I think you're reading symptoms that simply aren't there. Palinacousis? I've treated dozens of vets here and haven't seen a single case reported. And you watched me examine Ramón Hernandez. Did he seem off to you?"

"No," Carrie said. "Not at all."

Dr. Finley's puzzlement remained. "I've never seen a case of that in my whole career, and it's been a long career. But I have seen your work, and it's exemplary. There's no way you caused anything like that in these men. Impossible."

Carrie was not ready to back off. "What about the connection between Ramón Hernandez and Steve Abington," she said. "The two had met. I told you about the picture at Rita Abington's home."

Dr. Finley was unmoved. "I spoke to Cal about that and he did some digging. Steve was referred to the DARPA program through other channels, so their knowing each other is just a coincidence, that's all. But you can speak to Cal on that if you'd like."

Carrie agreed. For a moment she contemplated sharing her belief that Lee Taggart, the VA nurse, was also in the same photograph. But the evidence was not conclusive enough for her to stake that claim.

Dr. Finley leaned forward in his chair and set his hand over Carrie's in an avuncular gesture. In that moment, her convictions fell away and she felt foolish for confiding in Dr. Finley without first obtaining proof to support her claims.

If only she had found those men . . .

"But what about both Abington and Fasciani leaving AMA?" Carrie asked.

Dr. Finley shrugged it off. "Carrie, these men were unstable to begin with. And we exacerbate that problem by agitating them with the virtual reality."

Carrie saw the logic, but was not quite ready to back away. "And my getting run off the road and Sam dying on the same day? You don't see any connections there?"

Dr. Finley leaned back in his chair and cast Carrie a look of shock and disgust. His expression conveyed his belief that her insinuations bordered on the absurd.

"You said yourself it was road rage. Honestly, Carrie, I'm more worried I hired a conspiracy theorist than anything else. To be candid, I see you drawing a lot of lines between events that have no logical connections."

Carrie decided it was time to beat a hasty retreat. Dr. Finley was visibly bothered by her theory, his head shaking in disbelief. Several psychological causes explained conspiracy theorists, including anxiety disorders, paranoia, and psychosis. None of those labels would do her or her career any good.

While Carrie was not willing to abandon her search for the missing link that would connect these strange happenings in some logical manner, she would have to wait for the answers. Other questions of hers would have to wait as well. Was the jogger in the park really as harmless as he professed? Had someone other than Adam been in her room? Perhaps Dr. Finley was right, and those were unrelated events as well, but Carrie was not ready to concede. Surely the Goodwin recordings would reveal something—something that would convince Dr. Finley she was not a theorist at all.

Dr. Finley gathered his composure and stood. "So, can we put this behind us for the moment and concentrate on getting you better and getting us back to work?"

he asked. "I want us to finish what Sam and I started. We're on the verge of something important here, Carrie, and I'd rather focus our energies on the patients who want our help and not those who walked away."

"Yes," Carrie said. "I feel better just talking it out."

"Good," Dr. Finley said, clapping his hands together. "Now then, let's send you to war."

44

Carrie's stomach knotted when Dr. Finley pushed open the conference room door. What would she see through the looking glass? Would it help her better understand Adam, give her a glimpse into his world of constant fear? She could hardly imagine how horrible the simulation must have been, how real, how visceral, to elicit such a violent and disturbed reaction in Abington.

It was ironic, Carrie thought, that before she'd joined this endeavor to cure PTSD, she'd had no profoundly disturbing memories. Nothing of real substance she could draw upon as fodder for simulation. Now she had a whole host of experiences to use.

On the long table inside the windowless conference room, Carrie saw a laptop computer and some futuristic eyewear, a cross between ski goggles and wraparound sunglasses. The eyewear was connected to the laptop via a USB port. Calvin Trent stood to greet Carrie and Dr. Finley, wearing a blue suit that fit snugly against his broad shoulders. With Trent was the bald man Carrie had seen at grand rounds.

Trent extended a hand to Carrie, warmth entering his gray eyes. "Nice to see you again," he said. It was then he noticed Carrie's face. "Goodness, what happened to you?"

Carrie said, "Car accident."

Trent grimaced in solidarity. "Well, I'll make sure there are no car crashes in your simulation. I can imagine you have a little PTSD already from that experience. Wouldn't want to make things worse."

Carrie gave a little laugh. "Yeah, let's do that," she said.

Trent turned to his companion. "This is Bob Richardson," he said. "He's been helping with operations. Bob, this is Dr. Alistair Finley and Dr. Carrie Bryant with the VA."

Carrie watched Dr. Finley shake hands with Richardson for what appeared to be the first time, confirming her earlier belief that he had not been introduced to her at the grand rounds simply because the two had never met before.

A related question popped into Carrie's mind. "How many people are involved with this program?" she asked.

Trent said, "I'd say with all the technicians, and medical staff and such, we're probably close to a hundred."

"Close to a hundred," Carrie repeated. "Where is everybody?"

"Spread out," Trent said. "We don't have an official base of operations just yet. Believe it or not, the government is always looking to save a buck or two, so to minimize costs we utilize the workspace of our experts and consultants whenever possible."

"I explained to Carrie that there's a lot more going on here than just neurology and neurosurgery," Dr. Finley said.

Trent nodded in agreement. "That's correct. We have psychologists, physiologists, simulation technicians, a wide variety of specialists involved. There are even plans in the works for building a dormitory or semi-permanent housing, but for now vets in the program who come to us without a permanent residence have to settle for Motel Six, which is a lot nicer than the streets where most of them had been living. We have contracts in place with a car service to shuttle our program participants to all their various appointments."

Richardson said, "Having everything decentralized does create some operational challenges."

"I can't imagine driving Abington anywhere without an armed guard," Carrie said. The memory of Abington's assault replayed in her mind.

"I heard you had a terrible experience there," Richardson said in a sincerely apologetic tone.

Carrie said, "That's for sure."

Trent said, "We intentionally run the simulation on the premises here at the VA to minimize travel time. Once the DBS system is installed, most of the vets are a lot more docile, I can assure you. But I'm sorry about what happened to you."

"I'm assuming you know that he's gone," Carrie said to Trent. "Fasciani too. Both vanished."

Trent grimaced. "Yes, I'm aware. We're looking for both of them. Many in our program have issues with alcohol and drugs, which can lead to all sorts of erratic behavior."

"They left AMA," Carrie said. "We signed them out."

Trent looked at Dr. Finley. "Yes, Alistair told me. In fact, we have a meeting scheduled with Dr. Goodwin to come up with better protocols moving forward. We don't want this to become a trend. We're too close to finishing phase three."

"What's the next phase?" Carrie asked.

"Full deployment of the solution. Tested, validated, and FDA sanctioned. It's the game changer," Trent said.

Bob Richardson manipulated the laptop and did something to make the screen turn black.

"We're ready whenever you are, Cal," he said. Richardson spoke in a hard, dry voice. It was the voice of someone accustomed to commanding a crowd. He did not strike Carrie as a subordinate. Who was this guy, really?

"Are you ready, Carrie?" Trent asked.

Carrie had that funny feeling in the pit-in-her-stomach that preceded any roller coaster ride. "Sure thing," she said.

"We're using a simulation from one of our program participants," Richardson said. "But for privacy reasons, I'm not at liberty to tell you which one."

Carrie smiled politely. "Of course. I understand."

Carrie took a seat at the conference table with Richardson on her right, Trent on her left, and Dr. Finley across from her. The goggles were lightweight and fit over Carrie's head with minimum adjustments required. The earbuds slipped right into place. Through the lens Carrie could see only black.

"Are you ready?" Trent's voice was slightly muffled, but clear enough for Carrie to give him a thumbs-up sign.

Blackness gave way to light, and a desert scene unfolded in Carrie's view. A digitally rendered lone figure stood on a bridge that crossed over a sand-covered road. What appeared to be palm trees stood in the background, with a few scattered tufts of vegetation. In front of the bridge were two heavily armed and armored Humvees, and behind those vehicles were two kneeling soldiers, each holding automatic weapons.

While shadows and lighting enhanced the reality of the 3-D graphics, the scene itself still looked like something out of a video game. Adam could no longer play "Call of Duty," but Carrie had seen him shooting up the enemy enough times to be reminded of a light-weight version of that game.

The sound of Humvee engines rumbled in Carrie's ear, and the graphics began to move. First, the kneeling soldiers stood, and then the Humvees inched ahead. Carrie turned her head from side to side, but her field of view remained unchanged. This was more like watching a computer-generated movie than the total-immersion experience she had expected.

The Humvees rolled under the bridge with the two soldiers bringing up the rear. There was movement from the figure on the bridge, and Carrie saw him using what appeared to be a cell phone. The animation was close to the natural arcs and curves of the human body, but not quite there.

In her headphones, Carrie heard the sound of an explosion, and in the next instant the ground in front of the lead Humvee became a debris field. The now-mangled Humvee lifted several feet above the virtual ground before it crash-landed hard on four tires. The graphics showed the vehicle's shock absorbers doing their job as the wheels bounced several times before they finally settled. Dust and sand kicked skyward, but it was still video game dust and sand. While the whole sequence was surprising, Carrie did not find it overly frightening or hyper-realistic.

The gunmen on foot returned fire and shot at the man on the bridge, while three burned and bleeding soldiers crawled out from the wrecked Humvee. The graphics here were well done, and Carrie could see that two of the men had lost limbs, one an arm, and the other a leg. The third solider to climb out bled profusely from a head wound.

A second explosion followed. This one swallowed one of the two soldiers on foot. When that virtual dust cleared, the sand beneath the soldier's body was colored red, and he was without limbs. The surviving soldier fired at the man on the bridge, this time striking him somewhere—torso, head, it was difficult for Carrie to tell. The dead insurgent tumbled off the bridge and landed on the desert sand with a thud.

The scene faded to black and Carrie removed her headset.

Richardson appraised Carrie as if she might need to be sedated like Abington.

"Well, I hope that wasn't too traumatic for you," he said.

Carrie removed the earbuds and stared down at her lap for several seconds. When she looked up, Carrie's face showed signs of strain, and her composure was compromised.

"If you re-created my car accident, I'd be in tears right now," Carrie said. "I can only imagine what the soldiers go through after seeing their own worst nightmares replayed on screen."

Carrie glanced around the room and felt confident everyone believed her lie. She had expected so much more from the simulation, based on Abington's violent reaction.

Dr. Finley said, "The reconsolidation of the negative memory is a necessary albeit unfortunate step in the process. With the memory fresh in the mind, we can use electric stimulation to remove the emotion associated with the event. Ramón Hernandez can watch his virtual reality simulation now like it's the movie of the week, when before it would have sent him into a violent rage."

Carrie believed Adam could see a similar demo of his traumatic experience in Afghanistan, and while it might add a few notches to his blood pressure, that would be it. It was simply not believable enough, in her estimation, to incite such a strong emotional reaction. Carrie recalled the crazed look in Abington's eyes just before the attack, as well as the mysterious words he had uttered.

I don't belong here . . . I don't belong . . .

What had Trent really done to him prior to surgery?

By now, David had probably retrieved the recording device. Carrie could hardly wait to see him, to share what she had learned during the demo, and to listen in on Goodwin's private conversations. She had a strong feeling they would reveal something significant.

"Amazing, I'm really impressed," Carrie said. "Cal and Bob, I want to thank you for taking the time to arrange this demo for me. It really did open my eyes."

"You're very welcome," Trent said. "We view you as a vital part of this team, Carrie. I speak for Bob and the rest of the DARPA organization when I say how grateful we are to have you on board. And, not to be glib here, but I'm also hopeful you'll be able to operate with your injuries. If you asked Alistair, he'd say you're one of the best surgeons he's ever worked with. Everyone is simply devastated about what happened to Sam, but if we had to replace him, we're glad it's you at the helm."

Carrie returned a slight smile, no teeth showing. "I'm glad to be a part," she said. "And thank you for your endorsement. I really do appreciate it."

Carrie took out her phone and pretended to type a message. In reality, she had snapped a photo of Bob Richardson. With David's help, she hoped they could figure out who he really was.

45

Gabby, the little girl with pigtails, gave Carrie a delightful, gap-toothed smile and hugged her knees only because she was not tall enough to reach higher. Gabby's surprise embrace tugged at Carrie's heart. This complete sweetie pie paid no attention to Carrie's injuries. To her innocent eyes, Carrie was just a friend of her "Uncle David," as she called him, nothing more. There was no judgment, no pretense, nothing but total acceptance.

Carrie's heart warmed more when Gabby turned to David and gazed up at him with wide-eyed reverence.

"Can you play with me?" Gabby asked.

"In a little bit, sweetheart," David said. "I have some grown-up talk to do first."

Emma and Gabby had come up to David's apartment a minute or so after Carrie had arrived. At first Carrie felt a spark of jealousy when she saw how pretty Emma was, how put-together she seemed in her hip-hugging jeans and cute turquoise top, but the feeling passed quickly. Emma and David had an undeniable intimacy, but Carrie got the vibe it was not based on any romantic love. Try as she might, Carrie could not quite figure out what David did not see in Emma, or Emma in David, but she was not going to question it. She knew what she felt for David, and suspected he felt the same. Something was going to happen between them. She could see it in the way he looked at her, and feel it in the way his look made her skin tingle.

David took Carrie's phone and sent Emma the picture she'd taken.

Emma glanced at her phone's display and showed the photo to David and Carrie for confirmation. "This is the guy?"

The picture Carrie had taken included part of Cal Trent, but Bob Richardson was front and center.

"That's him," David said. "How good is the facial recognition software at the DMV?"

"Very good," Emma said. "We're required to run a one-to-many comparison before issuing a driver's license, permit, or ID."

"What's a one-to-many comparison?" Carrie asked.

Emma said, "One-to-many compares photos of an applicant with all the other customers on file at DMV. We get alerted if there are possible matches between customers under different names. We examine the possible matches to determine whether it's simply very similar-looking individuals, or possibly the same individual under different names."

"Sounds good to me," David said.

"Me too," Carrie said. "But what if he's not a licensed Massachusetts driver?"

Emma shrugged. "We have a new data-sharing

initiative to give law enforcement agencies more access to our data. I've helped with the rollout, so I have contacts who could do a search for me if I don't get any local hits. I used it before to locate Rita Abington's address. Give me a few days on this," Emma said.

"Thanks," David said. "I really appreciate it."

Emma collected Gabby from the toy corner, and together they left David's apartment with some substantial protests that could be heard while the pair descended the stairs.

"She's such a cutie pie," Carrie said.

"She's the best," David said. "Her dad doesn't know what he's missing."

Carrie suspected David would make a terrific father, someone who would be patient, kind, and capable. The thought made him more attractive to her. David's cozy apartment was similar to her old place in Brookline. It was bright, airy, and sparsely furnished. She wanted to take a closer look at the many photographs lining his wall, but that would have to wait. They had business to discuss.

"Tell me about the VR before we listen to the recording," David said.

Carrie recounted her experience in the neurology unit conference room in considerable detail.

David seemed troubled by what he heard. "There was no position tracking?" he asked after she had finished.

"No, it was more like watching a movie. The view didn't change when I moved my head."

"This is DARPA," David said, sounding incredulous. "You'd think they would have the most sophisticated technology available. A completely immersive experience."

"That's what I thought, too. Something didn't seem right about it."

"Let's have a listen to those recordings," David said.

He set up the two portable speakers on a scuffed coffee table and plugged in a connecting cable. While this was going on, an orange tabby cat padded out from the bedroom, gracefully leapt from the floor onto the sofa, and immediately began to knead the cushion with its claws.

"That's Bosra," David said. "This is his favorite spot. Well, mine too. We nap here a lot."

Within a few seconds the cat had condensed into a tight ball, so that no part of its body existed outside the beam of sunlight that streamed through the tall bay window. Bosra purred delightedly when Carrie scratched behind the ears.

"How long have you had him?" Carrie asked.

"Her," David corrected. "About a year. She's a rescue."

Carrie imagined David and Bosra taking long naps together on this very couch, and believed it had enough room for all three to partake.

As if reading her thoughts, David sat down on the other side of Carrie so Bosra would not be disturbed. He pressed Play on the recording device and a burst of static gave way to the sound of a phone ringing.

"It's noise-activated," David explained. "So there may be a lot of ringing phones before we hear any actual dialogue. Hopefully we won't have to listen to your colleague, Evan, having sex."

Carrie knew all about Evan's sexcapades in Goodwin's office, as well as David's gravity-defying stint underneath the desk. It was a glimpse into the lengths he would go for the story, and gave Carrie a keener understanding of how David had ended up a prisoner of the Syrian opposition forces.

The recorded phone rang once more. Somebody answered on the second ring, and Carrie knew the woman's voice immediately—Goodwin. Though Carrie was privy to only half of the conversation, she could tell it was a vendor calling about an intracranial pressure monitoring device. Goodwin sounded uninterested from the start. She ended the call with the terse parting words, "Let me get back to you when I have time."

A number of unrelated conversations had been recorded over several days, and Carrie and David listened to each without learning anything especially interesting about Goodwin. She chatted with Evan pleasantly enough, always about the VA. It was utterly unrevealing. Goodwin gave a resident some thoughtful advice, which Carrie thought a bit out of character for the ice queen. Twice Goodwin spoke by phone with her mother, and Carrie got the distinct impression a vendor call would have been more welcome.

It was not until the third day of recordings that Carrie heard a new voice, an older voice she recognized: Cal Trent. It took Carrie just a few seconds to realize Goodwin had an edge to her voice.

"Hello, Cal," Goodwin said. "Have a seat."

According to the time stamp on the recording device, the conversation took place two days after Carrie's accident.

"Thanks, Sandra. How are you?"

"I'm fine. Need anything to drink?"

"No, I'm fine. What's up? Why the urgency?"

"I'm worried," Goodwin said. "I think we need to scale back. Even go dark."

Cal's laugh expressed his utter contempt for the idea. "Good one," he said. "What's next on your agenda, Sandra?"

"Please, Cal."

"The pipeline is full. We're moving forward. That's the plan."

Carrie glanced at David's notepad, where he jotted the word "pipeline" and put a question mark after it.

"I don't think that's a good idea," Goodwin said on the recording.

"And how will the board take it when we pull funding for your movable prosthetics initiative?" Trent asked. "How many of the millions we've committed to the VA have already been spent? That's not something your bosses are going to give up on easily. A lot of questions will be raised. A lot of fingers will be pointed at you. And then I think you'll point them back at me. And we can't have that, can we? I'm not trying to be subtle or coy here, Sandy. I think you get my meaning. I've got a pipeline of patients to send your way and we're going to send them. You get that DBS surgery done. That's your job. And you let me do the rest."

Silence.

"Are we all set here?" Trent asked.

"We're all set," Goodwin said, her voice going soft.

Carrie and David heard background noise as Trent got up from his chair, opened the office door, and closed it. The recording picked up Goodwin's labored breathing and other sounds: a desk drawer opening up, a squeaking chair, and the click of Goodwin's key-board as she furiously typed a message.

David shut off the recorder and turned to face Carrie. "What exactly is a movable prosthetic?" He glanced at his notes. "I'm assuming it's not what's commonly out there."

David's eyes had gone wild. Bosra perked up her head, yawned, stretched, climbed down off the sofa, and padded away. Evidently the energy in the room had become too much for her to handle.

"I'm sure he's talking about reliable neural-interface technology, RE-NET," Carrie said. "I've attended a few lectures about it at different neurosurgery conferences over the years. One lecture showed a video demonstration of a man using targeted muscle re-innervation to pick up a coffee cup."

"Re-innervation?" David repeated for confirmation. "Is that like the re-animation of nerves?"

"Very much so," Carrie said, nodding. "There are still nerves firing even after a limb is severed. It's just that the signal doesn't go anywhere. With computers, robotics, and a whole lot of sophistication, a prosthetic can learn to recognize these signals and contract the muscles like a working limb. TRM-controlled prosthetics is very cutting-edge stuff."

"And there's nothing like it at the VA currently?"

She shook her head. "Not that I know of, but I'm just a technician, remember." Carrie said "technician" with exaggerated contempt.

"Is it possible that Trent is getting his DBS patients from outside the system?"

"That's what it sounded like to me," Carrie said. "Patients come to the VA through a very bureaucratic process. If someone is bypassing that system, there's got to be a good reason for it."

"Maybe Goodwin wanted to minimize your role at the VA to keep you from finding out what that circumvention was all about?"

Carrie processed David's words. "Maybe the last DBS surgeon got too close to that answer," she said.

Now it was David's turn to process. "What have you gotten yourself into here, Carrie?" he asked.

"I don't know," Carrie said. "I really don't know."

They listened to hours of Sandra being Sandra, and found nothing of further interest on those recordings—nothing incriminating, nothing to explain what she and Cal were doing.

David put his hands behind his head, stretched, and looked to the ceiling.

"Anneke is going to be pretty ticked off at me," David said.

"Yeah? Why's that?" Carrie asked.

"Because I got a feeling this story is going to take a hell of a long time for me to write."

46

Carrie returned to the VA the following morning, unsure what the next step should be. She had hoped David's plan would provide further clarity, but instead it created more seemingly unconnected threads. How did Abington's and Fasciani's disappearances relate to Goodwin's ambitions with regards to reliable neural-interface technology? How did Abington come to join the DBS program? How many vets had been treated? Where were they all living?

These were questions that extended far beyond her purview. She was at the VA to drill and to insert wires, and nothing more. Sandra Goodwin had erected a wall between her and the patients' postoperative care for a very specific reason. But what was it? And who exactly was Bob Richardson? Carrie felt confident he was more than a bit player in Cal Trent's world. In this way, Dr. Finley appeared marginalized as well. Trent's operation included a cast of unknowns, of people who played pivotal roles and were introduced only on a need-to-know basis.

In the intervening hours from when she heard the recording to her return to the hospital, Carrie did some digging on Cal Trent and sent an e-mail to David with a fairly exhaustive dossier. Admittedly, it gave them no real insights. Trent got his BS in mechanical engineering from the University of Miami, and went on to receive an MBA from Northwestern. He was an associate with the consulting firm McKinsey & Company, and worked for BEA Systems before he found employment with DARPA. Trent had been married for eighteen years, with two kids and a permanent residence in Bethesda. He seemed like a regular guy, though graft and corruption stained the noblest professions.

Carrie and David agreed not to play the recording for anybody—not Dr. Finley, and certainly not the police. They had nothing criminal to investigate, just a lot of innuendo. As for Dr. Finley, if he knew Carrie had secretly recorded Sandra Goodwin, she'd be fired in a heartbeat, and any hope of closure would be lost. So long as Dr. Finley employed her, Carrie could investigate Goodwin and Trent from the shadows.

Until Carrie was officially cleared to operate, all DBS procedures were on hold, and waiting patients would need to be rescheduled. During this downtime, Dr. Finley informed Carrie of his plans to conduct neurological exams on both DBS and regular VA patients, and get caught up on some backlogged paperwork. Carrie could not stay at home and do nothing all day, so she came to the VA to get caught up on her journal reading—or so she said to Dr. Finley. In reality, Carrie was there to keep her eyes and ears open.

When Dr. Finley invited Carrie to join him in examining another vet from the DBS program, Carrie jumped at the chance. It was Ramón Hernandez redux. This vet's name was Terry Bushman, an über-fit male in his early thirties with short-cropped blond hair, his arms covered with tattoos and scars. Carrie asked the same questions of Bushman as she had of Hernandez. The answers were decidedly similar. No experience with voice illusion, no issues with his DBS, and while he expressed lingering PTSD symptoms, they were not nearly as debilitating as before. Same as Hernandez, there was some asymmetry of Bushman's neck where the stimulating wires had been tunneled from the scalp, and he had small scars on the chest where the generator was placed.

Near the end of the exam, Carrie asked Bushman to tell her how he got involved in the program.

"I was living at a halfway house," Bushman said. He had a youthful voice, like a California surfer. "So, these guys from DARPA show up, give me all sorts of psych testing, and next I know I'm living at a different halfway house outside of Boston with wires in my head. Simple as that."

Carrie had wondered if Ramón had recruited Bushman, or if he had ever met Abington or Fasciani. The answers were no to all. Carrie got some background on Bushman, and it seemed he had a decent relationship with his family, nothing like Abington. Carrie was willing to accept a dead end when she hit one. But still something did not make sense. Why would two vets seem perfectly fine and two others exhibit strange neurological behaviors?

Carrie joined Dr. Finley in the cafeteria for a post-exam coffee. It was approaching dinnertime, and Bushman was Dr. Finley's last patient of the day.

He was exuberant as ever. "I think in another week you should be recovered enough to get back to the OR," he said. "When I first met Terry, he suffered from debilitating uncomplicated PTSD with persistent reexperiencing of the traumatic event, had trouble with crowds because he associated the stimuli with the trauma, and there was a lot of self-medicating going on. Now look at him."

"It is impressive," Carrie admitted.

"We have four cases like Terry Bushman and Ramón Hernandez. Four. Once we get to ten, I think we'll be able to trumpet success."

"What about the others?" Carrie asked.

Dr. Finley's glow dimmed. "Not everyone gets better, Carrie. Not every drug, not every therapy works a miracle. But these four represent the possibilities. We need to stay positive."

"Do you mind if I look over your patient records?"

Dr. Finley's prominent eyebrows rose an inch or so. "Um, I guess. Sure. Mind if I ask why?"

"Call it professional curiosity. I just really want to know these men."

Carrie got a quick nod of approval.

"Yes, of course," he said. "I'll pull them together for you and you can look at them in the morning."

Those files, Carrie believed, would show her whether other vets left the neuro recovery unit under special circumstances like Abington and Fasciani.

"Thanks, that would be great," she said.

Dr. Finley stood. "Time for me to go home," he said. "You should do the same. I'm worried you're going to push yourself too hard."

Carrie thanked him for his concern, and returned to her office to gather her things. She was there only a few minutes before someone knocked on her door. Carrie's heart nearly stopped at the sight of Sandra Goodwin lurking in the open doorway, as if she'd been there watching for some time.

Without an invitation, Goodwin entered Carrie's incommodious office, sporting a chilly smile. She wore her hair up in a tight bun, and the harsh glare of the fluorescents highlighted the severe angles of her face. Goodwin's sharp eyes bore down on Carrie in a way that turned her blood to ice.

"Carrie, I'm glad I caught you," Goodwin said in a honey-dripped voice. "Do you have a minute?"

"I was just heading out," Carrie said.

"This won't take long," Goodwin said coolly.

"Sure," Carrie said. "What can I do for you?"

"I think you and I got off on the wrong foot," Goodwin said. "And I'd like for us to be friends."

Because you know I'm on to you, Carrie thought.

"Sandra, I really don't know what you're talking about. I've kept a clear line between my job and what Evan does ever since our little chat. If you want to be professionally cordial, then perhaps you'll explain to me why you signed Abington and Fasciani out AMA." Carrie almost let slip something about reliable neural-interface technology, which could have been disastrous if Goodwin found out she'd been bugged.

"I told Dr. Finley I had little choice. They were both extremely insistent."

"I saw Fasciani after his surgery. He was so doped up on Valium I don't see how he could have done that."

Something flashed in Goodwin's expression that gave Carrie shivers. "You saw him?" Goodwin asked. "Could you explain yourself, please?"

Carrie's chest tightened. Goodwin had her trapped. *Dammit!*

"Yes, I went up to see him after my surgery," Carrie admitted. "I honestly think this policy of yours is ludicrous."

"Think what you will," Goodwin said in a sharp-edged voice. "It's my law, and I'm surprised and more than a little disappointed you decided to ignore the directive."

"Well, I apologize," Carrie said, rather insincerely. "But you need to see this from my point of view."

"You weren't credentialed by us, Carrie, and for that reason alone you have no business interacting with the patients outside the OR. I thought this was clear."

Goodwin leaned against a wall and let her white lab coat fall open to show off the scrubs she wore underneath, as if Carrie needed the reminder they both were surgeons.

"Eric could not have possibly given his consent," Carrie said. "He was too drugged."

"But he did," Goodwin retorted. "I was called to the floor and I signed the papers after he issued his demands. I spent time trying to talk him out of it. I'm sorry I don't have any of those conversations recorded so you could believe me." She gave Carrie a foxy grin.

Carrie held her breath, paralyzed, expecting any moment to be accused of spying.

"What do you want me to say, Sandra? I'm not at all comfortable with how you've handled this. I did an invasive procedure on two men who checked out AMA and subsequently vanished. Something isn't right."

Goodwin took a step into Carrie's office and gave a look meant to incite fear. "I'll tell you what isn't right," Goodwin said. "I have a presentation due in a couple days for an upcoming meeting with the top brass here. I have to go through every surgical procedure from the past year and catalogue every complication. That's going to take me hours. If you so want to be a part of this team, I think you should do the work."

"Me?" Carrie could not contain her incredulousness.

"It would be a shame to inform the VA of your unwillingness to follow my rules. I could get you suspended in about five minutes, and fired in a day. You'll be out of here quicker than it takes me to fill out an AMA form."

Carrie eyed Goodwin with disgust. "That's blackmail," she said.

"No, Carrie darling, it's called being a team player. Stay right here. I'll come down with the files. You don't have access to the electronic system, so I'm afraid paper will have to do. And I'm afraid you can't remove anything from the premises. But that's okay. You're used to working late nights, aren't you?"

The glimmer in Goodwin's eyes dimmed, along with her phony smile.

47

"Drained" did not capture Carrie's whole-body exhaustion. The stacks of medical records took up most of her desk space. The work was decidedly tedious and excruciatingly time-consuming. Many of the files Carrie reviewed were several inches thick and offered no means by which to conduct a keyword search for complications. Carrie had to painstakingly review each case down to the last period. She could have punted on the whole thing, done a half-baked job, but that was not in her nature. If she were going to do something, even scut work, she'd do it right.

That was just her wiring.

The complications Carrie recorded on her impressive spreadsheet were commonplace and did not denote a pattern of incompetence, or at least nothing Carrie could derive from the data. The VA might not have state-of-the-art equipment like White Memorial, but it appeared to be a first-class facility with top-notch surgeons. Even though Carrie thought Navarro was an ass, and Goodwin a shrew, they each performed their respective roles admirably and even, at times, in exemplary form.

Carrie's grueling residency had trained her for endurance work, and she probably could have gone another hour before giving in to fatigue. Thankfully, that was unnecessary. Carrie closed the last manila folder and fired off a tersely worded e-mail to Goodwin with her Excel spreadsheet attached. Her findings corresponded with well-established industry standards. Stereotactic radiosurgery, more commonly known as "gamma knife" surgery, had the lowest rate of complications. By contrast, transsphenoidal surgery, a relatively safe procedure, had a statistically significant number of issues. The other surgical complications Carrie came across ran the gamut and included hematomas, infection, and leakage of cerebrospinal fluid. There were a number of non-neurosurgical complications like deep venous thrombosis, and a few cases of pulmonary emboli, cardiac arrhythmias, blood sugar and electrolyte imbalances, but all in all, the VA seemed to be well within the norm of surgical maladies.

Carrie massaged her eyes and took a long drink of the Diet Coke that had kept her alert these many hours. While Goodwin may have won the battle, the victor in the larger war had yet to be determined. Carrie was going to blow the lid off Goodwin's dealings with Trent. It was just a matter of time.

Carrie shut down her computer, collected her purse, and turned out the lights. Her depleted resolve sparked back to life as she closed and locked her office door. But the feeling was fleeting. Her limbs were heavy with fatigue, and the idea of making the long drive home seemed intolerable, perhaps even dangerous. Studies proved drowsy driving was equivalent to drunk driving, and her eyes were already closing. The on-call room beckoned her, and Carrie gave in. Four or five hours or so of sleep and she could be back at her desk, looking through the files Dr. Finley had promised to provide by morning.

Carrie headed to the on-call room through hospital halls that were deathly quiet, eerily so. She reached the stairwell without encountering a single person, unusual for any time, day or night. The harsh glare of the white vinyl floor was like needles in her eyes. Carrie made an unusually quick ascent to the third floor. A creeping fear tickled at the back of her neck that hastened her strides. Maybe it was the jogger in the park, or the car crash, but the quiet made her jittery.

All three on-call rooms were vacant, and Carrie opted for the one at the far end of the hall. She locked the door behind her and glanced at the time on the analog clock mounted to the concrete wall.

Three o'clock in the morning.

What a brutal day.

Carrie plumped down on the thin, unforgiving mattress and heard every click in her stiff and achy joints. At least she had on scrubs, which were just as good as pajamas, if not better.

For a moment she felt incredibly alone and lonely and wished David was with her. But the feeling faded as Carrie closed her eyes. Even her resentment and anger toward Goodwin could not keep her from drifting off. Exhaustion took over, and thoughts of David and

Goodwin receded into the back of Carrie's consciousness. Her body melted into the bed, legs and arms became heavy as her breathing turned shallow.

The minute hand on the clock ticked off seconds like a hypnotic metronome. Then the noise was gone. All noise was gone.

Then sleep.

At last sleep, finally sleep.

Until something woke her.

Carrie's eyes fluttered open. She had no idea how long she'd been out. A few minutes? A few hours? The darkness was impenetrable, and she could not see the clock on the wall. Her body felt queasy, off-kilter from having woken up so suddenly. Her eyes would adjust to the dark, but right now Carrie could not make out any shapes at all. She might as well have been blindfolded. But her ears worked just fine and they picked up a faint noise, the slight sound of a metallic click. That noise must have awoken her. Carrie listened, but the only sound now was her heart slamming against her ribs.

The noise came again, and this time it was distinct and distinguishable. It was the sound of a doorknob turning ever so slightly. The soft jiggle of the handle boomed in Carrie's ears, and the click of the cylinder as it turned thundered loud as a crashing wave. She was about to call out that the room was occupied when a terrifying thought came to her. She had locked the door! The knob should not be turning at all, and yet it was. David had shown her how easily he manipulated those antiquated lock tumblers with a pick and a tension wrench. This was not just a resident looking for a place to crash. Somebody specifically wanted to get into her room.

Carrie's heart lodged in her throat, beating like a hummingbird's wings. Terror turned her skin clammy. She heard the noise again, a steady creak like the winding of a spring. Her thoughts raced. This corridor was empty. She could call out for help, but whoever was beyond that door would be on her in a flash. If he had a knife, a gun, her time in this life would be over.

The door opened a crack. Carrie held her breath and somehow managed to keep perfectly still. Her eyes remained open, but only as slits. She wanted to appear to be sleeping, the equivalent of playing dead.

Light from the hallway illuminated the silhouette of an imposing figure entering her room. He was at least six feet tall, and solidly built. Carrie's breathing turned ragged and every effort she made to slow it faltered. The intruder had to think she was sound asleep, unaware. Her body heated as fear took hold.

This can't be happening . . . this is a dream . . . a nightmare . . . Wake up, Carrie! Wake up!

But she was awake, and it was a battle not to scream.

The man closed the door behind him, but left it open so a bit of light seeped in. He needed to see to attack. It was enough light for Carrie to track his approach. Breathing through her nose, Carrie could not seem to take in enough air. If she hyperventilated, he would know she was awake.

The man took another silent step toward her. Carrie dug her fingers into the bedsheets as if she were dangling from a cliff. She saw the pillow in his hands, presumably one taken from an adjacent on-call room. He had not come here to sleep. She was certain this man had entered her room with the intention of smothering her to death.

As her mind clicked over, Carrie understood the plan's sickening simplicity. No blood. No screams. No loud noise of any sort. She could be disposed of in a relatively clean manner; her body could be removed from the building in a laundry bin.

The assassin remained absolutely calm. Carrie's panic induced feelings of paralysis she prayed to overcome. There would be a moment, a precise opportunity, when surprise would be her singular advantage.

He reached the edge of her bed and looked down at her. He watched her sleep. She could hear his soft breathing and feel his smothering presence. She kept her body rigid and still as the dead. Through her peripheral vision she watched the man lift up the pillow.

Wait, Carrie . . . wait . . . not yet . . .

The anticipation became agony. Carrie held her breath and tried to keep her face muscles from twitching.

The man took his time. She was asleep, after all. He maneuvered the pillow over her face like a bombardier setting his sights on a building below.

At the last possible second, Carrie lashed out with a punch that connected solidly with the man's unguarded testicles. She heard him make an agonized sound, one that gurgled up from his gut and came out as a hiss of air. The man dropped to his knees, disabled.

Wasting no time, Carrie scrambled off the bed and darted for the door.

48

From behind, Carrie heard the man call, "You bitch," and felt his strong hand grab her ankle. With her free leg, Carrie kicked blindly backward and connected hard with something—his face, his chest, something.

The blow was enough to knock him off balance. The man let out a yowl, more angry than hurt. His grip weakened and Carrie wiggled her ankle free from his grasp. Any hesitation could be fatal. Carrie bolted for the door, reaching it in one long stride. She spilled into the empty hallway at the same instant a scream, like a low, moaning train whistle, tumbled from her lips.

"Help me," Carrie wailed, breaking into a frantic sprint. "Please! Somebody!"

The VA was already like a crypt, and the on-call rooms were purposely out of the way, to maximize quiet. A cardiac care unit was on the other side of the floor, Carrie remembered, but she would never outrun her attacker.

The stairwell entrance was in front of her, about thirty feet away. On the wall adjacent to that door a red fire alarm caught Carrie's eye. Surviving meant reaching one of the lower levels. She slowed to keep from ramming the door full speed. Her feet skidded on the vinyl floor as if it were made of ice. With her left hand, Carrie ripped the stairwell door open, and with her right hand she reached out and pulled the alarm. The strobe mounted above the stairwell started to flash and a series of loud beeps sounded like a fleet of trucks backing up.

Carrie took only two steps and jumped the remaining stairs. Her momentum carried her into the concrete wall of the landing below. She bounced off the wall, but managed to stay on her feet. The piercing alarm drowned out most of her screams.

Above her, the man appeared in the doorway like some nightmare incarnate. He made the same leap Carrie did, just as she reached the bottom of the next set of stairs. Her pursuer ping-ponged off the concrete wall, but quickly regained his footing, and was soon on the move again.

Carrie knew police were nearby. The VA Police were well-armed officials with full police powers to enforce all federal laws. At least one VA Police officer would be stationed at the front entrance—with luck, more. Descending rapidly, Carrie heard her footfalls reverberate in the stairwell as she crossed the landing to the next flight of stairs. Behind her the man's wretched, rage-filled grunts intensified, and grew closer. His pace had quickened.

Carrie stumbled down the next flight of stairs and used her wrists to absorb most of the shock as her body careened off an unforgiving cement wall. One more flight to go.

She screamed as loud as her lungs permitted, "Help me!" Impossible to know if anyone heard her. The crack of a gunshot roared from somewhere above, followed by the sound of concrete splintering as a bullet struck the wall. Carrie made another long jumper's leap with a cat's grace. She reached the bottom landing just as another shot rang out and hit the wall near her head. The bullet sent shards of concrete in every direction. Carrie launched herself against the steel panic bar and used her body weight to throw the door open.

She tumbled out into the first-floor hallway. The fire alarm was loud, and strobe lights blinked everywhere. She would have to make a long run down an empty corridor to get help and would be an easy target even for a poor shot. Her eyes went to the wheelchair pushed up against the wall.

Wasting no time, Carrie gathered the folded wheelchair and took up position against the wall. A second later the hulking monster burst through the door with his weapon drawn.

With an explosive motion, Carrie shoved the wheelchair out in front of her, catching her attacker completely unaware. The strike connected at the lower part of the man's legs, and he went toppling forward, over the wheelchair, arms outstretched to brace his fall. He landed hard, and the force of his fall dislodged the gun from his hand. The weapon skated down the hall, maybe ten feet from Carrie. She was already headed in that direction, but so was her pursuer. His athleticism was nothing short of extraordinary as he got back to his feet in a blink.

Her focus was on the gun. It seemed counterintuitive, but going for the weapon would get her killed. He was fast as a puma and would be on her the second she picked up the gun. But there was another solution: keep *him* from getting the gun. Without breaking stride, Carrie gave the pistol a solid kick with her right foot, and it slid like a shuffleboard piece a good distance.

Carrie bellowed at the top of her lungs: "Somebody help me!"

"Bitch!" The man's harsh voice felt like claws raking her back.

Carrie gave the gun another solid kick. She made it halfway down the hall and prayed help was nearby. Up ahead, Carrie saw movement. Her focus sharpened on a police officer with his gun drawn. He came charging forward, and close on his heels were two sizable orderlies. Carrie kept up her sprint, but something told her the man behind her had slowed. She glanced over her shoulder and saw him turn to go the other direction. But from that end of the hall another armed police officer appeared, accompanied by two additional security guards. The VA might not have all the best medical equipment, but budget constraints did not extend to security. The hospital was a military target and therefore heavily guarded.

"Freeze!" one of the policemen shouted. "Hands in the air."

Carrie ran into the arms of an orderly. Soon, she was barricaded behind a wall of people. The man who had chased her was trapped between two groups of security personnel, and they were closing in fast.

Their sharp voices, audible over the piercing alarm, commanded him to get down on the ground. He wore hospital scrubs like an orderly, and filled them out like a football player, but she had never seen him at the VA before. But she had seen him, hadn't she? The jawline, perhaps that was most familiar. His face was handsome and covered with hard guy's stubble. His gray, wolflike eyes held a devilish glint as he slowly raised his hands. Carrie stayed locked on his every movement. He paused to bite his wrist as his hands came over his head. The curious smile on his face was directed right at Carrie.

Police approached with caution, and again ordered the man to get facedown on the floor. He obliged. Carrie stood back and watched the surreal events unfold from a safe distance. A second wave of security moved in, and quickly had the man's hands bound with steel handcuffs. He lifted his head slightly off the floor, still keeping his menacing gaze locked on Carrie. His hateful eyes held a secret; Carrie could feel it.

The police swarmed the area, speaking to each other and to their captive. Just then, the man started to grunt, not once but several times, as if he had something lodged in his throat. He began to writhe and froth at the mouth. His legs went completely spasmodic. He wiggled like a distressed worm. Carrie thought she knew what had happened. When he put his mouth to his wrist, he'd ingested something—sodium cyanide perhaps, the more lethal of the two cyanide salts.

The police realized their captive was in distress and flipped him on his back. "We need a doctor!" one police officer shouted.

Carrie rushed to help. The instinct to triage trumped what this monster had done to her, and what he almost did. She was a doctor, but this was a hopeless case.

She knew the highly toxic chemical interferes with the body's ability to use oxygen, and the brain dies within minutes of ingestion. It took four men to lift the convulsing detainee off the ground and onto a stretcher.

The man frothed at the mouth, gurgled and choked, until he went still and fell silent. Carrie knew he had expired, but they would try to revive him. Cyanokit and sodium thiosulfate were both cyanide antidotes administered intravenously.

At that point he was in full respiratory distress, and Carrie ran alongside his stretcher, administering chest compressions over the middle of the chest. It was at this moment Carrie noticed a mark on the man's neck. She looked closely.

A tattoo of a shamrock.

49

Detective Kowalski from the Boston PD would be showing up soon. Carrie tried to calm her crackling nerves, but was gripped by an icy terror. Six hours after the attack she could feel the man's powerful hand wrapped around her ankle. The VA Police arranged transport, since she was too rattled to drive, and they also set up the meeting with the Boston PD.

David drove up to the Bryants' home in a Zipcar rental and followed Carrie to her bedroom for a private conversation. The police would want to know why somebody had tried to kill her, and she wanted David's help with her answer. For a while, neither could speak. Carrie's body shook as though suffering a chill. She was exhausted physically and mentally and it was David's news that pulled her from the fog of fear.

"I know who Bob Richardson is," he announced. "Emma finally accessed the database the DMV shared with law enforcement and came up with a hundred percent facial match."

Bob Richardson, according to the bio David printed off the corporate Web site, was a senior vice president at CerebroMed, a Virginia-based biopharmaceutical company focused primarily on discovering drugs affecting cerebral function.

"What the heck is Bob Richardson doing giving me a virtual reality demo?"

"Are there any drug trials involved with what you're doing?" David asked.

Carrie felt her senses sharpening. Having something to focus on helped her to settle.

"No," Carrie said. "Unless Goodwin and Trent are doing something Dr. Finley and I don't know about."

"Which we know she is."

"But what?" Carrie asked.

"What if Goodwin is letting Trent experiment on these patients with a drug of some sort—maybe related to PTSD, maybe not—and in exchange she receives money for her advanced neurological procedures?"

Carrie mulled this over. "I thought the virtual reality was insufficient," she said. "But a drug? Now *that* could explain the palinacousis, some sort of side effect."

"Yeah, a side effect," David said. "One that Goodwin hid by getting those patients off the floor."

Carrie nodded. "She wanted them gone. They weren't exhibiting poor judgment after all. She *made* them sign out AMA."

"Not every patient has the side effect," David said. "That was always one of our working assumptions. You just happened to investigate two who did."

"It would explain why Goodwin didn't want me to

check in on any of my patients post-op. She didn't want me to discover the side effect and alert somebody. It would have thrown the program into disarray. The vets would be subjected to a battery of tests and maybe the drug would be discovered. Game over."

David thought. "You've got some success stories, though, right?"

"So far I've met Ramón Hernandez and Terry Bushman. But Dr. Finley mentioned two others."

"Maybe the side effects are temporary in some cases, so they just need time to clear."

"It's possible," Carrie said.

"Can you get access to the patient records of the vets who have been treated with DBS?"

"I had asked Dr. Finley if I could see them before I was attacked," Carrie said. "Why?"

"It would be interesting to see if any other vets left the neuro recovery unit like Abington and Fasciani. And speaking of your boss, what about him?"

Carrie looked incredulous. "Who? Alistair? No," she said. Alistair was Carrie's confidant, her mentor, the man who had given her career new life—but she could discount his involvement for other reasons, too.

"He didn't even know Richardson," Carrie said, "and he had plenty of opportunities to introduce him to me. I think I have a pretty good read on people, and Alistair's commitment is to the patients, to this program. He didn't care that I went looking for Abington and Fasciani. He encouraged it. The problem was Goodwin—who, by the way, signed those AMA forms. She's the last link in the chain. Alistair has had my back with Goodwin since day one. There's a reason Goodwin has had it out for me from the get-go. She didn't want me on staff, and was very vocal about it."

David looked intrigued. "Goodwin runs the surgical staff, right?"

"That's right," Carrie said.

"So what about Rockwell?"

Carrie said, "I was a special hire by Dr. Finley, but Sam Rockwell was on Goodwin's staff from the start, and a fully accredited VA neurosurgeon."

"So Goodwin didn't want you hired."

"Another reason I think the buck stops with her."

"She gave you that bogus assignment, knowing you would be at the hospital late," David said.

Carrie went pale. "You think Goodwin set me up to be killed?"

"It's possible," David said. "And perhaps she did the same to Rockwell."

"What do you mean?"

"What if Dr. Finley didn't know what Goodwin was up to, but Rockwell did?" David said.

Carrie considered this. "Rockwell knew," she said in a soft voice. "He had to. Maybe he wanted out, or was going to blow the whistle, or something. That's why they tried to kill him."

"And he was as good as dead, too," David said. "At least until he started to wake up."

A sour, acidic taste burned the back of Carrie's throat. "Goodwin must have known I was on my way to see him," she said.

"It's possible Rockwell's doc called Goodwin to report a change in his condition. He was her employee, after all, so they probably had some kind of relationship. The other doctor might have mentioned you were coming up to see him."

"And Goodwin told Trent," Carrie said. "So what do we tell the police?" Carrie stopped pacing and sat on the edge of the bed beside David.

"We don't have much evidence," David said. "We have a recording that really doesn't validate anything we just discussed. Everything here is conjecture, not proof. We go to the police with what we have, and the whole operation could go dark. Evidence could be destroyed, or worse, those missing vets might be permanently silenced—like Rockwell."

Carrie sat back on the bed and leaned against the wall to keep from tipping over. Fatigue seeped into her bones, leaving her completely enervated. A feeling of dread had wormed into her gut and Carrie clamped a hand over her mouth to stifle a sob.

"What have I gotten myself into?" she muttered, just barely holding it together.

David took hold of Carrie's hand. He held her gaze until the fear swirling inside calmed like a windless sea. In that moment, the only sound Carrie could hear was her own racing heart. She felt strangely hypnotized by the flecks of gold that ringed David's penetrating eyes.

For the first time, Carrie noticed the scar across David's cheek and wondered if he got that in Syria, or some other dangerous place he called the office. For a moment his touch completely possessed her, and blocked out all other sensations.

"Whatever you decide," David said, still holding her hand, "I'll be with you every step of the way."

Carrie's mother called from downstairs, "Sweetheart, Detective Kowalski is here."

Detective Kowalski sipped from the mug of tea Howard Bryant had replenished. After greetings and introductions, it was time to get down to business.

Everyone gathered around the kitchen table: Carrie, Irene, Howard, Adam, and David. Adam hung back, leaning against a wall, and made no effort to shield his glowering expression. His anger appeared reserved for—and directed solely at—David, for reasons Carrie could not fathom.

Everyone was dressed casually, but the proceedings carried an air of formality. To his credit, Detective Kowalski, a trim man in his fifties with a salt-and-pepper crew cut, a snub nose, and kind brown eyes, took his time getting started. His patience helped Carrie to relax, though her hand shook with a persistent tremor every time she sipped her tea. David's touch had quieted Carrie's nerves, but the horror of what she'd endured persisted. Irene stood behind her daughter, her hands perched protectively on Carrie's shoulders.

"So you've seen this guy before? That's what I heard." Kowalski spoke with a heavy South Boston accent.

It was an effort to focus, but she looked at the color picture of the dead man Kowalski put in front of her. The photograph did not show where he had taped the cyanide capsule to the inside of his wrist.

"At the park," Carrie said. "I thought he was following me. I guess he was." She glanced at Adam, who looked distraught.

"Any reason?" Kowalski asked. "I mean, I can't say

I've ever come across a stalker who carried cyanide capsules on him before."

"Can you order those online?" Howard asked.

Kowalski pondered the question. "Yeah, I think so," he said. "I remember some guy took a pill in court after he was convicted of arson. Couldn't do the time, I guess. Maybe our guy had a 'get caught' plan as well."

"Maybe," Irene said.

Carrie and David exchanged glances. This was the moment of truth—should they share what limited information they had? She gazed down at the photograph of the man with the shamrock tattoo, taken post-life, and felt five sets of eyes boring down on her.

"We've got no ID," Kowalski said. "Serial numbers are wiped clean from the gun. DNA testing will take some time, same as a dental match. For now he's a John Doe. I don't know why this guy was after you, where your paths might have crossed other than the park, but there's something here. A patient of yours, somebody you saw at the VA, one of your other jobs, during medical school, at a party? I don't know you. You tell me." Detective Kowalski took a long, unhurried drink and eyed Carrie over the rim of his mug.

Carrie shot David a sidelong glance and picked up the photograph. She studied it silently for half a minute, then set it back down on the table.

"I don't know why he attacked me," she finally said.

50

Everyone crammed into the compact foyer of the Bryants' home to say good-bye to Detective Kowalski.

At the door Kowalski paused and focused on Carrie once more. "You have my card," he said. "Anything changes, you let me know."

"I will," Carrie said. "And thank you, Detective, for everything you've done."

"Wish I could do more," Kowalski said. "I'm sorry this happened to you, I really am. Just know we're going to do everything possible to figure out who this guy was and what he wanted."

Carrie felt a stab of guilt, knowing it would be wasted effort. If the police even sniffed around DARPA, she firmly believed the whole operation would be shuttered, evidence purged, and everything Carrie had endured would be for naught. She owed it to Steve Abington and Eric Fasciani to hand the federal district attorneys an airtight case against Goodwin, Richardson, and Trent. Perhaps they would find the missing vets, or maybe evidence that Goodwin and Trent had plotted her murder, or that of Sam Rockwell.

Carrie had already formulated the next steps in her mind. What she needed now was time alone with David to finalize those plans. With Kowalski gone, Howard and Irene returned to the kitchen to clean up, and Carrie went outside for a breath of fresh air. David followed.

Carrie ambled down the walkway and David caught up with her just before she reached the driveway. He took her hand again and pulled her in close to him.

"You made the right call," David said.

"Right call about what?"

Carrie and David whirled at the sound of Adam's voice. He wore the same saturnine look Carrie had observed in the kitchen, something truly unsettled.

Adam folded his arms across his chest in a hostile manner, but kept his distance. "Right about what?" he repeated.

"Nothing, Adam," Carrie said. "Just something David and I were discussing. It's private."

Adam closed the gap between them until only a few feet remained.

"Here's what I think," Adam said, his voice directed solely at David. A shadow crossed Adam's face, a darkness Carrie found deeply troublesome. "I think since you two have been hanging out, a lot of bad things have happened to my sister."

David took a single step toward Adam. He remained calm and composed, nonthreatening, nonconfrontational. Of course, Adam did not see it that way. His eyes dared David to throw the first punch.

"Adam, no," David said. "This has nothing to do with me."

"Yeah? Well, I don't see it that way," Adam said. "Carrie's been followed, somebody broke into her bedroom, somebody ran her off the road, and now someone tried to kill her. All that happened when? When, David?"

Carrie came forward. She knew how close Adam was to exploding. "Adam, this isn't David's doing," Carrie said.

Adam maneuvered so close to David the two could almost touch noses. To his credit, David did not back away. But to Carrie's eyes, David was nervous, and rightly so.

"Let's be level-headed about this, Adam," David said.

"Yeah, let's," Adam said in David's face. "This is my sister and I love her, and I'd do anything to protect her. *Anything.* So I think the level-headed thing to do is stay away from her. Whatever you're doing is dangerous, and if something happens to my sister, something happens to you. How's that sound?"

Adam did not give an inch. His stare made Carrie hold her breath.

"Are you going to hit me again?" David asked in a calm voice.

By this point, Howard and Irene had noticed something going on, and they came outside to investigate.

Irene rushed down the walkway. "What's happening?" she called.

The spell seemed to break. *Not a second too soon,* Carrie thought.

Adam turned around. "Nothing, Mom," he said. He

locked eyes with David once more. "David was just leaving, and I came out to say good-bye."

Braxton Price stood on the bank of the Charles River and watched the sailboats carve graceful lines across the rippling water. Any minute now the call would come with his directive. *Fifty-fifty,* he thought. He knew which direction he wanted it to go. Gantry was a brother and a friend, and Carrie Bryant needed to die.

How a brain surgeon had taken down Gantry, a well-trained, hard-core soldier, was difficult for Price to fathom, but his friend was dead and that was that. The plan all along had been to take Carrie out in the parking lot early that morning, silent-like—certainly not in the hospital, which had a larger police presence. Gantry had evidently improvised, and somehow she got the better of him.

Pity.

Something like this was bound to happen, and Price had warned his employers on several occasions about the risk of continuing after Rockwell's decommissioning. But once a grunt, always a grunt, and Price knew the suits were not about to take that kind of strategic direction from a low-level operator. *Whatever.* At least the group within DARPA who got this program off the ground had listened to him when it mattered most.

Nothing about Price's motivations was especially patriotic. It was all about the money, and he'd balked at the notion of getting his muscle from a ragtag group of mercenaries whose loyalties could easily be compromised. Employing members from Price's former squad, like Gantry, assured him that even under extreme duress his team would not falter. As individuals, each one of them had been tested, and while bones and bodies broke over in Afghanistan, allegiances never did. Price did not fight for his country; he fought solely for his brothers. When Gantry took that pill, he'd metaphorically leapt on a grenade to save his comrades. So Price would avenge him. It was not a matter of if, but when.

The air was still and warm, not unusual for this time of year. Price wanted to remove his jacket, but it hid the wires that would scramble the expected call. It also concealed his favorite pistol, a Beretta 92FS with a fifteen-round magazine and impeccable long-range accuracy.

At four thirty the call came in. Price wore an earpiece, but that was commonplace these days, so nobody took notice of him talking to himself on the bank of the Charles River. Price reached into his jacket pocket and pushed the Talk button without needing to check the phone's display.

"Speak," Price said.

"It's a no-go," a man's voice said in his ear.

"Fine."

"Too much scrutiny right now. There's another way to get her removed."

"Are we going dark?"

"No."

"Bad idea. We should go dark."

"Not my call," the man said.

Price could not help but smile. "Yeah," he said with a chuckle. "We're all just players here."

51

Carrie woke to the sound of persistent knocking on her bedroom door. She panicked, thinking she was back in the on-call room, and whoever was knocking had come to do her harm.

"Carrie, are you awake?" Adam asked. "Can we talk?"

She shook her head to clear the cobwebs from her mind. "Yeah, come in," she said, her voice raspy with sleep.

Adam entered, looking distraught.

Dressed in the same clothes she had worn to her interview with Detective Kowalski, Carrie sat up in bed and spun around to put her feet on the floor. She eyed her brother with concern. "What's wrong?" she asked.

She knew what was wrong, of course. Adam was coming unhinged. It was obvious in the way he had threatened David. The encounter had left Carrie rattled and unnerved. David, to his credit, took it all in stride, but

Carrie wished Adam had apologized to him in some way. Perhaps Adam had experienced a change of heart.

Adam eyed Limbic before plopping down on Carrie's desk chair. He slouched forward, and Carrie waited for him to speak.

"What's going on, Adam?" she asked at last.

"David," Adam said in a hushed voice.

"I have his number. I'm sure he'd love to hear your apology."

"That's not why I came to talk to you." Adam's expression was grave, his haunted eyes encircled by dark rings.

Carrie felt the weight of his gaze. "What, then?" she asked.

"Outside, when I was toe to toe with him, I had thoughts that scared me."

"Thoughts?"

Adam bounced his legs up and down. Evidently, it was not enough to settle him, because he took a ballpoint pen from Carrie's desk and twirled it about his fingers like a miniature baton. He had learned the trick in high school and tried to teach Carrie the method, but she never quite caught on.

"I wanted to kill him," Adam said.

Carrie gasped. "Adam, what are you saying?"

The pen tumbled from Adam's hand and dropped to the floor. His gaze never left Carrie, and his cold stare sent a chill down her spine.

Adam's eyes turned red, and he looked on the verge of tears. "I'm saying I didn't just want to hurt him, I wanted to kill him." His hushed voice was almost hypnotic. "It took everything in me not to grab his head and break his neck. I could have done it, too. I don't know how I held back. If you hadn't been there, I don't think I would have."

Carrie was stunned. A hollow pit in her gut allowed all sorts of feelings to roll in: fear, disgust, sadness, hopelessness. It was a cocktail of emotions she could not process.

"Why are you telling me this?" she asked.

"I'm telling you because I need your help," Adam said.

Carrie's guard fell immediately. She could look past Adam's confession to focus instead on the guilt and fear that seemed to consume him. She reached for Adam's hand, but he jerked away from her touch and rose to his feet.

"What can I do to help?" Carrie asked, rising as well. "We'll talk to Mom and Dad. Maybe find you a new therapist."

"I don't need a therapist," Adam said through clenched teeth. "I need the wires."

Carrie blanched. "What did you say?"

"You heard me," Adam said. "I want those wires in my brain. Scramble this shit up so I stop thinking the way I do."

Carrie sank down onto her bed. "I can't do that," she said.

"What do you mean you can't? You're in charge of the thing."

"No, no. I'm just a surgeon." This was an odd bit of irony, to embrace the role Goodwin had tried to thrust upon her. But she did not know what else to say.

"You still have pull, don't you? You're the brain surgeon. You can get me in and get me cured."

"It's not that simple," Carrie said.

"Why?"

"Because it might not work." Carrie cringed inwardly, knowing her argument had holes.

"I was at dinner when you told Mom and Dad all about that Ramón guy. And who was the other one? Bushman or something. It worked for them. You said it worked for two others, too."

"But they're the exception, not the rule."

"So? What's the worst thing that can happen to me?" Adam asked. "I get some surgery that doesn't do anything. Then I go back to being a walking time bomb, but this time with actual wires in my body."

Carrie imagined Adam lying in a hospital bed, his head bandaged, muttering "Follow my light . . . follow my light . . . follow my light" the way Steve Abington had.

"No, it's not that simple," said Carrie. "I'm not entirely sure it's safe."

Adam looked flustered. "Have you done the surgery before?"

"Yes."

"And?"

"And two of my patients are missing."

"Because of the surgery?"

"No," Carrie said, but corrected herself. "I just don't know. I'm still trying to figure it all out."

Carrie did not know how much to say. Yes, the DBS procedure could produce a specific side effect, but that was almost secondary to what Sandra Goodwin and Cal Trent were cooking up. And she still did not know how Bob Richardson from CerebroMed fit in this equation. Until she had some answers, she would never put Adam forward as a candidate for the surgery. Never.

"There's a reason I've been followed and twice nearly killed," Carrie said.

Adam glowered. "Yeah. And I think that reason is David. Who knows who he's pissed off? Believe me, I've seen those embedded reporters in action. They can be like jackals. Maybe he dug up the wrong details on the wrong people and now that he's hanging out with you, you're a target, too."

"I don't think so," Carrie said.

Adam fell to his knees and clutched Carrie's hands with force. "Please," he said. "I need to feel better." He panted to catch his breath. His emotions choked back his voice, and his eyes brimmed with desperation.

"Until I know it's completely safe, I just can't do it. I'm sorry."

"I don't care about any damn side effects!" Adam shouted. His ferocity took Carrie by surprise and frightened her. "I'll take any side effect right now." Adam sprang to his feet and began to pace. "What I'm afraid of is that next time I feel like I did with David, I won't be able to hold back."

"I'm sorry, Adam," Carrie said. "But I just can't. And I don't want you to get your hopes up for this treatment, either. We need to focus on therapy. You need therapy."

Adam nodded glumly, several times in quick succession. Without another word, he marched out of Carrie's bedroom but left the door open. She had expected him to slam it shut.

Carrie exhaled loudly and took a moment to collect

her thoughts. Part of her believed Adam would be fine
if he did get the operation. That he'd be like Ramón or
Terry Bushman, one of the fab four for whom DBS
had been a life-saving procedure. Another part of her
worried he'd vanish without a trace, like Abington and
Fasciani. Until she had answers, there could be no wires.

A few minutes later, Carrie heard a loud crash followed by the shattering of glass. She raced downstairs,
arriving in the foyer at the same instant as her worried
parents.

Without words, Carrie followed her parents into the
living room, where Adam perched upon the couch so he
could reach the photographs on the wall. His face had
a wicked look, a darkness she had never seen. In his
hand, Adam wielded a massive hammer that Carrie recognized from his toolbox. He had already shattered
one photo, and now Adam swung the hammer at a
second, this one a picture of the siblings dressed in ski
gear, taken at Sunday River in Maine. The hammer
struck dead center, and the glass shattered into thousands of jagged pieces.

Adam was not selecting photos at random. Each
picture was of him and Carrie. He swung again, and this
time shattered the glass on a picture of brother and
sister taken in front of Big Ben when they were in their
teens. The face of the hammer put a large hole where
Carrie's head had been.

"Adam!" Irene screamed. "What are you doing?"
She sank to the floor, her hands covering her mouth
but not silencing her sobs.

Howard Bryant held Carrie back. Adam was in a
blind rage; who knew what he would do if she approached?

Adam cocked his arm back once more, and aimed the hammer at another photograph, but paused to shoot his mother an annoyed look.

"I'm just showing my sister the same kind of love she showed me," Adam said. He brought the hammer forward again, and the sound of breaking glass filled the room once more.

52

The next morning, Carrie was back in her mom's Volvo, making what had become a routine drive from Hopkinton to the VA. Adam had stormed out after his terrifying tirade and never returned. Where he'd gone, Carrie could not say. Part of her worried he'd never come back home, another part worried that he would. Carrie's distraught parents had left the house before she did, to continue to look for their son.

However, Adam was not Howard and Irene's only concern. Her parents had thought her return to work was too much, too soon, but Carrie had insisted. After all, the man the police believed to be an emotionally unstable, well-armed stalker was dead.

While Carrie sounded convincing, the reality was a far cry from her assurances. The drive to the VA proved tense, as Carrie remained on high alert. Until Goodwin and Trent were decommissioned, she remained a target, and certainly DARPA had more deadly resources to throw at her. So long as she kept with the crowds, on the roads, or in the halls of the VA, however, Carrie felt moderately safe.

What she would not do, misguided or not, was cower, go into hiding, or hire an armed detail to guard her 24/7. She had to live her life, terror be damned.

Bottom line: she was on a mission.

Her voice mail and e-mail were flooded with messages from concerned friends and former colleagues, many of whom had heard about Carrie's ordeal on the local news. Dr. Finley had called, but she let it go to voice mail too. He'd side with her mother and insist Carrie rest at home for the day. Among those checking in was Carrie's old pal Valerie from BCH, who called during the morning commute. Their conversation was brief, but Val's worry touched Carrie's heart. The former colleagues made plans to get together for drinks and dinner in the coming weeks.

"You have no idea who that man was?" Val asked.

"Police are still looking. They think they'll get an ID soon enough."

"Well, I'm just grateful you're all right. And I want you to know, Carrie, that you're deeply missed around here. I mean that."

Carrie's eyes welled, but she did not cry. No need to make Val feel worse. "I'm doing okay," she said. "I mean it."

Val, being Val, said, "You got somebody to talk to?"

"Like a therapist?" Carrie asked.

"Well, not exactly," Val said.

"Oh, that," Carrie said.

"Just saying, it would help."

Carrie laughed. "Yeah, I've got someone to talk to."

"Well, I want to hear all about him."

"Who said it's a he?"

Val scoffed. "It could be a woman. Don't matter to me. But I am pretty sure we're not talking about a stuffed animal here, darling. You can give me all the four-one-one when I see you. And take care of yourself, Carrie. I mean it."

"I will."

As she hung up with Val, the car in front, no signal given, abruptly changed lanes. Carrie had to hit the brakes hard to avoid a collision. She hit her horn, and muttered a string of expletives that would have made her mother blush first and cringe second.

The other driver's maneuver was not unusual during rush hour, and Carrie's outburst surprised her. *Stress-induced,* she figured, and in that moment she forgave Adam for everything. Her brother's anger, directed toward her and at David, was triggered by constant duress. In the aftermath of her own extreme stress, Carrie could better relate to Adam's persistent volatility. She called her parents to check on the search and was told they had been unable to locate Adam. They would resume the effort later, after they returned home from work. Carrie had her doubts they would have any success. Something about Adam's last tirade made Carrie believe she would never see her brother again.

Carrie remained extra vigilant as she navigated through the crush of morning traffic. At one point, she glanced in her rearview mirror and noticed a red Camaro a few cars back that looked a lot like Adam's. Of course that was impossible. If Adam had gotten that car fired up, they'd have seen a celebration worthy of Mardi Gras on his side of the garage. Curious, though, Carrie tried to get a look at the driver, but the car was too far back for her to see much of anything.

Frustrated with the pace of her commute, Carrie took the next exit, not her usual. A short time later the Camaro reappeared in her rearview. Carrie relived the sinking feeling she'd had in the park, when her future would-be murderer became something to fear. A block later, though, the Camaro turned down a side street; just like that, it was gone.

The uneasy feelings—the fear and paranoia, a sense that something horrible could happen any minute, a terror that pawed at the back of her neck—those feelings lasted all the way to the VA and followed her into the building.

Carrie braced herself for an onslaught of attention that did not come. Even in the busy main foyer, nobody took notice of her. In a way, the silence was a stark reminder of her low profile at the hospital. While her face had been splashed all over the TV, she was not a well-known figure here. Her role fit in that netherworld between employee and contractor. At the main entrance, Carrie flashed her ID to the security guard and walked in without fanfare.

Welcome back to the jungle; nice of you to come.

The morning hustle and bustle seemed so perfectly ordinary, which paradoxically made it all feel a little eerie. Although there was a heavier-than-usual VA Police presence, Carrie saw no crime scene tape, nothing cordoned off. The evidence, as Detective Kowalski indicated, had been gathered, documented, and photo-graphed in the intervening hours. Life at the VA, for all intents and purposes, had returned to normal.

Carrie's plan for the day was a simple one. With no surgery on the docket, she would spend time examin-ing Dr. Finley's case files, and start to gather evidence. David had the right instincts. Had other vets gone MIA like Abington or Fasciani? If Goodwin wanted to conceal a side effect such as palinacousis, the first step would be to get those patients off the neuro recov-ery floor, where residents were trained to look for cog-nitive issues.

Carrie showed up at Dr. Finley's office with two cups of coffee, but when she opened the closed door, she found three people inside. Sandra Goodwin and Evan Navarro sat on those uncomfortable metal chairs facing Dr. Finley.

Carrie's eyes turned to slits as she focused her atten-tion on Goodwin. She fought back the urge to scream, *Did you try to have me killed?* The outburst might have been satisfying, but Carrie knew it would serve no purpose. All that mattered was obtaining proof of Goodwin's wrongdoing. That required tact, not brute force.

Goodwin and Navarro both acted irritated by Car-rie's intrusion; no outward signs of empathy there. Dr. Finley's face, by contrast, revealed his deep concern, and it put a walnut-sized lump in Carrie's throat. He was effusive in expressing his utter relief.

Carrie presented Dr. Finley with the coffee she'd bought him. "I know it's not Starbucks, but it's the best we've got here," she said.

"The fact that you could think about me at all is

incredible," Dr. Finley said. He took the beverage with a grateful smile. He remained standing beside Carrie, his hire.

Carrie looked over at Goodwin and Navarro. "I hope I'm not interrupting anything," she said.

"Coincidentally enough," Goodwin said, "you were the subject of our conversation." The tone of her voice cooled the room a few degrees.

"Oh?"

"We're discussing the DBS program," Navarro said.

Carrie could not help feeling amazed at the lack of empathy. "Well, in case you or Sandra were curious, I'm doing just fine," she said. "Thank you very much for asking."

"I'm glad to hear it," Goodwin said, not sounding glad at all. "But my chief concern, as I was just explaining to Alistair, is the continuation of DBS surgeries in light of your incident."

"By 'incident,' I assume you mean my attempted murder." Carrie felt her whole body heat up. It took great restraint not to go at Goodwin the way Adam had threatened David.

"It's my opinion that a trauma such as what you experienced makes you a danger to the patients and to the program."

"Last I checked, I wasn't actually shot," Carrie countered. She saw where this conversation was headed, and she did not like it one bit.

"While you aren't physically injured," Goodwin said, "your mental status is questionable at best. Evan has been studying up on the DBS procedure, and I think he'll be fine to take over for you until a mental health professional clears you to operate."

"Evan?" Carrie could not hide her incredulity. "Is that why he came to the OR? To watch me work? Nice bit of subterfuge there, Sandra. Well played."

"I don't appreciate your innuendos, Carrie," Navarro said.

"I don't appreciate you poaching my job," Carrie snapped back.

"It would only be temporary," Dr. Finley said in a conciliatory tone.

Carrie frowned. "You're not on their side here, are you, Alistair?"

"No," Dr. Finley said. "I'm not. But we have another problem."

Sandra flashed a frigid smile. "I told Alistair that if we don't replace you with Evan, I'll go to the board with a formal complaint about your violating my procedures by interfering with patient care. Given all the scrutiny the VA is under these days, I'm sure you can imagine how poorly that will be received."

"They'll force me to let you go, Carrie," Dr. Finley said in a defeated voice.

"And Evan will continue in your place regardless. So really, Carrie, you have no choice in the matter."

"When is the next surgery?" Carrie asked.

"The day after tomorrow," Navarro said.

Carrie shot Dr. Finley a panicked look. "Is it a PTSD case?" she asked.

"Yes, it is," Navarro answered. "But don't worry, I'm ready, and it'll go just fine."

Dr. Finley cleared his throat, and Carrie noticed how uncomfortable he seemed. "Carrie, Dr. Goodwin has requested that you take a leave of absence until you're medically cleared to operate."

"I've seen how you like to interfere with my processes and procedures. I'm not one to give second chances, and I don't want to risk you inserting yourself where your services are not required."

"Alistair, I can't believe you're letting this happen," Carrie said. "Navarro doesn't know anything about DBS."

"Look at it this way, Carrie," Dr. Finley said. "I have no choice. That's the way it is in the VA. It's the military, and everyone has to take orders, including me. Navarro has a licensed M.D. after his name, and as far as the VA is concerned, that means he can do everything from heart surgery to delivering a baby if the VA says so."

"I strongly disagree with this," Carrie said. "How can you feel comfortable with someone who may be completely incompetent?"

"As I recall, Carrie," Navarro said, "you had no experience when you came on board."

"If you take some time away, I can get you back on the team," Dr. Finley said. "On a permanent basis, if you like. If you don't, Sandra will go to the board, and if she does that, your status here will be entirely out of my hands."

Carrie's arms fell to her sides. "What choice do I have?" she asked.

Goodwin stood. "None," she said.

53

With a scowl across her face, Carrie leaned against a wall outside Dr. Finley's office, arms folded tightly across her chest, and waited for Goodwin and Navarro to depart. As he walked out, Navarro shot Carrie a smarmy, sidelong glance that made her blood boil once more. But her real anger was saved for Goodwin, who refused to look Carrie in the eyes.

Are you surprised I'm still alive? Carrie wanted to shout.

Goodwin could not have been completely dissatisfied, though. She had played the same blackmail card twice, but this time to greater effect.

Carrie stormed back into Dr. Finley's office as soon as the other two were out of sight.

"I can't believe you let Goodwin do that to me," Carrie snapped as she closed the door behind her.

Seated at his desk, Dr. Finley looked utterly besieged. He let go a loud sigh and ran his fingers through an unruly tangle of hair.

"We can retreat now and regroup later, or Goodwin will put a permanent end to your career," he said. "She'll trash your reputation so that you'll never match for another residency, and I doubt you'll find a situation like this one at some other hospital. Think about what's best for your career here, Carrie. Take the time off. Let the dust settle and hope to allow cooler heads to prevail. The program has to be protected at all costs."

Though it stung to hear, Carrie was not entirely surprised by Dr. Finley's stance. Any threat to the program, in his view, had to be neutralized. He had gone out of his way to hire Carrie in a rather unorthodox manner to avoid significant delays following Rockwell's accident. He would do what was necessary to keep the OR active.

"Speaking of the program, did you know Bob Richardson works for CerebroMed?"

Dr. Finley's brow creased and he looked a little puzzled. "I'd never met Richardson before your demo. But I'm not entirely surprised."

"No? Why?"

"DARPA hired them."

"DARPA contracted with CerebroMed?" Carrie was surprised. "We deal in DBS, Alistair, not neurological drugs."

"I'm well aware," Dr. Finley said. "Cal Trent told me that CerebroMed has been developing software for studying and re-creating traumatic events. DARPA has been partnering with them, but that's all I know. It's part of the VR program, and not really within my area of expertise. How did you learn this, by the way?"

Carrie shrugged off the question. There was no use

debating. Carrie knew she had lost her greatest ally. This program was Dr. Finley's greatest love, and it meant more to him than the truth about Goodwin. That much was obvious. Until she could give him definitive proof, he would always find a logical explanation for any concern Carrie raised.

"Well, can I at least review the files I requested?" Carrie asked.

"Yes, of course," Dr. Finley said, and he presented Carrie with a large stack of files. Carrie glanced at them briefly.

"These are neurological reports," she said.

"Yes."

"I'm looking specifically for postoperative complications."

Dr. Finley grimaced a little. "I'm afraid that would require Dr. Goodwin's involvement."

Carrie just smiled and clutched Dr. Finley's files to her chest.

"No worries then," she said. "I'll just look over what I have."

Carrie retreated to her office. She set Dr. Finley's files on her desk. From her purse, she dug out Evan Navarro's hospital ID and log-on credentials. They were written on the same piece of scratch paper as the main number for the VA, which Carrie had jotted down the night Eric Fasciani disappeared. Carrie might not be able to view the medical records of DBS patients who had spent time on the neuro recovery floor, but Navarro could.

The electronic medical records system, known as VistA (for Veterans Health Information Systems and

Technology Architecture), offered a variety of specialized enterprise applications, including electronic health records. The system, one of the largest in the United States, contained the records of more than eight million veterans, and personal data for hundreds of thousands of medical personnel and operating staff. Carrie was interested in only a handful of patients, specifically vets like Abington and Fasciani who had DBS surgery to combat PTSD symptoms.

Carrie launched the VistA program and entered Navarro's ID into the log-on screen. It took her almost thirty minutes to figure out the system, but eventually Carrie got the hang of it. It was different from the electronic medical records system at BCH, but intuitive enough for her to search for Steve Abington's name. From there, Carrie was a few clicks away from the problem list detailed in the computerized patient record system, abbreviated on the graphical user interface as "CPRS."

Steve Abington's arrhythmia was logged as "inactive," but she could see the onset date, last update, and location of the incident, which was the neuro recovery floor. The application said nothing about Abington's transfer to the med ICU, probably because Navarro did not have access privileges to that part of his medical record. Navarro was a neurosurgeon, and it seemed the walls Goodwin had erected between her department and the rest of the VA applied to this software application as well. No matter. Using Abington's case file, Carrie retrieved the clinic-specific procedure code for DBS and used that to search all DBS patients in the past twelve months.

There they were. Some names Carrie recognized:

Steve Abington, Eric Fasciani, Don McCall, Ramón Hernandez, Gerald Wright, and Terry Bushman. Some she did not. Based on the patients who were fully anesthetized during their operation, it was easy to distinguish between DBS patients treated for movement disorders, and those treated for PTSD.

On a piece of paper, Carrie made a two-column table and filled it with information from Abington's patient record. She ignored details such as clinical reminders, recent lab results, patient record flags, postings, and active medications to focus solely on significant problems that might have resulted in a patient being transferred to another unit.

She started with the patients she knew, and in a matter of minutes had a list of four names, with one medical complication post-DBS among them.

Patient Name	Problem List
Abington, Steve	Ventricular Tachycardia
Hernandez, Ramón	None
Fasciani, Eric	None
Bushman, Terry	None

The next patient Carrie looked up was Jim Caldwell. According to the record, Sam Rockwell had done his surgery. Seven hours after the operation, Caldwell's blood sugar levels dropped. Carrie could not see in the VistA system whether he remained on the neuro recovery floor, but now she had another name for her expanding table.

Patient Name	Problem List
Caldwell, Jim	Hypoglycemia

This process went on for several hours. Carrie combed through the records of every vet who had come through the DARPA program seeking a cure for PTSD. Twenty names in total.

By this point Carrie's eyes were like sandpaper. But her mind was reeling, and her whole body pulsed with an intense energy like nothing she'd ever experienced. She scanned the list, utterly incredulous. Of the twenty patients in total, fifteen had experienced complications, eleven of which were not typically associated with the surgery.

Complication	Number of instances
Arrhythmia	4
Hypoglycemia	3
Hypotension	4
Severe Nausea	2
Vision Problem/NOS	2
No Complications	5

Carrie made a second table that summarized her findings.

Once again, Navarro's access restrictions prevented Carrie from seeing what happened to each patient following his medical complication, but she presumed many would have been transferred to the med ICU or some other acute care department within the hospital. Carrie was not certain of the percent of DBS surgeries that resulted in post-op complications, but she knew the number was not 75 percent.

It would be Goodwin's job to bring these astronomical numbers to Dr. Finley's attention—which, of course, she would not do if her intent was to hide them.

With Goodwin's philosophy of "turfing" so ingrained, by getting the patients off the floor, she essentially made them disappear.

Carrie tried to come up with ways those complications could be induced. Potassium certainly could produce arrhythmia, and insulin obviously made the blood sugar levels drop. Beta blockers were a possible cause for a sudden drop in blood pressure, but Carrie knew of several drugs that would induce hypotension.

Five patients appeared to have no postoperative side effects whatsoever, but that included Eric Fasciani, who had improbably overcome the effects of Valium to check out AMA. Two of the other five vets Carrie knew: Ramón Hernandez and Terry Bushman. The remaining two must have been the patients Dr. Finley said had results similar to Bushman and Hernandez.

Carrie thought back to the night Fasciani disappeared and recalled that only one nurse was working the floor, the same man she thought she'd recognized in the photograph at Rita Abington's home. If Nurse Taggart were involved, Fasciani could have been removed from the floor without intentionally inducing some medical complication.

Carrie took out her phone to call David, and tried to quell the intense feelings of anger that coursed through her veins.

David picked up on the second ring.

"Do you still have the temporary ID for Michael Stephen?" she asked.

"And hello to you, my dear," David said in a cheery voice. "I've been worried about you all day. How are you?"

"No time to chat. I need to know if you still have that ID."

"I've still got it," David said. "Why?"

"Because I'm now persona non grata on the neuro recovery floor, and in the VA as well, but you're not."

"And what, pray tell, will I be doing on the neuro recovery floor?"

"You'll be helping me figure out what really happens to Evan Navarro's very first DBS patient after his surgery is done."

54

David's temporary ID was good for the month, and he had no trouble getting inside the VA. He wore his easy-on, easy-off disguise—surgical scrubs and canvas sneakers—and just like that, he was one of the crew.

By now, he guessed, Carrie was parked in the back lot, watching the rear of the building. David flashed on his meeting with Carrie just hours ago at Java du Jour. While it had only been a day since he'd last seen her, his visit marred by that uncomfortable confrontation with Adam, David felt as if it had been weeks. He took in every detail of her, and even though she was grim-faced and tense, David felt exhilarated to be with her again.

They ordered cappuccinos and discussed the plan; just like the last time, their drinks went cold. Carrie might have lost access to the OR, but she still could read the surgical schedule. From that, she got the name of Navarro's first DBS patient: Garrett McGhee.

It was David who came up with the stakeout approach. It made sense to Carrie, because she did not know what happened to the patients after they left the neuro recovery floor. Were they even moved to a different unit?

"I think they get transferred," Carrie had said. "Dr. Finley showed me Abington's patient information from the med ICU."

David was not convinced. "But that was after you went there looking for him," he said.

"So?"

"Maybe he never even made it there," David said.

"Come to think of it, the nurse in the med ICU couldn't trace him when I showed up, but I thought that was some problem with the record system. Should we set up surveillance cameras in McGhee's hospital room?"

David shook his head. "Might be easy to detect. I think we should figure out what happens—*if* anything happens—see it for ourselves, and then we'll improvise how to get the proof we need."

Carrie clutched her arms tightly, as though staving off a sudden chill.

"These are killers, David," Carrie said. "I feel sick I'm so scared. I don't know if I can go through with this."

"I'm just as scared as you are," David said. "And I'll back out, but only if you want to."

It was obvious from Carrie's face that it was not an option.

"I've never wanted to be more wrong about something in my entire life," Carrie said.

"Stats don't lie," David said. "Based on what you found, we have a seventy-five percent chance of proving that you're right."

David wandered the halls of the VA, trying to look like he belonged. He made frequent visits to the cafeteria and the restroom to pass the time until the next shift change. Throughout it all, he remained in constant communication with Carrie using Motorola two-way radios, which he had bought at Walmart for sixty bucks.

Now, thirty minutes before showtime, David had Carrie on his mind as much as the mission. He snuck into an unoccupied quiet room and put the push-to-talk to his mouth.

"Ground control to Major Tom. Can you hear me, Major Tom?"

There was a crackle and he heard Carrie's voice say, "Not funny."

"It was a little funny," David said.

"What's going on? Where are you?"

"Shift change is happening soon. I'm getting ready to move into position. I just wanted to hear your voice before I headed out."

"Be careful, David," Carrie said. "I don't know what is going to happen."

"Careful is my middle name," David said.

"I thought you told me it was Charles."

David's eyes widened. "Wow, that's some steel-trap memory you've got there."

He imagined Carrie's smile and it filled him with joy.

"Just be careful," she repeated. "Radio me when you're in position."

At fifteen minutes before the hour, David headed

for the neuro recovery floor. According to Carrie's intel, the unit was already half full with non-DBS surgical patients, but Garrett McGhee was not scheduled to arrive for several more hours. At that moment, Navarro was still doing the job Carrie had done, and Dr. Finley was in the OR with him, guiding his every step.

The double doors to the unit were closed and locked when David arrived, but he did not want to be buzzed inside. Instead, he used his smartphone to look occupied as he waited for the next shift to show up. There would be a little commotion at that point, during which David could more easily slip inside undetected.

At five minutes until three o'clock the new crew emerged from the elevator in a clump, chatting noisily amongst each other. The unit doors buzzed open, and David fell into step right behind them. He walked purposefully down the hall. He was practiced at looking official in places where he did not belong, and from the corner of his eyes it did not appear anybody paid particularly close attention to him.

He was quick to locate the room with McGhee's name written on a whiteboard—the kind of reservation nobody wanted to have. Inside the cubicle space David found an adjustable hospital bed, along with a bunch of medical equipment he could not identify. The glass enclosure left David exposed, but at least there were no direct sight lines to the nurses' station.

As a precaution, David closed the flimsy curtain for privacy and slipped inside the freestanding wardrobe closet that was pushed up against the wall opposite the bed. He closed the doors and plunged into darkness. A thin crack between the closet doors offered some light, but not much.

He had hardly any space to move about, and David already dreaded the many hours he would spend inside waiting for Garrett McGhee's arrival. After five minutes or so, David's legs began to throb, so he removed the two-way from his pants pocket, twisted his body so his back pressed against one of the side walls, and sank to the closet floor. To fit better, David wrapped his arms around his knees, which were nearly in his mouth, but at least he could hold this position for a while, meditate if he had to. He put the two-way to his mouth and called Carrie.

"I'm in a closet on the neuro recovery floor," he said. He had the volume low for when Carrie answered back.

"Okay, I'm outside watching the back entrance. I'll wait to hear from you."

"Roger. Over and out. Or whatever you're supposed to say."

There was a brief period of silence during which David wished he had one more chance to hear Carrie's voice. A second later the radio crackled back to life.

"Thank you, David. I mean it. Thank you for everything."

"Roger, over and out," David said.

And that was enough for him.

Tedium.

The walls of David's hideout were made of thin particleboard, so he passed the time by listening to the nurses' chatter, or counting the beeps on whichever machine happened to be loudest. The antiseptic hospital smell, that sickly clean odor, was starting to get to him, making the hours even more unpleasant to endure. Adding to his discomfort, David's body heat had turned the cramped quarters oppressively stuffy, and the slat between the doors offered a limited supply of fresh air. He had checked in with Carrie about a dozen times, but now he had to go dark since McGhee could arrive at any minute.

David's phone battery had run down, but he guessed it was close to 7:00 P.M., going by the last time he spoke with Carrie. Four hours jammed like a pretzel inside a closet; this was becoming a habit for him, it seemed. He felt achy all over, and the throbbing pain in his knees had gone from uncomfortable to deeply unpleasant. He could stretch his arms above his head, and that lessened the soreness somewhat. He wondered when—if—McGhee would finally show up.

The minutes passed slowly and without mercy until maybe another hour had ticked off the clock. What if there were complications? What if McGhee died during surgery? Maybe Navarro was as incompetent as he was devious. At some point during the long stretch of time with nothing happening, David felt pressure building in his bladder.

"Oh, great," he muttered.

I can hold it, was his first thought.

McGhee better get here soon, was the next thing to cross his mind.

A minute passed, then another, and all David could think about was peeing. When the pressure finally got too intense, David pushed open the closet door and clambered out like the Tin Man before he got oiled. The curtain kept David mostly out of sight while he used a portable urinal to relieve himself. The overwhelming feeling of relief extended to his arms and legs, and

David absolutely despised the thought of jamming himself back into the wardrobe. But then he heard the squeaky wheels of a stretcher in motion.

David scrambled into the closet and got the doors closed a few seconds before the stretcher came rolling into the room. The portable toilet was a tight fit under his legs, but he could not leave it half full of his urine for the nurses to find. There was a lot of commotion and dialogue as the patient, who David presumed was McGhee, was transferred from the stretcher to the bed. Two nurses took their time getting McGhee's vitals and hooking up his IV.

Now began the waiting game, and with each passing minute, each agonizing hour, David grew more weary. If nothing happened—and statistically that was a 25 percent possibility—he would find a way to sneak out of McGhee's room and get back to Carrie. Mission aborted for the night. His thoughts were dulled from inactivity and waiting.

The nurses came and went. They chatted playfully amongst themselves, but it was obvious they had tremendous competence in their craft, and deep caring for the patients. David was not interested in evaluating their skills as nursing professionals. He was waiting for the complication.

It must have been eleven, because another shift change arrived. He heard them talking, discussing medications, treatment, and such. A doctor poked her head in and did some exam on McGhee, but it was brief.

Thirty minutes after the eleven o'clock shift change took place—it had to be thirty—David heard someone enter the room. That was odd, because the new duty nurse had been in to see McGhee not long ago. The muscles in the back of David's neck tightened to the point he thought they might snap, but he turned his head anyway to get a look out the crack in the closet door. He could see a shape, the outline of a man with dark skin, lurking over McGhee's bed.

"How are we feeling tonight, Garrett?" the male nurse asked while glancing at a clipboard.

David watched the nurse extract something from the pocket of his uniform and had to squint to make out the syringe in the nurse's hand. The nurse inserted the syringe into the IV. Nothing happened for several minutes, until the nurse said, "Open your eyes, Garrett. The drug I gave you should make you less groggy . . . good . . . that's real good. Can you hear my voice?"

McGhee groaned, and then said in a mumbling voice, with almost exaggerated torpidity, "Yeah, yeah, stop saying it. Stop it."

"Oh, good," the nurse said. "I'm going to give you a little something else."

"A little something else . . . little something else . . . little something . . ." McGhee spoke as though in a daze, but he pronounced the words clearly so they were easy to understand.

David thought immediately of the auditory illusion, palinacousis, Carrie had so accurately described. It sounded as though McGhee was acting out her very description. Still peering through that crack in the closet, David watched the nurse inject something else into McGhee's IV, and a minute later he took out a smartphone and made a call.

"Rear entrance twenty minutes," the nurse said. "Keep the van running. It'll be quick."

David felt elated. At last they had proof Carrie was

right. Something truly sinister was going on here, even if he had no idea what exactly caused the auditory illusion, or where this nurse was taking McGhee, or what would happen to him once he got there, or why they were doing it. Carrie was watching the rear entrance right now, and she needed to know trouble was headed her way.

55

Hours of doing nothing made it hard to ignore the ever-present fear. It also gave Carrie lots of idle time to think about Adam. Nobody had heard from him since he left in such a rage. Her parents naturally continued to worry, and contemplated canceling evening plans to wait at home for him to show, but Carrie cajoled them into going out. If Adam was going to show, he would do so when he felt ready, she advised. So her parents went out, and soon after, Carrie did the same.

Had Adam returned home, Carrie would not have known. She kept her phone in her purse and the radio off, worried she might miss something of consequence if distracted. But there was a whole lot of nothing going on, and this gave Carrie time to fret and ponder the mission's many open questions. Would McGhee even have a medical complication induced? Would he be transferred to another unit, or moved out of the hospital entirely? Would they bring him back? If so, when?

The plan itself was all a bit "squishy," as Carrie said to David, which ran counter to her ethos of procedures and planning. Then again, she had long ago abandoned her comfort zone and proved to herself, many times over, just how adaptable she had become.

For want of something to do, Carrie ran through the plan's many permutations in her head for the umpteenth time. David was going to trail McGhee off the unit floor, assuming he experienced some sort of medical problem that required transfer. If McGhee left the hospital entirely, it would be Carrie's job to pick David up in her car, unless that maneuver would cause her to lose sight of the patient. For that reason, David had a Zipcar on standby in the visitor parking lot. If they became separated, she and David could communicate their locations via the two-way radios, which had a thirty-five-mile range.

That was the plan.

Squishy.

It had been hours since David made contact, and in that time Carrie's concern had grown—not to panic levels, but close. She knew McGhee must have been on the neuro recovery unit for several hours by now, but how long it would be until somebody might try to sneak him off the floor was anybody's guess.

The crackle of the radio sent Carrie's heart revving. She felt a surge of excitement, like the first tug on a once-slack fishing line.

"Carrie, are you there?" David spoke in a hushed voice.

"I'm here. What's the status?"

"A male nurse just left McGhee's hospital room. I think he injected something into his IV. Said something about a van coming to the rear entrance in about twenty minutes. Do you copy?"

Carrie scanned her surroundings—the rear entrance was in sight of where she was parked. "I got it. Where are you right now?" she asked.

"Um, that would be a closet in McGhee's cubicle."

"David, you've got to get out of there."

"Well, that's my plan. I'll meet you at the rear entrance, and we'll see if that van shows up."

In the background, Carrie heard loud beeping sounds. Right away she understood that one of the machines hooked to McGhee had just gone haywire. Another alarm sounded, this one much louder.

"Oh no, David," Carrie said into the radio. "Get out of there. Get out right now!"

In a matter of seconds, McGhee's cramped quarters had two nurses at his bedside. Through the slat between the closet doors, David watched them work as a team.

McGhee muttered under his breath, "I feel dizzy . . . dizzy . . . dizzy."

After a minute or so of silence, one of the nurses said, "Blood pressure is eighty-five over forty, heart rate hundred twenty bpm, respiratory sixteen breaths."

"He feels clammy to me," the other nurse said. "Shaking, sweating—does he have diabetes?"

"Not according to the EMR."

"Check his blood sugar anyway."

From out of David's view, a new voice spoke up. It was the same person who had earlier injected McGhee with something.

"What's happening?" the male nurse said. "I was just down the hall when I heard the alarm."

"Nurse Taggart, hello. I think our friend here might be having a blood sugar problem."

"Oh," was all Taggart said.

"I can give two milligrams IM glucagon," said one nurse, "and see what that does for him. I'd like a doctor to see him right away, please."

David felt dizzy and sweaty as well. He could pretty much follow the procedures as they took place, and soon after McGhee got the glucagon, a woman showed up, dark skinned, thin, petite, and introduced herself as Dr. Nisha Kapur.

"Fifty cc D50 stat," Dr. Kapur said. "We treat him first and then confirm with the lab results."

"FS zero," said a nurse. "I sent a venous level to the stat lab."

Dr. Kapur performed a battery of tests on McGhee just as David's left leg started to go numb. Prolonged pressure had cut off communication between the nerves in David's leg and his brain, producing an array of sensations that included warmth, numbness, and a wholly unpleasant tingling.

"How are you feeling, Mr. McGhee?" Kapur said in an overly loud voice.

"How are you feeling . . . how are you feeling . . . how are you feeling. Stop asking me!"

Sounds of flailing and twisting limbs alerted David that McGhee was likely quite agitated and might need to be restrained.

"He's a bit delirious from the DBS surgery still," one nurse said.

Somebody else entered the room. "What's going on?"

"Oh, Dr. Goodwin," Dr. Kapur said. "I didn't know you were here."

"Well, I'm helping out Evan because he was doing DBS surgery today."

Dr. Kapur explained the situation to Dr. Goodwin.

"Don't you think we should transfer him to the med ICU?"

"I can do that," Nurse Taggart said. "It's not a problem."

"Great. Thanks. And I'll head down to alert them that he's on his way," Goodwin said as she rushed out of the room.

While this took place, David's leg became miserably numb. The feeling of pins and needles digging into his skin was agonizing in ways he had never experienced. He tried everything to stretch the leg, but the burning sensation only intensified.

David watched the nurses unhook the monitors, and soon enough Nurse Taggart wheeled Garrett McGhee out of the room. The two nurses who stayed behind set to work putting the cubicle back together, which was now down one bed. Massaging his leg, David tried to ease the torturous sensation, but to no avail. He had to stretch the leg completely to get any relief, and every second the nurses remained inside the empty unit was excruciating. They chatted pleasantly, taking their sweet time.

A minute passed . . . then two . . .

The leg had to move. David flexed his hips and lifted the leg up a few inches. The relief was not quite enough, but it was something. He raised the leg a little bit higher, but this time his right leg moved as well. As it did, he knocked over the portable toilet with his urine inside. The plastic container landed with a soft sound that might not have attracted any attention, but the top came open and the liquid spilled out. David watched in horror as his urine trickled out the bottom of the closet door and cascaded to the floor like a golden waterfall. He could not move an inch to create a dam without pushing open the closet doors.

It did not really matter. A few seconds of the River David was enough for a nurse to take notice. The closet doors swung open with force, and David smiled awkwardly at the startled woman, who let fly a thunderous shriek.

David wasted no time. He sprang from the closet like a jack-in-the-box cut loose from its spring. His right leg landed just fine, but with his left leg asleep, his foot buckled from what he hoped was a temporary paralysis. He nearly collapsed to the floor. The nurse closest to him stumbled back and screamed again, a look of shock stretched across her face. Both nurses were frozen in place, which gave David a head start to hop out of the room. He could feel the sensation in his foot slowly return through the pins and needles. The strength came back fully by the time he reached the stairwell.

From behind, David heard tremendous tumult and commotion, but one phrase stuck out above all others.

"He took the stairs! Call the police!"

David descended one level and went out the first exit he came to, entering the hallway directly below the neuro recovery unit. He tried the nearest door, but it was locked. Time was going to run out on him. He put the radio to his lips.

"Carrie, listen, abort! Abort! I've been spotted. Do you hear me? Respond!"

"David, what's going on?"

David could not answer, because footsteps like a stampede could be heard headed his way. Security was heightened in the aftermath of Carrie's lethal encounter, and David was not surprised by the speed and effectiveness of the response.

He retreated back to the stairs, his only way out. The stairwell door boomed shut behind him. Breathless with anxiety, David shouted into the radio, "I've been spotted and they've called the police."

His voice echoed in the stairwell. From below David heard, "You, up there. Come down with your hands up!"

Nobody was going to wait for David to comply. Loud footsteps were on their way up to greet him.

It would be a hell of an escape, but David was not ready to give up just yet. He left the stairwell for a second time, and reentered the hallway he had just exited. This time, two uniformed police officers were running his way. With no available options, David darted back into the stairwell, where another police officer had just come into view.

"Hands up! Hands up!" David heard.

The officer stood five stairs away and removed what looked like a gun from his holster. David had just put the radio to his lips when the officer flicked his wrist. A square-shaped cartridge spat out the front end of what David now saw was a Taser.

"Carrie, abort! Aboooorr—"

A knifelike pain ripped through David's body the instant those contact points penetrated his right thigh. The pain was like nothing he had ever experienced. His skin felt on fire, immolation from the inside out. Maybe a scream escaped his lips. Hard for him to say. His body vibrated so violently it threatened to break apart.

Twitching, David fell to the concrete, landing hard on his back. Through the slits of his eyes, pushing beyond the pain, the burn, the earthquake of his body, David fixed his gaze on the radio that had tumbled from his grasp. He reached for it, but felt another pinch. A second lightning bolt of electricity coursed through him. His teeth knocked together in a violent chatter as his arms went spastic.

The radio, his lifeline to Carrie, was within reach, but miles away.

56

Carrie was on the two-way, trying to reach David, when a van pulled up to the rear entrance of the VA. The white cargo van without any windows was the kind that gave Carrie shivers anytime she passed one on the road. She set the radio down on the seat beside her and did not move. Twelve thirty in the morning. Flood-lights partially illuminated the back lot, but not Carrie's Volvo, which was parked directly opposite the van, maybe a hundred feet away. The van idled for a minute or two. No action. Just waiting.

Even though she was parked in the shadows, Carrie sank lower in her seat and peered out over the car's front dash. She caught a flash of movement near the van. The hospital rear doors had come open, and out stepped Lee Taggart, dressed in street clothes and pushing a wheel-chair. Seated in that wheelchair was a limp-looking man covered in a gray blanket, wearing a baseball cap on his head, which was slumped forward onto his chest. He looked unresponsive, likely very sedated.

It had to be Garrett McGhee.

The van's rear doors sprang open and a huge figure emerged out the back. Carrie recognized him right away. It was Ramón Hernandez.

She'd suspected Taggart, but Hernandez? What was he doing here?

Confusion paralyzed Carrie's mind. Pieces were on the table, but she still could not put them all into the puzzle.

Hernandez jumped to the ground and waited for Taggart to reach him. Together, the two men lifted the wheelchair holding McGhee into the back of the van with ease. To Carrie, to anybody, it looked like a hospital discharge, not a kidnapping. Seconds later, the van slipped into reverse and headed for the exit. And just like that, McGhee was gone.

Carrie waited until the van got some distance before she started her car's engine. She was short of breath, but not determination. The van took a left out of the lot and Carrie followed. She glanced at the two-way radio on the seat beside her. No way to reach David now. He was probably in handcuffs by this point.

Sick as she was about David, she could call somebody for help. From her purse, Carrie retrieved her phone without losing sight of the van. At that moment, the van made a sudden left turn and Carrie pulled to a quick stop on the side of the road, confused.

The turn made no sense to her. The van had gone down the access road to the VA's long-abandoned construction project on the hospital annex. The access road was a dead end, not a through street. Nothing was down that way but the boarded-up brick building.

A few seconds of contemplation, nothing more. She had to follow.

Carrie shut off her car's headlights and took the same turn as the van. It was dark, and hard to see, but Carrie managed not to drive off the potholed road and into a ditch. The four-story building loomed large in front of her. Battered chain-link fencing surrounded the annex, a symbolic "keep out" gesture at best. The structure was built on what appeared to be a weed-strewn sandlot dotted with rusted trash barrels. At the rear of the annex, beyond the fencing, was a dense patch of scraggly-looking trees and a sea of unruly brush.

When Carrie reached the halfway point, she let up on the gas and pulled over to the side of the road. She could see the van in front of her, and that meant the people inside would be able to see her.

The van drove up to the fence and Taggart got out. He pried the fence open where there was not any gate, and secured the pliable metal flap using two bungee cords, creating a makeshift entrance wide enough for the van to drive through. They must have cut the fence so from a distance the perimeter would not appear to have been breached.

Hernandez brought the van close to the building, but kept the engine running. Taggart stayed with McGhee, while Hernandez put the van in reverse and drove back through the fence opening. Carrie panicked, thinking he would drive right past her car, but instead he drove off the road and down what appeared to be a path that cut through the growth behind the annex.

Just like that, the van was gone.

A moment later, Hernandez emerged from a thicket of trees and brush. He went back through the fence and undid the bungee cords holding the flap in place. He caught up to Taggart, who waited for him at what must have been a rear entrance into the abandoned building. Sure enough, Taggart opened a door, and soon all three men vanished inside.

Carrie rolled down her window to battle back a sudden wave of nausea. Only then did she realize she was completely soaked in sweat. She watched the building for a few minutes and felt certain nobody was coming out. Why would Hernandez have hidden the van if he planned to go somewhere anytime soon? *The plan,* Carrie thought. *Get the evidence.* Maybe there was a window, some way for her to take a picture without entering the building.

A voice inside her head spoke up. She was unarmed, outnumbered, and untrained, while Hernandez was solid muscle and a skilled combat vet. No contest.

"Be smart here, Carrie," she said aloud.

Then she remembered the call she'd been about to make. Carrie retrieved her smartphone and dialed a number stored in her contacts. The phone rang four times before somebody finally answered.

Dr. Finley sounded logy. "Yeah, hello?"

"Alistair, it's Carrie. There's an emergency. I need your help." Her speech came out hurried and short of breath.

"Carrie, what on earth? What's going on?"

"The VA Police have my friend David Hoffman in custody right now. You have to tell them he's not a threat. He's with me."

"In custody? Why? And what do you mean he's with you? What are you doing?"

"I don't have time to explain, but there's something terrible happening at the VA. Sandra Goodwin and Cal Trent are kidnapping the DBS patients."

"What?" Dr. Finley sounded fully awake now, and appropriately alarmed.

"They've been experimenting on people, Alistair," Carrie said. "It's not DBS that's curing them. It's some sort of drug they've been given, I'm sure of it—something from CerebroMed, but it doesn't always work. There are side effects like palinacousis, maybe others. And Ramón Hernandez, he's involved, same as the nurse from the VA, Lee Taggart. I just watched them take Garrett McGee off of the neuro recovery unit."

"Carrie, you realize you sound absolutely mad."

"It's happening, whether you want to believe me or not. Now, please—help my friend David and call the police."

"Where are you?"

"I'm at the VA hospital annex construction site. That's where they brought McGhee."

"Okay, okay. Just get out of there. Get out now. I'll call the police and I'll call you right back."

Carrie ended the call. She knew the smart thing to do: get out. Of course she should do just that.

But a thought came to her. *What if the van takes off with McGhee inside before the police arrive?* More proof gone. She should at least get the license plate. It might be a vital bit of evidence the police would need.

Carrie scolded herself for not taking video of the two men lifting McGhee into the back of the van. So much had happened so fast she had not been thinking clearly. She could at least get a picture of the license plate, and then get out of there. For Abington, for Fasciani, for all the vets who had been hurt because of Goodwin and Trent—she owed it to them.

Carrie fired up the engine, but kept the lights off as she drove ahead. If anybody saw her coming, she could slam the car into reverse and make a quick escape. A hundred feet from the chain-link fence, Carrie pulled to the side of the road. She kept the engine running as she got out.

Her feet crunched on the hard-packed dirt, and the glow of city lights in the distance shone like an artificial dawn. Blood pounded in her ears, but she could still hear the drone of millions of buzzing insects that infested the woods where the van had been hidden.

Carrie's nerves were crackling. To her left she saw the path down which Hernandez had driven the van. She vanished inside the forest that bordered the access road and reached the van in a matter of feet. Her hands shook violently, but she managed to get a few pictures of the Massachusetts license plate.

The van itself was completely unremarkable, scuffed up some, dented in places. She did not linger and was soon headed down the path, back to her idling car. The whole trip took a few minutes at most. Carrie settled into the driver's seat and let the feeling of relief wash over her.

As soon as her hands found the steering wheel, Carrie felt a presence rise behind her. Her eyes went to the rearview mirror and she took it all in: the short-cropped hair, strong jawline, broad shoulders. Almost immedi-

ately Carrie recognized the silhouette of Terry Bushman, the second vet she had examined.

"Never turn your back on a marine," Bushman said.
"We're sneaky bastards."

Carrie screamed and tried to get out, but Bushman
reached his powerful arm over the seat and brought it
down alongside Carrie's neck. Bushman's left hand
pushed against his right wrist. He made a muscle with
his right arm that bulged into the side of Carrie's neck.
The pressure was directly on her two carotid arteries,
thankfully not her larynx or throat.

One second.

Carrie struggled to break free.

Two seconds.

She tried to scream.

Three seconds.

Her world was gone.

57

The first thing Carrie noticed was the smell. It was damp and mildewed, like the fetid water of a marsh. There was a whiff of urine, too, as well as a rank body-odor smell that made her want to gag. She felt tender soreness on both sides of her neck, but nothing on her throat. A sick, flulike feeling made it hard to focus. She wondered if she'd been drugged. Probably. What had happened?

As her awareness became more acute, Carrie heard moaning and what sounded like people mumbling. The noises came from both her left and right, and it was different men who spoke. They made strange groaning and grunting sounds. Disturbed. Panicked. She could make out some of the words.

"Get down! Get down!"

The voice that spoke was sharp-edged, but muted, and the words were slurred like somebody talking in their sleep.

A different voice said, "We're taking fire from the north side. Where they at? Where they at?"

More voices blended together. The chatter was best described as incessant, like the buzzing of the insects that occupied the woods behind the annex—only these were human voices, maybe half a dozen in total, mumbling simultaneously.

"I'm hit! I'm hit!"

"Talk, talk, talk to me."

"Oscar Mike! Oscar Mike!"

"Go! Go!"

"Clear!"

"The rounds are firing downwind."

On and on it went, without letup, until the chorus of voices became a single droning noise that Carrie could ignore. Her eyes fluttered open and she focused on what appeared to be the stripes of a mattress. It smelled, too—truly foul, just like the rest of this space.

With great effort Carrie managed to push onto her hands and knees. She lifted her head groggily and blinked rapidly. Her vision must not have cleared entirely, because what she saw made no sense to her. It looked like she was inside a dog kennel of some kind. Galvanized tubular frames held in place heavy-duty-gauge chain-link wire. The wire covered all sides of the welded structure, including the top. The single door, framed with galvanized tubes and covered in wire, was secured with a heavy chain and a heavy-duty padlock.

Carrie looked right and saw three additional kennels all in a row. Inside each wired enclosure was a thin and dirty man. Each of the three men sported a different stage of facial hair growth, as if it marked the length of his stay here. One had stubble, one had a full beard, and one looked like the Taliban. The man in the cage closest to Carrie rested on a grimy mattress, while the other two paced about their enclosures like animals at the zoo. Each man had sunken, hollow eyes, and a vacant stare. Those who moved about ambled with a zombie's gait. They wore blue hospital scrubs that were soiled and tattered and in such deplorable condition it made them look like shipwreck survivors. Affixed to each man's arm was an IV drip, secured in place with tape and hooked to a rolling metal IV stand. All three men muttered to themselves and seemed completely oblivious to Carrie's presence.

Inside each kennel was a blue bucket, into which Carrie watched one man urinate. Water bottles were strewn about, and trays with food scraps attracted a large congregation of buzzing flies. The cement floor, the color of rust, was damp with puddles and chipped in spots. Carrie noticed several coiled-up hoses outside the cages—showers, she thought—and drains spaced throughout to capture any excess water.

Lining a concrete wall to Carrie's left was a bank of decrepit-looking washing machines and dryers, some fallen over, some with broken glass and dimpled sides, all industrial strength. She knew then that this was the abandoned laundry facility of the old annex building. A tall pile of industrial laundry machines, like a mini-mountain of junkyard scrap, occupied a sizable area in the center of the cavernous space. Carrie believed she was in a subterranean room, with thick concrete columns peppered throughout to distribute and support the building's substantial weight. Overhead banks of fluorescent lights lit the old laundry facility from above, and flickered on and off as if they were sending Morse code.

"Hey, why are you standing? Get the hell down, or get shot!"

Carrie spun her head in the direction of the voice. Three more kennels stood to her left, but only two had people inside them. The far cage appeared to hold the man Carrie believed to be Garrett McGhee. The person in the cage closest to her, who had ordered her down, caused Carrie's jaw to come unhinged. It was Eric Fasciani! He was skeletal-looking, fierce with his gaze, haunted in every way imaginable.

Like the others, Fasciani wore soiled scrubs. His thin arms were covered in scabbed-over scratches, and Carrie noticed gruesome scratches on his neck as well. His face was bearded like the other men. Nobody shaved them. Nobody took care of them. Lab rats were treated better than this, at least for a while.

"Eric, what are you doing here? What is this place?"

Carrie spoke in a hushed whisper, afraid someone might come for her.

"What are you doing . . . what are you doing . . . stop saying that . . . got Taliban crawling all over this place. We gonna have to shoot our way out."

"Eric, please, talk to me. Tell me what's happening here."

"He can't hear you, Carrie Bryant, not really. Not in the way you understand it."

Carrie's breath caught at the sound of the man's voice. Her heart sank and her spirit cracked wide open. For a few frozen moments, Carrie could not move. She swallowed a jet of bile as the fear set in and anger cooked inside. With gritted teeth, Carrie wheeled and set her frightened gaze on the man who spoke.

Dr. Alistair Finley.

58

"What the hell are you doing?" Carrie screamed at Dr. Finley. "Let me go! Let me out of here!"

Dressed in his trademark oxford shirt and khaki pants, Dr. Finley had a pressed, clean appearance that made the other men's condition look even more deplorable. He approached with honest sympathy in his eyes. Almost a look of heartache, as though he knew Carrie's fate and deeply regretted it. He came over to her kennel and locked his fingers around the wire.

Meanwhile, Fasciani continued to bark and mutter and speak unintelligibly, but Carrie no longer concentrated on what he said. Her entire focus remained on Dr. Finley and three men who accompanied him into this dank cellar: Terry Bushman, Ramón Hernandez, and Lee Taggart, who held in his hand a long rodlike implement with two pointed prongs on the end. A few of the men in cages took notice of the cattle prod in Taggart's hand, and sank to the back of their kennels as though they'd been conditioned to react that way.

Carrie lunged at the wire, causing Dr. Finley to rip his hands away before she could grab them. With as much force as she could muster, Carrie shook the cage, but managed to make it rattle and nothing more. These kennels were bolted into the cement and would not budge no matter how much she tried. None of the men down here, those inside the cages or out, reacted to Carrie's rage.

"You need to calm down, Carrie," Dr. Finley said. "Nobody can hear you scream. Your outbursts will do you no good, and I have questions to ask. Important questions. If you yell, or don't cooperate, Braxton will administer a painful shock with this livestock prod."

"Braxton?" Carrie said.

Dr. Finley became aware of Carrie's confusion. "Ah, of course, Nurse Lee Taggart is in actuality Braxton Price, and he's as skilled as these other two gentlemen, if not more so. So you'll need to cooperate now, Carrie. It's vital for you."

Carrie focused her thoughts to compartmentalize her fear and terror. "What is this? What is going on here?"

Dr. Finley kept some distance from the cage as he removed his spectacles and rubbed at his eyes.

"This, Carrie," Dr. Finley said, gesturing to the kennels of men, "is how we're going to cure PTSD."

Carrie hated to hear Dr. Finley speak her name. It felt like another violation of her trust. She shook her head, disbelieving. She focused on the words the men in these cages spoke—playacted, it now seemed—and Carrie understood in a way she had not before that they seemed to be trapped inside a virtual reality simulation, one of war and bloodshed, a place where the gunfire never let up.

"What have you done to them?"

Easy does it, Carrie warned herself. *Don't lose your temper. They'll hurt you if you do.*

"I'm helping them," Dr. Finley said. "Well, not them exactly, but others like them. These men are pioneers, Carrie. These are men who will give us a window into the secret world of the traumatized brain. These men are heroes."

Carrie's sense of Dr. Finley's program was coming into sharper focus. A sickly chill overtook her.

"They're all homeless, aren't they?" she whispered. "Like Steve, like Eric, these men are vets who were living on the street, people nobody noticed and nobody missed."

"They fit the criteria we needed."

"And you!" Carrie's eyes turned fierce as she set her gaze on Ramón Hernandez and Terry Bushman. "You were like them, you were on the streets, too. How could you let this happen to these men?"

"Actually," Dr. Finley said, "Ramón and Terry weren't like them at all. They're both former members of Braxton's military squad. And they helped to—oh, let's call it *recruit* vets for our program. I was quite impressed when you discovered Ramón had a connection to Steve Abington that preceded our efforts here. You're a very clever woman."

Carrie gripped the wires again. "But you cured them both," she said.

"No," Dr. Finley answered. "I performed DBS surgery on them, and that's all. These men never had PTSD. And their implants produce no electrical discharge. To be blunt, they are part of our dog-and-pony show for the federal government, to ensure we continue to receive more funding. You see, Cal Trent needed to show progress to the higher-ups at DARPA, and sadly vets like Steve Abington were not going to do the trick. Not yet, anyway."

"What is this?" Carrie said, gesturing to Eric's IV drip. "What is in those IVs?" What had she gotten herself into?

"You actually had it figured out, Carrie," Dr. Finley said. "You just didn't quite put it all together."

"CerebroMed," Carrie said. "Bob Richardson."

"Richardson and CerebroMed," Dr. Finley repeated. "But it's not all Bob's doing, not by a long shot. I had the basis for the chemical properties of Deleritum and brought it to Richardson's attention."

"Deleritum?" Carrie asked.

"From the Latin verb meaning 'to erase.' "

Dr. Finley's ego and overweening pride would keep him talking, revealing secrets Carrie longed to know, but dreaded to hear.

"What is Deleritum?" Carrie spat out the word.

"It's a drug, Carrie, that reconsolidates bad memories causing PTSD symptoms," Dr. Finley answered matter-of-factly. "The drug is a highly modified form of MDMA, which you know better as the street drug ecstasy. Our lab is located down here, but I'm sure you had no idea. There are no nasty fumes, and not a lot of highly suspicious chemicals involved. Richardson is our supplier, and that service can't be undervalued. CerebroMed has been after something like this for years. Richardson stands to make a lot of money from this discovery, but money isn't everything."

Carrie was aware that the compounds found in MDMA had been shown to dampen the amygdala, which would allow people to re-engage with the negative experiences without significant consequence.

"It all has to do with perseverating memory," Dr. Finley continued. "We needed a way to trigger the memory so that it persisted in the amygdala, where we could then use DBS to neutralize the emotion. The problem was getting the memory to perseverate properly."

Carrie's eyes went wide with a look of horror. "Virtual reality didn't work, did it? You needed drugs to make it happen," she said.

"We needed drugs and a way to test them. Animals aren't very good at telling us their feelings. It might not look to you like we're close to a breakthrough here, but we are. A few more trials and we'll have something truly remarkable."

"But these drugs don't work," Carrie said. "These men are lost."

"Well, they do in some ways. It's a process, you see."

Carrie's thoughts were gelling, and those disparate threads Dr. Finley had referenced connected in ways she could not possibly have imagined. The word that flashed in her mind like neon on Broadway was "perseverate." It meant a thought or action repeated long after a stimulus that prompted a response had ceased. For some of these men, Deleritum made the war live on in their minds. Their trauma continued unabated—*perseverated,* in medical parlance—but for some, that perseveration manifested as palinacousis.

Dr. Finley observed Carrie thoughtfully. "So you do understand now, don't you?"

Carrie felt gravely ill, weak throughout her body. "Have you cured anybody?" she asked.

Dr. Finley appeared a bit contrite. "There are flashes

of real lucidity, yes, and the length varies—sometimes weeks—but eventually significant deteriorations recur. A few of the patients just have the palinacousis side effect, no lingering PTSD symptoms, but that's happened only a handful of times. Of course those are the ones we're most excited about."

Carrie felt confused. "Steve Abington—he communicated with me. He talked about his friend Roach before he attacked me. Was he one of those men? Is he still alive?"

"No, I'm afraid not. The sedatives we gave him pre-op dampened the effects of Deleritum significantly, but as soon as those drugs wore off he was completely lost. Same as your friend Eric, here."

Carrie looked down the row of cages. None of them appeared to be engaged with reality.

"But you said some people just have the palinacousis side effect. Where are those men?"

"They didn't make it."

"*Make* it? What do you do, Alistair—just execute them?"

"They might have trouble with hearing," Dr. Finley said, "but their mouths work just fine."

"You're a monster," Carrie said. "All of you. Monsters!"

Hernandez took a threatening step toward Carrie's cage. She retreated a few steps, forgetting for a moment the barrier between them.

"These guys were gone anyway," Hernandez said. "Why not put the body and mind to good use?"

"And what do you get out of this deal?" Carrie asked bitterly.

"Me?" Hernandez touched a finger to his chest.

"I'm helping to fix one of the biggest problems in the military and make a fortune doing it. What more do you want?"

"Is that it for you, Alistair?" Carrie asked. "Is it about the money?"

"No," Dr. Finley said with a shake of his head. "It's about the results. Think about what a drug like Delerium can do for the world. The trauma of war, of rape, of child abuse, fatal accidents, death and grief, all of it can be neutralized. I can bring happiness to the world. True peace of mind. What's that worth, Carrie? I think it's worth the sacrifice of these men."

"I think you don't want to go through the proper channels and develop a drug under the guidelines of the FDA. I think you want your glory and you want it now."

Dr. Finley shrugged off the rebuke. "There's a certain truth to what you say," he admitted. "I would like to be alive when I finally get the recognition and respect I deserve. Who wouldn't want to go down in history as the person who unlocked the secrets of the mind?"

"And Sandra Goodwin will have a state-of-the-art neurosurgical practice to run. I guess she gets something out of the deal, too," Carrie said.

"We all have our motivators in life," Dr. Finley said.

Carrie shook on the inside and out. Whether it was hubris or ego, Dr. Finley needed Carrie to understand his motives, to accept them if possible.

"Sam Rockwell knew what you were doing, didn't he?"

Dr. Finley got a distant look in his eyes, almost a

pained expression. "Sam was a dear friend. And he supported us from the start. He saw the greater good."

"By 'us,' you mean Navarro and Goodwin."

Dr. Finley scoffed. "Sandra yes, but Evan, no. That boy is a flea whom I utterly despise, as does Sandra. But he's a good soldier and he does as Sandra says. Unlike you."

Carrie felt nauseated all over again. *Turfing.* Sandra Goodwin had fostered the perfect work culture to make these patients disappear. "When these vets leave the floor they become other people's problems," Carrie said, almost to herself. "Navarro never bothered to look at the number of medical complications associated with DBS. To him it was just one less thing to worry about. So you killed Sam because why? He didn't want to play along?"

"So to speak," Dr. Finley said. "But believe me, I did not want to hurt him. Same as I don't want to hurt you. Sam left me no choice. I do have a heart, Carrie. We could have killed him when the accident didn't." Dr. Finley put the word "accident" inside air quotes. "But I told Braxton to leave him be. In his condition his family at least had a sprig of hope for his recovery, and he was no threat to me."

"Until he woke up."

A dark cloud crossed Dr. Finley's face. "If you hadn't been on your way to see him, we might have been able to handle it differently. As it was, you forced us to improvise. Why couldn't you have just done your job and inserted those wires while we did the rest?"

"It's not who I am."

"That, I'm afraid, was my miscalculation. Now I

need to know: besides David Hoffman, who else have you told?"

Cold terror seeped into Carrie's bones. "No, no, not David. He doesn't know anything."

Dr. Finley returned an annoyed look. "Don't play me for a fool," he said. "Who else have you told?"

Carrie would not answer.

"Your entire family is in danger now, Carrie. Be honest here. Who else have you told?"

"Go screw yourself." Carrie bent down, grabbed the empty blue bucket beside her, and hurled it as hard as she could against the wire. The bucket bounced back and nearly hit her in the face before it clattered noisily to the ground.

Dr. Finley turned his attention to Braxton. "Come with me to the lab. I'd like to have a word with you in private before we go and deal with Mr. Hoffman."

Braxton showed Carrie a syringe. "I used this to take care of Sam Rockwell after I ran you off the road," he said, a cold glint in his eyes. Ruefully, he added, "Guess I should have taken you out that day, after all."

Dr. Finley took a single step toward the exit, but turned back to address Carrie once more.

"I'm so sorry it's come to this," he said. "I really thought we could continue our efforts with you on board. The thought of landing a top-notch neurosurgeon so soon after we dealt with Sam was simply out of the question. I figured we'd have to go dark for some time. But then you came along. Like a miracle, really. The timing honestly could not have been better. And given your . . . past, well, I assumed you'd follow the rules and just do your job. Insert wires. Go home. Why would you rock the boat? You should have been the ultimate good soldier, Carrie. Sandra was right about you. You really were a loose cannon all along."

Braxton followed Dr. Finley to the exit.

"What are you going to do to me?" Carrie yelled.

Dr. Finley turned to Braxton. "He was your friend."

Braxton looked over at Carrie and then to Bushman. "Shooting an unarmed woman inside a cage isn't really my style. Bushman, kill the bitch."

Bushman's eyes flared as he took a pistol from an ankle holster. "As you wish," he said.

Braxton and Dr. Finley disappeared through an exit door. The vets' mumbling flooded Carrie's ears once again.

Bushman and Hernandez consulted one another for a bit, out of Carrie's earshot. When Bushman approached, he had venom in his eyes. Then he softened. For a second, Carrie thought he was going to let her go.

"It won't hurt, I promise," he said, almost apologetically.

Carrie fell to her knees as tears streamed down her face.

"Any last words?" Hernandez asked.

Carrie began to convulse. The fear, the pure terror of knowing these were her final few seconds, overwhelmed her. She really had no way out. Death had come for her.

In that moment Carrie's resolve thickened. She caught her breath and with great effort, fixed her gaze on Bushman. She would not die with her eyes closed. She would stare into the face of her killer. It was the last bit of humanity she had left.

Bushman's outstretched arm was like a steel rod. The pistol in his hand did not waver.

"Do you have anything to say?" Bushman asked.

"Yeah, get the fuck away from my sister."

Carrie heard an enormous bang, a bright flash of light that came from her right. In the very next instant, Terry Bushman's entire head vanished inside an explosion of blood, brains, and bone.

59

All Carrie could see was the blur of her brother, Adam, as he charged into the room, his rifle aimed at Ramón Hernandez. Bushman had crumpled to the floor, his face no longer recognizable beneath a gruesome crimson mask. The gun tumbled from Bushman's lifeless hand and skidded close to Fasciani's cage, far out of Carrie's reach. Several flashes erupted from the barrel of Adam's rifle, but Hernandez dropped to the floor with startling quickness, and as he did, removed a pistol from his holster.

"Look out, Adam!" Carrie screamed. As she spoke those words, bright flashes erupted from Hernandez's gun, aimed in Adam's direction.

Trapped inside their cages, the vets reacted to the sudden tumult as though they were part of the action. Some took cover, while others held up their arms and fired make-believe weapons at invisible targets.

With his feet in constant motion, Adam zigzagged using quick cuts that avoided the hail of bullets. The muffled pops from Hernandez's weapon rang out in the hollow enclosure. Feeling helpless beyond measure, Carrie grabbed the chain-link wire of her prison cell and pulled futilely, watching the scene unfold as if in slow motion.

Adam, surefooted and dexterous, veered left, then right in a series of sharp turns that closed the gap between him and Hernandez considerably. Seeking protection, Adam took shelter behind one of the many thick concrete support columns and opened a line of fire at Hernandez, who immediately returned volley. Bright flashes hindered her vision, but Carrie saw a few bullets fired by Hernandez smack into the concrete column that shielded her brother. Several more hit the ground near Adam's feet.

Hernandez's fire paused, during which Adam leaned out and got off several shots. Adam had a pistol strapped to his waist, but he seemed to prefer the accuracy of his rifle.

Of the six or so shots Adam fired, one hit the intended target. A geyser of blood erupted from Hernandez's punctured arm. He let out a savage scream. Clamping his hand over the wound, Hernandez found cover behind the tall pile of detritus laundry machines discarded nearby. For the moment, at least, he was out of Adam's direct firing line.

Adam let fly several shots, but those did nothing against Hernandez's massive steel barricade. To Carrie's horror, Adam unsheathed an enormous bowie knife from an ankle holster and slipped out from behind the protection of the support column. Holding the rifle one-handed, Adam fired several more shots designed to hold Hernandez in place. He set the rifle on the ground without making a sound. His finger went to his lips, urging Carrie's silence.

Adam approached the fortification of laundry machines stealthily, taking quick steps. Hernandez may have been reloading, or recovering, during the short respite, which allowed Adam to reach the barricade without incident. With a sudden burst of motion, Adam shot forward and ascended the metal mountain with the skill and grace of a ram.

Hernandez, sensing imminent danger, came up from his hiding place and raised his weapon to fire. At that same instant, Adam reached the top of the pile, and he leapt down on Hernandez, arms and legs spread-eagled, the knife clutched in his hand like a deadly talon.

The two entangled men vanished behind the metal mound, out of Carrie's sight. When they finally emerged, Adam had the knife poised above Hernandez's head, pressing with all his might. Hernandez grimaced as he parried the knife attack with his right hand, while his left clutched Adam's throat. The two men tussled and spun in a violent ballet.

Adam's color began to change, alarming red to terrifying blue, and the strength in his arm began to fade. Hernandez managed to bend the wrist enough to turn the blade against Adam. Then Hernandez applied tremendous pressure that bent the arm and inched the blade closer to Adam's heart.

Adam grunted and snorted as he tried to battle back.

The blade still moved closer.

"No!" Carrie screamed.

But there was no stopping it now. Hernandez plunged the knife into Adam's chest, burying it up to the hilt.

Adam's mouth fell open, but no sound escaped. As he stumbled backward, Adam used his right hand to retrieve the pistol from its holster. He flicked his wrist and fired a shot that struck Hernandez in the stomach. Adam shot again, in the heart this time, and Hernandez went slack as his eyes bugged out. They fell on top of each other and Adam fired two more times, into the stomach area. Those bullets exploded out Hernandez's back and made his body jump as if it had been electrocuted.

Adam rolled Hernandez off of him, and fished a ring full of keys from the dead man's pockets. With great exertion, Adam staggered to his feet, with the knife still protruding from his chest. Tears streamed down Carrie's face as Adam stumbled toward her cage. Blood sputtered from Adam's throat, painting the floor with bright red dots. He fumbled with the keys, but dropped to his knees before he could put one in the lock.

Carrie fell to the floor with him and stuck her hands through the wire to hold her brother upright. She moved her hands up a few holes in the wire to caress Adam's bloodstained face. His body listed from side to side, unsteady in her grasp, as if he were being tossed by waves.

"Adam, Adam, what are you doing here? Oh, Adam."

"I . . . followed . . . you. Been following you." The rasp in Adam's voice, the rattle in his chest, cleaved Carrie's heart.

Carrie recalled the Camaro she had seen in her rearview mirror. She'd thought little of it, but the car *had* belonged to her brother.

"I saw you," Carrie said.

Adam broke into that trademark smile of his, but this time flashed Carrie teeth that were stained bloodred.

"You followed them," Adam managed. "And I followed you. Protect, you—finally got the damn car working. Didn't tell you . . . told nobody, didn't want you to spot me. Guess you did anyway . . ."

There were certainly opportunities for Adam to come and go without anybody at home to notice. Maybe her parents had seen his car was gone, but with her phone shut off they had no way to reach her.

Adam's eyes glazed over.

"No," Carrie whimpered, and she held on tighter. "Don't you die on me. Don't you do it."

"Love you, sis," Adam said. It was obvious that incredible strength was required for Adam to push the key ring toward Carrie's cage. "Get out. Get out of here."

"No, I'm not letting go."

Adam glanced down at the knife buried in his chest. "I am," he said. "I am."

With that, Adam's body went limp. The eyes Carrie had seen full of both laughter and rage turned glassy and vacant. His expression, drained, became nearly serene.

Carrie sobbed and stretched through the wire to clutch her brother in her arms. She was still holding on to him when Braxton Price and Dr. Finley returned to the laundry room and saw the incredible carnage. Price drew his gun and took aim at Carrie, who would not for a second let go of her brother. She put her head up against the wire, desperate to feel more connected to Adam. Her eyes closed and she waited for death to come.

"They don't pay me enough," Price said.

A gunshot rang out, and then another.

Carrie looked just as a bullet lodged dead center into Price's skull. Price went limp, and he dropped to the ground like a marionette separated from its strings. A third gunshot sounded; this one hit Dr. Finley in the neck. Clutching the wound, Dr. Finley spun around in frantic circles, blood spewing through his fingers, spraying in all directions, a look of horror on his face. He tumbled to the floor near Price's inert body, where he convulsed and gurgled on the blood that now filled his throat, until his spasms stopped and he went perfectly still.

Confused by who had fired, Carrie turned her head in the direction of those gunshots. She saw Eric Fasciani, on his feet in a firing stance, IV in his arm, holding Bushman's smoking pistol in his right hand.

Fasciani looked over at Carrie and said, "Sergeant! Sergeant! I got two confirmed kills here, that's two confirmed kills."

EPILOGUE

Only certain sections of the Arlington Cemetery allow private headstone markers to be placed. Adam's marker was a simple design, dignified, and appropriate for a military setting. The inscription was factual: name, rank, date of birth, date of death, and a short phrase that required special approval. It read: *Remember those with invisible wounds.*

Spring days, like this seventy-degree delight in mid April, are seldom so spectacular, and the warm breeze made the freshly bloomed cherry blossoms smell even sweeter. The cemetery was mostly deserted at that mid-day hour, except for Howard and Irene Bryant, who were walking arm in arm back to their rental car parked nearby—and for David and Carrie, who lingered behind, holding hands, gazing at Adam's gravestone with somber expressions.

Carrie clutched in her hand the qualification number from her recent running of the Boston Marathon. She put the number on the grass in front of Adam's grave and used a rock she'd brought with her to hold it in place. When she stood, her eyes were filled with tears, and she clutched David's hand for comfort.

"I didn't do great, little brother," Carrie said, her voice cracking with emotion. "But I finished. Can't believe we lived in Hopkinton all those years and never bothered to run the big race. Well, I ran it for you. For Steve, for Eric, for all the vets. I raised about two thousand dollars for the Red Sox's Home Base Program, too, which I guess is pretty good. It'll help other vets suffering from PTSD, so I hope you're pleased."

Carrie's throat closed. She tried to take a breath, but a sob came out instead. It took time before she could speak again. When she did, her voice was soft and it trembled.

"I miss you every day, and I love you so very much," Carrie said through her gathering tears. "So here's the big news Mom and Dad told you I was going to share. Sandra Goodwin was finally sentenced today. That's really why we came down. I wanted to be here when it happened so I could tell you personally. It took *a year* for the trial," Carrie said. "Can you believe it's been a year? Well, she's going to spend the rest of her life in prison for what she did. Cal Trent and Bob Richardson—well, their trials are still under way, but they'll get the same, don't you worry about it."

Carrie fished a tissue from her purse and used it to wipe away the tears. She remembered something else to tell her brother.

"They found a burial site."

Buried. Burned.

Carrie had heard all about the gruesome details of

the killings, since she became close with the new secretary of Veterans Affairs. There had been eleven killings, they thought, but it could be more. Bodies turned to ash. The former secretary had resigned in disgrace, along with the medical director at the Boston VA, even though he claimed no involvement with Dr. Finley's program, no knowledge that DARPA's blood money funded a nightmare factory.

"Not much new to report on Eric's condition, or the others," Carrie said. "They're still suffering significant neurological damage. But the irony is, Dr. Finley might have been onto something all along. We've gone through his case files and there's something there. Using DBS to cure PTSD is not so far-fetched after all."

Carrie's composure cracked again, and she took a moment to recover. David gripped her hand tighter, but the heavy sadness felt like a boulder on her chest.

"I know it sounds horrible to say, but I'd rather you and the others didn't die in vain. And I guess on that note, I have some more good news to share. I matched with a residency program at the Cleveland Clinic. I'll be starting in September, and they want me to continue work on treating PTSD and other trauma using DBS. I've given this a lot of thought, and I've decided I'm not going to back away. There's an answer to the problem, a way to do the treatment that's safe and effective. It'll take years, and lots of hard work to figure it out, but the effort will pay off one day, I know it. What these people did was horrible, beyond words, but I'm choosing to blame the doctors, not the medicine."

Carrie leaned her head on David's shoulder as a

strong wind kicked up. She brushed the hair from her face and gave a strained smile.

"I feel the wind. Is that you talking, Adam? I sure hope so. I hope you approve. Anyway, I think about you every day. Mom and Dad do, too. We all love you so much."

Carrie shut her eyes tight, but those tears leaked out anyway. After a few minutes, she and David turned and walked over to where Howard and Irene stood, and all four embraced.

"We'll meet you for dinner later?" Irene asked, dabbing at her eyes with a handkerchief.

"Yeah," Carrie said. "Just text me the place and the time and we'll be there."

Howard leaned over to kiss Carrie on the forehead, and pulled her into his arms. "I love you so much, kiddo," he said in a shaky voice. "I'm so proud to call you my daughter."

Carrie hugged her father hard as she ever had. Then they were apart, two pairs headed for separate cars. Howard and Irene got into their sedan, while Carrie climbed into the driver's seat of Adam's fire-red Camaro, with David taking the passenger seat beside her. The car had made the long journey from Hopkinton to D.C. without one mechanical problem. Evidently, Adam needed inspiration to get it working right, and watching out for his sister's safety had provided more than enough.

Carrie fired up the engine and started to drive when David's cell phone rang.

"David here," he answered.

There was a long series of pauses as David said

things like, "Uh-huh, oh good, yeah, sure, of course, that sounds fine, of course."

He ended the call and said nothing.

Carrie looked over at him. "Well?"

"Well what?" David asked.

"Who called?"

"Anneke from the *Lowell Observer*."

"What about?"

"The Pulitzer," David said. "I won."

Carrie laughed. "That's how you celebrate?"

"Not a real celebratory occasion, and it's a story I wish I didn't have to write."

"David, it's fantastic news. I'm so proud of you. I really am."

Carrie used one hand to drive, and the other to give David's hand a squeeze.

"There's more," David said. "I've apparently been offered an assignment for *The New York Times*. They want me to go to Sierra Leone for a couple months."

"Oh my. That sounds dangerous."

"I'm a stringer, Carrie. I go where the story is."

Carrie pulled her hand away and focused on the road.

"What?" David asked.

"I'm moving to Cleveland soon," Carrie said. "We haven't really talked about us, and now you're going away."

David smiled and touched Carrie's face with much tenderness. "I'm a stringer," he said. "I go where the story is. And you're the story I want to follow for the rest of my life."

Carrie took David's hand and this time gave it a

kiss. She pressed down on the gas, and the Camaro shot forward like a rocket ship. For a moment Carrie felt Adam's presence in the seat behind her, his hand resting on her shoulder, a broad grin on his face, that twinkle in his eyes.

And on she drove.

She drove.

A NOTE FROM DANIEL PALMER

Dear Readers:

Every September, after submitting his latest novel to St. Martin's Press, my father would immediately begin to brainstorm. What kind of story would he be sharing with his readers next? Autumn 2013 was no exception. Pop knew he wanted his twentieth thriller to return to the hospital setting that was the hallmark of his earlier works. The protagonist would be a young female resident who encounters a desperate patient with the repeated claim, "I don't belong here." The doctor begins to believe the patient, investigates, and soon descends into a labyrinth of murder and corruption.

Dad's next story was in place. Then, in October of 2013, my father died suddenly.

I don't know how long my dad would have kept writing. He had no plans to stop. He had journals and file folders filled with ideas. With each novel, my father aimed to deliver his very best because he cared deeply for his readers. When news broke of his passing, my inbox flooded with messages from fans around the world.

Even though he was a bestselling novelist published in over thirty languages, the business of writing was sometimes lonely for my dad. It meant blank pages, solitude, and deadlines. But something changed for him in 2009. That was the year I landed my first publishing contract.

I was working from home doing consulting and writing. My dad was at his office, too, some sixty miles to the south. I'd leave my iChat application running all day so whenever Pop wanted a little face time, he could just dial me up online and there I'd be. Or me and his grandkids, or all of us plus his daughter-in-law. We would jawbone about plots until our fingers grew itchy to do some key tapping. I learned the craft of writing from my father during those long talks. Remembering them gave me confidence that I could run with his great premise for TRAUMA.

Working on the book proved to be a remarkable and deeply emotional journey. When the e-mail from Dad's beloved editor Jennifer Enderlin came in accepting the manuscript, I said aloud, "We did it, Pop."

I can't replace my father; nobody can. But I can continue his legacy, and that's a thrill and an honor that leaves me humbled and incredibly grateful.

In friendship,

Daniel Palmer

Read on for an excerpt from

MERCY

by Michael Palmer
and Daniel Palmer

Available in May 2016
in hardcover from St. Martin's Press

1

You really don't know what you've got till it's gone.

On nights like this, when Walter McKenna could barely get air into his lungs, and each breath came ragged and raw, the lyrics from the Joni Mitchell tune popped into his head and he'd grimace, thinking she was right. Damn right. In Walter's case, it was heart disease that had paved over the paradise of his good health. It zapped most of Walter's remaining strength and left him perpetually exhausted.

With great effort, Walter managed to sit up in his hospital bed. He had to do something to take the pressure off his bedsores—decubitus ulcers, his doctors called them—that had again formed on his buttocks and back.

Even in this new position, Walter felt them rubbing on the bed sheets. The pain brought him to tears. To keep new ulcers from forming, Walter endured daily chemical debridement. But that was better than the hives that had broken out a few weeks ago. Those were brutal little suckers. The pale red bumps came on like a speeding train, coating his entire body, and causing horrible itching that antihistamines could barely subdue.

If he were back home, Walter at least could enjoy some familiar comforts, but he was long past that possibility. Walter cursed softly. The hospital was his home now, and had been for months. Tomorrow's debridement was just another bit of suffering to add to his growing list of miseries.

He shifted position again, but it was impossible to get comfortable. His legs and arms were weighted with so much fluid he felt like a human water balloon. He also felt intense pressure on his bladder, and relieved himself into his catheter. Peeing into a tube, shitting into a bedpan: this was life with end-stage heart disease.

You don't know what you've got till it's gone . . .

In the morning, Melinda would show up, Walter's wife of twenty-five years, and they would watch television together and talk pleasantly during the commercials. She would bring him updates from the high school track team where he ran as a boy and coached as a man, and this would make him feel both happy and sad. She would try to hold his hand, but his fingers were stiff and achy, grotesquely engorged, and it hurt to be touched.

Now, just the thought of Melinda tightened Walter's chest, squeezing his heart. His oxygen made a loud sucking sound, like the last gasp of a dying breath. But it was not his last gasp. Even though Walter's arteries were clogged with plaque, the surrounding muscles starved for oxygen, and his ventricular function had downshifted from a sprint to a limp, he was still very much alive. A permanent resident in what he morbidly referred to as God's waiting room.

When the figure appeared in the doorway, Walter wondered for a second if he were dreaming. But the pain was present as always, and thank goodness his dreams were not that cruel. Still, doctors rarely stopped in at night unless they had good reason. Walter listened to the beeps, hums, and buzzes—the white noise of all the monitors attached to him—without a sense that anything was abnormal.

But the doctor was here, so Walter figured he had to have a good reason. This doc wore a waist-level, white lab coat, a crisply pressed shirt, and a bold red tie. He was Walter's hospitalist, a specialist in administering general medical care to hospitalized patients. Lots of different hospitalists looked after Walter—so many, in fact, that he had taken to calling all of them "Doc."

"What's up, Doc?" Walter croaked. He needed a sip of water, but was too weak to reach the glass himself. Doc noticed and gave Walter a drink.

"Just making rounds," Doc said.

"This late?"

Doc said nothing. From a black leather medical bag, Doc removed a bag of medicine, some clear liquid, and hooked it up to Walter's IV.

"Hey, I've got more bags hanging on that IV tree than a luggage carousel at Logan. What's with the new meds?"

Doc returned a half smile. "Just a refresh of your ACE inhibitor," he said.

Walter, who had taught high school physics for more than two decades, had little trouble absorbing all the medical jargon tossed his way. The angiotensin-converting-enzyme inhibitor would lower his blood pressure by decreasing oxygen demand from the heart.

It was all duct tape and glue to keep a leaky vessel afloat another day longer, but Walter preferred that to the alternative.

Doc titrated the new IV medication and did a quick check of Walter's vitals.

"How you feeling, Walt?" Doc asked.

"Like I'm dying," Walt said.

"Everyone is dying, Walt. We're just moving at different rates of speed, is all."

Walter could not argue there.

"Any unusual discomfort?" Doc asked.

Walter paused, as if he could have a new pain to which he was not yet attuned, but, no, nothing was out of the ordinary. He said as much.

"So, any big plans for tomorrow?" Doc's tone was a bit too sardonic, but Walter appreciated any hint of levity, even if it was gallows humor.

Several loud beeps rang out, and Walter's EKG burst into an erratic series of peaks and valleys.

"Just the meds kicking in," Doc said as he adjusted something on Walter's EKG monitor. "I gave you a big dose, so it will take effect right away." The beeping stopped, but Walter's heartbeat revved up several notches. His lungs, already thick with fluid, felt as if they'd been put in a vise.

The evening nurse popped her head in. "Oh—hi, Doctor. I was just checking on him because his monitor is alarming."

"Thank you, Judy. We're all set here. With his paperwork, I mean."

The nurse returned a look of grim acknowledgment that set Walter on edge. Paperwork. Walter thought he understood the reference. Alarms were a constant on this floor, and he had a signed DNR that meant care-givers were not to perform CPR if his breathing should stop or his heart stop beating.

I'm having a reaction to the meds, Walter thought in a panic. *Got to relax. Take it easy. I'm not ready.*

"What'd you give me, Doc?" Walter asked. A stab of chest pain took his breath away.

"Just a little something to take care of people who have no business living," Doc said.

Walter waited for a hint of a smile, some indication this was Doc's tasteless humor on display once more, but his expression was cold as stone. Walter glanced to-ward the doorway, hopeful the nurse would reappear, but she had already left, probably headed back to the nurse's station. No rush. No urgency. *Damn that DNR.*

Walter found himself gasping for breath. His body grew hot, and sweat blanketed his forehead. Gripping the bedsheets like horse's reins, Walter tried to slow the canter of his heart.

"I feel kind of funny, Doc," Walter wheezed.

Stinging drops of perspiration rolled into Walter's eyes. The pressure on his chest intensified. Walter took in several sharp, short breaths, but could not seem to fill his lungs.

A sharp, crushing pain took away what little breath remained. Unable to speak, Walter pawed the air, try-ing to get Doc's attention. A wave of nausea overtook him, and a strange pressure built up at the base of his neck. Walter's fingers turned a horrifying shade of dark violet. The gurgling in his lungs bubbled up to his throat. His heart skittered with irregular beats. A spasm of coughing shook Walter's ribs so violently he thought they would break. His arms began to ache, and Walter felt an overwhelming sense of dread, of impending doom. Something was terribly wrong with him.

"Doc . . . Doc," Walter coughed in breathless sputters. "I think . . . I'm . . . having . . . heart attack."

Doc titrated the IV once more. "You are, Walt. A big one. *The* big one, in fact."

Walter's eyes rolled into the back of his head. His heart seemed to bounce freely around his chest. From somewhere in the whiteness and the blackness of this strange place where Walter now found himself, he heard a familiar sound. A melody. Some song. A tune he once loved. Yes, there it was, echoing softly in his mind. The words came to him, as did the angelic glow of Melinda's face.

You don't know what you've got till it's gone . . .

2

There was no "normal" to Dr. Julie Devereux's workday. Life as a critical care doc at White Memorial, a
500-bed hospital in the heart of Boston, was suited to
people who could roll with it when the Emergency Department interrupted morning rounds for an immediate consultation, or when a patient who had been stable
moments ago was suddenly and inexplicably teeter-
ing on death.

Having Trevor, her twelve-year-old son, tag along
for the day was not on Julie's schedule. But go with the
flow, right? In no way did that mean Julie was pleased.
If this were some official take-your-kid-to-work day,
she would have had a different attitude. But this was a
Take Your Kid to Work Because He Got Suspended
from School for Fighting day. Not endearing. Not by a
long shot.

Trevor, a lanky, sweet-faced kid with thick, shoulder-
length brown hair just like his father's, brooded behind
Julie as she headed for her office down the hall.

"Wish I didn't have to be here," Trevor grumbled.

Julie stopped walking, turned around, and gave her son a hard-edged stare. "Well, I'm sorry, Trevor, but people do have to work for a living."

Two nurses strode past and said a warm hello to Julie. She was beloved here—a lot more than at home, it seemed.

Julie reminded herself to be patient with her son. Change was not easy, and Trevor, her only child, had to adjust to the fact that his mother would soon be remarried. She wondered if this acting out was Trevor's way of processing a stew of conflicted emotions. He liked Sam, or maybe tolerated was the better word, but resented the idea of a man other than his father living with them. He had said as much to Julie. Maybe the kid held out hope that Julie and Paul would reconcile one day. That was not going to happen.

Perhaps once she and Sam were married and living together, Trevor's recent string of bad behavior would come to an end.

"I still don't see why you couldn't have left me at home like I wanted. I would have been fine on my own. Better than being stuck in your office all day."

Julie shook her head in frustration. "Getting suspended two days for fighting isn't exactly how to earn trust," she said, in a matter-of-fact tone.

"Well, he started it," Trevor shot back.

Julie sighed. Trevor always had an answer for everything.

"How come I can't just stay with Dad?"

"Because your father isn't home. Believe me. I called."

"Where is he?"

"In New Hampshire, collecting scrap metal for his next sculpture."

Trevor seemed to think this was cool. His dad was cool. Of course he would think that. His dad thought homework was a waste of time and sugared cereal was a four-course meal.

"Dad let me weld the last time I was there." Trevor made this seem like an off-the-cuff remark when he knew he had tossed a barb that would sting.

"He did what?" Julie arched one of her delicate eyebrows and tried to block all sorts of horrible images from her mind. She had seen enough third-degree burns in her career to have some stern words with her ex-husband before this day was over. Paul had good intentions, but when it came to good judgment, he could be worse than Trevor.

"If it sells, I'm going to get a cut," Trevor announced with pride.

"Well, before you pick out a new iPad with your earnings, ask your father how many sculptures he's sold in the last five years."

Trevor looked away because he knew the answer was zero. Paul was quite talented, and his art fairly inventive, but he was not particularly ambitious or motivated. He did not make much money from his sculptures. Julie accepted that, as long as he paid the court-ordered child support. Paul could do this because of a substantial inheritance from a grandmother, one that allowed him to lead an artist's life. Paul paid his share of the child support on time and with no grumblings, but still Julie wished he'd be a stronger role model for his son.

Sam Talbot would never replace Paul as a father—nor

would he ever try—but with his kindness, maturity, and stability, Sam was sure to be important in Trevor's life. As a high school history teacher, Sam was not exactly rolling in the dough, but the way he loved her and the way she loved him made Julie feel like the richest woman in the world.

Julie set a hand on Trevor's delicate shoulder. Her son might have been obstinate, disrespectful at times, a little mouthy, but he was still her pride and joy.

"Look, kiddo, you're here for the day," Julie said, "so do your homework and try to make the best of it. And I hope you brought a good book, because you're not going to be glued to your electronics all day."

Julie tugged on her white lab coat so it fit better over her beige blouse. Everything fit better since she'd lost the weight gained during the divorce. She told people it was diet and exercise, but really the weight came off after she jettisoned the stress. For that, Julie had motorcycles to thank—a Honda Rebel 250, to be precise, which Sam, an avid rider, had bought for her as an engagement gift. Julie was looking forward to their upcoming ride to the Berkshires, and showing Sam the new hip-hugging leather pants she'd bought online from Cycle Gear. But the weekend was several days away, which meant plenty of time for Julie to work, look after Trevor, and feel like she was shortchanging both.

Since her separation from Paul, Julie had come to know a lot of single, career-oriented mothers who tried to be all and do all. Her advice to them, whenever asked: go ride a motorcycle. The worries and doubt wouldn't go away, but they'd have a blast forgetting them for a while.

Julie's first patient of the day was Shirley Mitchell, a 77-year-old woman with a nasty case of pneumonia to go along with the initial stages of peripheral artery disease. Despite her illness, Shirley had a fairly decent quality of life. This could not be said for many of Julie's critically ill patients in the 33-bed unit, who sometimes endured debilitating and costly treatments to squeeze out only a few more months of life.

Julie was an advocate for death with dignity. She wrote papers and frequently spoke at conferences with the goal of bringing about policy change. Self-determination was a fundamental right, and the courts were beginning to agree. It was coming to health care whether the providers liked it or not. High-profile cases like Brittany Maynard, the 29-year-old woman dying of brain cancer who ended her suffering on her own terms, would continue to be a force for change. Death with dignity laws did not, as some critics said, kill people who did not wish to die. Julie could produce thirty years of data as proof.

She, and others who thought like her, wanted to take government out of the equation and let the patient and the patient's doctor come to a decision on what was best. The option to have an option was what Julie fought for, not some death mandate, as her opponents feared.

Her activism, of course, was controversial among her colleagues who viewed her stance as anathema to their profession. *It violates the Hippocratic oath to do no harm. It demeans the value of human life. It will lead to abuse or reduce palliative care options.* All valid arguments, but Julie believed that even those most vocal in their opposition had at some point wrestled with doubt while helping to keep alive a supremely sick patient who wished only to die.

Sometimes dead is better.

Shirley's nurse was Amber, a petite, 26-year-old blonde who one day—not quite yet—might turn Trevor's head. For now, Trevor seemed oblivious to Amber's beauty and was content to wave hello from the doorway after Julie made introductions.

"Trevor, you know where my office is. Why don't you go there now and wait. I'll come get you for lunch."

Trevor gave a nearly imperceptible head nod, and away he went.

Amber somehow had managed to turn Shirley onto her side, not a simple feat given this particular patient's size, and was applying moisturizer to the backside of her body. ICU nurses were some of the most compassionate Julie had ever worked with. They did an incredible amount of work, almost always with a smile regardless of the unpleasantness of the task.

Shirley was not aware of Amber. She was sleeping soundly, thanks to the Propofol, and breathing normally through the endotracheal tube inserted down her throat.

"How was her night?" Julie asked. Since this was the morning shift, Julie would get Amber's take on what the night nurse had relayed.

"I heard she had a pretty good night," Amber said in a cheery voice. "Fever is down to 101. WBC is fifteen thousand."

"Fifteen thousand for the white blood count," Julie repeated, sounding pleased. "That's approaching normal."

"And there's less secretion in her endotracheal tube," Amber added.

"Less secretions, eh?"

Another bit of good news. When Shirley arrived at

the ICU, her chest X-ray showed substantial infiltrate clogging her lungs.

Amber said, "The respiratory therapist titrated down her oxygen and now she's only on forty-five percent. When I left yesterday she was on sixty."

Julie went to the Medi-Vac unit mounted on the wall and inserted a catheter down the tube. She engaged the suction, producing a whirring sound, and up came a soupy, yellowish, highly viscous, putrid-smelling liquid. It was less than Julie had expected.

"Looks like Shirley really is getting better," Julie said. "Maybe today you can give her a wake-up and lighten the Propofol."

Amber acted disappointed. "Shirley can be a handful. I'm really going to miss the Milk of Amnesia," she said.

Julie smiled at the long-running ICU joke; the milky white drug had the same color and consistency as the popular over-the-counter laxative. A sleeping patient makes no trouble, said the adage on the floor. But staying on the ventilator long-term increased the likelihood of going from sleeping to dead. The breathing tube keeping Shirley alive was also a gateway for getting bacteria into the lungs. Ventilator-associated pneumonia was a real risk. For people already seriously ill, it could be a death sentence.

"Let me know how Shirley is doing when she's awake. Maybe we can reduce the ventilator further, and if that goes well, we'll move on with a spontaneous breathing trial."

If Shirley were able to breathe for two hours under her own power, Julie would consider taking her off the ventilator.

"I'll get her awake right away," Amber said.

"Good," Julie answered.

So far the day was off to a banner start.

A raven-haired nurse named Lisa, dressed in floral scrubs, poked her head into Shirley's cubicle.

"Dr. Devereux, I need some help. It's the quarterback. I'm worried. We're cranking vasopressors, but his BP is unstable and trending down."

Julie darted out of the room and Lisa fell into step behind her. ICU nurses were not only compassionate but were some of the best trained in the field. They seldom worried over nothing.